The Castle Inn

The Castle Inn

STANLEY WEYMAN

ÆGYPAN PRESS

1898

The Castle Inn
A publication of
ÆGYPAN PRESS

www.aegypan.com

Chapter I

A KNIGHT-ERRANT

*A*bout a hundred and thirty years ago, when the third George, whom our grandfathers knew in his blind dotage, was a young and sturdy bridegroom; when old Q., whom 1810 found peering from his balcony in Piccadilly, deaf, toothless, and a skeleton, was that gay and lively spark, the Earl of March; when *bore* and *boreish* were words of *haut ton*, unknown to the vulgar, and the price of a borough was 5,000*l.*; when gibbets still served for sign-posts, and railways were not and highwaymen were — to be more exact, in the early spring of the year 1767, a traveling chariot-and-four drew up about five in the evening before the inn at Wheatley Bridge, a short stage from Oxford on the Oxford road. A gig and a couple of post-chaises, attended by the customary group of stablemen, topers, and gossips already stood before the house, but these were quickly deserted in favor of the more important equipage. The drawers in their aprons trooped out, but the landlord, foreseeing a rich harvest, was first at the door of the carriage, and opened it with a bow such as is rarely seen in these days.

"Will your lordship please to alight?" he said.

"No, rascal!" cried one of those within. "Shut the door!"

"You wish fresh horses, my lord?" the obsequious host replied. "Of course. They shall be —"

"We wish nothing," was the brisk answer. "D'ye hear? Shut the door, and go to the devil!"

Puzzled, but obedient, the landlord fell back on the servants, who had descended from their seat in front and were beating their hands one on another, for the March evening was chill. "What is up, gentlemen?" he said.

"Nothing. But we will put something down, by your leave," they answered.

"Won't they do the same?" He cocked his thumb in the direction of the carriage.

"No. You have such an infernal bad road, the dice roll," was the answer. "They will finish their game in quiet. That is all. Lord, how your folks stare! Have they never seen a lord before?"

"Who is it?" the landlord asked eagerly. "I thought I knew his Grace's face."

Before the servant could answer or satisfy his inquisitiveness, the door of the carriage was opened in haste, and the landlord sprang to offer his shoulder. A tall young man whose shaped riding-coat failed to hide that which his jeweled hands and small French hat would alone have betrayed — that he was dressed in the height of fashion — stepped down. "A room and a bottle of your best claret," he said. "And bring me ink and a pen."

"Immediately, my lord. This way, my lord. Your lordship will perhaps honor me by dining here?"

"Lord, no! Do you think I want to be poisoned?" was the frank answer. And looking about him with languid curiosity, the young peer, followed by a companion, lounged into the house.

The third traveler — for three there were — by a gesture directed the servant to close the carriage door, and, keeping his seat, gazed sleepily through the window. The loitering crowd, standing at a respectful distance, returned his glances with interest, until an empty post-chaise, approaching from the direction of Oxford, rattled up noisily and split the group asunder. As the steaming horses stopped within a few paces of the chariot, the gentleman seated in the latter saw one of the ostlers go up to the post-chaise and heard him say, "Soon back, Jimmie?"

"Aye, and I ha' been stopped too," the postboy answered as he dropped his reins.

"No!" in a tone of surprise. "Was it Black Jack?"

"Not he. 'Twas a woman!"

A murmur of astonishment greeted the answer. The postboy grinned, and sitting easily in his pad prepared to enjoy the situation. "Aye, a woman!" he said. "And a rare pair of eyes to that. What do you think she wanted, lads?"

"The stuff, of course."

"Not she. Wanted one of them I took" — and he jerked his elbow contemptuously in the direction whence he had come — "to fight a duel for her. One of they! Said, was he Mr. Berkeley, and would he risk his life for a woman."

The head ostler stared. "Lord! and who was it he was to fight?" he asked at last.

"She did not say. Her spark maybe, that has jilted her."

"And would they, Jimmie?"

"They? Shoo! They were Methodists," the postboy answered contemptuously, "Scratch wigs and snuff-color. If she had not been next door to a Bess of Bedlam and in a main tantrum, she would have seen that. But 'Are you Mr. Berkeley?' she says, all on fire like. And 'Will you fight for a woman?' And when they shrieked out, banged the door on them. But I tell you she was a pretty piece as you'd wish to see. If she had asked me, I would not have said no to her." And he grinned.

The gentleman in the chariot opened a window. "Where did she stop you, my man?" he asked idly.

"Half a mile this side of Oxford, your worship," the postboy answered, knuckling his forehead. "Seemed to me, sir, she was a play actress. She had that sort of way with her."

The gentleman nodded and closed the window. The night had so far set in that they had brought out lights; as he sat back, one of these, hung in the carriage, shone on his features and betrayed that he was smiling. In this mood his face lost the air of affected refinement — which was then the mode, and went perfectly with a wig and ruffles — and appeared in its true cast, plain and strong, yet not uncomely. His features lacked the insipid regularity which, where all shaved, passed for masculine beauty; the nose ended largely, the cheekbones were high, and the chin projected. But from the risk and even the edge of ugliness it was saved by a pair of grey eyes, keen, humorous, and kindly, and a smile that showed the eyes at their best. Of late those eyes had been known to express weariness and satiety; the man was tiring of the round of costly follies and aimless amusements in which he passed his life. But at twenty-six pepper is still hot in the mouth, and Sir George Soane continued to drink, game, and fribble, though the first pungent flavor of those delights had vanished, and the things themselves began to pall upon him.

When he had sat thus ten minutes, smiling at intervals, a stir about the door announced that his companions were returning. The landlord preceded them, and was rewarded for his pains with half a guinea; the crowd with a shower of small silver. The postillions cracked their whips, the horses started forward, and amid a shrill hurrah my lord's carriage rolled away from the door.

"Now, who casts?" the peer cried briskly, arranging himself in his seat. "George, I'll set you. The old stakes?"

"No, I am done for tonight," Sir George answered yawning without disguise.

"What! crabbed, dear lad?"

"Aye, set Berkeley, my lord. He's a better match for you."

"And be robbed by the first highwayman we meet? No, no! I told you, if I was to go down to this damp hole of mine — fancy living a hundred miles from White's! I should die if I could not game every day — you were to play with me, and Berkeley was to ensure my purse."

"He would as soon take it," Sir George answered languidly, gazing through the glass.

"Sooner, by — !" cried the third traveler, a saturnine, dark-faced man of thirty-four or more, who sat with his back to the horses, and toyed with a pistol that lay on the seat beside him. "I'm content if your lordship is."

"Then have at you! Call the main, Colonel. You may be the devil among the highwaymen — that was Selwyn's joke, was it not? — but I'll see the color of your money."

"Beware of him. He *doved* March," Sir George said indifferently.

"He won't strip me," cried the young lord. "Five is the main. Five to four he throws crabs! Will you take, George?"

Soane did not answer, and the two, absorbed in the rattle of the dice and the turns of their beloved hazard, presently forgot him; his lordship being the deepest player in London and as fit a successor to the luckless Lord Mountford as one drop of water to another. Thus left to himself, and as effectually screened from remark as if he sat alone, Sir George devoted himself to an eager scrutiny of the night, looking first through one window and then through the other; in which he persevered though darkness had fallen so completely that only the hedges showed in the lamplight, gliding giddily by in endless walls of white. On a sudden he dropped the glass with an exclamation, and thrust out his head.

"Pull up!" he cried. "I want to descend."

The young lord uttered a peevish exclamation. "What is to do?" he continued, glancing round; then, instantly returning to the dice, "if it is my purse they want, say Berkeley is here. That will scare them. What are you doing, George?"

"Wait a minute," was the answer; and in a twinkling Soane was out, and was ordering the servant, who had climbed down, to close the door. This effected, he strode back along the road to a spot where a figure, cloaked, and hooded, was just visible, lurking on the fringe of the lamplight. As he approached it, he raised his hat with an exaggeration of politeness.

"Madam," he said, "you asked for me, I believe?"

The woman — for a woman it was, though he could see no more of her than a pale face, staring set and Gorgonlike from under the hood — did not answer at once. Then, "Who are you?" she said.

"Colonel Berkeley," he answered with assurance, and again saluted her.

"Who killed the highwayman at Hounslow last Christmas?" she cried.

"The same, madam."

"And shot Farnham Joe at Roehampton?"

"Yes, madam. And much at your service."

"We shall see," she answered, her voice savagely dubious. "At least you are a gentleman and can use a pistol? But are you willing to risk something for justice' sake?"

"And the sake of your *beaux veux*, madam?" he answered, a laugh in his voice. "Yes."

"You mean it?"

"Prove me," he answered.

His tone was light; but the woman, who seemed to labor under strong emotion, either failed to notice this or was content to put up with it. "Then send on your carriage," she said.

His jaw fell at that, and had there been light by which to see him he would have looked foolish. At last, "Are we to walk?" he said.

"Those are the lights of Oxford," she answered. "We shall be there in ten minutes."

"Oh, very well," he said, "A moment, if you please."

She waited while he went to the carriage and told the astonished servants to leave his baggage at the Mitre; this understood, he put in his head and announced to his host that he would come on next day. "Your lordship must excuse me tonight," he said.

"What is up?" my lord asked, without raising his eyes or turning his head. He had taken the box and thrown nicks three times running, at five guineas the cast; and was in the seventh heaven. "Ha! five is the main. Now you are in it, Colonel. What did you say, George? Not coming! What is it?"

"An adventure."

"What! a petticoat?"

"Yes," Sir George answered, smirking.

"Well, you find 'em in odd places. Take care of yourself. But shut the door, that is a good fellow. There is a d——d draft."

Sir George complied, and, nodding to the servants, walked back to the woman. As he reached her the carriage with its lights whirled away, and left them in darkness.

Soane wondered if he were not a fool for his pains, and advanced a step nearer to conviction when the woman with an impatient "Come!" started along the road; moving at a smart pace in the direction which the chariot had taken, and betraying so little shyness or timidity as to seem unconscious of his company. The neighborhood of Oxford is low and flat, and except where a few lights marked the outskirts of the city a wall of darkness shut them in, permitting nothing to be seen that lay more than a few paces away. A grey drift of clouds, luminous in comparison with the gloom about them, moved slowly overhead, and out of the night the raving of a farm-dog or the creaking of a dry bough came to the ear with melancholy effect.

The fine gentleman of that day had no taste for the wild, the rugged, or the lonely. He lived too near the times when those words spelled danger. He found at Almack's his most romantic scene, at Ranelagh his *terra incognita,* in the gardens of Versailles his ideal of the charming and picturesque. Sir George, no exception to the rule, shivered as he looked round. He began to experience a revulsion of spirits; and to consider that, for a gentleman who owned Lord Chatham for a patron, and was even now on his roundabout way to join that minister — for a gentleman whose fortune, though crippled and impaired, was still tolerable, and who, where it had suffered, might look with confidence to see it made good at the public expense — or to what end patrons or ministers? — he began to reflect, I say, that for such an one to exchange a peer's coach and good company for a night trudge at a woman's heels was a folly, better befitting a boy at school than a man of his years. Not that he had ever been so wild as to contemplate anything serious; or from the first had entertained the most remote intention of brawling in an unknown cause. That was an extravagance beyond him; and he doubted if the girl really had it in her mind. The only adventure he had proposed, when he left the carriage, was one of gallantry; it was the only adventure then in vogue. And for that, now the time was come, and the *incognita* and he were as much alone as the most ardent lover could wish, he felt singularly disinclined.

True, the outline of her cloak, and the indications of a slender, well-formed shape which it permitted to escape, satisfied him that the postboy had not deceived him; but that his companion was both young and handsome. And with this and his bargain it was to be supposed he would be content. But the pure matter-of-factness of the girl's manner, her silence, and her uncompromising attitude, as she walked by his side, cooled whatever ardor her beauty and the reflection that he had jockeyed Berkeley were calculated to arouse; and it was with an effort that he presently lessened the distance between them.

"Et vera incessu patuit dea!" he said, speaking in the tone between jest and earnest which he had used before. "'And all the goddess in her step appears.' Which means that you have the prettiest walk in the world, my dear — but whither are you taking me?"

She went steadily on, not deigning an answer.

"But — my charmer, let us parley," he remonstrated, striving to maintain a light tone. "In a minute we shall be in the town and —"

"I thought that we understood one another," she answered curtly, still continuing to walk, and to look straight before her; in which position her hood, hid her face. "I am taking you where I want you."

"Oh, very well," he said, shrugging his shoulders. But under his breath he muttered, "By heaven, I believe that the pretty fool really thinks — that I am going to fight for her!"

To a man who had supped at White's the night before, and knew his age to be the *âge des philosophes*, it seemed the wildest fancy in the world. And his distaste grew. But to break off and leave her — at any rate until he had put it beyond question that she had no underthought — to break off and leave her after placing himself in a situation so humiliating, was too much for the pride of a Macaroni. The lines of her head and figure too, half guessed and half revealed, and wholly light and graceful, had caught his fancy and created a desire to subjugate her. Reluctantly, therefore, he continued to walk beside her, over Magdalen Bridge, and thence by a path which, skirting the city, ran across the low wooded meadows at the back of Merton.

A little to the right the squat tower of the college loomed against the lighter rack of clouds, and rising amid the dark lines of trees that beautify that part of the outskirts, formed a *coup d'oeil* sufficiently impressive. Here and there, in such of the chamber windows as looked over the meadows, lights twinkled cheerfully; emboldened by which, yet avoiding their scope, pairs of lovers of the commoner class sneaked to and fro under the trees. Whether the presence of these recalled early memories which Sir George's fastidiousness found unpalatable, or he felt his fashion, smirched by the vulgarity of this Venus-walk, his impatience grew; and was not far from bursting forth when his guide turned sharply into an alley behind the cathedral, and, after threading a lane of mean houses, entered a small court.

The place, though poor and narrow, was not squalid. Sir George could see so much by the light which shone from a window and fell on a group of five or six persons, who stood about the nearest door and talked in low, excited voices. He had a good view of one man's face, and read in it gloom and anger. Then the group made way for the girl, eyeing her, as he thought, with pity and a sort of deference; and cursing the folly that had brought him into such a place and situation, wondering what on earth it all meant or in what it would end, he followed her into the house.

She opened a door on the right-hand side of the narrow passage, and led the way into a long, low room. For a moment he saw no more than two lights on a distant table, and kneeling at a chair beside them a woman with grey disheveled hair, who seemed to be praying, her face hidden. Then his gaze, sinking instinctively, fell on a low bed between him and the woman; and there rested on a white sheet, and on the solemn outlines — so certain in their rigidity, so unmistakable by human eyes — of a body laid out for burial.

Chapter II

A MISADVENTURE

*T*o be brought up short in an amorous quest by such a sight as that was a shock alike to Soane's better nature and his worse dignity. The former moved him to stand silent and abashed, the latter to ask with an indignant curse why he had been brought to that place. And the latter lower instinct prevailed. But when he raised his head to put the question with the necessary spirt of temper, he found that the girl had left his side and passed to the other hand of the dead; where, the hood thrown back from her face, she stood looking at him with such a gloomy fire in her eyes as it needed but a word, a touch, a glance to kindle into a blaze.

At the moment, however, he thought less of this than of the beauty of the face which he saw for the first time. It was a southern face, finely molded, dark and passionate, full-lipped, yet wide of brow, with a generous breadth between the eyes. Seldom had he seen a woman more beautiful; and he stood silent, the words he had been about to speak dying stillborn on his lips.

Yet she seemed to understand them; she answered them. "Why have I brought you here?" she cried, her voice trembling; and she pointed to the bed. "Because he is — he was my father. And he lies there. And because the man who killed him goes free. And I would — I would kill *him!* Do you hear me? I would kill him!"

Sir George tried to free his mind from the influence of her passion and her eyes, from the nightmare of the room and the body, and to see things in a sane light. "But — my good girl," he said, slowly and not unkindly, "I know nothing about it. Nothing. I am a stranger here."

"For that reason I brought you here," she retorted.

"But — I cannot interfere," he answered, shaking his head. "There is the law. You must apply to it. The law will punish the man if he has done wrong."

"But the law will *not* punish him!" she cried with scorn. "The law? The law is your law, the law of the rich. And he" — she pointed to the bed — "was poor and a servant. And the man who killed him was his master. So he goes free — of the law!"

"But if he killed him?" Sir George muttered lamely.

"He did!" she cried between her teeth. "And I would have you kill him!"

He shook his head. "My good girl," he said kindly, "you are distraught. You are not yourself. Or you would know a gentleman does not do these things."

"A gentleman!" she retorted, her smoldering rage flaming up at last. "No; but I will tell you what he does. He kills a man to save his purse! Or his honor! Or for a mis-word at cards! Or the lie given in drink! He will run a man through in a dark room, with no one to see fair play! But for drawing his sword to help a woman, or avenge a wrong, a gentleman — a gentleman does not do these things. It is true! And may —"

"Oh, have done, have done, my dear!" cried a wailing, tearful voice; and Sir George, almost cowed by the girl's fierce words and the fiercer execration that was on her lips, hailed the intervention with relief. The woman whom he had seen on her knees had risen and now approached the girl, showing a face wrinkled, worn, and plain, but not ignoble; and for the time lifted above the commonplace by the tears that rained down it. "Oh, my lovey, have done," she cried. "And let the gentleman go. To kill another will not help him that is dead. Nor us that are left alone!"

"It will not help him!" the girl answered, shrilly and wildly; and her eyes, leaving Soane, strayed round the room as if she were that moment awakened and missed someone. "No! But is he to be murdered, and no one suffer? Is he to die and no one pay? He who had a smile for us, go in or out, and never a harsh word or thought; who never did any man wrong or wished any man ill? Yet he lies there! Oh, mother, mother," she continued, her voice broken on a sudden by a tremor of pain, "we are alone! We are alone! We shall never see him come in at that door again!"

The old woman sobbed helplessly and made no answer; on which the girl, with a gesture as simple as it was beautiful, drew the grey head to her shoulder. Then she looked at Sir George. "Go," she said; but he saw that the tears were welling up in her eyes, and that her frame was beginning to tremble. "Go! I was not myself — a while ago — when I fetched you. Go, sir, and leave us."

Moved by the abrupt change, as well as by her beauty, Sir George lingered; muttering that perhaps he could help her in another way. But she shook her head, once and again; and, instinctively respecting the grief which had found at length its proper vent, he turned and, softly lifting the latch, went out into the court.

The night air cooled his brow, and recalled him to sober earnest and the eighteenth century. In the room which he had left, he had marked nothing out of the common except the girl. The mother, the furniture, the very bed on which the dead man lay, all were appropriate, and such as he would expect to find in the house of his under-steward. But the girl? The girl was gloriously handsome; and as eccentric as she was beautiful. Sir George's head turned and his eyes glowed as he thought of her. He considered what a story he could make of it at White's; and he put up his spying-glass, and looked through it to see if the towers of the cathedral still overhung the court. "Gad, sir!" he said aloud, rehearsing the story, as much to get rid of an unfashionable sensation he had in his throat as in pure whimsy, "I was surprised to find that it was Oxford. It should have been Granada, or Baghdad, or Florence! I give you my word, the houris that the Montagu saw in the Hammam at Stamboul were nothing to her!"

The persons through whom he had passed on his way to the door were still standing before the house. Glancing back when he had reached the mouth of the court, he saw that they were watching him; and, obeying a sudden impulse of curiosity, he turned on his heel and signed to the nearest to come to him. "Here, my man," he said, "a word with you."

The fellow moved towards him reluctantly, and with suspicion. "Who is it lies dead there?" Sir George asked.

"Your honor knows," the man answered cautiously.

"No, I don't."

"Then you will be the only one in Oxford that does not," the fellow replied, eyeing him oddly.

"Maybe," Soane answered with impatience. "Take it so, and answer the question,"

"It is Masterson, that was the porter at Pembroke."

"Ah! And how did he die?"

"That is asking," the man answered, looking shiftily about. "And it is an ill business, and I want no trouble. Oh, well" — he continued, as Sir George put something in his hand — "thank your honor, I'll drink your health. Yes, it is Masterson, poor man, sure enough; and two days ago he was as well as you or I — saving your presence. He was on the gate that evening, and there was a supper on one of the staircases: all the bloods of the College, your honor will understand. About an hour before midnight the Master sent him to tell the gentlemen he could not sleep for the noise. After that it is not known just what happened, but the party had him in and gave him wine; and whether he went then and returned again when the company were gone is a question. Any way, he was found in the morning, cold and dead at the foot of the stairs, and his neck broken. It is said by some a trap was laid for him on the staircase. And if it was," the man continued, after a pause, his true feeling finding sudden vent, "it is a black shame that the law does not punish it! But the coroner brought it in an accident."

Sir George shrugged his shoulders. Then, moved by curiosity and a desire to learn something about the girl, "His daughter takes it hardly," he said.

The man grunted. "Ah," he said, "maybe she has need to. Your honor does not come from him?"

"From Whom? I come from no one."

"To be sure, sir, I was forgetting. But, seeing you with her — but there, you are a stranger."

Soane would have liked to ask him his meaning, but felt that he had condescended enough. He bade the man a curt good-night, therefore, and turning away passed quickly into St. Aldate's Street. Thence it was but a step to the Mitre, where he found his baggage and servant awaiting him.

In those days distinctions of dress were still clear and unmistakable. Between the peruke — often forty guineas' worth — the tie-wig, the scratch, and the man who went content with a little powder, the intervals were measurable. Ruffles cost five pounds a pair; and velvets and silks, cut probably in Paris, were morning wear. Moreover, the dress of the man who lost or won his thousand in a night at Almack's, and was equally well known at Madame du Deffand's in Paris and at Holland House, differed as much from the dress of the ordinary well-to-do gentleman as that again differed from the lawyer's or the doctor's. The Mitre, therefore, saw in Sir George a very fine gentleman indeed, set him down to an excellent supper in its best room, and promised a post-chaise-and-four for the following morning — all with much bowing and scraping, and much mention of my lord to whose house he would post. For in those days, if a fine gentleman was a very fine gentleman, a peer was also a peer. Quite recently they had ventured to hang one; but with apologies, a landau-and-six, and a silken halter.

Sir George would not have had the least pretension to be the glass of fashion and the mold of form, which St. James's Street considered him, if he had failed to give a large share of his thoughts while he supped to the beautiful woman he had quitted. He knew very well what steps Lord March or Tom Hervey would take, were either in his place; and though he had no greater taste for an irregular life than became a man in his station who was neither a Methodist nor Lord Dartmouth, he allowed his thoughts to dwell, perhaps longer than was prudent, on the girl's perfections, and on what might have been were his heart a little harder, or the not overrigid rule which he observed a trifle less stringent. The father was dead. The girl was poor: probably her ideal of a gallant was a College beau, in second-hand lace and stained linen, drunk on ale in the forenoon. Was it likely that the fortress would hold out long, or that the maiden's heart would prove to be more obdurate than Danäe's?

Soane, considering these things and his self-denial, grew irritable over his Chambertin. He pictured Lord March's friend, the Rena, and found this girl immeasurably before her. He painted the sensation she would make and the fashion he could give her, and vowed that she was a Gunning with sense and wit added; to sum up all, he blamed himself for a saint and a Scipio. Then, late as it was, he sent for the landlord, and to get rid of his thoughts, or in pursuance of them, inquired of that worthy if Mr. Thomasson was in residence at Pembroke.

"Yes, Sir George, he is," the landlord answered; and asked if he should send for his reverence.

"No," Soane commanded. "If there is a chair to be had, I will go to him."

"There is one below, at your honor's service. And the men are waiting."

So Sir George, with the landlord, lighting him and his man attending with his cloak, descended the stairs in state, entered the sedan, and was carried off to Pembroke.

Chapter III

TUTOR AND PUPILS — OLD STYLE

Doctor Samuel Johnson, of Johnson's Court, Fleet Street, had at this time some name in the world; but not to the pitch that persons entering Pembroke College hastened to pay reverence to the second floor over the gateway, which he had vacated thirty years earlier — as persons do now. Their gaze, as a rule, rose no higher than the first-floor oriel, where the shapely white shoulder of a Parian statue, enhanced by a background of dark-blue silken hanging, caught the wandering eye. What this lacked of luxury and mystery was made up — almost to the Medmenham point in the eyes of the city — by the gleam of girandoles, and the glow, rather felt than seen, of Titian-copies in Florence frames. Sir George, borne along in his chair, peered up at this well-known window — well-known, since in the Oxford of 1767 a man's rooms were furnished if he had tables and chairs, store of beef and October, an apple-pie and Common Room port — and seeing the casement brilliantly lighted, smiled a trifle contemptuously.

"The Reverend Frederick is not much changed," he muttered. "Lord, what a beast it was! And how we hazed him! Ah! At home, is he?" — this to the servant, as the man lifted the head of the chair. "Yes, I will go up."

To tell the truth, the Reverend Frederick Thomasson had so keen a scent for Gold Tufts or aught akin to them, that it would have been strange if the instinct had not kept him at home; as a magnet, though unseen, attracts the needle. The same prepossession brought him, as soon as he heard of his visitor's approach, hurrying to the head of the stairs; where, if he had had his way, he would have clasped the baronet in his arms, slobbered over him, after the mode of Paris — for that was a trick of his — and perhaps even wept on his shoulder. But Soane, who knew his ways, coolly defeated the maneuver by fending him off with his cane; and the Reverend Frederick was reduced to raising his eyes and hands to heaven in token of the joy which filled him at the sight of his old pupil.

"Lord! Sir George, I am inexpressibly happy!" he cried. "My dear sir, my very dear sir, welcome to my poor rooms! This is joy indeed! Gaudeamus! Gaudeamus! To see you once more, fresh from the groves of Arthur's and the scenes of your triumphs! Pardon me, my dear sir, I must and will shake you by the hand again!" And succeeding at last in seizing Sir George's hand, he fondled and patted it in both of his — which were fat and white — the while with every mark of emotion he led him into the room.

"Gad!" said Sir George, standing and looking round. "And where is she, Tommy?"

"That old name! What a pleasure it is to hear it!" cried the tutor, affecting to touch his eyes with the corner of a dainty handkerchief; as if the gratification he mentioned were too much for his feelings.

"But, seriously, Tommy, where is she?" Soane persisted, still looking round with a grin.

"My dear Sir George! My honored friend! But you would always have your joke."

"And, plainly, Tommy, is all this frippery yours?"

"Tut, tut!" Mr. Thomasson remonstrated. "And no man with a finer taste. I have heard Mr. Walpole say that with a little training no man would excel Sir George Soane as a connoisseur. An exquisite eye! A nice discrimination! A —"

"Now, Tommy, to how many people have you said that?" Sir George retorted, dropping into a chair, and coolly staring about him. "But, there, have done, and tell me about yourself. Who is the last sprig of nobility you have been training in the way it should grow?"

"The last pupil who honored me," the Reverend Frederick answered, "as you are so kind as to ask after my poor concerns, Sir George, was my Lord E——'s son. We went to Paris, Marseilles, Genoa, Florence; visited the mighty monuments of Rome, and came home by way of Venice, Milan, and Turin. I treasure the copy of Tintoretto which you see there, and these bronzes, as memorials of my lord's munificence. I brought them back with me."

"And what did my lord's son bring back?" Sir George asked, cruelly. "A Midianitish woman?"

"My honored friend!" Mr. Thomasson remonstrated. "But your wit was always mordant — mordant! Too keen for us poor folk!"

"D'ye remember the inn at Cologne, Tommy?" Sir George continued, mischievously reminiscent. "And Lord Tony arriving with his charmer? And you giving up your room to her? And the trick we played you at Calais, where we passed the little French dancer on you for Madame la

Marquise de Personne?"

Mr. Thomasson winced, and a tinge of color rose in his fat pale face. "Boys, boys!" he said, with an airy gesture. "You had an uncommon fancy even then, Sir George, though you were but a year from school! Ah, those were charming days! Great days!"

"And nights!" said Sir George, lying back in his chair and looking at the other with eyes half shut, and insolence half veiled. "Do you remember the faro bank at Florence, Tommy, and the three hundred livres you lost to that old harridan, Lady Harrington? Pearls cast before swine you styled them, I remember."

"Lord, Sir George!" Mr. Thomasson cried, vastly horrified. "How can you say such a thing? Your excellent memory plays you false."

"It does," Soane answered, smiling sardonically. "I remember. It was seed sown for the harvest, you called it — in your liquor. And that touches me. Do you mind the night Fitzhugh made you so prodigiously drunk at Bonn, Tommy? And we put you in the kneading-trough, and the servants found you and shifted you to the horse-trough? Gad! you would have died of laughter if you could have seen yourself when we rescued you, lank and dripping, with your wig like a sponge!"

"It must have been — uncommonly diverting!" the Reverend Frederick stammered; and he smiled widely, but with a lack of heart. This time there could be no doubt of the pinkness that overspread his face.

"Diverting? I tell you it would have made old Dartmouth laugh!" Sir George said, bluntly.

"Ha, ha! Perhaps it would. Perhaps it would. Not that I have the honor of his lordship's acquaintance."

"No? Well, he would not suit you, Tommy. I would not seek it."

The Reverend Frederick looked doubtful, as weighing the possibility of anything that bore the name of lord being alien from him. From this reflection, however, he was roused by a new sally on Soane's part. "But, crib me! you are very fine tonight, Mr. Thomasson," he said, staring about him afresh. "Ten o'clock, and you are lighted as for a drum! What is afoot?"

The tutor smirked and rubbed his hands. "Well, I — I was expecting a visitor, Sir George."

"Ah, you dog! She is not here, but you are expecting her."

Mr. Thomasson grinned; the jest flattered him. Nevertheless he hastened to exonerate himself. "It is not Venus I am expecting, but Mars," he said with a simper. "The Honorable Mr. Dunborough, son to my Lord Dunborough, and the same whose meritorious services at the Havanna you, my dear friend, doubtless remember. He is now cultivating in peace the gifts which in war —"

"Sufficed to keep him out of danger!" Sir George said bluntly. "So he is your last sprig, is he? He should be well seasoned."

"He is four-and-twenty," Mr. Thomasson answered, pluming himself and speaking in his softest tones. "And the most charming, I assure you, the most debonair of men. But do I hear a noise?"

"Yes," said Sir George, listening. "I hear something."

Mr. Thomasson rose. "What — what is it, I wonder?" he said, a trifle nervously. A dull sound, as of a hive of bees stirred to anger, was becoming audible.

"Devil if I know!" Sir George answered. "Open the window."

But the Reverend Frederick, after approaching the window with the intention of doing so, seemed disinclined to go nearer, and hovered about it. "Really," he said, no longer hiding his discomposure. "I fear that it is something — something in the nature of a riot. I fear that that which I anticipated has happened. If my honorable friend had only taken my advice and remained here!" And he wrung his hands without disguise.

"Why, what has he to do with it?" Soane asked, curiously.

"He — he had an accident the other night," Mr. Thomasson answered. "A monstrous nuisance for him. He and his noble friend, Lord Almeric Doyley, played a little trick on a — on one of the College servants. The clumsy fellow — it is marvelous how awkward that class of persons is — fell down the stairs and hurt himself."

"Seriously?"

"Somewhat. Indeed — in fact he is dead. And now there is a kind of feeling about it in the town. I persuaded Mr. Dunborough to take up his quarters here for the night, but he is so spirited he would dine abroad. Now I fear, I really fear, he may be in trouble!"

"If it is he they are hooting in St. Aldate's," Sir George answered dryly, "I should say he was in trouble! But in my time the gownsmen would have sallied out and brought him off before this. And given those yelpers a cracked crown or two!"

The roar of voices in the narrow streets was growing clearer and more threatening. "Ye-es?" said the Reverend Frederick, moving about the room, distracted between his anxiety and his respect for his companion. "Perhaps so. But there is a monstrous low, vulgar set in College nowadays; a man of spirit has no chance with them. Yesterday they had the insolence to break into my noble friend's rooms and throw his furniture out of window! And, I vow, would have gone on to — but Lord! this is frightful! What a shocking howling! My dear sir, my very dear Sir George," Mr. Thomasson continued, his voice tremulous and his fat cheeks grown on a sudden loose and flabby, "do you think that there is any danger?"

"Danger?" Sir George answered, with cruel relish — he had gone to the window, and was looking out. "Well, I should say that Madam Venus there would certainly have to stand shot. If you are wise you will put out some of those candles. They are entering the lane now. Gad, Tommy, if they think your lad of spirit is here, I would not give much for your window-glass!"

Mr. Thomasson, who had hastened to take the advice, and had extinguished all the candles but one, thus reducing the room to partial darkness, wrung his hands and moaned for answer. "Where are the proctors?" he said. "Where are the constables? Where are the — Oh, dear, dear, this is dreadful!"

And certainly, even in a man of firmer courage a little trepidation might have been pardoned. As the unseen crowd, struggling and jostling, poured from the roadway of St. Aldate's into the narrow confines of Pembroke Lane, the sound of its hooting gathered sudden volume, and from an intermittent murmur, as of a remote sea, swelled in a moment into a roar of menace. And as a mob is capable of deeds from which the members who compose it would severally shrink, as nothing is so pitiless, nothing so unreasoning, so in the sound of its voice is a note that appalls all but the hardiest. Soane was no coward. A year before he had been present at the siege of Bedford House by the Spitalfields weavers, where swords were drawn and much blood was spilled, while the gentlemen of the clubs and coffee-houses looked on as at a play; but even he felt a slackening of the pulse as he listened. And with the Reverend Frederick it was different. He was not framed for danger. When the smoking glare of the links which the ringleaders carried began to dance and flicker on the opposite houses, he looked about him with a wild eye, and had already taken two steps towards the door, when it opened.

It admitted two men about Sir George's age, or a little younger. One, after glancing round, passed hurriedly to the window and looked out; the other sank into the nearest chair, and, fanning himself with his hat, muttered a querulous oath.

"My dear lord!" cried the Reverend Frederick, hastening to his side — and it is noteworthy that he forgot even his panic in the old habit of reverence — "What an escape! To think that a life so valuable as your lordship's should lie at the mercy of those wretches! I shudder at the thought of what might have happened."

"Fan me, Tommy" was the answer. And Lord Almeric, an excessively pale, excessively thin young man, handed his hat with a gesture of exhaustion to the obsequious tutor. "Fan me; that is a good soul. Positively I am suffocated with the smell of those creatures! Worse than horses, I assure you. There, again! What a pother about a common fellow! 'Pon honor, I don't know what the world is coming to!"

"Nor I," Mr. Thomasson answered, hanging over him with assiduity and concern on his countenance. "It is not to be comprehended."

"No, 'pon honor it is not!" my lord agreed. And then, feeling a little recovered, "Dunborough," he asked, "what are they doing?"

"Hanging you, my dear fellow!" the other answered from the window, where he had taken his place within a pace of Soane, but without discovering him. He spoke in the full boisterous tone of one in perfect health and spirits, perfectly satisfied with himself, and perfectly heedless of others.

"Oh, I say, you are joking?" my lord answered. "Hanging me? Oh, ah! I see. In effigy!"

"And your humble servant," said Mr. Dunborough. "I tell you, Tommy, we had a near run for it. Curse their impudence, they made us sweat. For a very little I would give the rascals something to howl for."

Perhaps he meant no more than to put a bold face on it before his creatures. But unluckily the rabble, which had come provided with a cart and gallows, a hangman, and a paunchy, red-faced fellow in canonicals, and which hitherto had busied itself with the mock execution, found leisure at this moment to look up at the window. Catching sight of the object of their anger, they vented their rage in a roar of execration, so much louder than all that had gone before that it brought the sentence which Mr. Thomasson was uttering to a quavering end. But the demonstration, far from intimidating Mr. Dunborough, provoked him to fury. Turning from the sea of brandished hands and upturned faces, he strode to a table, and in a moment returned. The window was open, he flung it wider, and stood erect, in full view of the mob.

The sight produced a momentary silence, of which he took advantage. "Now, you tailors, begone!" he cried harshly. "To your hovels, and leave gentlemen to their wine, or it will be the worse for you. Come, march! We have had enough of your fooling, and are tired of it."

The answer was a shout of "Cain!" and "Murderer!" One voice cried "Ferrers!" and this caught the fancy of the crowd. In a moment a hundred were crying, "Aye, Ferrers! Come down, and we'll Ferrers you!"

He stood a moment irresolute, glaring at them; then something struck and shattered a pane of the window beside him, and the fetid smell of a bad egg filled the room. At the sound Mr. Thomasson uttered a cry and shrank farther into the darkness, while Lord Almeric rose hastily and looked about for a refuge. But Mr. Dunborough did not flinch.

"D——n you, you rascals, you will have it, will you?" he cried; and in the darkness a sharp click was heard. He raised his hand. A shriek in the street below answered the movement; some who stood nearest saw that he held a pistol and gave the information to others, and there was a wild rush to escape. But before the hammer dropped, a hand closed on his, and Soane, crying, "Are you mad, sir?" dragged him back.

Dunborough had not entertained the least idea that anyone stood near him, and the surprise was as complete as the check. After an instinctive attempt to wrench away his hand, he stood glaring at the person who held him. "Curse you!" he said. "Who are you? And what do you mean?"

"Not to sit by and see murder done," Sir George answered firmly. "Tomorrow you will thank me."

"For the present I'll thank you to release my hand," the other retorted in a freezing tone. Nevertheless, Sir George thought that the delay had sobered him, and complied. "Much obliged to you," Dunborough continued. "Now perhaps you will walk into the next room, where there is a light, and we can be free from that scum."

Mr. Thomasson had already set the example of a prudent retreat thither; and Lord Almeric, with a feeble, "Lord, this is very surprising! But I think that the gentleman is right, Dunny," was hovering in the doorway. Sir George signed to Mr. Dunborough to go first, but he would not, and Soane, shrugging his shoulders, preceded him.

The room into which they all crowded was no more than a closet, containing a dusty bureau propped on three legs, a few books, and Mr. Thomasson's robes, boots, and wig-stand. It was so small that when they were all in it, they stood perforce close together, and had the air of persons sheltering from a storm. This nearness, the glare of the lamp on their faces, and the mean surroundings gave a kind of added force to Mr. Dunborough's rage. For a moment after entering he could not speak; he had dined largely, and sat long after dinner; and his face was suffused with blood. But then, "Tommy, who is — this — fellow?" he cried, blurting out the words as if each must be the last.

"Good heavens!" cried the tutor, shocked at the low appellation. "Mr. Dunborough! Mr. Dunborough! You mistake. My dear sir, my dear friend, you do not understand. This is Sir George Soane, whose name must be known to you. Permit me to introduce him."

"Then take that for a meddler and a coxcomb, Sir George Soane!" cried the angry man; and quick as thought he struck Sir George, who was at elbows with him, lightly in the face.

Sir George stepped back, his face crimson. "You are not sober, sir!"

he said.

"Is not that enough?" cried the other, drowning both Mr. Thomasson's exclamation of horror and Lord Almeric's protest of, "Oh, but I say, you know —" under the volume of his voice. "You have a sword, sir, and I presume you know how to use it. If there is not space here, there is a room below, and I am at your service. You will not wipe that off by rubbing it," he added coarsely.

Sir George dropped his hand from his face as if it stung him. "Mr. Dunborough," he said trembling — but it was with passion, "if I thought you were sober and would not repent tomorrow what you have done tonight —"

"You would do fine things," Dunborough retorted. "Come, sir, a truce to your impertinence! You have meddled with me, and you must maintain it. Must I strike you again?"

"I will not meet you tonight," Sir George answered firmly. "I will be neither Lord Byron nor his victim. These gentlemen will bear me out so far. For the rest, if you are of the same mind tomorrow, it will be for me and not for you to ask a meeting."

"At your service, sir," Mr. Dunborough said, with a sarcastic bow. "But suppose, to save trouble in the morning, we fix time and place now."

"Eight — in Magdalen Fields," Soane answered curtly. "If I do not hear from you, I am staying at the Mitre Inn. Mr. Thomasson, I bid you good-night. My lord, your servant."

And with that, and though Mr. Thomasson, wringing his hands over what had occurred and the injury to himself that might come of it, attempted some feeble remonstrances, Sir George bowed sternly, took his hat and went down. He found his chair at the foot of the stairs, but in consideration of the crowd he would not use it. The college porters, indeed, pressed him to wait, and demurred to opening even the wicket. But he had carried forbearance to the verge, and dreaded the least appearance of timidity; and, insisting, got his way. The rabble admired so fine a gentleman, and so resolute a bearing, gave place to him with a jest, and let him pass unmolested down the lane.

It was well that they did, for he had come to the end of his patience. One man steps out of a carriage, picks up a handkerchief, and lives to wear a Crown. Another takes the same step; it lands him in a low squabble from which he may extricate himself with safety, but scarcely with an accession of credit. Sir George belonged to the inner circle of fashion, to which neither rank nor wealth, nor parts, nor power, of necessity admitted. In the sphere in which he moved, men seldom quarreled and as seldom fought. Of easiest habit among themselves, they left bad manners and the duello to political adventurers and cubbish peers, or to the gentlemen of the quarter sessions and the local ordinary. It was with a mighty disgust, therefore, that Sir George considered alike the predicament into which a caprice had hurried him, and the insufferable young Hector whom fate had made his antagonist. They would laugh at White's. They would make a jest of it over the cakes and fruit at Betty's. Selwyn would turn a quip. And yet the thing was beyond a joke. He must be a target first and a butt afterwards — if any afterwards there were.

As he entered the Mitre, sick with chagrin, and telling himself he might have known that something of this kind would come of stooping to vulgar company, he bethought him — for the first time in an hour — of the girl. "Lord!" he said, thinking of her request, her passion, and her splendid eyes; and he stood. For the *âge des philosophes*, destiny seemed to be taking too large a part in the play. This must be the very man with whom she had striven to embroil him!

His servant's voice broke in on his thoughts. "At what hour will your honor please to be called?" he asked, as he carried off the laced coat and wig.

Soane stifled a groan. "Called?" he said. "At half-past six. Don't stare, booby! Half-past six, I said. And do you go now, I'll shift for myself. But first put out my dispatch-case, and see there is pen and ink. It's done? Then be off, and when you come in the morning bring the landlord and another with you."

The man lingered. "Will your honor want horses?" he said.

"I don't know. Yes! No! Well, not until noon. And where is my sword?"

"I was taking it down to clean it, sir."

"Then don't take it; I will look to it myself. And mind you, call me at the time I said."

Chapter IV

PEEPING TOM OF WALLINGFORD

*T*o be an attorney-at-law, avid of practice and getting none; to be called Peeping Tom of Wallingford, in the place where you would fain trot about busy and respected; to be the sole support of an old mother, and to be come almost to the toe of the stocking — these circumstances might seem to indicate an existence and prospects bare, not to say arid. Eventually they presented themselves in that light to the person most nearly concerned — by name Mr. Peter Fishwick; and moving him to grasp at the forlorn hope presented by a vacant stewardship at one of the colleges, brought him by coach to Oxford. There he spent three days and his penultimate guineas in canvassing, begging, bowing, and smirking; and on the fourth, which happened to be the very day of Sir George's arrival in the city, was duly and handsomely defeated without the honor of a vote.

Mr. Fishwick had expected no other result; and so far all was well. But he had a mother, and that mother entertained a fond belief that local jealousy and nothing else kept down her son in the place of his birth. She had built high hopes on this expedition; she had thought that the Oxford gentlemen would be prompt to recognize his merit; and for her sake the sharp-featured lawyer went back to the Mitre a rueful man. He had taken a lodging there with intent to dazzle the town, and not because his means were equal to it; and already the bill weighed upon him. By nature as cheerful a gossip as ever wore a scratch wig and lived to be inquisitive, he sat mum through the evening, and barely listened while the landlord talked big of his guest upstairs, his curricle and fashion, the sums he lost at White's, and the plate in his dressing-case.

Nevertheless the lawyer would not have been Peter Fishwick if he had not presently felt the stirrings of curiosity, or, thus incited, failed to be on the move between the stairs and the landing when Sir George came in and passed up. The attorney's ears were as sharp as a ferret's nose, and he was notably long in lighting his humble dip at a candle which by chance stood outside Sir George's door. Hence it happened that Soane — who after dismissing his servant had gone for a moment into the adjacent chamber — heard a slight noise in the room he had left; and, returning quickly to learn what it was, found no one, but observed the outer door shake as if someone tried it. His suspicions aroused, he was still staring at the door when it moved again, opened a very little way, and before his astonished eyes admitted a small man in a faded black suit, who, as soon as he had squeezed himself in, stood bowing with a kind of desperate audacity.

"Hallo!" said Sir George, staring anew. "What do you want, my man?"

The intruder advanced a pace or two, and nervously crumpled his hat in his hands. "If your honor pleases," he said, a smile feebly propitiative appearing in his face, "I shall be glad to be of service to you."

"Of service?" said Sir George, staring in perplexity. "To me?"

"In the way of my profession," the little man answered, fixing Sir George with two eyes as bright as birds'; which eyes somewhat redeemed his small keen features. "Your honor was about to make your will." "My will?" Sir George cried, amazed; "I was about to —" and then in an outburst of rage, "and if I was — what the devil business is it of yours?" he cried. "And who are you, sir?"

The little man spread out his hands in deprecation. "I?" he said. "I am an attorney, sir, and everybody's business is my business."

Sir George gasped. "You are an attorney!" he cried. "And — and everybody's business is your business! By God, this is too much!" And seizing the bell-rope he was about to overwhelm the man of law with a torrent of abuse, before he had him put out, when the absurdity of the appeal and perhaps a happy touch in Peter's last answer struck him; he held his hand, and hesitated. Then, "What is your name, sir?" he said sternly.

"Peter Fishwick," the attorney answered humbly.

"And how the devil did you know — that I wanted to make a will?"

"I was going upstairs," the lawyer explained. "And the door was ajar."

"And you listened?"

"I wanted to hear," said Peter with simplicity.

"But what did you hear, sir?" Soane retorted, scarcely able to repress a smile.

"I heard your honor tell your servant to lay out pen and paper, and to bring the landlord and another upstairs when he called you in the morning. And I heard you bid him leave your sword. And putting two and two together, respected sir," Peter continued manfully, "and knowing that it is only of a will you need three witnesses, I said to myself, being an attorney —"

"And everybody's business being your business," Sir George muttered irritably.

"To be sure, sir — it is a will, I said, he is for making. And with your honor's leave," Peter concluded with spirit, "I'll make it."

"Confound your impudence," Sir George answered, and stared at him, marveling at the little man's shrewdness.

Peter smiled in a sickly fashion. "If your honor would but allow me?" he said. He saw a great chance slipping from him, and his voice was plaintive.

It moved Sir George to compassion. "Where is your practice?" he asked ungraciously.

The attorney felt a surprising inclination to candor. "At Wallingford," he said, "it should be. But —" and there he stopped, shrugging his shoulders, and leaving the rest unsaid.

"*Can* you make a will?" Sir George retorted.

"No man better," said Peter with confidence; and on the instant he drew a chair to the table, seized the pen, and bent the nib on his thumbnail; then he said briskly, "I wait your commands, sir."

Sir George stared in some embarrassment — he had not expected to be taken so literally; but, after a moment's hesitation, reflecting that to write down his wishes with his own hand would give him more trouble, and that he might as well trust this stranger as that, he accepted the situation. "Take down what I wish, then," he said. "Put it into form afterwards, and bring it to me when I rise. Can you be secret?"

"Try me," Peter answered with enthusiasm. "For a good client I would bite off my tongue."

"Very well, then, listen!" Sir George said. And presently, after some humming and thinking, "I wish to leave all my real property to the eldest son of my uncle, Anthony Soane," he continued.

"Right, sir. Child already in existence, I presume? Not that it is absolutely necessary," the attorney continued glibly. "But —"

"I do not know," said Sir George.

"Ah!" said the lawyer, raising his pen and knitting his brows while he looked very learnedly into vacancy. "The child is expected, but you have not yet heard, sir, that —"

"I know nothing about the child, nor whether there is a child," Sir George answered testily. "My uncle may be dead, unmarried, or alive and married — what difference does it make?"

"Certainty is very necessary in these things," Peter replied severely. The pen in his hand, he became a different man. "Your uncle, Mr.

Anthony Soane, as I understand, is alive?"

"He disappeared in the Scotch troubles in '45," Sir George reluctantly explained, "was disinherited in favor of my father, sir, and has not since been heard from."

The attorney grew rigid with alertness; he was like nothing so much as a dog, expectant at a rat-hole. "Attainted?" he said.

"No!" said Sir George.

"Outlawed?"

"No."

The attorney collapsed: no rat in the hole. "Dear me, dear me, what a sad story!" he said; and then remembering that his client had profited, "but out of evil — ahem! As I understand, sir, you wish all your real property, including the capital mansion house and demesne, to go to the eldest son of your uncle Mr. Anthony Soane in tail, remainder to the second son in tail, and, failing sons, to daughters — the usual settlement, in a word, sir."

"Yes."

"No exceptions, sir."

"None."

"Very good," the attorney answered with the air of a man satisfied so far. "And failing issue of your uncle? To whom then, Sir George?"

"To the Earl of Chatham."

Mr. Fishwick jumped in his seat; then bowed profoundly.

"Indeed! Indeed! How very interesting!" he murmured under his breath. "Very remarkable! Very remarkable, and flattering."

Sir George stooped to explain. "I have no near relations," he said shortly. "Lord Chatham — he was then Mr. Pitt — was the executor of my grandfather's will, is connected with me by marriage, and at one time acted as my guardian."

Mr. Fishwick licked his lips as if he tasted something very good. This was business indeed! These were names with a vengeance! His face shone with satisfaction; he acquired a sudden stiffness of the spine. "Very good, sir," he said. "Ve — ry good," he said. "In fee simple, I understand?"

"Yes."

"Precisely. Precisely; no uses or trusts? No. Unnecessary of course. Then as to personalty, Sir George?"

"A legacy of five hundred guineas to George Augustus Selwyn, Esquire, of Matson, Gloucestershire. One of the same amount to Sir Charles Bunbury, Baronet. Five hundred guineas to each of my executors; and to each of these four a mourning ring."

"Certainly, sir. All very noble gifts!" And Mr. Fishwick smacked his lips.

For a moment Sir George looked his offence; then seeing that the attorney's ecstasy was real and unaffected, he smiled. "To my land-steward two hundred guineas," he said; "to my house-steward one hundred guineas, to the housekeeper at Estcombe an annuity of twenty guineas. Ten guineas and a suit of mourning to each of my upper servants not already mentioned, and the rest of my personalty —"

"After payment of debts and funeral and testamentary expenses," the lawyer murmured, writing busily.

Sir George started at the words, and stared thoughtfully before him: he was silent so long that the lawyer recalled his attention by gently repeating, "And the residue, honored sir?"

"To the Thatched House Society for the relief of small debtors," Sir George answered, between a sigh and a smile. And added, "They will not gain much by it, poor devils!"

Mr. Fishwick with a rather downcast air noted the bequest. "And that is all, sir, I think?" he said with his head on one side. "Except the appointment of executors."

"No," Sir George answered curtly. "It is not all. Take this down and be careful. As to the trust fund of fifty thousand pounds" — the attorney gasped, and his eyes shone as he seized the pen anew. "Take this down carefully, man, I say," Sir George continued. "As to the trust fund left by my grandfather's will to my uncle Anthony Soane or his heirs conditionally on his or their returning to their allegiance and claiming it within the space of twenty-one years from the date of his will, the interest in the meantime to be paid to me for my benefit, and the principal sum, failing such return, to become mine as fully as if it had vested in me from the beginning —"

"Ah!" said the attorney, scribbling fast, and with distended cheeks.

"I leave the said fund to go with the land."

"To go with the land," the lawyer repeated as he wrote the words. "Fifty thousand pounds! Prodigious! Prodigious! Might I ask, sir, the date of your respected grandfather's will?"

"December, 1746," Sir George answered.

"The term has then nine months to run?"

"Yes."

"With submission, then it comes to this," the lawyer answered thoughtfully, marking off the points with his pen in the air. "In the event of — of this will operating — all, or nearly all of your property, Sir George, goes to your uncle's heirs in tail — if to be found — and failing issue of his body to my Lord Chatham?"

"Those are my intentions."

"Precisely, sir," the lawyer answered, glancing at the clock. "And they shall be carried out. But — ahem! Do I understand, sir, that in the event of a claimant making good his claim before the expiration of the nine months, you stand to lose this stupendous, this magnificent sum — even in your lifetime?"

"I do," Sir George answered grimly. "But there will be enough left to pay your bill."

Peter stretched out his hands in protest, then, feeling that this was unprofessional, he seized the pen. "Will you please to honor me with the names of the executors, sir?" he said.

"Dr. Addington, of Harley Street."

"Yes, sir."

"And Mr. Dagge, of Lincoln's Inn Fields, attorney-at-law."

"It is an honor to be in any way associated with him," the lawyer muttered, as he wrote the name with a flourish. "His lordship's man of business, I believe. And now you may have your mind at ease, sir," he continued. "I will put this into form before I sleep, and will wait on you for your signature — shall I say at —"

"At a quarter before eight," said Soane. "You will be private?"

"Of course, sir. It is my business to be private. I wish you a very good night."

The attorney longed to refer to the coming meeting, and to his sincere hope that his new patron would leave the ground unscathed. But a duel was so alien from the lawyer's walk in life, that he knew nothing of the punctilios, and he felt a delicacy. Tamely to wish a man a safe issue seemed to be a common compliment incommensurate with the occasion; and a bathos. So, after a moment of hesitation, he gathered up his papers, and tiptoed out of the room with an absurd exaggeration of respect, and a heart bounding jubilant under his flapped waistcoat.

Left to himself, Sir George heaved a sigh, and, resting his head on his hand, stared long and gloomily at the candles. "Well, better be run through by this clown," he muttered after a while, "than live to put a pistol to my own head like Mountford and Bland. Or Scarborough, or poor Bolton. It is not likely, and I wish that little pettifogger had not put it into my head; but if a cousin were to appear now, or before the time is up, I should be in Queer Street. Estcombe is dipped: and of the money I raised, there is no more at the agent's than I have lost in a night at Quinze! D——n White's and that is all about it. And d——n it, I shall, and finely, if old Anthony's lad turn up and sweep off the three thousand a year that is left. Umph, if I am to have a steady hand tomorrow I must get to bed. What unholy chance brought me into this scrape?"

Chapter V

THE MEETING

Sir George awoke next morning, and, after a few lazy moments of semi-consciousness, remembered what was before him, it is not to be denied that he felt a chill. He lay awhile, thinking of the past and the future — or the no future — in a way he seldom thought, and with a seriousness for which the life he had hitherto led had left him little time and less inclination.

But he was young; he had a digestion as yet unimpaired, and nerves still strong; and when he emerged an hour later and, more soberly dressed than was his wont, proceeded down the High Street towards the Cherwell Bridge, his spirits were at their normal level. The spring sunshine which gilded the pinnacles of Magdalen tower, and shone cool and pleasant on a score of hoary fronts, wrought gaily on him also. The milksellers and such early folk were abroad, and filled the street with their cries; he sniffed the fresh air, and smiled at the good humor and morning faces that everywhere greeted him; and d——d White's anew, and vowed to live cleanly henceforth, and forswear Pam. In a word, the man was of such a courage that in his good resolutions he forgot his errand, and whence they arose; and it was with a start that, as he approached the gate leading to the college meadows, he marked a chair in waiting, and beside it Mr. Peter Fishwick, from whom he had parted at the Mitre ten minutes before.

Soane did not know whether the attorney had preceded him or followed him: the intrusion was the same, and flushed with annoyance, he strode to him to mark his sense of it. But Peter, being addressed, wore his sharpest business air, and was entirely unconscious of offence. "I have merely purveyed a surgeon," he said, indicating a young man who stood beside him. "I could not learn that you had provided one, sir."

"Oh!" Sir George answered, somewhat taken aback, "this is the gentleman."

"Yes, sir."

Soane was in the act of saluting the stranger, when a party of two or three persons came up behind, and had much ado not to jostle them in the gateway. It consisted of Mr. Dunborough, Lord Almeric, and two other gentlemen; one of these, an elderly man, who wore black and hair-powder, and carried a gold-topped cane, had a smug and well-pleased expression, that indicated his stake in the meeting to be purely altruistic. The two companies exchanged salutes.

On this followed a little struggle to give precedence at the gate, but eventually all went through. "If we turn to the right," someone observed, "there is a convenient place. No, this way, my lord."

"Oh Lord, I have such a head this morning!" his lordship answered; and he looked by no means happy. "I am all of a twitter! It is so confounded early, too. See here: cannot this be — ?"

The gentleman who had spoken before drowned his voice. "Will this do, sir?" he said, raising his hat, and addressing Sir George. The party had reached a smooth glade or lawn encompassed by thick shrubs, and to all appearance a hundred miles from a street. A fairy-ring of verdure, glittering with sunlight and dewdrops, and tuneful with the songs of birds, it seemed a morsel of paradise dropped from the cool blue of heaven. Sir George felt a momentary tightening of the throat as he surveyed its pure brilliance, and then a sudden growing anger against the fool who had brought him thither.

"You have no second?" said the stranger.

"No," he answered curtly; "I think we have witnesses enough."

"Still — if the matter can be accommodated?"

"It can," Soane answered, standing stiffly before them. "But only by an unreserved apology on Mr. Dunborough's part. He struck me. I have no more to say."

"I do not offer the apology," Mr. Dunborough rejoined, with a horse-laugh. "So we may as well go on, Jerry. I did not come here to talk."

"I have brought pistols," his second said, disregarding the sneer. "But my principal, though the challenged party, is willing to waive the choice of weapons."

"Pistols will do for me," Sir George answered.

"One shot, at a word. If ineffective, you will take to your swords," the second continued; and he pushed back his wig and wiped his forehead, as if his employment were not altogether to his taste. A duel was a fine thing — at a distance. He wished, however, that he had someone with whom to share the responsibility, now it was come to the point; and he cast a peevish look at Lord Almeric. But his lordship was, as he had candidly said, "all of a twitter," and offered no help.

"I suppose that I am to load," the unlucky second continued. "That being so, you, Sir George, must have the choice of pistols."

Sir George bowed assent, and, going a little aside, removed his hat, wig, and cravat; and was about to button his coat to his throat, when he observed that Mr. Dunborough was stripping to his shirt. Too proud not to follow the example, though prudence suggested that the white linen made him a fair mark, he stripped also, and in a trice the two, kicking off their shoes, moved to the positions assigned to them; and in their breeches and laced lawn shirts, their throats bare, confronted one another.

"Sir George, have you no one to represent you?" cried the second again, grown querulous under the burden. His name, it seemed, was Morris. He was a major in the Oxfordshire Militia.

Soane answered with impatience. "I have no second," he said, "but my surgeon will be a competent witness."

"Ah! to be sure!" Major Morris answered, with a sigh of relief. "That is so. Then, gentlemen, I shall give the signal by saying One, two, three! Be good enough to fire together at the word Three! Do you understand?"

"Yes," said Mr. Dunborough. And "Yes," Sir George said more slowly.

"Then, now, be ready! Prepare to fire! One! two! th —"

"Stay!" flashed Mr. Dunborough, while the word still hung in the air. "You have not given us our pistols," he continued, with an oath.

"What?" cried the second, staring.

"Man, you have not given us our pistols."

The major was covered with confusion. "God bless my soul! I have not!" he cried; while Lord Almeric giggled hysterically. "Dear me! dear me! it is very trying to be alone!" He threw his hat and wig on the grass, and again wiped his brow, and took up the pistols. "Sir George? Thank you. Mr. Dunborough, here is yours." Then: "Now, are you ready? Thank you."

He retreated to his place again. "Are you ready, gentlemen? Are you quite ready?" he repeated anxiously, amid a breathless silence. "One! two! *three!*"

Sir George's pistol exploded at the word; the hammer of the other clicked futile in the pan. The spectators, staring, and expecting to see one fall, saw Mr. Dunborough start and make a half turn. Before they had time to draw any conclusion he flung his pistol a dozen paces away, and cursed his second. "D——n you, Morris!" he cried shrilly; "you put no powder in the pan, you hound! But come on, sir," he continued, addressing Sir George, "I have this left." And rapidly changing his sword from his left hand, in which he had hitherto held it, to his right, he rushed upon his opponent with the utmost fury, as if he would bear him down by main force.

"Stay!" Sir George cried; and, instead of meeting him, avoided his first rush by stepping aside two paces. "Stay, sir," he repeated; "I owe you a shot! Prime afresh. Reload, sir, and —"

But Dunborough, blind and deaf with passion, broke in on him unheeding, and as if he carried no weapon; and crying furiously, "Guard yourself!" plunged his half-shortened sword at the lower part of Sir George's body. The spectators held their breath and winced; the assault was so sudden, so determined, that it seemed that nothing could save Sir George from a thrust thus delivered. He did escape, however, by a bound, quick as a cat's; but the point of Dunborough's weapon ripped up his breeches on the hip, the hilt rapped against the bone, and the two men came together bodily. For a moment they wrestled, and seemed to be going to fight like beasts.

Then Sir George, his left forearm under the other's chin, flung him three paces away; and shifting his sword into his right hand — hitherto he had been unable to change it — he stopped Dunborough's savage rush with the point, and beat him off and kept him off — parrying his lunges, and doing his utmost the while to avoid dealing him a fatal wound. Soane was so much the better swordsman — as was immediately apparent to all the onlookers — that he no longer feared for himself; all his fears were for his opponent, the fire and fury of whose attacks he could not explain to himself, until he found them flagging; and flagging so fast that he sought a reason. Then Dunborough's point beginning to waver, and his feet to slip, Sir George's eyes were opened; he discerned a crimson patch spread and spread on the other's side — where unnoticed Dunborough had kept his hand — and with a cry for help he sprang forward in time to catch the falling man in his arms.

As the others ran in, the surgeons quickly and silently, Lord Almeric more slowly, and with exclamations, Sir George lowered his burden gently to the ground. The instant it was done, Morris touched his arm and signed to him to stand back. "You can do no good, Sir George," he urged. "He is in skillful hands. He would have it; it was his own fault. I can bear witness that you did your best not to touch him."

"I did not touch him," Soane muttered.

The second looked his astonishment. "How?" he said. "You don't mean to say that he is not wounded? See there!" And he pointed to the blood which dyed the shirt. They were cutting the linen away.

"It was the pistol," Sir George answered.

Major Morris's face fell, and he groaned. "Good G——d!" he said, staring before him. "What a position I am in! I suppose — I suppose, sir, his pistol was not primed?"

"I am afraid not," Soane answered.

He was still in his shirt, and bareheaded; but as he spoke one of several onlookers, whom the clatter of steel had drawn to the spot, brought his coat and waistcoat, and held them while he put them on. Another handed his hat and wig, a third brought his shoes and knelt and buckled them; a fourth his kerchief. All these services he accepted freely, and was unconscious of them — as unconscious as he was of the eager deference, the morbid interest, with which they waited on him, eyed him, and stared at him. His own thoughts, eyes, attention, were fixed on the group about the fallen man; and when the elder surgeon glanced over his shoulder, as wanting help, he strode to them.

"If we had a chair here, and could move him at once," the smug gentleman whispered, "I think we might do."

"I have a chair. It is at the gate," his colleague answered.

"Have you? A good thought of yours!"

"The credit should lie — with my employer," the younger man answered in a low voice. "It was his thought; here it comes. Sir George, will you be good enough —" But then, seeing the baronet's look of mute anxiety, he broke off. "It is dangerous, but there is hope — fair hope," he answered. "Do you, my dear sir, go to your inn, and I will send thither when he is safely housed. You can do no good here, and your presence may excite him when he recovers from the swoon."

Sir George, seeing the wisdom of the advice, nodded assent; and remarking for the first time the sensation of which he was the center, was glad to make the best of his way towards the gates. He had barely reached them — without shaking off a knot of the more curious, who still hung on his footsteps — when Lord Almeric, breathless and agitated, came up with him.

"You are for France, I suppose?" his lordship panted. And then, without waiting for an answer: "What would you advise me to do?" he babbled. "Eh? What do you think? It will be the devil and all for me, you know."

Sir George looked askance at him, contempt in his eye. "I cannot advise you," he said. "For my part, my lord, I remain here."

His lordship was quite taken aback. "No, you don't?" he said. "Remain here! — You don't mean it,"

"I usually mean — what I say," Soane answered in a tone that he thought must close the conversation.

But Lord Almeric kept up with him. "Aye, but will you?" he babbled in vacuous admiration. "Will you really stay here? Now that is uncommon bold of you! I should not have thought of that — of staying here, I mean. I should go to France till the thing blew over. I don't know that

I shall not do so now. Don't you think I should be wise, Sir George? My position, you know. It is uncommon low, is a trial, and —"

Sir George halted so abruptly that will-he, nill-he, the other went on a few paces. "My lord, you should know your own affairs best," he said in a freezing tone. "And, as I desire to be alone, I wish your lordship a very good day."

My lord had never been so much astonished in his life. "Oh, good morning," he said, staring vacantly, "good morning!" but by the time he had framed the words, Sir George was a dozen paces away.

It was an age when great ladies wept out of wounded vanity or for a loss at cards — yet made a show of their children lying in state; when men entertained the wits and made their wills in company, before they bowed a graceful exit from the room and life. Doubtless people felt, feared, hoped, and perspired as they do now, and had their ambitions apart from Pam and the loo table. Nay, Rousseau was printing. But the "Nouvelle Héloïse," though it was beginning to be read, had not yet set the mode of sensibility, or sent those to rave of nature who all their lives had known nothing but art. The suppression of feeling, or rather the cultivation of no feeling, was still the mark of a gentleman; his maxim; honored alike at Medmenham and Marly, to enjoy — to enjoy, be the cost to others what it might.

Bred in such a school, Sir George should have viewed what had happened with polite indifference, and put himself out no further than was courteous, or might serve to set him right with a jury, if the worst came to the worst. But, whether because he was of a kindlier stuff than the common sort of fashionables, or was too young to be quite spoiled, he took the thing that had occurred with unexpected heaviness; and, reaching his inn, hastened to his room to escape alike the curiosity that dogged him and the sympathy that, for a fine gentleman, is never far to seek. To do him justice, his anxiety was not for himself, or the consequences to himself, which at the worst were not likely to exceed a nominal verdict of manslaughter, and at the best would be an acquittal; the former had been Lord Byron's lot, the latter Mr. Brown's, and each had killed his man. Sir George had more *savoir faire* than to trouble himself about this; but about his opponent and his fate he felt a haunting — and, as Lord Almeric would have said, a low — concern that would let him neither rest nor sit. In particular, when he remembered the trifle from which all had arisen, he felt remorse and sorrow; which grew to the point of horror when he recalled the last look which Dunborough, swooning and helpless, had cast in his face.

In one of these paroxysms he was walking the room when the elder surgeon, who had attended his opponent to the field, was announced.

Soane still retained so much of his life habit as to show an unmoved front; the man of the scalpel thought him hard and felt himself repelled; and though he had come from the sick-room hot-foot and laden with good news, descended to a profound apology for the intrusion.

"But I thought that you might like to hear, sir," he continued, nursing his hat, and speaking as if the matter were of little moment, "that Mr. Dunborough is as — as well as can be expected. A serious case — I might call it a most serious case," he continued, puffing out his cheeks. "But with care — with care I think we may restore him. I cannot say more than that."

"Has the ball been extracted?"

"It has, and so far well. And the chair being on the spot, Sir George, so that he was moved without a moment's delay — for which I believe we have to thank Mr. — Mr. —"

"Fishwick," Soane suggested.

"To be sure — *that* is so much gained. Which reminds me," the smug gentleman continued, "that Mr. Attorney begged me to convey his duty and inform you that he had made the needful arrangements and provided bail, so that you are at liberty to leave, Sir George, at any hour."

"Ah!" Soane said, marveling somewhat. "I shall stay here, nevertheless, until I hear that Mr. Dunborough is out of danger."

"An impulse that does you credit, sir," the surgeon said impressively. "These affairs, alas! are very greatly to be de —"

"They are d——d inconvenient," Sir George drawled. "He is not out of danger yet, I suppose?"

The surgeon stared and puffed anew. "Certainly not, sir," he said.

"Ah! And where have you placed him?"

"The Honorable Mr. —, the sufferer?"

"To be sure! Who else, man?" Soane asked impatiently.

"In some rooms at Magdalen," the doctor answered, breathing hard. And then, "Is it your wish that I should report to you tomorrow, sir?"

"You will oblige me. Thank you. Good-day."

Chapter VI

A FISH OUT OF WATER

Sir George spent a long day in his own company, and heedless that on the surgeon's authority he passed abroad for a hard man and a dashed unfeeling fellow, dined on Lord Lyttelton's "Life of King Henry the Second," which was a new book in those days, and the fashion; and supped on gloom and good resolutions. He proposed to call and inquire after his antagonist at a decent hour in the morning, and if the report proved favorable, to go on to Lord ——'s in the afternoon.

But his suspense was curtailed, and his inquiries were converted into a matter of courtesy, by a visit which he received after breakfast from Mr. Thomasson. A glance at the tutor's smiling, unctuous face was enough. Mr. Thomasson also had had his dark hour — since to be mixed up with, a fashionable fracas was one thing, and to lose a valuable and influential pupil, the apple of his mother's eye, was another; but it was past, and he gushed over with gratulations.

"My dear Sir George," he cried, running forward and extending his hands, "how can I express my thankfulness for your escape? I am told that the poor dear fellow fought with a fury perfectly superhuman, and had you given ground must have ran you through a dozen times. Let us be thankful that the result was otherwise." And he cast up his eyes.

"I am," Sir George said, regarding him rather grimly. "I do not know that Mr. Dunborough shares the feeling."

"The dear man!" the tutor answered, not a whit abashed. "But he is better. The surgeon has extracted the ball and pronounces him out of danger."

"I am glad to hear it," Soane answered heartily. "Then, now I can get away."

"À volonté!" cried Mr. Thomasson in his happiest vein. And then with a roguish air, which some very young men found captivating, but which his present companion stomached with difficulty, "I will not say that you have come off the better, after all, Sir George," he continued.

"Ah!"

"No," said the tutor roguishly. "Tut-tut. These young men! They will at a woman by hook or crook."

"So?" Sir George said coldly. "And the latest instance?"

"His Chloe — and a very obdurate, disdainful Chloe at that — has come to nurse him," the tutor answered, grinning. "The prettiest high-stepping piece you ever saw, Sir George — that I will swear! — and would do you no discredit in London. It would make your mouth water to see her. But he could never move her; never was such a prude. Two days ago he thought he had lost her for good and all — there was that accident, you understand. And now a little blood lost — and she is at his pillow!"

Sir George reddened at a sudden thought he had. "And her father unburied!" he cried, rising to his feet. This Macaroni was human, after all.

Mr. Thomasson stared in astonishment. "You know?" he said. "Oh fie, Sir George, have you been hunting already? Fie! Fie! And all London to choose from!"

But Sir George simply repeated, "And her father not buried, man?"

"Yes," Mr. Thomasson answered with simplicity. "He was buried this morning. Oh, that is all right."

"This morning? And the girl went from that — to Dunborough's bedside?" Sir George exclaimed in indignation.

"It was a piece of the oddest luck," Mr. Thomasson answered, smirking, and not in the least comprehending the other's feeling. "He was lodged in Magdalen yesterday; this morning a messenger was dispatched to Pembroke for clothes and suchlike for him. The girl's mother has always nursed in Pembroke, and they sent for her to help. But she was that minute home from the burial, and would not go. Then up steps the girl and 'I'll go,' says she — heaven knows why or what took her, except the contrariness of woman. However, there she is! D'ye see?" And Mr. Thomasson winked.

"Tommy," said Sir George, staring at him, "I see that you're a d——d rascal!"

The tutor, easy and smiling, protested. "Fie, Sir George," he said. "What harm is in it? To tend the sick, my dear sir, is a holy office. And if in this case harm come of it —" and he spread out his hands and paused.

"As you know it will," Sir George cried impulsively.

But Mr. Thomasson shrugged his shoulders. "On the contrary, I know nothing," he answered. "But — if it does, Mr. Dunborough's position is such that — hem! Well, we are men of the world, Sir George, and the girl might do worse."

Sir George had heard the sentiment before, and without debate or protest. Now it disgusted him. "Faugh, man!" he said, rising. "Have done! You sicken me. Go and bore Lord Almeric — if he has not gone to Paris to save his ridiculous skin!"

But Mr. Thomasson, who had borne abuse of himself with Christian meekness, could not hear that unmoved. "My dear Sir George, my dear friend," he urged very seriously, and with a shocked face, "you should not say things like that of his lordship. You really should not! My lord is a most excellent and —"

"Pure ass!" said Soane with irritation. "And I wish you would go and divert him instead of boring me."

"Dear, dear, Sir George!" Mr. Thomasson wailed. "But you do not mean it? And I brought you such good news, as I thought. One might — one really might suppose that you wished our poor friend the worst."

"I wish him no worse a friend!" Sir George responded sharply; and then, heedless of his visitor's protestations and excuses and offers of assistance, would see him to the door.

It was more easy, however, to be rid of him — the fine gentleman of the time standing on scant ceremony with his inferiors — than of the annoyance, the smart, the vexation, his news left behind him. Sir George was not in love. He would have laughed at the notion. The girl was absolutely and immeasurably below him; a girl of the people. He had seen her once only. In reason, therefore — and polite good breeding enforced the demand — he should have viewed Mr. Dunborough's conquest with easy indifference, and complimented him with a jest founded on the prowess of Mars and the smiles of Venus.

But the girl's rare beauty had caught Sir George's fancy; the scene in which he had taken part with her had captivated an imagination not easily inveigled. On the top of these impressions had come a period of good resolutions prescribed by imminent danger; and on the top of that twenty-four hours of solitude — a thing rare in the life he led. Result, that Sir George, picturing the girl's fate, her proud, passionate face, and her future, felt a sting at once selfish and unselfish, a pang at once generous and vicious. Perhaps at the bottom of his irritation lay the feeling that if she was to be any man's prey she might be his. But on the whole his feelings were surprisingly honest; they had their root in a better nature, that, deep sunk under the surface of breeding and habit, had been wholesomely stirred by the events of the last few days.

Still, the good and the evil in the man were so far in conflict that, had he been asked as he walked to Magdalen what he proposed to do should he get speech with the girl, it is probable he would not have known what to answer. Courtesy, nay, decency required that he should, inquire after his antagonist. If he saw the girl — and he had a sneaking desire to see her — well. If he did not see her — still well; there was an end of a foolish imbroglio, which had occupied him too long already. In an hour he could be in his post-chaise, and a mile out of town.

As it chanced, the surgeons in attendance on Dunborough had enjoined quiet, and forbidden visitors. The staircase on which the rooms lay — a bare, dusty, unfurnished place — was deserted; and the girl herself opened the door to him, her finger on her lips. He looked for a blush and a glance of meaning, a little play of conscious eyes and hands, a something of remembrance and coquetry; and had his hat ready in his hand and a smile on his lips. But she had neither smile nor blush for him; on the contrary, when the dim light that entered the dingy staircase disclosed who awaited her, she drew back a pace with a look of dislike and embarrassment.

"My good girl," he said, speaking on the spur of the moment — for the reception took him aback — "what is it? What is the matter?"

She did not answer, but looked at him with solemn eyes, condemning him.

Even so Sir George was not blind to the whiteness of her throat, to the heavy coils of her dark hair, and the smooth beauty of her brow. And suddenly he thought he understood; and a chill ran through him. "My G——d!" he said, startled; "he is not dead?"

She closed the door behind her, and stood, her hand on the latch. "No, he is not dead," she said stiffly, voice and look alike repellent. "But he has not you to thank for that."

"Eh?"

"How can you come here with that face," she continued with sudden passion — and he began to find her eyes intolerable — "and ask for him? You who — fie, sir! Go home! Go home and thank God that you have not his blood upon your hands — you — who might today be Cain!"

He gasped. "Good Lord!" he said unaffectedly. And then, "Why, you are the girl who yesterday would have me kill him!" he cried with indignation; "who came out of town to meet me, brought me in, and would have matched me with him as coolly as ever sportsman set cock in pit! Aye, you! And now you blame me! My girl, blame yourself! Call yourself Cain, if you please!"

"I do," she said unblenching. "But I have my excuse. God forgive me nonetheless!" Her eyes filled as she said it. "I had and have my excuse. But you — a gentleman! What part had you in this? Who were you to kill your fellow-creature — at the word of a distraught girl?"

Sir George saw his opening and jumped for it viciously. "I fear you honor me too much," he said, in the tone of elaborate politeness, which was most likely to embarrass a woman in her position. "Most certainly you do, if you are really under the impression that I fought Mr. Dunborough on your account, my girl!"

"Did you not?" she stammered; and the newborn doubt in her eyes betrayed her trouble.

"Mr. Dunborough struck me, because I would not let him fire on the crowd," Sir George explained, blandly raising his quizzing glass, but not using it. "That was why I fought him. And that is my excuse. You see, my dear," he continued familiarly, "we have each an excuse. But I am not a hypocrite."

"Why do you call me that?" she exclaimed; distress and shame at the mistake she had made contending with her anger.

"Because, my pretty Methodist," he answered coolly, "your hate and your love are too near neighbors. Cursing and nursing, killing and billing, come not so nigh one another in my vocabulary. But with women — some women — it is different."

Her cheeks burned with shame, but her eyes flashed passion. "If I were a lady," she cried, her voice low but intense, "you would not dare to insult me."

"If you were a lady," he retorted with easy insolence, "I would kiss you and make you my wife, my dear. In the meantime, and as you are not — give up nursing young sparks and go home to your mother. Don't roam the roads at night, and avoid traveling-chariots as you would the devil. Or the next knight-errant you light upon may prove something ruder than — Captain Berkeley!"

"You are not Captain Berkeley?"

"No."

She stared at him, breathing hard. Then, "I was a fool, and I pay for it in insult," she said.

"Be a fool no longer then," he retorted, his good-humor restored by the success of his badinage; "and no man will have the right to insult you, *ma belle.*"

"I will never give *you* the right!" she cried with intention.

"It is rather a question of Mr. Dunborough," he answered, smiling superior, and flirting his spy-glass to and fro with his fingers. "Say the same to him, and — but are you going, my queen? What, without ceremony?"

"I am not a lady, and *noblesse oblige* does not apply to me," she cried. And she closed the door in his face — sharply, yet without noise.

He went down the stairs a step at a time — thinking. "Now, I wonder where she got that!" he muttered. *"Noblesse oblige!* And well applied too!" Again, "Lord, what beasts we men are!" he thought. "Insult? I suppose

I did insult her; but I had to do that or kiss her. And she earned it, the little firebrand!" Then standing and looking along the High — he had reached the College gates — "D——n Dunborough! She is too good for him! For a very little — it would be mean, it would be low, it would be cursed low — but for two pence I would speak to her mother and cheat him. She is too good to be ruined by that coarse-tongued boaster! Though I suppose she fancies him. I suppose he is an Adonis to her! Faugh! Tommy, my lord, and Dunborough! What a crew!"

The good and evil, spleen and patience, which he had displayed in his interview with the girl rode him still; for at the door of the Mitre he paused, went in, came out, and paused again. He seemed to be unable to decide what he would do; but in the end he pursued his way along the street with a clouded brow, and in five minutes found himself at the door of the mean house in the court, whence the porter of Pembroke had gone out night and morning. Here he knocked, and stood. In a moment the door was opened, but to his astonishment by Mr. Fishwick.

Either the attorney shared his surprise, or had another and more serious cause for emotion; for his perky face turned red, and his manner as he stood holding the door half-open, and gaping at the visitor, was that of a man taken in the act, and thoroughly ashamed of himself. Sir George might have wondered what was afoot, if he had not espied over the lawyer's shoulder a round wooden table littered with papers, and guessed that Mr. Fishwick was doing the widow's business — a theory which Mr. Fishwick's first words, on recovering himself, bore out.

"I am here — on business," he said, cringing and rubbing his hands. "I don't — I don't think that you can object, Sir George."

"I?" said Soane, staring at him in astonishment and some contempt. "My good man, what has it to do with me? You got my letter?"

"And the draft, Sir George!" Mr. Fishwick bowed low. "Certainly, certainly, sir. Too much honored. Which, as I understood, put an end to any — I mean it not offensively, honored sir — to any connection between us?"

Sir George nodded. "I have my own lawyers in London," he said stiffly. "I thought I made it clear that I did not need your services further."

Mr. Fishwick rubbed his hands. "I have that from your own lips, Sir George," he said. "Mrs. Masterson, my good woman, you heard that?"

Sir George glowered at him. "Lord, man?" he said. "Why so much about nothing? What on earth has this woman to do with it?"

Mr. Fishwick trembled with excitement. "Mrs. Masterson, you will not answer," he stammered.

Sir George first stared, then cursed his impudence; then, remembering that after all this was not his business, or that on which he had come, and being one of those obstinates whom opposition but precipitates to their ends, "Hark ye, man, stand aside," he said. "I did not come here to talk to you. And do you, my good woman, attend to me a moment. I have a word to say about your daughter."

"Not a word! Mrs. Masterson," the attorney cried his eyes almost bursting from his head with excitement.

Sir George was thunderstruck. "Is the man an idiot?" he exclaimed, staring at him. And then, "I'll tell you what it is, Mr. Fishwick, or whatever your name is — a little more of this, and I shall lay my cane across your back."

"I am in my duty," the attorney answered, dancing on his feet.

"Then you will suffer in it!" Sir George retorted. "With better men. So do not try me too far. I am here to say a word to this woman which I would rather say alone."

"Never," said the attorney, bubbling, "with my good will!"

Soane lost patience at that. "D——n you!" he cried. "Will you be quiet?" And made a cut at him with his cane. Fortunately the lawyer evaded it with nimbleness; and having escaped to a safe distance hastened to cry, "No malice! I bear you no malice, sir!" with so little breath and so much good nature that Sir George recovered his balance. "Confound you, man!" he continued. "Why am I not to speak? I came here to tell this good woman that if she has a care for this girl the sooner she takes her from where she is the better! And you cannot let me put a word in."

"You came for that, sir?"

"For what else, fool?"

"I was wrong," said the attorney humbly. "I did not understand. Allow me to say, sir, that I am entirely of your opinion. The young lady — I mean she shall be removed tomorrow. It — the whole arrangement is improper — highly improper."

"Why, you go as fast now as you went slowly before," Sir George said, observing him curiously.

Mr. Fishwick smiled after a sickly fashion. "I did not understand, sir," he said. "But it is most unsuitable, most unsuitable. She shall return tomorrow at the latest."

Sir George, who had said what he had to say, nodded, grunted, and went away; feeling that he had performed an unpleasant — and somewhat doubtful — duty under most adverse circumstances. He could not in the least comprehend the attorney's strange behavior; but after some contemptuous reflection, of which nothing came, he dismissed it as one of the low things to which he had exposed himself by venturing out of the charmed circle in which he lived. He hoped that the painful series was now at an end, stepped into his post-chaise, amid the reverent salaams of the Mitre, the landlord holding the door; and in a few minutes had rattled over Folly Bridge, and left Oxford behind him.

Chapter VII

ACHILLES AND BRISEIS

*T*he honorable Mr. Dunborough's collapse arising rather from loss of blood than from an injury to a vital part, he was sufficiently recovered even on the day after the meeting to appreciate his nurse's presence. Twice he was heard to chuckle without apparent cause; once he strove, but failed, to detain her hand; while the feeble winks which from time to time he bestowed on Mr. Thomasson when her back was towards him were attributed by that gentleman, who should have known the patient, to reflections closely connected with her charms.

His rage was great, therefore, when three days after the duel, he awoke, missed her, and found in her place the senior bedmaker of Magdalen — a worthy woman, learned in simples and with hands of horn, but far from beautiful. This good person he saluted with a vigor which proved him already far on the road to recovery; and when he was tired of swearing, he wept and threw his nightcap at her. Finally, between one and the other, and neither availing to bring back his Briseis, he fell into a fever; which, as he was kept happed up in a box-bed, in a close room, with every window shut and every draft kept off by stuffy curtains — such was the fate of sick men then — bade fair to postpone his recovery to a very distant date.

In this plight he sent one day for Mr. Thomasson, who had the nominal care of the young gentleman; and the tutor being brought from the club tavern in the Corn Market which he occasionally condescended to frequent, the invalid broke to him his resolution.

"See here, Tommy," he said in a voice weak but vicious. "You have got to get her back. I will not be poisoned by this musty old witch any longer."

"But if she will not come?" said Mr. Thomasson sadly.

"The little fool threw up the sponge when she came before," the patient answered, tossing restlessly. "And she will come again, with a little pressure. Lord, I know the women! So should you."

"She came before because — well, I do not quite know why she came," Mr. Thomasson confessed.

"Any way, you have got to get her back."

The tutor remonstrated, "My dear good man," he said unctuously, "you don't think of my position. I am a man of the world, I know —"

"All of it, my Macaroni!"

"But I cannot be — be mixed up in such a matter as this, my dear sir."

"All the same, you have got to get her," was the stubborn answer. "Or I write to my lady and tell her you kept mum about my wound. And you will not like that, my tulip."

On that point he was right; for if there was a person in the world of whom Mr. Thomasson stood in especial awe, it was of Lady Dunborough. My lord, the author of "Pomaria Britannica" and "The Elegant Art of Pomiculture as applied to Landscape Gardening," was a quantity he could safely neglect. Beyond his yew-walks and his orchards his lordship was a cipher. He had proved too respectable even for the peerage; and of late had cheerfully resigned all his affairs into the hands of his wife, formerly the Lady Michal M'Intosh, a penniless beauty, with the pride of a Scotchwoman and the temper of a Hervey. Her enemies said that my lady had tripped in the merry days of George the Second, and now made up for past easiness by present hardness. Her friends — but it must be confessed her ladyship had no friends.

Be that as it might, Mr. Thomasson had refrained from summoning her to her son's bedside; partly because the surgeons had quickly pronounced the wound a trifle, much more because the little he had seen of her ladyship had left him no taste to see more. He knew, however, that the omission would weigh heavily against him were it known; and as he had hopes from my lady's aristocratic connections, and need in certain difficulties of all the aid he could muster, he found the threat not one to be sneezed at. His laugh betrayed this.

However, he tried to put the best face on the matter. "You won't do that," he said. "She would spoil sport, my friend. Her ladyship is no fool, and would not suffer your little amusements."

"She is no fool," Mr. Dunborough replied with emphasis. "As you will find, Tommy, if she comes to Oxford, and learns certain things. It will be farewell to your chance of having that milksop of a Marquis for a pupil!"

Now, it was one of Mr. Thomasson's highest ambitions at this time to have the young Marquis of Carmarthen entrusted to him; and Lady Dunborough was connected with the family, and, it was said, had interest there. He was silent.

"You see," Mr. Dunborough continued, marking with a chuckle the effect his words had produced, "you have got to get her."

Mr. Thomasson did not admit that that was so, but he writhed in his chair; and presently he took his leave and went away, his plump pale face gloomy and the crow's feet showing plain at the corners of his eyes. He had given no promise; but that evening a messenger from the college requested Mrs. Masterson to attend at his rooms on the following morning.

She did not go. At the appointed hour, however, there came a knock on the tutor's door, and that gentleman, who had sent his servant out of the way, found Mr. Fishwick on the landing. "Tut-tut!" said the don with some brusqueness, his hand still on the door; "do you want me?" He had seen the attorney after the duel, and in the confusion attendant on the injured man's removal; and knew him by sight, but no farther.

"I — hem — I think you wished to see Mrs. Masterson?" was Mr. Fishwick's answer, and the lawyer, but with all humility, made as if he would enter.

The tutor, however, barred the way. "I wished to see Mrs. Masterson," he said dryly, and with his coldest air of authority. "But who are you?"

"I am here on her behalf," Mr. Fishwick answered, meekly pressing his hat in his hands.

"On her behalf?" said Mr. Thomasson stiffly. "Is she ill?"

"No, sir, I do not know that she is ill."

"Then I do not understand," Mr. Thomasson answered in his most dignified tone. "Are you aware that the woman is in the position of a college servant, inhabiting a cottage the property of the college? And liable to be turned out at the college will?"

"It may be so," said the attorney.

"Then, if you please, what is the meaning of her absence when requested by one of the Fellows of the college to attend?"

"I am here to represent her," said Mr. Fishwick.

"Represent her! Represent a college laundress! Pooh! I never heard of such a thing."

"But, sir, I am her legal adviser, and —"

"Legal adviser!" Mr. Thomasson retorted, turning purple — he was really puzzled. "A bedmaker with a legal adviser! It's the height of impudence! Begone, sir, and take it from me, that the best advice you can give her is to attend me within the hour."

Mr. Fishwick looked rather blue. "If it has nothing to do with her property," he said reluctantly, and as if he had gone too far.

"Property!" said Mr. Thomasson, gasping.

"Or her affairs."

"Affairs!" the tutor cried. "I never heard of a bedmaker having affairs."

"Well," said the lawyer doggedly, and with the air of a man goaded into telling what he wished to conceal, "she is leaving Oxford. That is the fact."

"Oh!" said Mr. Thomasson, falling on a sudden into the minor key. "And her daughter?"

"And her daughter."

"That is unfortunate," the tutor answered, thoughtfully rubbing his hands. "The truth is — the girl proved so good a nurse in the case of my noble friend who was injured the other day — my lord Viscount Dunborough's son, a most valuable life — that since she absented herself, he has not made the same progress. And as I am responsible for him —"

"She should never have attended him!" the attorney answered with unexpected sharpness.

"Indeed! And why not, may I ask?" the tutor inquired.

Mr. Fishwick did not answer the question. Instead, "She would not have gone to him in the first instance," he said, "but that she was under a misapprehension."

"A misapprehension?"

"She thought that the duel lay at her door," the attorney answered; "and in that belief was impelled to do what she could to undo the consequences. Romantic, but a most improper step!"

"Improper!" said the tutor, much ruffled. "And why, sir?"

"Most improper," the attorney repeated in a dry, businesslike tone. "I am instructed that the gentleman had for weeks past paid her attentions which, his station considered, could scarcely be honorable, and of which she had more than once expressed her dislike. Under those circumstances, to expose her to his suit — but no more need be said," the attorney added, breaking off and taking a pinch of snuff with great enjoyment, "as she is leaving the city."

Mr. Thomasson had much ado to mask his chagrin under a show of contemptuous incredulity. "The wench has too fine a conceit of herself!" he blurted out. "Hark you, sir — this is a fable! I wonder you dare to put it about. A gentleman of the station of my lord Dunborough's son does not condescend to the gutter!"

"I will convey the remark to my client," said the attorney, bristling all over.

"Client!" Mr. Thomasson retorted, trembling with rage — for he saw the advantage he had given the enemy. "Since when had laundry maids lawyers? Client! Pho! Begone, sir! You are abusive. I'll have you looked up on the rolls. I'll have your name taken!"

"I would not talk of names if I were you," cried Mr. Fishwick, reddening in his turn with rage. "Men give a name to what you are doing this morning, and it is not a pleasant one. It is to be hoped, sir, that Mr. Dunborough pays you well for your services!"

"You — insolent rascal!" the tutor stammered, losing in a moment all his dignity and becoming a pale flabby man, with the spite and the terror of crime in his face. "You — begone! Begone, sir."

"Willingly," said the attorney, swelling with defiance. "You may tell your principal that when he means marriage, he may come to us. Not before. I take my leave, sir. Good morning." And with that he strutted out and marched slowly and majestically down the stairs.

He bore off the honors of war. Mr. Thomasson, left among his Titian copies, his gleaming Venuses, and velvet curtains, was a sorry thing. The man who preserves a cloak of outward decency has always this vulnerable spot; strip him, and he sees himself as others see or may see him, and views his ugliness with griping qualms. Mr. Thomasson bore the exposure awhile, sitting white and shaking in a chair, seeing himself and seeing the end, and, like the devils, believing and trembling. Then he rose and staggered to a little cupboard, the door of which was adorned with a pretty Greek motto, and a hovering Cupid painted in a blue sky; whence he filled himself a glass of cordial. A second glass followed; this restored the color to his cheeks and the brightness to his eyes. He shivered; then smacked his lips and began to reflect what face he should put upon it when he went to report to his pupil.

In deciding that point he made a mistake. Unluckily for himself and others, in the version which he chose he was careful to include all matters likely to arouse Dunborough's resentment; in particular he laid malicious stress upon the attorney's scornful words about a marriage. This, however — and perhaps the care he took to repeat it — had an unlooked-for result. Mr. Dunborough began by cursing the rogue's impudence, and did it with all the heat his best friend could desire. But, being confined to his room, haunted by the vision of his flame, yet debarred from any attempt to see her, his mood presently changed; his heart became as water, and he fell into a maudlin state about her. Dwelling constantly on memories of his Briseis — whose name, by the way, was

Julia — having her shape and complexion, her gentle touch and her smile, always in his mind, while he was unable in the body to see so much as the hem of her gown, Achilles grew weaker in will as he grew stronger in body. Headstrong and reckless by nature, unaccustomed to thwart a desire or deny himself a gratification, Mr. Dunborough began to contemplate paying even the last price for her; and one day, about three weeks after the duel, dropped a word which frightened Mr. Thomasson.

He was well enough by this time to be up, and was looking through one window while the tutor lounged in the seat of another. On a sudden "Lord!" said he, with a laugh that broke off short in the middle. "What was the queer catch that fellow sang last night? About a bailiff's daughter. Well, why not a porter's daughter?"

"Because you are neither young enough, nor old enough, nor mad enough!" said Mr. Thomasson cynically, supposing the other meant nothing.

"It is she that would be mad," the young gentleman answered, with a grim chuckle. "I should take it out of her sooner or later. And, after all, she is as good as Lady Macclesfield or Lady Falmouth! As good? She is better, the saucy baggage! By the Lord, I have a good mind to do it!"

Mr. Thomasson sat dumbfounded. At length, "You are jesting! You cannot mean it," he said.

"If it is marriage or nothing — and, hang her, she is as cold as a church pillar — I do mean it," the gentleman answered viciously; "and so would you if you were not an old insensible sinner! Think of her ankle, man! Think of her waist! I never saw a waist to compare with it! Even in the Havanna! She is a pearl! She is a jewel! She is incomparable!"

"And a porter's daughter!"

"Faugh, I don't believe it." And he took his oath on the point.

"You make me sick!" Mr. Thomasson said; and meant it. Then, "My dear friend, I see how it is," he continued. "You have the fever on you still, or you would not dream of such things."

"But I do dream of her — every night, confound her!" Mr. Dunborough said; and he groaned like a love-sick boy. "Oh, hang it, Tommy," he continued plaintively, "she has a kind of look in her eyes when she is pleased — that makes you think of dewy mornings when you were a boy and went fishing."

"It *is* the fever!" Mr. Thomasson said, with conviction. "It is heavy on him still." Then, more seriously, "My very dear sir," he continued, "do you know that if you had your will you would be miserable within the week. Remember —

"'Tis tumult, disorder, 'tis loathing and hate;
  Caprice gives it birth, and contempt is its fate!"

"Gad, Tommy!" said Mr. Dunborough, aghast with admiration at the aptness of the lines. "That is uncommon clever of you! But I shall do it all the same," he continued, in a tone of melancholy foresight. "I know I shall. I am a fool, a particular fool. But I shall do it. Marry in haste and repent at leisure!"

"A porter's daughter become Lady Dunborough!" cried Mr. Thomasson with scathing sarcasm.

"Oh yes, my tulip," Mr. Dunborough answered with gloomy meaning. "But there have been worse. I know what I know. See Collins's Peerage, volume 4, page 242: 'Married firstly Sarah, widow of Colonel John Clark, of Exeter, in the county of Devon' — all a hum, Tommy! If they had said spinster, of Bridewell, in the county of Middlesex, 'twould have been as true! I know what I know."

After that Mr. Thomasson went out of Magdalen, feeling that the world was turning round with him. If Dunborough were capable of such a step as this — Dunborough, who had seen life and service, and of whose past he knew a good deal — where was he to place dependence? How was he to trust even the worst of his acquaintances? The matter shook the pillars of the tutor's house, and filled him with honest disgust.

Moreover, it frightened him. In certain circumstances he might have found his advantage in fostering such a *mésalliance*. But here, not only had he reason to think himself distasteful to the young lady whose elevation was in prospect, but he retained too vivid a recollection of Lady Dunborough to hope that that lady would forget or forgive him! Moreover, at the present moment he was much straitened for money; difficulties of long standing were coming to a climax. Venuses and Titian copies have to be paid for. The tutor, scared by the prospect, to which he had lately opened his eyes, saw in early preferment or a wealthy pupil his only way of escape. And in Lady Dunborough lay his main hope, which a catastrophe of this nature would inevitably shatter. That evening he sent his servant to learn what he could of the Mastersons' movements.

The man brought word that they had left the town that morning; that the cottage was closed, and the key had been deposited at the college gates.

"Did you learn their destination?" the tutor asked, trimming his fingernails with an appearance of indifference.

The servant said he had not; and after adding the common gossip of the court, that Masterson had left money, and the widow had gone to her own people, concluded, "But they were very close after Masterson's death, and the neighbors saw little of them. There was a lawyer in and out, a stranger; and it is thought he was to marry the girl, and that that had set them a bit above their position, sir."

"That will do," said the tutor. "I want to hear no gossip," And, hiding his joy, he went off hot-foot to communicate the news to his pupil.

But Mr. Dunborough laughed in his face. "Pooh!" he said. "I know where they are."

"You know? Then where are they?" Thomasson asked.

"Ah, my good Tommy, that is telling."

"Well," Mr. Thomasson answered, with an assumption of dignity. "At any rate they are gone. And you must allow me to say that I am glad of it — for your sake!"

"That is as may be," Mr. Dunborough answered. And he took his first airing in a sedan next day. After that he grew so reticent about his affairs, and so truculent when the tutor tried to sound him, that Mr. Thomasson was at his wits' end to discern what was afoot. For some time, however, he got no clue. Then, going to Dunborough's rooms one day, he found them empty, and, bribing the servant, learned that his master had gone to Wallingford. And the man told him his suspicions. Mr. Thomasson was aghast; and by that day's post — after much searching of heart and long pondering into which scale he should throw his weight — he dispatched the following letter to Lady Dunborough:

"HONORED MADAM, —

"The peculiar care I have of that distinguished and excellent gentleman, your son, no less than the profound duty I owe to my lord and your ladyship, induces me to a step which I cannot regard without misgiving; since, once known, it must deprive me of the influence with Mr. Dunborough which I have now the felicity to enjoy, and which, heightened by the affection he is so good as to bestow on me, renders his society the most agreeable in the world. Nevertheless, and though considerations of this sort cannot but have weight with me, I am not able to be silent, nor allow your honored repose among the storied oaks of Papworth to be roughly shattered by a blow that may still be averted by skill and conduct.

"For particulars, Madam, the young gentleman — I say it with regret — has of late been drawn into a connection with a girl of low origin and suitable behavior, Not that your ladyship is to think me so wanting in *savoir-faire* as to trouble your ears with this, were it all; but the person concerned — who (I need scarcely tell one so familiar with Mr. Dunborough's amiable disposition) is solely to blame — has the wit to affect virtue, and by means of this pretence, often resorted to by creatures of that class, has led my generous but misguided pupil to the point of matrimony. Your ladyship shudders? Alas! it is so. I have learned within the hour that he has followed her to Wallingford, whither she has withdrawn herself, doubtless to augment his passion; I am forced to conclude that nothing short of your ladyship's presence and advice can now stay his purpose. In that belief, and with the most profound regret, I pen these lines; and respectfully awaiting the favor of your ladyship's commands, which shall ever evoke my instant compliance,

"I have the honor to be while I live, Madam,

Your ladyship's most humble obedient servant,

"FREDERICK THOMASSON

"*Nota bene.* — I do not commend the advantage of silence in regard to this communication, this being patent to your ladyship's sagacity."

Chapter VIII

THE OLD BATH ROAD

*I*n the year 1757 — to go back ten years from the spring with which we are dealing — the ordinary Englishman was a Balbus despairing of the State. No phrase was then more common on English lips, or in English ears, than the statement that the days of England's greatness were numbered, and were fast running out. Unwitting the wider sphere about to open before them, men dwelt fondly on the glories of the past. The old babbled of Marlborough's wars, of the entrance of Prince Eugene into London, of choirs draped in flags, and steeples reeling giddily for Ramillies and Blenheim. The young listened, and sighed to think that the day had been, and was not, when England gave the law to Europe, and John Churchill's warder set troops moving from Hamburg to the Alps.

On the top of such triumphs, and the famous reign of good Queen

Anne, had ensued forty years of peace, broken only by one inglorious war. The peace did its work: it settled the dynasty, and filled the purse; but men, considering it, whispered of effeminacy and degeneracy, and the like, as men will to the end of time. And when the clouds, long sighted on the political horizon, began to roll up, they looked fearfully abroad and doubted and trembled; and doubted and trembled the more because in home affairs all patriotism, all party-spirit, all thought of things higher than ribbon or place or pension, seemed to be dead among public men. The Tories, long deprived of power, and discredited by the taint or suspicion of Jacobitism, counted for nothing. The Whigs, agreed on all points of principle, and split into sections, the Ins and Outs, solely by the fact that all could not enjoy places and pensions at once, the supply being unequal to the demand — had come to regard politics as purely a game; a kind of licensed hazard played for titles, orders, and emoluments, by certain families who had the *entrée* to the public table by virtue of the part they had played in settling the succession.

Into the midst of this state of things, this world of despondency, mediocrity, selfishness, and chicanery, and at the precise crisis when the disasters which attended the opening campaigns of the Seven Years' War — and particularly the loss of Minorca — seemed to confirm the gloomiest prognostications of the most hopeless pessimists, came William Pitt; and in eighteen months changed the face of the world, not for his generation only, but for ours. Indifferent as an administrator, mediocre as a financier, passionate, haughty, headstrong, with many of the worst faults of an orator, he was still a man with ideals — a patriot among placemen, pure where all were corrupt. And the effect of his touch was magical. By infusing his own spirit, his own patriotism, his own belief in his country, and his own belief in himself, into those who worked with him — aye, and into the better half of England — he wrought a seeming miracle.

See, for instance, what Mr. Walpole wrote to Sir Horace Mann in September, 1757. "For how many years," he says, "have I been telling you that your country was mad, that your country was undone! It does not grow wiser, it does not grow more prosperous! . . . How do you behave on these lamentable occasions? Oh, believe me, it is comfortable to have an island to hide one's head in! . . ." Again he writes in the same month, "It is time for England to slip her own cables, and float away into some unknown ocean."

With these compare a letter dated November, 1759. "Indeed," he says to the same correspondent, "one is forced to ask every morning what victory there is, for fear of missing one." And he wrote with reason. India, Canada, Belleisle, the Mississippi, the Philippines, the Havanna,

Martinique, Guadaloupe — there was no end to our conquests. Wolfe fell in the arms of victory, Clive came home the satrap of sovereigns; but day by day ships sailed in and couriers spurred abroad with the news that a new world and a nascent empire were ours. Until men's heads reeled and maps failed them, as they asked each morning "What new land, today?" Until those who had despaired of England awoke and rubbed their eyes — awoke to find three nations at her feet, and the dawn of a new and wider day breaking in the sky.

And what of the minister? They called him the Great Commoner, the heaven-born statesman; they showered gold boxes upon him; they bore him through the city, the center of frantic thousands, to the effacement even of the sovereign. Where he went all heads were bared; while he walked the rooms at Bath and drank the water, all stood; his very sedan, built with a boot to accommodate his gouty foot, was a show followed and watched wherever it moved. A man he had never seen left him a house and three thousand pounds a year; this one, that one, the other one, legacies. In a word, for a year or two he was the idol of the nation — the first great People's Minister.

Then, the crisis over, the old system lifted its head again; the mediocrities returned; and, thwarted by envious rivals and a jealous king, Pitt placed the crown alike on his services and his popularity by resigning power when he could no longer dictate the policy which he knew to be right. Nor were events slow to prove his wisdom. The war with Spain which he would have declared, Spain declared. The treasure fleet which he would have seized, escaped us. Finally, the peace when it came redounded to his credit, for in the main it secured his conquests — to the disgrace of his enemies, since more might have been obtained.

Such was the man who, restored to office and lately created an earl by the title of Chatham, lay ill at Bath in the spring of '67. The passage of time, the course of events, the ravages of gout, in a degree the acceptance of a title, had robbed his popularity of its first gloss. But his name was still a name to conjure with in England. He was still the idol of the City. Crowds still ran to see him where he passed. His gaunt figure racked with gout, his eagle nose, his piercing eyes, were still England's picture of a minister. His curricle, his troop of servants, the very state he kept, the ceremony with which he traveled, all pleased the popular fancy. When it was known that he was well enough to leave Bath, and would lie a night at the Castle Inn at Marlborough, his suite requiring twenty rooms, even that great hostelry, then reputed one of the best, as it was certainly the most splendid in England, and capable, it was said, of serving a dinner of twenty-four covers on silver, was in an uproar. The landlord, who knew the tastes of half the peerage, and which bin

Lord Sandwich preferred, and which Mr. Rigby, in which rooms the Duchess or Lady Betty liked to lie, what Mr. Walpole took with his supper, and which shades the Princess Amelia preferred for her card-ta-ble — even he, who had taken his glass of wine with a score of dukes, from Cumberland the Great to Bedford the Little, was put to it; the notice being short, and the house somewhat full.

Fortunately the Castle Inn, on the road between London and the west, was a place of call, not of residence. Formerly a favorite residence of the Seymour family, and built, if tradition does not lie, by a pupil of Inigo Jones, it stood — and for the house, still stands — in a snug fold of the downs, at the end of the long High Street of Marlborough; at the precise point where the route to Salisbury debouches from the Old Bath Road. A long-fronted, stately mansion of brick, bosomed in trees, and jealous of its historic past — it had sheltered William of Orange — it presented to the north and the road, from which it was distant some hundred yards, a grand pillared portico flanked by projecting wings. At that portico, and before those long rows of shapely windows, forty coaches, we are told, changed horses every day. Beside the western wing of the house a green sugarloaf mound, reputed to be of Druidical origin, rose above the trees; it was accessible by a steep winding path, and crowned at the date of this story by a curious summer-house. Travelers from the west who merely passed on the coach, caught, if they looked back as they entered the town, a glimpse of groves and lawns laid out by the best taste of the day, between the southern front and the river. To these a doorway and a flight of stone steps, corresponding in position with the portico in the middle of the north front, conducted the visitor, who, if a man of feeling, was equally surprised and charmed to find in these shady retreats, stretching to the banks of the Kennet, a silence and beauty excelled in few noblemen's gardens. In a word, while the north front of the house hummed with the revolving wheels, and echoed the chatter of half the fashionable world bound for the Bath or the great western port of Bristol, the south front reflected the taste of that Lady Hertford who had made these glades and trim walks her principal hobby.

With all its charms, however, the traveler, as we have said, stayed there but a night or so. Those in the house, therefore, would move on, and so room could be made. And so room was made; and two days later, a little after sunset, amid a spasm of final preparation, and with a great parade of arrival, the earl's procession, curricle, chariot, coaches, chaises, and footmen, rolled in from the west. In a trice lights flashed everywhere, in the road, at the windows, on the mound, among the trees; the crowd thickened — every place seemed peopled with the Pitt liveries. Women, vowing that they were cramped to death, called languidly for chaise-doors to be opened; and men who had already descended, and were stretching their limbs in the road, ran to open them. This was in the rear of the procession; in front, where the throng of townsfolk closed most thickly round the earl's traveling chariot, was a sudden baring of heads, as the door of the coach was opened. The landlord, bowing lower than he had ever bowed to the proud Duke of Somerset, offered his shoulder. And then men waited and bent nearer; and nothing happening, looked at one another in surprise. Still no one issued; instead, something which the nearest could not catch was said, and a tall lady, closely hooded, stepped stiffly out and pointed to the house. On which the landlord and two or three servants hurried in; and all was expectation.

The men were out again in a moment, bearing a great chair, which they set with nicety at the door of the carriage. This done, the gapers saw what they had come to see. For an instant, the face that all England knew and all Europe feared — but blanched, strained, and drawn with pain — showed in the opening. For a second the crowd was gratified with a glimpse of a gaunt form, a star and ribbon; then, with a groan heard far through the awestruck silence, the invalid sank heavily into the chair, and was borne swiftly and silently into the house.

Men looked at one another; but the fact was better than their fears. My lord, after leaving Bath, had had a fresh attack of the gout; and when he would be able to proceed on his journey only Dr. Addington, his physician, whose gold-headed cane, great wig, and starched aspect did not foster curiosity, could pretend to say. Perhaps Mr. Smith, the landlord, was as much concerned as any; when he learned the state of the case, he fell to mental arithmetic with the assistance of his fingers, and at times looked blank. Counting up the earl and his gentleman, and his gentleman's gentleman, and his secretary, and his private secretary, and his physician, and his three friends and their gentlemen, and my lady and her woman, and the children and nurses, and a crowd of others, he could not see where tomorrow's travelers were to lie, supposing the minister remained. However, in the end, he set that aside as a question for tomorrow; and having seen Mr. Rigby's favorite bin opened (for Dr. Addington was a connoisseur), and reviewed the cooks dishing up the belated dinner — which an endless chain of servants carried to the different apartments — he followed to the principal dining room, where the minister's company were assembled; and between the intervals of carving and seeing that his guests ate to their liking, enjoyed the conversation, and, when invited, joined in it with tact and self-respect. As became a host of the old school.

By this time lights blazed in every window of the great mansion; the open doors emitted a fragrant glow of warmth and welcome; the rattle of plates and hum of voices could be heard in the road a hundred paces away. But outside and about the stables the hubbub had somewhat subsided, the road had grown quiet, and the last townsfolk had withdrawn, when a little after seven the lamps of a carriage appeared in the High Street, approaching from the town. It swept round the church, turned the flank of the house, and in a twinkling drew up before the pillars.

"Hilloa! House!" cried the postillion. "House!" And, cracking his whip on his boot, he looked up at the rows of lighted windows.

A man and a maid who traveled outside climbed down. As the man opened the carriage door, a servant bustled out of the house. "Do you want fresh horses?" said he, in a kind of aside to the footman.

"No — rooms!" the man answered bluntly.

Before the other could reply, "What is this?" cried a shrewish voice from the interior of the carriage. "Hoity toity! This is a nice way of receiving company! You, fellow, go to your master and say that I am here."

"Say that the Lady Dunborough is here," an unctuous voice repeated, "and requires rooms, dinners, fire, and the best he has. And do you be quick, fellow!"

The speaker was Mr. Thomasson, or rather Mr. Thomasson plus the importance which comes of traveling with a viscountess. This, and perhaps the cramped state of his limbs, made him a little long in descending. "Will your ladyship wait? or will you allow me to have the honor of assisting you to descend?" he continued, shivering slightly from the cold. To tell the truth, he was not enjoying his honor on cheap terms. Save the last hour, her ladyship's tongue had gone without ceasing, and Mr. Thomasson was sorely in need of refreshment.

"Descend? No!" was the tart answer. "Let the man come! Sho! Times are changed since I was here last. I had not to wait then, or break my shins in the dark! Has the impudent fellow gone in?"

He had, but at this came out again, bearing lights before his master. The host, with the civility which marked landlords in those days — the halcyon days of inns — hurried down the steps to the carriage. "Dear me! Dear me! I am most unhappy!" he exclaimed. "Had I known your ladyship was traveling, some arrangement should have been made. I declare, my lady, I would not have had this happen for twenty pounds! But —"

"But what, man! What is the man mouthing about?" she cried impatiently.

"I am full," he said, extending his palms to express his despair. "The Earl of Chatham and his lordship's company traveling from Bath occupy all the west wing and the greater part of the house; and I have positively no rooms fit for your ladyship's use. I am grieved, desolated, to have to say this to a person in your ladyship's position," he continued glibly, "and an esteemed customer, but —" and again he extended his hands.

"A fig for your desolation!" her ladyship cried rudely. "It don't help me, Smith."

"But your ladyship sees how it is."

"I am hanged if I do!" she retorted, and used an expression too coarse for modern print. "But I suppose that there is another house, man."

"Certainly, my lady — several," the landlord answered, with a gesture of deprecation. "But all full. And the accommodation not of a kind to suit your ladyship's tastes."

"Then — what are we to do?" she asked with angry shrillness.

"We have fresh horses," he ventured to suggest. "The road is good, and in four hours, or four and a half at the most, your ladyship might be in Bath, where there is an abundance of good lodgings."

"Bless the man!" cried the angry peeress. "Does he think I have a skin of leather to stand this jolting and shaking? Four hours more! I'll lie in my carriage first!"

A small rain was beginning to fall, and the night promised to be wet as well as cold. Mr. Thomasson, who had spent the last hour, while his companion slept, in visions of the sumptuous dinner, neat wines, and good beds that awaited him at the Castle Inn, cast a despairing glance at the doorway, whence issued a fragrance that made his mouth water. "Oh, positively," he cried, addressing the landlord, "something must be done, my good man. For myself, I can sleep in a chair if her ladyship can anyway be accommodated."

"Well," said the landlord dubiously, "if her ladyship could allow her woman to lie with her?"

"Bless the man! Why did you not say that at once?" cried my lady. "Oh, she may come!" This last in a voice that promised little comfort for the maid.

"And if the reverend gentleman — would put up with a couch below stairs?"

"Yes, yes," said Mr. Thomasson; but faintly, now it came to the point.

"Then I think I can manage — if your ladyship will not object to sup with some guests who have just arrived, and are now sitting down? Friends of Sir George Soane," the landlord hastened to add, "whom your ladyship probably knows."

"Drat the man! — too well!" Lady Dunborough answered, making a wry face. For by this time she had heard all about the duel. "He has nearly cost me dear! But, there — if we must, we must. Let me get my tooth in the dinner, and I won't stand on my company." And she proceeded to descend, and, the landlord going before her, entered the house.

In those days people were not so punctilious in certain directions as they now are. My lady put off her French hood and traveling cloak in the lobby of the east wing, gave her piled-up hair a twitch this way and that, unfastened her fan from her waist, and sailed in to supper, her maid carrying her gloves and scent-bottle behind her. The tutor, who wore no gloves, was a little longer. But having washed his hands at a pump in the scullery, and dried them on a roller-towel — with no sense that the apparatus was deficient — he tucked his hat under his arm and, handling his snuff-box, tripped after her as hastily as vanity and an elegant demeanor permitted.

He found her in the act of joining, with an air of vast condescension, a party of three; two of whom her stately salute had already frozen in their places. These two, a slight perky man of middle age, and a frightened rustic-looking woman in homely black — who, by the way, sat with her mouth, open and her knife and fork resting points upward on the table — could do nothing but stare. The third, a handsome girl, very simply dressed, returned her ladyship's gaze with mingled interest and timidity.

My lady noticed this, and the girl's elegant air and shape, and set down the other two for her duenna and her guardian's man of business. Aware that Sir George Soane had no sister, she scented scandal, and lost not a moment in opening the trenches.

"And how far have you come today, child?" she asked with condescension, as soon as she had taken her seat.

"From Reading, madam," the girl answered in a voice low and restrained. Her manner was somewhat awkward, and she had a shy air, as if her surroundings were new to her, But Lady Dunborough was more and more impressed with her beauty, and a natural air of refinement that was not to be mistaken.

"The roads are insufferably crowded," said the peeress. "They are intolerable!"

"I am afraid you suffered some inconvenience," the girl answered timidly.

At that moment Mr. Thomasson entered. He treated the strangers to a distant bow, and, without looking at them, took his seat with a nonchalant ease, becoming a man who traveled with viscountesses, and was at home in the best company. The table had his first hungry glance. He espied roast and cold, a pair of smoking ducklings just set on, a dish of trout, a round of beef, a pigeon-pie, and hot rolls. Relieved, he heaved a sigh of satisfaction.

"'Pon honor this is not so bad!" he said. "It is not what your ladyship is accustomed to, but at a pinch it will do. It will do!"

He was not unwilling that the strangers should know his companion's rank, and he stole a glance at them, as he spoke, to see what impression it made. Alas! the deeper impression was made on himself. For a moment he stared; the next he sprang to his feet with an oath plain and strong.

"Drat the man!" cried my lady in wrath. He had come near to oversetting her plate. "What flea has bitten you now?"

"Do you know — who these people are?" Mr. Thomasson stammered, trembling with rage; and, resting both hands on the back of his chair, he glared now at them and now at Lady Dunborough. He could be truculent where he had nothing to fear; and he was truculent now.

"These people?" my lady drawled in surprise; and she inspected them through her quizzing-glass as coolly as if they were specimens of a rare order submitted to her notice. "Not in the least, my good man. Who are they? Should I know them?"

"They are —"

But the little man, whose seat happened to be opposite the tutor's, had risen to his feet by this time; and at that word cut him short. "Sir!" he cried in a flutter of agitation. "Have a care! Have a care what you say! I am a lawyer, and I warn you that anything defamatory will — will be —"

"Pooh!" said Mr. Thomasson. "Don't try to browbeat me, sir. These persons are impostors, Lady Dunborough! Impostors!" he continued. "In this house, at any rate. They have no right to be here!"

"You shall pay for this!" shrieked Mr. Fishwick. For he it was.

"I will ring the bell," the tutor continued in a high tone, "and have them removed. They have no more to do with Sir George Soane, whose name they appear to have taken, than your ladyship has."

"Have a care! Have a care, sir," cried the lawyer, trembling.

"Or than I have!" persisted Mr. Thomasson hardily, and with his head in the air; "and no right or title to be anywhere but in the servants' room. That is their proper place. Lady Dunborough," he continued, his eyes darting severity at the three culprits, "are you aware that this young person whom you have been so kind as to notice is — is —"

"Oh, Gadzooks, man, come to the point!" cried her ladyship, with one eye on the victuals.

"No, I will not shame her publicly," said Mr. Thomasson, swelling with virtuous self-restraint. "But if your ladyship would honor me with two words apart?"

Lady Dunborough rose, muttering impatiently; and Mr. Thomasson, with the air of a just man in a parable, led her a little aside; but so that the three who remained at the table might still feel that his eye and his reprehension rested on them. He spoke a few words to her ladyship; whereon she uttered a faint cry, and stiffened. A moment and she turned and came back to the table, her face crimson, her headdress nodding. She looked at the girl, who had just risen to her feet.

"You baggage!" she hissed, "begone! Out of this house! How dare you sit in my presence?" And she pointed to the door.

Chapter IX

ST. GEORGE AND THE DRAGON

*T*he scene presented by the room at this moment was sufficiently singular. The waiters, drawn to the spot by the fury of my lady's tone, peered in at the half-opened door, and asking one another what the fracas was about, thought so; and softly called to others to witness it. On one side of the table rose Lady Dunborough, grim and venomous; on the other the girl stood virtually alone — for the elder woman had fallen to weeping helplessly, and the attorney seemed to be unequal to this new combatant. Even so, and though her face betrayed trouble and some irresolution, she did not blench, but faced her accuser with a slowly rising passion that overcame her shyness.

"Madam," she said, "I did not clearly catch your name. Am I right in supposing that you are Lady Dunborough?"

The peeress swallowed her rage with difficulty. "Go!" she cried, and pointed afresh to the door. "How dare you bandy words with me? Do you hear me? Go!"

"I am not going at your bidding," the girl answered slowly. "Why do

you speak to me like that?" And then, "You have no right to speak to
me in that way!" she continued, in a flush of indignation.

"You impudent creature!" Lady Dunborough cried. "You shameless,
abandoned baggage! Who brought you in out of the streets? You, a
kitchen-wench, to be sitting at this table smiling at your betters! I'll —
Ring the bell! Ring the bell, fool!" she continued impetuously, and
scathed Mr. Thomasson with a look. "Fetch the landlord, and let me
see this impudent hussy thrown out! Aye, madam, I suppose you are
here waiting for my son; but you have caught me instead, and I'll be
bound. I'll —"

"You'll disgrace yourself," the girl retorted with quiet pride. But she
was very white. "I know nothing of your son."

"A fig for the lie, mistress!" cried the old harridan; and added, as was
too much the fashion in those days, a word we cannot print. The
Duchess of Northumberland had the greater name for coarseness; but
Lady Dunborough's tongue was known in town. "Aye, that smartens
you, does it?" she continued with cruel delight; for the girl had winced
as from a blow. "But here comes the landlord, and now out you go. Aye,
into the streets, mistress! Hoity-toity, that dirt like you should sit at
tables! Go wash the dishes, slut!"

There was not a waiter who saw the younger woman's shame who did
not long to choke the viscountess. As for the attorney, though he had
vague fears of privilege before his eyes, and was clogged by the sex of
the assailant, he could remain silent no longer.

"My lady," he cried, in a tone of trembling desperation, "you will —
you will repent this! You don't know what you are doing. I tell you that
tomorrow —"

"What is this?" said a quiet voice. It was the landlord's; he spoke as
he pushed his way through the group at the door. "Has your ladyship
some complaint to make?" he continued civilly, his eye taking in the
scene — even to the elder woman, who through her tears kept muttering,
"Deary, we ought not to have come here! I told him we ought not to
come here!" And then, before her ladyship could reply, "Is this the party
— that have Sir George Soane's rooms?" he continued, turning to the
nearest servant.

Lady Dunborough answered for the man. "Aye!" she said, pitiless in
her triumph. "They are! And know no more of Soane than the hair of
my head! They are a party of fly-by-nights; and for this fine madam, she
is a kitchen dish-washer at Oxford! And the commonest, lowest slut
that —"

"Your ladyship has said enough," the landlord interposed, moved by
pity or the girl's beauty. "I know already that there has been some

mistake here, and that these persons have no right to the rooms they occupy. Sir George Soane has alighted within the last few minutes —"

"And knows nothing of them!" my lady cried, clapping her hands in triumph.

"That is so," the landlord answered ominously. Then, turning to the bewildered attorney, "For you, sir," he continued, "if you have anything to say, be good enough to speak. On the face of it, this is a dirty trick you have played me."

"Trick?" cried the attorney.

"Aye, trick, man. But before I send for the constable —"

"The constable?" shrieked Mr. Fishwick. Truth to tell, it had been his own idea to storm the splendors of the Castle Inn; and for certain reasons he had carried it in the teeth of his companions' remonstrances. Now between the suddenness of the onslaught made on them, the strangeness of the surroundings, Sir George's inopportune arrival, and the scornful grins of the servants who thronged the doorway, he was cowed. For a moment his wonted sharpness deserted him; he faltered and changed color. "I don't know what you mean," he said. "I gave — I gave the name of Soane; and you — you assigned me the rooms. I thought it particularly civil, sir, and was even troubled about the expense —"

"Is your name Soane?" Mr. Smith asked with blunt-ness; he grew more suspicious as the other's embarrassment increased.

"No," Mr. Fishwick admitted reluctantly. "But this young lady's name —"

"Is Soane?"

"Yes."

Mr. Thomasson stepped forward, grim as fate. "That is not true," he said coldly. "I am a Fellow of Pembroke College, Oxford, at present in attendance on her ladyship; and I identify this person" — he pointed to the girl — "as the daughter of a late servant of the College, and this woman as her mother. I have no doubt that the last thing they expected to find in this place was one who knew them."

The landlord nodded. "Joe," he said, turning to a servant, "fetch the constable. You will find him at the Falcon."

"That is talking!" cried my lady, clapping her hands gleefully. "That is talking!" And then addressing the girl, "Now, madam," she said, "I'll have your pride pulled down! If I don't have you in the stocks for this, tease my back!"

There was a snigger at that, in the background, by the door; and a crush to get in and see how the rogues took their exposure; for my lady's shrill voice could be heard in the hall, and half the inn was running to listen. Mrs. Masterson, who had collapsed at the mention of the constable, and could now do nothing but moan and weep, and the attorney, who spluttered vain threats in a voice quavering between fear and passion evoked little sympathy. But the girl, who through all remained silent, white, and defiant, who faced all, the fingers of one hand drumming on the table before her, and her fine eyes brooding scornfully on the crowd, drew from more than one the compliment of a quicker breath and a choking throat. She was the handsomest piece they had seen, they muttered, for many a day — as alien, from the other two as light from darkness; and it is not in man's nature to see beauty humiliated, and feel no unpleasant emotion. If there was to be a scene, and she did not go quietly — in that case more than one in the front rank, who read the pride in her eyes, wished he were elsewhere.

Suddenly the crowd about the door heaved. It opened slowly, and a voice, airy and indifferent, was heard remarking, "Ah! These are the people, are they? Poor devils!" Then a pause; and then, in a tone of unmistakable surprise, "Hallo!" the newcomer cried as he emerged and stared at the scene before him. "What is this?"

The attorney almost fell on his knees. "Sir George!" he screamed. "My dear Sir George! Honored sir, believe me I am innocent of any ill-meaning."

"Tut-tut!" said Sir George, who might have just stepped out of his dressing-closet instead of his carriage, so perfect was his array, from the ruffles that fell gracefully over his wrists to the cravat that supported his chin. "Tut-tut! Lord, man, what is the meaning of this?"

"We are going to see," the landlord answered dryly, forestalling the lawyer's reply. "I have sent for the constable, Sir George."

"But, Sir George, you'll speak for us?" Mr. Fishwick cried piteously, cutting the other short in his turn. "You will speak for us? You know me. You know that I am a respectable man. Oh, dear me, if this were told in Wallingford!" he continued; "and I have a mother aged seventy! It is a mistake — a pure mistake, as I am prepared to prove. I appeal to you, sir. Both I and my friends —"

He was stopped on that word; and very strangely. The girl turned on him, her cheeks scarlet. "For shame!" she cried with indignation that seemed to her hearers inexplicable. "Be silent, will you?"

Sir George stared with the others. "Oh!" said Lady Dunborough, "so you have found your voice, have you, miss — now that there is a gentleman here?"

"But — what is it all about?" Sir George asked.

"They took your rooms, sir," the landlord explained respectfully.

"Pooh! is that all?" Soane answered contemptuously. What moved him he could not tell; but in his mind he had chosen his side. He did not like Lady Dunborough.

"But they are not," the landlord objected, "they are not the persons they say they are, Sir George."

"Chut!" said Soane carelessly. "I know this person, at any rate. He is respectable enough. I don't understand it at all. Oh, is that you, Thomasson?"

Mr. Thomasson had fallen back a pace on Sir George's entrance; but being recognized he came forward. "I think that you will acknowledge, my dear sir," he said persuasively — and his tone was very different from that which he had taken ten minutes earlier — "that at any rate — they are not proper persons to sit down with her ladyship."

"But why should they sit down with her?" said Sir George the fashionable, slightly raising his eyebrows.

"Hem — Sir George, this is Lady Dunborough," replied Mr. Thomasson, not a little embarrassed.

Soane's eyes twinkled as he returned the viscountess's glance. But he bowed profoundly, and with a sweep of his hat that made the rustics stare. "Your ladyship's most humble servant," he said. "Allow me to hope that Mr. Dunborough is perfectly recovered. Believe me, I greatly regretted his mischance."

But Lady Dunborough was not so foolish as to receive his overtures according to the letter. She saw plainly that he had chosen his side — the impertinent fop, with his airs and graces! — and she was not to be propitiated. "Pray leave my son's name apart," she answered, tossing her head contemptuously. "After what has happened, sir, I prefer not to discuss him with you."

Sir George raised his eyebrows, and bowed as profoundly as before. "That is entirely as your ladyship pleases," he said. Nevertheless he was not accustomed to be snubbed, and he set a trifle to her account.

"But for that creature," she continued, trembling with passion, "I will not sleep under the same roof with her."

Sir George simpered. "I am sorry for that," he said. "For I am afraid that the Falcon in the town is not the stamp of house to suit your ladyship."

The viscountess gasped. "I should like to know why you champion her," she cried violently. "I suppose you came here to meet her."

"Alas, madam, I am not so happy," he answered — with such blandness that a servant by the door choked, and had to be hustled out in disgrace. "But since Miss — er — Masterson is here, I shall be glad to place my rooms at her — mother's disposal."

"There are no rooms," said the landlord. Between the two he was growing bewildered.

"There are mine," said Sir George dryly.

"But for yourself, Sir George?"

"Oh, never mind me, my good man. I am here to meet Lord Chatham, and some of his people will accommodate me."

"Well, of course," Mr. Smith answered, rubbing his hands dubiously — for he had sent for the constable — "of course, Sir George — if you wish it. I did not understand for whom the rooms were ordered, or — or this unpleasantness would not have arisen."

"To be sure," Sir George drawled good-naturedly. "Give the constable half-a-crown, Smith, and charge it to me." And he turned on his heel.

But at this appearance of a happy issue, Lady Dunborough's rage and chagrin, which had been rising higher and higher with each word of the dialogue, could no longer be restrained. In an awful voice, and with a port of such majesty that an ordinary man must have shaken in his shoes before her towering headdress, "Am I to understand," she cried, "that, after all that has been said about these persons, you propose to harbor them?"

The landlord looked particularly miserable; luckily he was saved from the necessity of replying by an unexpected intervention.

"We are much obliged to your ladyship," the girl behind the table said, speaking rapidly, but in a voice rather sarcastic than vehement. "There were reasons why I thought it impossible that we should accept this gentleman's offer. But the words you have applied to me, and the spirit in which your ladyship has dealt with me, make it impossible for us to withdraw and lie under the — the vile imputations, you have chosen to cast upon me. For that reason," she continued with spirit, her face instinct with indignation, "I do accept from this gentleman — and with gratitude — what I would fain refuse. And if it be any matter to your ladyship, you have only your unmannerly words to thank for it."

"Ho! ho!" the viscountess cried in affected contempt. "Are we to be called in question by creatures like these? You vixen! I spit upon you!"

Mr. Thomasson smiled in a sickly fashion. For one thing, he began to feel hungry; he had not supped. For another, he wished that he had kept his mouth shut, or had never left Oxford. With a downcast air, "I think it might be better," he said, "if your ladyship were to withdraw from this company."

But her ladyship was at that moment as dangerous as a tigress. "You think?" she cried. "You think? I think you are a fool!"

A snigger from the doorway gave point to the words; on which Lady Dunborough turned wrathfully in that direction. But the prudent landlord had slipped away, Sir George also had retired, and the servants and others, concluding the sport was at an end, were fast dispersing. She saw that redress was not to be had, but that in a moment she would be left alone with her foes; and though she was bursting with spite, the prospect had no charms for her. For the time she had failed; nothing she could say would now alter that. Moreover her ladyship was vaguely conscious that in the girl, who still stood pitilessly behind the table, as expecting her to withdraw, she had met her match. The beautiful face and proud eyes that regarded her so steadfastly had a certain terror for the battered great lady, who had all to lose in a conflict, and saw dimly that coarse words had no power to hurt her adversary.

So Lady Dunborough, after a moment's hesitation, determined to yield the field. Gathering her skirts about her with a last gesture of contempt, she sailed towards the door, resolved not to demean herself by a single word. But halfway across the room her resolution, which had nearly cost her a fit, gave way. She turned, and withering the three travelers with a glance, "You — you abandoned creature!" she cried. "I'll see you in the stocks yet!" And she swept from the room.

Alas! the girl laughed: and my lady heard her!

Perhaps it was that; perhaps it was the fact that she had not dined, and was leaving her supper behind her; perhaps it was only a general exasperation rendered her ladyship deaf. From one cause or another she lost something which her woman said to her — with no small appearance of excitement — as they crossed the hall. The maid said it again, but with no better success; and pressing nearer to say it a third time, when they were halfway up the stairs, she had the misfortune to step on her mistress's train. The viscountess turned in a fury, and slapped her cheek.

"You clumsy slut!" she cried. "Will that teach you to be more careful?"

The woman shrank away, one side of her face deep red, her eyes glittering. Doubtless the pain was sharp; and though the thing had happened before, it had never happened in public. But she suppressed her feelings, and answered whimpering, "If your ladyship pleases, I wished to tell you that Mr. Dunborough is here."

"Mr. Dunborough? Here?" the viscountess stammered.

"Yes, my lady, I saw him alighting as we passed the door."

Chapter X

MOTHER AND SON

*L*ady Dunborough stood, as if turned to stone by the news. In the great hall below, a throng of servants, the Pitt livery prominent among them, were hurrying to and fro, with a clatter of dishes and plates, a ceaseless calling of orders, a buzz of talk, and now and then a wrangle. But the lobby and staircase of the west wing, on the first floor of which she stood — and where the great man lay, at the end of a softly lighted passage, his door guarded by a man and a woman seated motionless in chairs beside it — were silent by comparison; the bulk of the guests were still at supper or busy in the east or inferior wing; and my lady had a moment to think, to trace the consequences of this inopportune arrival, and to curse, now more bitterly than before, the failure of her attempt to eject the girl from the house.

However, she was not a woman to lie down to her antagonists, and in the depth of her stupor she had a thought. Her brow relaxed; she clutched the maid's arm. "Quick," she whispered, "go and fetch Mr. Thomasson — he is somewhere below. Bring him here, but do not let Mr. Dunborough see you as you pass! Quick, woman — run!"

The maid flew on her errand, leaving her mistress to listen and fret on the stairs, in a state of suspense almost unbearable. She caught her son's voice in the entrance hall, from which stately arched doorways led to the side lobbies; but happily he was still at the door, engaged in railing at a servant; and so far all was well. At any moment, however, he might stride into the middle of the busy group in the hall; and then if he saw Thomasson before the tutor had had his lesson, the trick, if not the game, was lost. Her ladyship, scarcely breathing, hung over the balustrade, and at length had the satisfaction of seeing Thomasson and the woman enter the lobby at the foot of the stairs. In a trice the tutor, looking scared, and a trifle sulky — for he had been taken from his meat — stood at her side.

Lady Dunborough drew a breath of relief, and by a sign bade the maid begone. "You know who is below?" she whispered.

Mr. Thomasson nodded. "I thought it was what you wished," he said, with something in his tone as near mutiny as he dared venture. "I understood that your ladyship desired to overtake him and reason with him."

"But with the girl here?" she muttered. And yet it was true. Before she had seen this girl, she had fancied the task of turning her son to be well within her powers. Now she gravely doubted the issue; nay, was inclined to think all lost if the pair met. She told the tutor this, in curt phrase; and continued: "So, do you go down, man, at once, and meet him at the door; and tell him that I am here — he will discover that for himself — but that the hussy is not here. Say she is at Bath or — or anywhere you please."

Mr. Thomasson hesitated. "He will see her," he said.

"Why should he see her?" my lady retorted. "The house is full. He must presently go elsewhere. Put him on a false scent, and he will go after her hot-foot, and not find her. And in a week he will be wiser."

"It is dangerous," Mr. Thomasson faltered, his eyes wandering uneasily.

"So am I," the viscountess answered in a passion. "And mind you, Thomasson," she continued fiercely, "you have got to side with me now! Cross me, and you shall have neither the living nor my good word; and without my word you may whistle for your sucking lord! But do my bidding, help me to checkmate this baggage, and I'll see you have both. Why, man, rather than let him marry her, I'd pay you to marry her! I'd rather pay down a couple of thousand pounds, and the living too. D'ye hear me? But it won't come to that if you do my bidding."

Still Mr. Thomasson hesitated, shrinking from the task proposed, not because he must lie to execute it, but because he must lie to Dunborough, and would suffer for it, were he found out. On the other hand, the bribe was large; the red gabled house, set in its little park, and as good as a squire's, the hundred-acre glebe, the fat tithes and Easter dues — to say nothing of the promised pupil and freedom from his money troubles — tempted him sorely. He paused; and while he hesitated he was lost. For Mr. Dunborough, with the landlord beside him, entered the side-hall, booted, spurred, and in his horseman's coat; and looked up and saw the pair at the head of the staircase. His face, gloomy and discontented before, grew darker. He slapped his muddy boot with his whip, and, quitting the landlord without ceremony, in three strides was up the stairs. He did not condescend to Mr. Thomasson, but turned to the viscountess.

"Well, madam," he said with a sneer. "Your humble servant. This is an unforeseen honor! I did not expect to meet you here."

"I expected to meet *you*," my lady answered with meaning.

"Glad to give you the pleasure," he said, sneering again. He was evidently in the worst of tempers. "May I ask what has set *you* traveling?" he continued.

"Why, naught but your folly!" the viscountess cried.

"Thank you for nothing, my lady," he said. "I suppose your spy there" — and he scowled at the tutor, whose knees shook under him — "has set you on this. Well, there is time. I'll settle accounts with him by-and-by."

"Lord, my dear sir," Mr. Thomasson cried faintly, "you don't know your friends!"

"Don't I? I think I am beginning to find them out," Mr. Dunborough answered, slapping his boot ominously, "and my enemies!" At which the tutor trembled afresh.

"Never mind him," quoth my lady. "Attend to me, Dunborough. Is it a lie, or is it not, that you are going to disgrace yourself the way I have heard?"

"Disgrace myself?" cried Mr. Dunborough hotly.

"Aye, disgrace yourself."

"I'll flay the man that says it!"

"You can't flay me," her ladyship retorted with corresponding spirit. "You impudent, good-for-nothing fellow! D'you hear me? You are an impudent, good-for-nothing fellow, Dunborough, for all your airs and graces! Come, you don't swagger over me, my lad! And as sure as you do this that I hear of, you'll smart for it. There are Lorton and Swanton — my lord can do as he pleases with *them*, and they'll go from you; and your cousin Meg, ugly and long in the tooth as she is, shall have them! You may put this beggar's wench in my chair, but you shall smart for it as long as you live!"

"I'll marry whom I like!" he said.

"Then you'll buy her dear," cried my lady, ashake with rage.

"Dear or cheap, I'll have her!" he answered, inflamed by opposition and the discovery that the tutor had betrayed him. "I shall go to her now! She is here."

"That is a lie!" cried Lady Dunborough. "Lie number one."

"She is in the house at this moment!" he cried obstinately. "And I shall go to her."

"She is at Bath," said my lady, unmoved. "Ask Thomasson, if you do not believe me."

"She is not here," said the tutor with an effort.

"Dunborough, you'll outface the devil when you meet him!" my lady added — for a closing shot. She knew how to carry the war into the enemy's country.

He glared at her, uncertain what to believe. "I'll see for myself," he said at last; but sullenly, and as if he foresaw a check.

He was in the act of turning to carry out his intention, when Lady Dunborough, with great presence of mind, called to a servant who was passing the foot of the stairs. The man came. "Go and fetch this gentleman the book," she said imperiously, "with the people's names. Bring it here. I want to see it."

The man went, and in a moment returned with it. She signed to him to give it to Mr. Dunborough. "See for yourself," she said contemptuously.

She calculated, and very shrewdly, that as the lawyer and his companions had given the name of Soane and taken possession of Sir George's rooms, only the name of Soane would appear in the book. And so it turned out. Mr. Dunborough sought in vain for the name of Masterson or for a party of three, resembling the one he pursued; he found only the name of Sir George Soane entered when the rooms were ordered.

"Oh!" he said with an execration. "He is here, is he? Wish you joy of him, my lady! Very well, I go on. Good night, madam!" The viscountess knew that opposition would stiffen him. "Stop!" she cried.

But he was already in the hall, ordering fresh saddle-horses for himself and his man. My lady heard the order, and stood listening. Mr. Thomasson heard it, and stood quaking. At any moment the door of the room in which the girl was supping might open — it was adjacent to the hall — and she come out, and the two would meet. Nor did the suspense last a moment or two only. Fresh horses could not be ready in a minute, even in those times, when day and night post-horses stood harnessed in the stalls. Even Mr. Dunborough could not be served in a moment. So he roared for a pint of claret and a crust, sent one servant flying this way, and another that, hectored up and down the entrance, to the admiration of the peeping chambermaids; and for a while added much to the bustle. Once in those minutes the fateful door did open, but it emitted only a waiter. And in the end, Mr. Dunborough's horses being announced, he strode out, his spurs ringing on the steps, and the viscountess heard him clatter away into the night, and drew a deep breath of relief. For a day or two, at any rate, she was saved. For the time, the machinations of the creature below stairs were baffled.

Chapter XI

DR. ADDINGTON

*I*t did not occur to Lady Dunborough to ask herself seriously how a girl in the Mastersons' position came to be in such quarters as the Castle Inn, and to have a middle-aged and apparently respectable attorney for a traveling companion. Or, if her ladyship did ask herself those questions, she was content with the solution, which the tutor out of his knowledge of human nature had suggested; namely, that the girl, wily as she was beautiful, knew that a retreat in good order, flanked after the fashion of her betters by duenna and man of business, doubled her virtue; and by so much improved her value, and her chance of catching Mr. Dunborough and a coronet.

There was one in the house, however, who did set himself these riddles, and was at a loss for an answer. Sir George Soane, supping with Dr. Addington, the earl's physician, found his attention wander from the conversation, and more than once came near to stating the problem which troubled him. The cozy room, in which the two sat, lay at the bottom of a snug passage leading off the principal corridor of the west wing; and was as remote from the stir and bustle of the more public part of the house as the silent movements of Sir George's servant were from the clumsy haste of the helpers whom the pressure of the moment had compelled the landlord to call in.

The physician had taken his supper earlier, but was gourmet enough to follow, now with an approving word, and now with a sigh, the different stages of Sir George's meal. In public, a starched, dry man, the ideal of a fashionable London doctor of the severer type, he was in private a benevolent and easy friend; a judge of port, and one who commended it to others; and a man of some weight in the political world. In his early days he had been a mad doctor; and at Batson's he could still disconcert the impertinent by a shrewd glance, learned and practiced among those unfortunates.

With such qualifications, Dr. Addington was not slow to perceive Sir

George's absence of mind; and presuming on old friendship — he had attended the younger man from boyhood — he began to probe for the cause. Raising his half-filled glass to the light, and rolling the last mouthful on his tongue, "I am afraid," he said, "that what I heard in town was true?"

"What was it?" Soane asked, rousing himself.

"I heard, Sir George, that my Lady Hazard had proved an inconstant mistress of late?"

"Yes. Hang the jade! And yet — we could not live without her!"

"They are saying that you lost three thousand to my Lord March, the night before you left town?"

"Halve it."

"Indeed? Still — an expensive mistress?"

"Can you direct me to a cheap one?" Sir George said rather crustily.

"No. But doesn't it occur to you a wife with money — might be cheaper?" the doctor asked with a twinkle in his eye.

Sir George shrugged his shoulders for answer, and turning from the table — the servant had withdrawn — brushed the crumbs from his breeches, and sat staring at the lire, his glass in his hand. "I suppose — it will come to that presently," he said, sipping his wine.

"Very soon," the doctor answered, dryly, "unless I am in error."

Sir George looked at him. "Come, doctor!" he said. "You know something! What is it?"

"I know that it is town talk that you lost seven thousand last season; and God knows how many thousands in the three seasons before it!"

"Well, one must live," Sir George answered lightly.

"But not at that rate."

"In that state of life, doctor, into which God has been pleased — you know the rest."

"In that state of life into which the devil!" retorted the doctor with heat. "If I thought that my boy would ever grow up to do nothing better than — than — but there, forgive me. I grow warm when I think of the old trees, and the old pictures, and the old Halls that you fine gentlemen at White's squander in a night! Why, I know of a little place in Oxfordshire, which, were it mine by inheritance — as it is my brother's — I would not stake against a Canons or a Petworth!"

"And Stavordale would stake it against a bootjack — rather than not play at all!" Sir George answered complacently.

"The more fool he!" snapped the doctor.

"So I think."

"Eh?"

"So I think," Sir George answered coolly. "But one must be in the fashion, doctor."

"One must be in the Fleet!" the doctor retorted. "To be in the fashion you'll ruin yourself! If you have not done it already," he continued with something like a groan. "There, pass the bottle. I have not patience with you. One of these fine days you will awake to find yourself in the Rules."

"Doctor," Soane answered, returning to his point, "you know something."

"Well —"

"You know why my lord sent for me."

"And what if I do?" Dr. Addington answered, looking thoughtfully through his wine. "To tell the truth, I do, Sir George, I do, and I wish I did not; for the news I have is not of the best. There is a claimant to that money come forward. I do not know his name or anything about him; but his lordship thinks seriously of the matter. I am not sure," the doctor continued, with his professional air, and as if his patient in the other room were alone in his mind, "that the vexation attending it has not precipitated this attack. I'm not — at all — sure of it. And Lady Chatham certainly thinks so."

Sir George was some time silent. Then, with a fair show of indifference, "And who is the claimant?" he asked.

"That I don't know," Dr. Addington answered. "He purports, I suppose, to be your uncle's heir. But I do know that his attorney has forwarded copies of documents to his lordship, and that Lord Chatham thinks the matter of serious import."

"The worse for me," said Sir George, forcing a yawn. "As you say, doctor, your news is not of the best."

"Nor, I hope, of the worst," the physician answered with feeling. "The estate is entailed?"

Sir George shook his head. "No," he said. "It is mortgaged. But that is not the same thing."

The doctor's face showed genuine distress. "Ah, my friend, you should not have done that," he said reproachfully. "A property that has been in the family — why, since —"

"My great-grandfather the stay-maker's time," Sir George answered flippantly, as he emptied his glass. "You know Selwyn's last upon that? It came by bones, and it is going by bones."

"God forbid!" said the physician, rubbing his gold-rimmed glasses with an air of kindly vexation, not unmixed with perplexity. "If I thought that my boy would ever come to — to —"

"Buzz the gold-headed cane?" Sir George said gravely. "Yes, doctor, what would you do?"

But the physician, instead of answering, looked fixedly at him, nodded, and turned away. "You would deceive some, Sir George," he said quietly, "but you do not deceive me. When a man who is not jocular by nature makes two jokes in as many minutes, he is hard hit."

"Insight?" drawled Sir George lazily. "Or instinct."

"Experience among madmen — some would call it," the doctor retorted with warmth. "But it is not. It is what you fine gentlemen at White's have no part in! Good feeling."

"Ah!" said Soane; and then a different look came into his face. He stooped and poked the fire. "Pardon me, doctor," he said soberly. "You are a good fellow. It is — well, of course, it's a blow. If your news be true, I stand to lose fifty thousand; and shall be worth about as much as a Nabob spends yearly on his liveries."

Dr. Addington, in evident distress, thrust back his wig. "Is it as bad as that?" he said. "Dear, dear, I did not dream of this."

"Nor I," Sir George said dryly. "Or I should not have betted with March."

"And the old house!" the doctor continued, more and more moved. "I don't know one more comfortable."

"You must buy it," said Soane. "I have spared the timber, and there is a little of the old wine left."

"Dear, dear!" the doctor answered; and his sigh said more than the words. Apparently it was also more effectual in moving Sir George. He rose and began to pace the room, choosing a part where his face evaded the light of the candles that stood in heavy silver sconces on the dark mahogany. Presently he laughed, but the laugh was mirthless.

"It is quite the Rake's Progress," he said, pausing before one of Hogarth's prints which hung on the wall. "Perhaps I have been a little less of a fool and a little more of a rogue than my prototype; but the end is the same. D——n me, I am sorry for the servants, doctor — though I dare swear that they have robbed me right and left. It is a pity that clumsy fool, Dunborough, did not get home when he had the chance the other day."

The doctor took snuff, put up his box, filled his glass and emptied it before he spoke. Then, "No, no, Sir George, it has not come to that yet," he said heartily. "There is only one thing for it now. They must do something for you." And he also rose to his feet, and stood with his back to the fire, looking at his companion.

"Who?" Soane asked, though he knew very well what the other meant.

"The Government," said the doctor. "The mission to Turin is likely to be vacant by-and-by. Or, if that be too much to ask, a consulship, say at Genoa or Leghorn, might be found, and serve for a stepping-stone to Florence. Sir Horace has done well there, and you —"

"Might toady a Grand-duke and bear-lead sucking peers — as well as another!" Soane answered with a gesture of disgust. "Ugh, one might as well be Thomasson and ruin boys. No, doctor, that will not do. I had sooner hang myself at once, as poor Fanny Braddock did at Bath, or put a pistol to my head like Bland!"

"God forbid!" said the doctor solemnly.

Sir George shrugged his shoulders, but little by little his face lost its hardness. "Yes, God forbid," he said gently. "But it is odd. There is poor Tavistock with a pretty wife and two children, and another coming; and Woburn and thirty thousand a year to inherit, broke his neck last week with the hounds; and I, who have nothing to inherit, why nothing hurts me!"

Dr. Addington disregarded his words.

"They must do something for you at home then," he said, firmly set on his benevolent designs. "In the Mint or the Customs. There should not be the least difficulty about it. You must speak to his lordship, and it is not to be supposed that he will refuse."

Sir George grunted, and might have expressed his doubts, but at that moment the sound of voices raised in altercation penetrated the room from the passage. A second later, while the two stood listening, arrested by the noise, the door was thrown open with such violence that the candles flickered in the draft. Two persons appeared on the threshold, the one striving to make his way in, the other to resist the invasion.

The former was our friend Mr. Fishwick, who having succeeded in pushing past his antagonist, stared round the room with a mixture of astonishment and chagrin. "But — this is *not* his lordship's room!" he cried. "I tell you, I will see his lordship!" he continued. "I have business with him, and —" here his gaze alighted on Sir George, and he stood confounded.

Dr. Addington took advantage of the pause. "Watkins," he said in an awful voice, "what is the meaning of this unmannerly intrusion? And who is this person?"

"He persisted that he must see his lordship," the servant, a sleek, respectable man in black, answered. "And rather than have words about it at his lordship's door — which I would not for twice the likes of him!" he added with a malevolent glance at the attorney — "I brought him here. I believe he is mad. I told him it was out of the question, if he was the king of England or my lord duke. But he would have it that he had an appointment."

"So I have!" cried Mr. Fishwick with heat and an excited gesture. "I have an appointment with Lord Chatham. I should have been with his lordship at nine o'clock."

"An appointment? At this time of night?" Dr. Addington returned with a freezing mien. "With Lord Chatham? And who may you please to be, sir, who claim this privilege?"

"My name is Fishwick, sir, and I am an attorney," our friend replied.

"A mad attorney?" Dr. Addington answered, affecting to hear him amiss.

"No more mad, sir, than you are!" Mr. Fishwick retorted, kindling at the insinuation. "Do you comprehend me, sir? I come by appointment. My lord has been so good as to send for me, and I defy anyone to close his door on me!"

"Are you aware, sir," said the doctor, frowning under his wig with the port of an indignant Jupiter, "what hour it is? It is ten o'clock."

"It may be ten o'clock or it may be eleven o'clock," the attorney answered doggedly. "But his lordship has honored me with a summons, and see him I must. I insist on seeing him."

"You may insist or not as you please," said Dr. Addington contemptuously. "You will not see him. Watkins," he continued, "what is this cock-and-bull story of a summons? Has his lordship sent for anyone?"

"About nine o'clock he said that he would see Sir George Soane if he was in the house," Watkins answered. "I did not know that Sir George was here, and I sent the message to his apartments by one of the men."

"Well," said Dr. Addington in his coldest manner, "what has that to do with this gentleman?"

"I think I can tell you," Sir George said, intervening with a smile. "His party have the rooms that were reserved for me. And doubtless by an error the message which was intended for me was delivered to him."

"Ah!" said Dr. Addington gruffly. "I understand."

Alas! poor Mr. Fishwick understood too; and his face, as the truth dawned on him, was one of the most comical sights ever seen. A nervous, sanguine man, the attorney had been immensely elated by the honor paid to him; he had thought his cause won and his fortune made. The downfall was proportionate: in a second his pomp and importance were gone, and he stood before them timidly rubbing one hand on another. Yet even in the ridiculous position in which the mistake placed him — in the wrong and with all his heroics wasted — he retained a sort of manliness. "Dear me, dear me," he said, his jaw fallen, "I — Your most humble servant, sir! I offer a thousand apologies for the intrusion! But having business with his lordship, and receiving the message," he continued in a tone of pathetic regret, "it was natural I should think it was intended for me. I can say no more than that I humbly crave pardon for intruding on you, honorable gentlemen, over your wine."

Dr. Addington bowed stiffly; he was not the man to forgive a liberty.

But Sir George had a kindly impulse. In spite of himself, he could not refrain from liking the little man who so strangely haunted his steps. There was a spare glass on the table. He pushed it and the bottle towards Mr. Fishwick.

"There is no harm done," he said kindly. "A glass of wine with you, sir."

Mr. Fishwick in his surprise and nervousness, dropped his hat, picked it up, and dropped it again; finally he let it lie while he filled his glass. His hand shook; he was unaccountably agitated. But he managed to acquit himself fairly, and with a "Greatly honored, Sir George. Good-night, gentlemen," he disappeared.

"What is his business with Lord Chatham?" Dr. Addington asked rather coldly. It was plain that he did not approve of Sir George's condescension.

"I have no notion," Soane answered, yawning. "But he has got a very pretty girl with him. Whether she is laying traps for Dunborough —"

"The viscountess's son?"

"Just so — I cannot say. But that is the old harridan's account of it."

"Is she here too?"

"Lord, yes; and they had no end of a quarrel downstairs. There is a story about the girl and Dunborough. I'll tell it you some time."

"I began to think — he was here on your business," said the doctor.

"He? Oh, no," Sir George answered without suspicion, and turned to look for his candlestick. "I suppose that he is in the case I am in — wants something and comes to the fountain of honor to get it."

And bidding the other good-night, he went to bed; not to sleep, but to lie awake and reckon and calculate, and add a charge here to interest there, and set both against income, and find nothing remain.

He had sneered at the old home because it had been in his family only so many generations. But there is this of evil in an old house — it is bad to live in, but worse to part from. Sir George, straining his eyes in the darkness, saw the long avenue of elms and the rooks' nests, and the startled birds circling overhead; and at the end of the vista the wide doorway, *aed. temp.* Jac. 1 — saw it all more lucidly than he had seen it since the September morning when he traversed it, a boy of fourteen, with his first gun on his arm. Well, it was gone; but he was Sir George, macaroni and fashionable, arbiter of elections at White's, and great at Almack's, more powerful in his sphere than a belted earl! But, then, that was gone too, with the money — and — and what was left? Sir George groaned and turned on his pillow and thought of Bland and Fanny Braddock. He wondered if anyone had ever left the Castle by the suicide door, and, to escape his thoughts, lit a candle and read "La Belle

Héloïse," which he had in his mail.

Chapter XII

JULIA

*I*t is certain that if Sir George Soane had borne any other name, the girl, after the conversation which had taken place between them on the dingy staircase at Oxford, must have hated him. There is a kind of condescension from man to woman, in which the man says, "My good girl, not for me — but do take care of yourself," which a woman of the least pride finds to be of all modes of treatment the most shameful and the most humiliating. The masterful overtures of such a lover as Dunborough, who would take all by storm, are still natural, though they lack respect; a woman would be courted, and sometimes would be courted in the old rough fashion. But, for the other mode of treatment, she may be a Grizel, or as patient — a short course of that will sharpen not only her tongue, but her fingernails.

Yet this, or something like it, Julia, who was far from being the most patient woman in the world, had suffered at Sir George's hands; believing at the time that he was someone else, or, rather, being ignorant then and for just an hour afterwards that such a person as Sir George Soane existed. Enlightened on this point and on some others connected with it (which a sagacious reader may divine for himself) the girl's first feeling in face of the astonishing future opening before her had been one of spiteful exultation. She hated him, and he would suffer. She hated him with all her heart and strength, and he would suffer. There were balm and sweet satisfaction in the thought.

But presently, dwelling on the matter, she began to relent. The very completeness of the revenge which she had in prospect robbed her of her satisfaction. The man was so dependent on her, so deeply indebted to her, must suffer so much by reason of her, that the maternal instinct, which is said to be developed even in half-grown girls, took him under its protection; and when that scene occurred in the public room of the Castle Inn and he stood forward to shield her (albeit in an arrogant, careless, half-insolent way that must have wounded her in other circumstances), she was not content to forgive him only — with a smile; but long after her companion had fallen asleep, Julia sat brooding over the fire, her arms clasped about her knees; now reading the embers with parted lips and shining eyes, and now sighing gently — for "la femme propose, mais Dieu dispose." And nothing is certain.

After this, it may not have been pure accident that cast her in Sir George's way when he strolled out of the house next morning. A coach had come in, and was changing horses before the porch. The passengers were moving to and fro before the house, grooms and horse-boys were shouting and hissing, the guard was throwing out parcels. Soane passed through the bustle, and, strolling to the end of the High Street, saw the girl seated on a low parapet of the bridge that, near the end of the inn gardens, carries the Salisbury road over the Kennet. She wore a plain riding-coat, such as ladies then affected when they traveled and would avoid their hoops and patches. A little hood covered her hair, which, undressed and unpowdered, hung in a club behind; and she held up a plain fan between her complexion and the sun.

Her seat, though quiet and remote from the bustle — for the Salisbury road is the less frequented of the two roads — was in view of the gates leading to the Inn; and her extreme beauty, which was that of expression as well as feature, made her a mark for a dozen furtive eyes, of which she affected to be unconscious. But as soon as Sir George's gaze fell on her, her look met his frankly and she smiled; and then again her eyes dropped and studied the road before her, and she blushed in a way Soane found enchanting. He had been going into the town, but he turned and went to her and sat down on the bridge beside her, almost with the air of an old acquaintance. He opened the conversation by saying that it was a prodigious fine day; she agreed. That the Downs were uncommonly healthy; she said the same. And then there was silence.

"Well?" he said after a while; and he looked at her.

"Well?" she answered in the same tone. And she looked at him over the edge of her fan, her eyes laughing.

"How did you sleep, child?" he asked; while he thought, "Lord! How handsome she is!"

"Perfectly, sir," she answered, "thanks to your excellency's kindness."

Her voice as well as her eyes laughed. He stared at her, wondering at the change in her. "You are lively this morning," he said.

"I cannot say the same of you, Sir George," she answered. "When you came out, and before you saw me, your face was as long as a coach-horse's."

Sir George winced. He knew where his thoughts had been. "That was before I saw you, child," he said. "In your company —"

"You are scarcely more lively," she answered saucily. "Do you flatter yourself that you are?"

Sir George was astonished. He was aware that the girl lacked neither wit nor quickness; but hitherto he had found her passionate at one time, difficult and *farouche* at another, at no time playful or coquettish. Here, and this morning, she did not seem to be the same woman. She spoke with ease, laughed with the heart as well as the lips, met his eyes with freedom and without embarrassment, countered his sallies with sportiveness — in a word, carried herself towards him as though she were an equal; precisely as Lady Betty and the Honorable Fanny carried themselves. He stared at her.

And she, seeing the look, laughed in pure happiness, knowing what was in his mind, and knowing her own mind very well. "I puzzle you?" she said.

"You do," he answered. "What are you doing here? And why have you taken up with that lawyer? And why are you dressed, child —"

"Like this?" she said, rising, and sitting down again. "You think it is above my station?"

He shrugged his shoulders, declining to put his views into words; instead, "What does it all mean?" he said.

"What do you suppose?" she asked, averting her eyes for the first time.

"Well, of course — you may be here to meet Dunborough," he answered bluntly. "His mother seems to think that he is going to marry you."

"And what do you think, sir?"

"I?" said Sir George, reverting to the easy, half-insolent tone she hated. And he tapped his Paris snuff-box and spoke with tantalizing slowness. "Well, if that be the case, I should advise you to see that Mr. Dunborough's surplice — covers a parson."

She sat still and silent for a full half-minute after he had spoken. Then she rose without a word, and without looking at him; and, walking away to the farther end of the bridge, sat down there with her shoulder turned to him.

Soane felt himself rebuffed, and for a moment let his anger get the better of him. "D——n the girl, I only spoke for her own good!" he muttered; then reflecting that if he followed her she might remove again and make him ridiculous, he rose to go into the house. But apparently that was not what she wished. He was scarcely on his legs before she turned her head, saw that he was going, and imperiously beckoned to him.

He went to her, wondering as much at her audacity as her pettishness. When he reached her, "Sir George," she said, retaining her seat and looking gravely at him, while he stood before her like a boy undergoing correction, "you have twice insulted me — once in Oxford when, believing Mr. Dunborough's hurt lay at my door, I was doing what I could to repair it; and again today. If you wish to see more of me, you must refrain from doing so a third time. You know, a third time — you know what a third time does. And more — one moment, if you please. I must ask you to treat me differently. I make no claim to be a gentlewoman, but my condition is altered. A relation has left me a — a fortune, and when I met you here last night I was on my way to Bath to claim it."

Sir George passed from the surprise into which the first part of this speech had thrown him, to surprise still greater. At last, "I am vastly glad to hear it," he said. "For most of us it is easier to drop a fortune than to find one."

"Is it?" she said, and laughed musically, Then, moving her skirt to show him that he might sit down, "Well, I suppose it is. You have no experience of that, I hope, sir?"

He nodded.

"The gaming-table?" she said.

"Not this time," he answered, wondering why he told her. "I had a grandfather, who made a will. He had a fancy to wrap up a bombshell in the will. Now — the shell has burst."

"I am sorry," she said; and was silent a moment. At length, "Does it make — any great difference to you?" she asked naïvely.

Sir George looked at her as if he were studying her appearance. Then, "Yes, child, it does," he said.

She hesitated, but seemed to make up her mind. "I have never asked you where you live," she said softly; "have you no house in the country?"

He suppressed something between an oath and a groan. "Yes," he said, "I have a house."

"What do you call it?"

"Estcombe Hall. It is in Wiltshire, not far from here."

She looked at her fan, and idly flapped it open, and again closed it in the air. "Is it a fine place?" she said carelessly.

"I suppose so," he answered, wincing.

"With trees, and gardens, and woods?"

"Yes."

"And water?"

"Yes. There is a river."

"You used to fish in it as a boy?"

"Yes."

"Estcombe! it is a pretty name. And shall you lose it?"

But that was too much for Soane's equanimity. "Oh, d——n the girl!" he cried, rising abruptly, but sitting down again. Then, as she recoiled, in anger real or affected, "I beg your pardon," he said formally. "But — it is not the custom to ask so many questions upon private matters."

"Really, Sir George?" she said, receiving the information gravely, and raising her eyebrows. "Then Estcombe is your Mr. Dunborough, is it?"

"If you will," he said, almost sullenly.

"But you love it," she answered, studying her fan, "and I do not love — Mr. Dunborough!"

Marveling at her coolness and the nimbleness of her wit, he turned so that he looked her full in the face. "Miss Masterson," he said, "you are too clever for me. Will you tell me where you learned so much? 'Fore Gad, you might have been at Mrs. Chapone's, the way you talk."

"Mrs. Chapone's?" she said.

"A learned lady," he explained.

"I was at a school," she answered simply, "until I was fifteen. A godfather, whom I never knew, left money to my father to be spent on my schooling."

"Lord!" he said. "And where were you at school?"

"At Worcester."

"And what have you done since? — if I may ask."

"I have been at home. I should have taught children, or gone into service as a waiting-woman; but my father would keep me with him. Now I am glad of it, as this money has come to me."

"Lord! it is a perfect romance!" he exclaimed. And on the instant he fancied that he had the key to the mystery, and her beauty. She was illegitimate — a rich man's child! "Gad, Mr. Richardson should hear of it," he continued with more than his usual energy. "Pamela — why you might be Pamela!"

"That if you please," she said quickly, "for certainly I shall never be Clarissa."

Sir George laughed. "With such charms it is better not to be too sure!" he answered. And he looked at her furtively and looked away again. A coach bound eastwards came out of the gates; but it had little of his attention, though he seemed to be watching the bustle. He was thinking that if he sat much longer with this strange girl, he was a lost man. And then again he thought — what did it matter? If the best he had to expect was exile on a pittance, a consulship at Genoa, a governorship at

Guadeloupe, where would he find a more beautiful, a wittier, a gayer companion? And for her birth — a fico! His great-grandfather had made money in stays; and the money was gone! No doubt there would be gibing at White's, and shrugging at Almack's; but a fico, too, for that — it would not hurt him at Guadeloupe, and little at Genoa. And then on a sudden the fortune of which she had talked came into his head, and he smiled. It might be a thousand; or two, three, four, at most five thousand. A fortune! He smiled and looked at her.

He found her gazing steadily at him, her chin on her hand. Being caught, she reddened and looked, away. He took the man's privilege, and continued to gaze, and she to flush; and presently, "What are you looking at?" she said, moving uneasily.

"A most beautiful face," he answered, with the note of sincerity in his voice which a woman's ear never fails to appreciate.

She rose and curtsied low, perhaps to hide the tell-tale pleasure in her eyes. "Thank you, sir," she said. And she drew back as if she intended to leave him.

"But you are not — you are not offended, Julia?"

"Julia?" she answered, smiling. "No, but I think it is time I relieved your Highness from attendance. For one thing, I am not quite sure whether that pretty flattery was addressed to Clarissa — or to Pamela. And for another," she continued more coldly, seeing Sir George wince under this first stroke — he was far from having his mind made up — "I see Lady Dunborough watching us from the windows at the corner of the house. And I would not for worlds relieve her ladyship's anxiety by seeming unfaithful to her son."

"You can be spiteful, then?" Soane said, laughing.

"I can — and grateful," she answered. "In proof of which I am going to make a strange request, Sir George. Do not misunderstand it. And yet — it is only that before you leave here — whatever be the circumstances under which you leave — you will see me for five minutes."

Sir George stared, bowed, and muttered "Too happy." Then observing, or fancying he observed, that she was anxious to be rid of him, he took his leave and went into the house.

For a man who had descended the stairs an hour before, hipped to the last degree, with his mind on a pistol, it must be confessed that he went up with a light step; albeit, in a mighty obfuscation, as Dr. Johnson might have put it. A kinder smile, more honest eyes he swore he had never seen, even in a plain face. Her very blushes, of which the memory set his *blasé* blood dancing to a faster time, were a character in themselves. But — he wondered. She had made such advances, been so friendly, dropped such hints — he wondered. He was fresh from the masquerades, from Mrs. Cornely's assemblies, Lord March's converse, the Chudleigh's fantasies; the girl had made an appointment — he wondered.

For all that, one thing was unmistakable. Life, as he went up the stairs, had taken on another and a brighter color; was fuller, brisker, more generous. From a spare garret with one poor casement it had grown in an hour into a palace, vague indeed, but full of rich vistas and rosy distances and quivering delights. The corridor upstairs, which at his going out had filled him with distaste — there were boots in it, and water-cans — was now the Passage Beautiful; for he might meet her there. The day which, when he rose, had lain before him dull and monotonous — since Lord Chatham was too ill to see him, and he had no one with whom to game — was now full-furnished with interest, and hung with recollections — recollections of conscious eyes and the sweetest lips in the world. In a word, Julia had succeeded in that which she had set herself to do. Sir George might wonder. He was nonetheless in love.

Chapter XIII

A SPOILED CHILD

*J*ulia was right in fancying that she saw Lady Dunborough's face at one of the windows in the southeast corner of the house. Those windows commanded both the Marlborough High Street and the Salisbury road, welcomed alike the London and the Salisbury coach, overlooked the loungers at the entrance to the town, and supervised most details of the incoming and outgoing worlds. Lady Dunborough had not been up and about half-an-hour before she remarked these advantages. In an hour her ladyship was installed in that suite, which, though in the east wing, was commonly reckoned to be one of the best in the house. Heaven knows how she did it. There is a pertinacity, shameless and violent, which gains its ends, be the crowd between never so dense. It is possible that Mr. Smith would have ousted her had he dared. It is possible he had to pay forfeit to the rightful tenants, and in private cursed her for an old jade and a brimstone. But when a viscountess sits herself down in the middle of a room and declines to budge, she cannot with decency be taken up like a sack of hops and dumped in the passage.

Her ladyship, therefore, won, and had the pleasure of viewing from the coveted window the scene between Julia and Sir George; a scene which gave her the profoundest satisfaction. What she could not see — her eyes were no longer all that they had been — she imagined. In five minutes she had torn up the last rag of the girl's character, and proved her as bad as the worst woman that ever rode down Cheapside in a cart. Lady Dunborough was not mealy-mouthed, nor one of those who mince matters.

"What did I tell you?" she cried. "She will be on with that stuck-up before night, and be gone with morning. If Dunborough comes back he may whistle for her!"

Mr. Thomasson did not doubt that her ladyship was right. But he spoke with indifferent spirit. He had had a bad night, had lain anywhere, and dressed nowhere, and was chilly and unkempt. Apart from the awe in which he stood of her ladyship, he would have returned to Oxford by the first coach that morning.

"Dear me!" Lady Dunborough announced presently. "I declare he is leaving her! Lord, how the slut ogles him! She is a shameless baggage if ever there was one; and ruddled to the eyes, as I can see from here. I hope the white may kill her! Well, I'll be bound it won't be long before he is to her again! My fine gentleman is like the rest of them — a damned impudent fellow!"

Mr. Thomasson turned up his eyes. "There was something a little odd — does not your lady think so?" — he ventured to say, "in her taking possession of Sir George's rooms as she did."

"Did I not say so? Did I not say that very thing?"

"It seems to prove an understanding between them before they met here last night."

"I'll take my oath on it!" her ladyship cried with energy. Then in a tone of exultation she continued, "Ah! here he is again, as I thought! And come round by the street to mask the matter! He has down beside her again. Oh, he is limed, he is limed!" my lady continued, as she searched for her spying-glass, that she might miss no wit of the love-making.

The tutor was all complacence. "It proves that your ladyship's strata-gem," he said, "was to the point last night."

"Oh, Dunborough will live to thank me for that!" she answered. "Gadzooks, he will! It is first come first served with these madams. This will open his eyes if anything will."

"Still — it is to be hoped she will leave before he returns," Mr. Thomasson said, with a slight shiver of anticipation. He knew Mr. Dunborough's temper.

"Maybe," my lady answered. "But even if she does not —" There she broke of, and stood peering through the window. And suddenly, "Lord's sake!" she shrieked, "what is this?"

The fury of her tone, no less than the expletive — which we have ventured to soften — startled Mr. Thomasson to his feet. Approaching the window in trepidation — for her ladyship's wrath was impartial, and as often alighted on the wrong head as the right — the tutor saw that she had dropped her quizzing-glass, and was striving with shaking hands — but without averting her eyes from the scene outside — to recover and readjust it. Curious as well as alarmed, he drew up to her, and, looking over her shoulder, discerned the seat and Julia; and, alas! seated on the bench beside Julia, not Sir George Soane, as my lady's indifferent sight, prompted by her wishes, had persuaded her, but Mr. Dunborough!

The tutor gasped. "Oh, dear!" he said, looking round, as if for a way of retreat. "This is — this is most unfortunate."

My lady in her wrath did not heed him. Shaking her fist at her unconscious son, "You rascal!" she cried. "You paltry, impudent fellow! You would do it before my eyes, would you? Oh, I would like to have the brooming of you! And that minx! Go down you," she continued, turning fiercely on the trembling, wretched Thomasson — "go down this instant, sir, and — and interrupt them! Don't stand gaping there, but down to them, booby, without the loss of a moment! And bring him up before the word is said. Bring him up, do you hear?"

"Bring him up?" said Mr. Thomasson, his breath coming quickly. "I?"

"Yes, you! Who else?"

"I — I — but, my dear lady, he is — he can be very violent," the unhappy tutor faltered, his teeth chattering, and his cheek flabby with fright. "I have known him — and perhaps it would be better, considering my sacred office, to — to —"

"To what, craven?" her ladyship cried furiously.

"To leave him awhile — I mean to leave him and presently —"

Lady Dunborough's comment was a swinging blow, which the tutor hardly avoided by springing back. Unfortunately this placed her lady-ship between him and the door; and it is not likely that he would have escaped her cane a second time, if his wits, and a slice of good fortune, had not come to his assistance. In the midst of his palpitating "There, there, my lady! My dear good lady!" his tune changed on a sudden to

"See; they are parting! They are parting already. And — and I think — I really think — indeed, my lady, I am sure that she has refused him! She has not accepted him?"

"Refused him!" Lady Dunborough ejaculated in scorn. Nevertheless she lowered the cane and, raising her glass, addressed herself to the window. "Not accepted him? Bosh, man!"

"But if Sir George had proposed to her before?" the tutor suggested. "There — oh, he is coming in! He has — he has seen us."

It was too true. Mr. Dunborough, approaching the door with a lowering face, had looked up as if to see what witnesses there were to his discomfiture. His eyes met his mother's. She shook her fist at him. "Aye, he has," she said, her tone more moderate. "And, Lord, it must be as you say! He is in a fine temper, if I am any judge."

"I think," said Mr. Thomasson, looking round, "I had better — better leave — your ladyship to see him alone."

"No," said my lady firmly.

"But — but Mr. Dunborough," the tutor pleaded, "may like to see you alone. Yes, I am sure I had better go."

"No," said my lady more decisively; and she laid her hand on the hapless tutor's arm.

"But — but if your ladyship is afraid of — of his violence," Mr. Thomasson stuttered, "it will be better, surely, for me to call some — some of the servants."

"Afraid?" Lady Dunborough cried, supremely contemptuous. "Do you think I am afraid of my own son? And such a son! A poor puppet," she continued, purposely raising her voice as a step sounded outside, and Mr. Dunborough, flinging open the door, appeared like an angry Jove on the threshold, "who is fooled by every ruddled woman he meets! Aye, sir, I mean you! You! Oh, I am not to be browbeaten, Dunborough!" she went on; "and I will trouble you not to kick my furniture, you unmannerly puppy. And out or in's no matter, but shut the door after you."

Mr. Dunborough was understood to curse everybody; after which he fell into the chair that stood next the door, and, sticking his hands into his breeches-pockets, glared at my lady, his face flushed and somber.

"Hoity-toity! are these manners?" said she. "Do you see this reverend gentleman?"

"Aye, and G—— d—— him!" cried Mr. Dunborough, with a very strong expletive; "but I'll make him smart for it by-and-by. You have ruined me among you."

"Saved you, you mean," said Lady Dunborough with complacency, "if you are worth saving — which, mind you, I very much doubt,

Dunborough."

"If I had seen her last night," he answered, drawing a long breath, "it would have been different. For that I have to thank you two. You sent me to lie at Bath and thought you had got rid of me. But I am back, and I'll remember it, my lady! I'll remember you too, you lying sneak!"

"You common, low fellow!" said my lady.

"Aye, talk away!" said he; and then no more, but stared at the floor before him, his jaw set, and his brow as black as a thundercloud. He was a powerful man, and, with that face, a dangerous man. For he was honestly in love; the love was coarse, brutal, headlong, a passion to curse the woman who accepted it; but it was not the less love for that. On the contrary, it was such a fever as fills the veins with fire and drives a man to desperate things; as was proved by his next words.

"You have ruined me among you," he said, his tone dull and thick, like that of a man in drink. "If I had seen her last night, there is no knowing but what she would have had me. She would have jumped at it. You tell me why not! But she is different this morning. There is a change in her. Gad, my lady," with a bitter laugh, "she is as good a lady as you, and better! And I'd have used her gently. Now I shall carry her off. And if she crosses me I will wring her handsome neck!"

It is noticeable that he did not adduce any reason why the night had changed her. Only he had got it firmly into his head that, but for the delay they had caused, all would be well. Nothing could move him from this.

"Now I shall run away with her," he repeated.

"She won't go with you," my lady cried with scorn.

"I shan't ask her," he answered. "When there is no choice she will come to it. I tell you I shall carry her off. And if I am taken and hanged for it, I'll be hanged at Papworth — before your window."

"You poor simpleton!" she said. "Go home to your father."

"All right, my lady," he answered, without lifting his eyes from the carpet. "Now you know. It will be your doing. I shall force her off, and if I am taken and hanged I will be hanged at Papworth. You took fine pains last night, but I'll take pains today. If I don't have her I shall never have a wife. But I will have her."

"Fools cry for the moon," said my lady. "Any way, get out of my room. You are a fine talker, but I warrant you will take care of your neck."

"I shall carry her off and marry her," he repeated, his chin sunk on his breast, his hand rattling the money in his pocket.

"It is a distance to Gretna," she answered. "You'll be nearer it outside my door, my lad. So be stepping, will you? And if you take my advice, you will go to my lord."

"All right; you know," he said sullenly. "For that sneak there, if he comes in my way, I'll break every bone in his body. Good-day, my lady. When I see you again I will have Miss with me."

"Like enough; but not Madam," she retorted. "You are not such a fool as that comes to. And there is the Act besides!"

That was her parting shot; for all the feeling she had shown, from the opening to the close of the interview, she might have been his worst enemy. Yet after a fashion, and as a part of herself, she did love him; which was proved by her first words after the door had closed upon him.

"Lord!" she said uneasily. "I hope he will play no Ferrers tricks, and disgrace us all. He is a black desperate fellow, is Dunborough, when he is roused."

The crestfallen tutor could not in a moment recover himself; but he managed to say that he did not think Mr. Dunborough suspected Sir George; and that even if he did, the men had fought once, in which case there was less risk of a second encounter.

"You don't know him," my lady answered, "if you say that. But it is not that I mean. He'll do some wild thing about carrying her off. From a boy he would have his toy. I've whipped him till the blood ran, and he's gone to it."

"But without her consent," said Mr. Thomasson, "it would not be possible."

"I mistrust him," the viscountess answered. "So do you go and find this baggage, and drop a word to her — to go in company you understand. Lord! he might marry her that way yet. For once away she would have to marry him — aye, and he to marry her to save his neck. And fine fools we should look."

"It's — it's a most surprising, wonderful thing she did not take him," said the tutor thoughtfully.

"It's God's mercy and her madness," quoth the viscountess piously. "She may yet. And I would rather give you a bit of a living to marry her — aye, I would, Thomasson — than be saddled with such a besom!"

Mr. Thomasson cast a sickly glance at her ladyship. The evening before, when the danger seemed imminent, she had named two thousand pounds and a living. Tonight, the living. Tomorrow — what? For the living had been promised all along and in any case. Whereas now, a remote and impossible contingency was attached to it. Alas! the tutor saw very clearly that my lady's promises were pie-crust, made to be broken.

She caught the look, but attributed it to another cause. "What do you fear, man?" she said. "Sho! he is out of the house by this time."

Mr. Thomasson would not have ventured far on that assurance, but he had himself seen Mr. Dunborough leave the house and pass to the stables; and anxious to escape for a time from his terrible patroness, he professed himself ready. Knowing where the rooms, which the girl's party occupied, lay, in the west wing, he did not call a servant, but went through the house to them and knocked at the door.

He got no answer, so gently opened the door and peeped in. He discovered a pleasant airy apartment, looking by two windows over a little grass plot that flanked the house on that side, and lay under the shadow of the great Druid mound. The room showed signs of occupancy — a lady's cloak cast over a chair, a great litter of papers on the table. But for the moment it was empty.

He was drawing back, satisfied with his survey, when he caught the sound of a heavy tread in the corridor behind him. He turned; to his horror he discerned Mr. Dunborough striding towards him, a whip in one hand, and in the other a note; probably the note was for this very room. At the same moment Mr. Dunborough caught sight of the tutor, and bore down on him with a view halloa. Mr. Thomasson's hair rose, his knees shook under him, he all but sank down where he was. Fortunately at the last moment his better angel came to his assistance. His hand was still on the latch of the door; to open it, to dart inside, and to shoot the bolt were the work of a second. Trembling he heard Mr. Dunborough come up and slash the door with his whip, and then, contented with this demonstration, pass on, after shouting through the panels that the tutor need not flatter himself — he would catch him by-and-by.

Mr. Thomasson devoutly hoped he would not; and, sweating at every pore, sat down to recover himself. Though all was quiet, he suspected the enemy of lying in wait; and rather than run into his arms was prepared to stay where he was, at any risk of discovery by the occupants. Or there might be another exit. Going to one of the windows to ascertain this, he found that there was; an outside staircase of stone affording egress to the grass plot. He might go that way; but no! — at the base of the Druid mound he perceived a group of townsfolk and rustics staring at the flank of the building — staring apparently at him. He recoiled; then he remembered that Lord Chatham's rooms lay in that wing, and also looked over the gardens. Doubtless the countryfolk were watching in the hope that the great man would show himself at a window, or that, at the worst, they might see the crumbs shaken from a tablecloth he had used.

This alone would have deterred the tutor from a retreat so public:

besides, he saw something which placed him at his ease. Beyond the group of watchers he espied three people strolling at their leisure, their backs towards him. His sight was better than Lady Dunborough's; and he had no difficulty in making out the three to be Julia, her mother, and the attorney. They were moving towards the Bath road. Freed from the fear of interruption, he heaved a sigh of relief, and, choosing the most comfortable chair, sat down on it.

It chanced to stand by the table, and on the table, as has been said, lay a vast litter of papers. Mr. Thomasson's elbow rested on one. He went to move it; in the act he read the heading: "This is the last will and testament of me Sir Anthony Cornelius Soane, baronet, of Estcombe Hall, in the county of Wilts."

"Tut-tut!" said the tutor. "That is not Soane's will, that is his grandfather's." And between idleness and curiosity, not unmingled with surprise, he read the will to the end. Beside it lay three or four narrow slips; he examined these, and found them to be extracts from a register. Apparently someone was trying to claim under the will; but Mr. Thomasson did not follow the steps or analyze the pedigree — his mind was engrossed by perplexity on another point. His thoughts might have been summed up in the lines —

"Not that the things themselves are rich or rare,
The wonder's how the devil they got there" —

in a word, how came the papers to be in that room? "These must be Soane's rooms," he muttered at last, looking about him. "And yet — that's a woman's cloak. And that old cowskin bag is not Sir George's. It is odd. Ah! What is this?"

This was a paper, written and folded brief-wise, and indorsed: "Statement of the Claimant's case for the worshipful consideration of the Eight Honorable the Earl of Chatham and others the trustees of the Estcombe Hall Estate. Without Prejudice."

"So!" said the tutor. "This may be intelligible." And having assured himself by a furtive glance through the window that the owners of the room were not returning, he settled himself to peruse it. When he again looked up, which was at a point about one-third of the way through the document, his face wore a look of rapt, incredulous, fatuous astonishment.

Chapter XIV

A GOOD MAN'S DILEMMA

*T*en minutes later Mr. Thomasson slid back the bolt, and opening the door, glanced furtively up and down the passage. Seeing no one, he came out, closed the door behind him, and humming an air from the "Buona Figlinola," which was then the fashion, returned slowly, and with apparent deliberation, to the east wing. There he hastened to hide himself in a small closet of a chamber, which he had that morning secured on the second floor, and having bolted the door behind him, he plumped down on the scanty bed, and stared at the wall, he was the prey of a vast amazement.

"Jupiter!" he muttered at last, "what a — a Pactolus I have missed! Three months ago, two months ago, she would have gone on her knees to marry me! And with all that money — Lord! I would have died Bishop of Oxford. It is monstrous! Positively, I am fit to kill myself when I think of it!"

He paused awhile to roll the morsel on the palate of his imagination, and found that the pathos of it almost moved him to tears. But before long he fell from the clouds to more practical matters. The secret was his, but what was he going to do with it? Where make his market of it? One by one he considered all the persons concerned. To begin with, there was her ladyship. But the knowledge did not greatly affect the viscountess, and he did not trust her. He dismissed the thought of applying to her. It was the same with Dunborough; money or no money was all one to him, he would take the girl if he could get her. He was dismissed as equally hopeless. Soane came next; but Sir George either knew the secret, or must know it soon; and though his was a case the tutor pondered long, he discerned no profit he could claim from him. Moreover, he had not much stomach for driving a bargain with the baronet; so in the end Sir George too was set aside.

There remained only the Buona Figliuola — the girl herself. "I might pay my court to her," the tutor thought, "but she would have a spite against me for last night's work, and I doubt I could not do much. To be sure, I might put her on her guard against Dunborough, and trust to her gratitude; but it is ten to one she would not believe me. Or I could let him play his trick — if he is fool enough to put his neck in a noose — and step in and save her at the last moment. Ah!" Mr. Thomasson continued, looking up to the ceiling in a flabby ecstasy of appreciation, "If I had the courage! That were a game to play indeed, Frederick Thomasson!"

It was, but it was hazardous; and the schemer rose and walked the floor, striving to discover a safer mode of founding his claim. He found none, however; and presently, with a wry face, he took out a letter which he had received on the eve of his departure from Oxford — a letter from a dun, threatening process and arrest. The sum was one which a year's stipend of a fat living would discharge; and until the receipt of the letter the tutor, long familiar with embarrassment, had taken the matter lightly. But the letter was to the point, and meant business — a spunging house and the Fleet; and with the cold shade of the Rules in immediate prospect, Mr. Thomasson saw himself at his wits' end. He thought and thought, and presently despair bred in him a bastard courage.

Buoyed up by this he tried to picture the scene; the lonely road, the carriage, the shrieking girl, the ruffians looking fearfully up and down as they strove to silence her; and himself running to the rescue; as Mr. Burchell ran with the big stick, in Mr. Goldsmith's novel, which he had read a few months before. Then the struggle. He saw himself knocked — well, pushed down; after all, with care, he might play a fine part without much risk. The men might fly either at sight of him, or when he drew nearer and added his shouts to the girl's cries; or — or someone else might come up, by chance or summoned by the uproar! In a minute it would be over; in a minute — and what a rich reward he might reap.

Nevertheless he did not feel sure he would be able to do it. His heart thumped, and his smile grew sickly, and he passed his tongue again and again over his dry lips, as he thought of the venture. But do it or not when the time came, he would at least give himself the chance. He would attend the girl wherever she went, dog her, watch her, hang on her skirts; so, if the thing happened, he would be at hand, and if he had the courage, would save her.

"It should — it should stand me in a thousand!" he muttered, wiping his damp brow, "and that would put me on my legs."

He put her gratitude at that; and it was a great sum, a rich bribe. He thought of the money lovingly, and of the feat with trembling, and took his hat and unlocked his door and went downstairs. He spied about him cautiously until he learned that Mr. Dunborough had departed;

then he went boldly to the stables, and inquired and found that the gentleman had started for Bristol in a post-chaise. "In a middling black temper," the ostler added, "saving your reverence's presence."

That ascertained, the tutor needed no more. He knew that Dunborough, on his way to foreign service, had lain ten days in Bristol, whistling for a wind; that he had landed there also on his return, and made — on his own authority — some queer friends there. Bristol, too, was the port for the plantations; a slave-mart under the rose, with the roughest of all the English seatown populations. There were houses at Bristol where crimping was the least of the crimes committed; in the docks, where the great ships, laden with sugar and tobacco, sailed in and out in their seasons, lay sloops and skippers, ready to carry all comers, criminal and victim alike, beyond the reach of the law. The very name gave Mr. Thomasson pause; he could have done with Gretna — which Lord Hardwicke's Marriage Act had lately raised to importance — or Berwick, or Harwich, or Dover. But Bristol had a grisly sound. From Marlborough it lay no more than forty miles away by the Chippenham and Marshfield road; a post-chaise and four stout horses might cover the distance in four hours.

He felt, as he sneaked into the house, that the die was cast. The other intended to do it then. And that meant — "Oh, Lord," he muttered, wiping his brow, "I shall never dare! If he is there himself, I shall never dare!" As he crawled upstairs he went hot one moment and shivered the next; and did not know whether he was glad or sorry that the chance would be his to take.

Fortunately, on reaching the first floor he remembered that Lady Dunborough had requested him to convey her compliments to Dr. Addington, with an inquiry how Lord Chatham did. The tutor felt that a commonplace interview of this kind would settle his nerves; and having learned the position of Dr. Addington's apartments, he found his way down the snug passage of which we know and knocked at the door. A voice, disagreeably raised, was speaking on the other side of the door, but paused at the sound of his knock. Someone said "Come in," and he entered.

He found Dr. Addington standing on the hearth, stiff as a poker, and swelling with dignity. Facing him stood Mr. Fishwick. The attorney, flustered and excited, cast a look at Mr. Thomasson as if his entrance were an added grievance; but that done, went on with his complaint.

"I tell you, sir," he said, "I do not understand this. His lordship was able to travel yesterday, and last evening he was well enough to see Sir George Soane."

"He did not see him," the physician answered stiffly. There is no class which extends less indulgence to another than the higher grade of professional men to the lower grade. While to Sir George Mr. Fishwick was an odd little man, comic, and not altogether inestimable, to Dr. Addington he was an anathema.

"I said only, sir, that he was well enough to see him," the lawyer retorted querulously. "Be that as it may, his lordship was not seriously ill yesterday. Today I have business of the utmost importance with him, and am willing to wait upon him at any hour. Nevertheless you tell me that I cannot see him today, nor tomorrow —"

"Nor in all probability the next day," the doctor answered grimly.

Mr. Fishwick's voice rose almost to a shriek. "Nor the next day?" he cried.

"No, nor the next day, so far as I can judge."

"But I must see him! I tell you, sir, I must see him," the lawyer ejaculated. "I have the most important business with him!"

"The most important?"

"The most important!"

"My dear sir," Dr. Addington said, raising his hand and clearly near the end of his patience, "my answer is that you shall see him — when he is well enough to be seen, and chooses to see you, and not before! For myself, whether you see him now or never see him, is no business of mine. But it *is* my business to be sure that his lordship does not risk a life which is of inestimable value to his country."

"But — but yesterday he was well enough to travel!" murmured the lawyer, somewhat awed. "I — I do not like this!"

The doctor looked at the door.

"I — I believe I am being kept from his lordship!" Mr. Fishwick persisted, stuttering nervously. "And there are people whose interest it is to keep me from his lordship. I warn you, sir, that if anything happens in the meantime —"

The doctor rang the bell.

"I shall hold you responsible!" Mr. Fishwick cried passionately. "I consider this a most mysterious illness. I repeat, I —"

But apparently that was the last straw. "Mysterious?" the doctor cried, his face purple with indignation. "Leave the room, sir! You are not sane, sir! By God, you ought to be shut up, sir! You ought not to be allowed to go about. Do you think that you are the only person who wants to see His Majesty's Minister? Here is a courier come today from His Grace the Duke of Grafton, and tomorrow there will be a score, and a king's messenger from His Majesty among them — and all this trouble is given by a miserable, little, paltry, petti — Begone, sir, before I say too much!" he continued trembling with anger. And then to the servant, "John, the door! the door! And see that this person does not trouble me again. Be good enough to communicate in writing, sir, if you have anything to say."

With which poor Mr. Fishwick was hustled out, protesting but not convinced. It is seldom the better side of human nature that lawyers see; nor is an attorney's office, or a barrister's chamber, the soil in which a luxuriant crop of confidence is grown. In common with many persons of warm feelings, but narrow education, Mr. Fishwick was ready to believe on the smallest evidence — or on no evidence at all — that the rich and powerful were leagued against his client; that justice, if he were not very sharp, would be denied him; that the heavy purse had a knack of outweighing the righteous cause, even in England and in the eighteenth century. And the fact that all his hopes were staked on this case, that all his resources were embarked in it, that it had fallen, as it were, from heaven into his hands — wherefore the greater the pity if things went amiss — rendered him peculiarly captious and impracticable. After this every day, nay, every hour, that passed without bringing him to Lord Chatham's presence augmented his suspense and doubled his anxiety. To be put off, not one day, but two days, three days — what might not happen in three days! — was a thing intolerable, insufferable; a thing to bring the heavens down in pity on his head! What wonder if he rebelled hourly; and being routed, as we have seen him routed, muttered dark hints in Julia's ear, and, snubbed in that quarter also, had no resource but to shut himself up in his sleeping-place, and there brood miserably over his suspicions and surmises?

Even when the lapse of twenty-four hours brought the swarm of couriers, messengers, and expresses which Dr. Addington had foretold; when the High Street of Marlborough — a name henceforth written on the page of history — became but a slowly moving line of coaches and chariots bearing the select of the county to wait on the great Minister; when the little town itself began to throb with unusual life, and to take on airs of fashion, by reason of the crowd that lay in it; when the Duke of Grafton himself was reported to be but a stage distant, and there detained by the Earl's express refusal to see him; when the very *KING*, it was rumored, was coming on the same business; when, in a word, it became evident that the eyes of half England were turned to the Castle Inn at Marlborough, where England's great statesman lay helpless, and gave no sign, though the wheels of state creaked and all but stood still — even then Mr. Fishwick refused to be satisfied, declined to be comforted. In place of viewing this stir and bustle, this coming and going as a perfect confirmation of Dr. Addington's statement, and a proof of his integrity, he looked askance at it. He saw in it a demonstration of the powers ranked against him and the principalities he had to combat; he felt, in face of it, how weak, how poor, how insignificant he was; and at one time despaired, and at another was in a frenzy, at one time wearied Julia with prophecies of treachery, at another poured his forebodings into the more sympathetic bosom of the elder woman. The reader may laugh; but if he has ever staked his all on a cast, if he has taken up a hand of twelve trumps, only to hear the ominous word "misdeal!" he will find something in Mr. Fishwick's attitude neither unnatural nor blameworthy.

Chapter XV

AMORIS INTEGRATIO

During the early days of the Minister's illness, when, as we have seen, all the political world of England were turning their coaches and six towards the Castle Inn, it came to be the custom for Julia to go every morning to the little bridge over the Kennet, thence to watch the panorama of departures and arrivals; and for Sir George to join her there without excuse or explanation, and as if, indeed, nothing in the world were more natural. As the Earl's illness continued to detain all who desired to see him — from the Duke of Grafton's parliamentary secretary to the humblest aspirant to a tide-waitership — Soane was not the only one who had time on his hands and sought to while it away in the company of the fair. The shades of Preshute churchyard, which lies in the bosom of the trees, not three bowshots from the Castle Inn and hard by the Kennet, formed the chosen haunt of one couple. A second pair favored a seat situate on the west side of the Castle Mound, and well protected by shrubs from the gaze of the vulgar. And there were others.

These Corydons, however, were at ease; they basked free from care in the smiles of their Celias. But Soane, in his philandering, had to do with black care that would be ever at his elbow; black care, that always when he was not with Julia, and sometimes while he talked to her, would jog his thoughts, and draw a veil before the future. The prospect of losing Estcombe, of seeing the family Lares broken and cast out, and the family stem, tender and young, yet not ungracious, snapped off short, wrung a heart that belied his cold exterior. Moreover, when all these had been sacrificed, he was his own judge how far he could without means pursue the life which he was living. Suspense, anxiety, sordid calculation were ever twitching his sleeve, and would have his attention. Was the claim a valid claim, and must it prevail? If it prevailed, how was he to live; and where, and on what? Would the Minister grant his suit for a place or a pension? Should he prefer that suit, or might he still by one deep night and one great hand at hazard win back the thirty thousand guineas he had lost in five years?

Such questions, troubling him whether he would or no, and forcing themselves on his attention when they were least welcome, ruffled at last the outward composure on which as a man of fashion he plumed himself. He would fall silent in Julia's company, and turning his eyes from her, in unworthy forgetfulness, would trace patterns in the dust with his cane, or stare by the minute together at the quiet stream that moved sluggishly beneath them.

On these occasions she made no attempt to rouse him. But when he again awoke to the world, to the coach passing in its cloud of dust, or the gaping urchin, or the clang of the distant dinner-bell, he would find her considering him with an enigmatical smile, that lay in the region between amusement and pity; her shapely chin resting on her hand, and the lace falling from the whitest wrist in the world. One day the smile lasted so long, was so strange and dubious, and so full of a weird intelligence, that it chilled him; it crept to his bones, disconcerted him, and set him wondering. The uneasy questions that had haunted him at the first, recurred. Why was this girl so facile, who had seemed so proud, and whose full lips curved so naturally? Was she really won, or was she with some hidden motive only playing with him? The notion was not flattering to a fine gentleman's vanity; and in any other case he would have given himself credit for conquest. But he had discovered that this girl was not as other girls; and then there was that puzzling smile. He had surprised it half a dozen times before.

"What is it?" he said abruptly, holding her eyes with his. This time he was determined to clear up the matter.

"What?" she asked in apparent innocence. But she colored, and he saw that she understood.

"What does your smile mean, Pulcherrima?"

"Only — that I was reading your thoughts, Sir George," she answered.

"And they were not of me."

"Impossible!" he said. "I vow, Julia —"

"Don't vow," she answered quickly, "or when you vow — some other time — I may not be able to believe you! You were not thinking of me, Sir George, but of your home, and the avenue of which you told me, and the elms in which the rooks lived, and the river in which you used to fish. You were wondering to whom they would go, and who would possess them, and who would be born in the room in which you were born, and who would die in the room in which your father died."

"You are a witch!" he said, a spasm of pain crossing his face.

"Thank you," she answered, looking at him over her fan. "Last time you said, 'D——n the girl!' It is clear I am improving your manners, Sir George. You are now so polite, that presently you will consult me."

So she could read his very thoughts! Could set him on the rack! Could perceive when pain and not irritation underlay the oath or the compliment. He was always discovering something new in her; something that piqued his curiosity, and kept him amused. "Suppose I consult you now?" he said.

She swung her fan to and fro, playing with it childishly, looking at the light through it, and again dropping it until it hung from her wrist by a ribbon. "As your highness pleases," she said at last. "Only I warn you, that I am not the Bottle Conjuror."

"No, for you are here, and he was not there," Sir George answered, affecting to speak in jest. "But tell me; what shall I do in this case? A claim is made against me."

"It's the bomb," she said, "that burst, Sir George, is it not?"

"The same. The point is, shall I resist the claim, or shall I yield to it? What do you say, ma'am?"

She tossed up her fan and caught it deftly, and looked to him for admiration. Then, "It depends," she said. "Is it a large claim?"

"It is a claim — for all I have," he answered slowly. It was the first time he had confessed that to anyone, except to himself in the night watches.

If he thought to touch her, he succeeded. If he had fancied her unfeeling before, he did so no longer. She was red one minute and pale the next, and the tears came into her eyes. "Oh," she cried, her breast heaving, "you should not have told me! Oh, why did you tell me?" And she rose hurriedly as if to leave him; and then sat down again, the fan quivering in her hand.

"But you said you would advise me!" he answered in surprise.

"I! Oh, no! no!" she cried.

"But you must!" he persisted, more deeply moved than he would show. "I want your advice. I want to know how the case looks to another. It is a simple question. Shall I fight, Julia, or shall I yield to the claim?"

"Fight or yield?" she said, her voice broken by agitation. "Shall you fight or yield? You ask me?"

"Yes."

"Then fight! Fight!" she answered, with surprising emotion: and she rose again to her feet. And again sat down. "Fight them to the last, Sir George!" she cried breathlessly. "Let the creatures have nothing! Not a penny! Not an acre!"

"But — if it is a righteous claim?" he said, amazed at her excitement.

"Righteous?" she answered passionately. "How can a claim be righteous that takes all that a man has?"

He nodded, and studied the road awhile, thinking less of her advice than of the strange fervor with which she had given it. At the end of a minute he was surprised to hear her laugh. He felt hurt, and looked up to learn the reason; and was astounded to find her smiling at him as lightly and gaily as if nothing had occurred to interrupt her most whimsical mood; as if the question he had put to her had not been put, or were a farce, a jest, a mere pastime!

"Sho, Sir George," she said, "how silly you must think me to proffer you advice; and with an air as if the sky were falling? Do you forgive me?"

"I forgive you *that*," Sir George answered. But, poor fellow, he winced under her sudden change of tone.

"That is well," she said confidently. "And there again, do you know you are changed; you would not have said that a week ago. I have most certainly improved your manners."

Sir George made an effort to answer her in the same strain. "Well, I should improve," he said. "I come very regularly to school. Do you know how many days we have sat here, *ma belle*?"

A faint color tinged her cheek. "If I do not, that dreadful Mr. Thomasson does," she answered. "I believe he never lets me go out of his sight. And for what you say about days — what are days, or even weeks, when it is a question of reforming a rake, Sir George? Who was it you named to me yesterday," she continued archly, but with her eyes on the toe of her shoe which projected from her dress, "who carried the gentleman into the country when he had lost I don't know how many thousand pounds? And kept him there out of harm's way?"

"It was Lady Carlisle," Sir George answered dryly; "and the gentleman was her husband."

It was Julia's turn to draw figures in the dust of the roadway, which she did very industriously; and the two were silent for quite a long time,

while someone's heart bumped as if it would choke her. At length —
"He was not quite ruined, was he?" she said, with elaborate carelessness;
her voice was a little thick — perhaps by reason of the bumping.

"Lord, no!" said Sir George. "And I am, you see."

"While I am not your wife!" she answered; and flashed her eyes on
him in sudden petulance; and then, "Well, perhaps if my lady had her
choice — to be wife to a rake can be no bed of roses, Sir George! While
to be wife to a ruined rake — perhaps to be wife to a man who, if he
were not ruined, would treat you as the dirt beneath his feet, beneath
his notice, beneath —"

She did not seem to be able to finish the sentence, but rose choking,
her face scarlet. He rose more slowly. "Lord!" he said humbly, looking
at her in astonishment, "what has come to you suddenly? What has
made you angry with me, child?"

"Child?" she exclaimed. "Am I a child? You play with me as if I were!"

"Play with you?" Sir George said, dumfounded; he was quite taken
aback by her sudden vehemence. "My dear girl, I cannot understand
you. I am not playing with you. If anyone is playing, it is you. Sometimes
— I wonder whether you hate me or love me. Sometimes I am happy
enough to think the one; sometimes — I think the other —"

"It has never struck you," she said, speaking with her head high, and
in her harshest and most scornful tone, "that I may do neither the one
nor the other, but be pleased to kill my time with you — since I must
stay here until my lawyer has done his business?"

"Oh!" said Soane, staring helplessly at the angry beauty, "if that be
all —"

"That is all!" she cried. "Do you understand? That is all."

He bowed gravely. "Then I am glad that I have been of use to you.
That at least," he said.

"Thank you," she said dryly. "I am going into the house now. I need
not trouble you farther."

And sweeping him a curtsey that might have done honor to a duchess,
she turned and sailed away, the picture of disdain. But when her face
was safe from his gaze and he could no longer see them, her eyes filled
with tears of shame and vexation; she had to bite her trembling lip to
keep them back. Presently she slackened her speed and almost stopped
— then hurried on, when she thought that she heard him following. But
he did not overtake her, and Julia's step grew slow again, and slower
until she reached the portico.

Between love and pride, hope and shame, she had a hard fight;
happily a coach was unloading, and she could stand and feign interest
in the passengers. Two young fellows fresh from Bath took fire at her

eyes; but one who stared too markedly she withered with a look, and, if the truth be told, her fingers tingled for his ears. Her own ears were on the alert, directed backwards like a hare's. Would he never come? Was he really so simple, so abominably stupid, so little versed in woman's ways? Or was he playing with her? Perhaps, he had gone into the town? Or trudged up the Salisbury road; if so, and if she did not see him now, she might not meet him until the next morning; and who could say what might happen in the interval? True, he had promised that he would not leave Marlborough without seeing her; but things had altered between them since then.

At last — at last, when she felt that her pride would allow her to stay no longer, and she was on the point of going in, the sound of his step cut short her misery. She waited, her heart beating quickly, to hear his voice at her elbow. Presently she heard it, but he was speaking to another; to a coarse rough man, half servant half loafer, who had joined him, and was in the act of giving him a note. Julia, outwardly cool, inwardly on tenterhooks, saw so much out of the corner of her eye, and that the two, while they spoke, were looking at her. Then the man fell back, and Sir George, purposely averting his gaze and walking like a man heavy in thought, went by her; he passed through the little crowd about the coach, and was on the point of disappearing through the entrance, when she hurried after him and called his name.

He turned, between the pillars, and saw her. "A word with you, if you please," she said. Her tone was icy, her manner freezing.

Sir George bowed. "This way, if you please," she continued imperiously; and preceded him across the hall and through the opposite door and down the steps to the gardens, that had once been Lady Hertford's delight. Nor did she pause or look at him until they were halfway across the lawn; then she turned, and with a perfect change of face and manner, smiling divinely in the sunlight,

"Easy her motion seemed, serene her air,"

she held out her hand.

"You have come — to beg my pardon, I hope?" she said.

The smile she bestowed on him was an April smile, the brighter for the tears that lurked behind it; but Soane did not know that, nor, had he known it, would it have availed him. He was utterly dazzled, conquered, subjugated by her beauty. "Willingly," he said. "But for what?"

"Oh, for — everything!" she answered with supreme assurance.

"I ask your divinity's pardon for everything," he said obediently.

"It is granted," she answered. "And — I shall see you tomorrow, Sir

George?"

"Tomorrow?" he said. "Alas, no; I shall be away tomorrow."

He had eyes; and the startling fashion in which the light died out of her face, and left it grey and colorless, was not lost on him. But her voice remained steady, almost indifferent. "Oh!" she said, "you are going?" And she raised her eyebrows.

"Yes," he answered; "I have to go to Estcombe."

She tried to force a laugh, but failed. "And you do not return? We shall not see you again?" she said.

"It lies with you," he answered slowly. "I am returning tomorrow evening by the Bath road. Will you come and meet me, Julia — say, as far as the Manton turning? It's on your favorite road. I know you stroll there every evening. I shall be there a little after five. If you come tomorrow, I shall know that, notwithstanding your hard words, you will take in hand the reforming of a rake — and a ruined rake, Julia. If you do not come —"

He hesitated. She had to turn away her head that he might not see the light that had returned to her eyes. "Well, what then?" she said softly.

"I do not know."

"But Lady Carlisle was his wife," she whispered, with a swift sidelong shot from eyes instantly averted. "And — you remember what you said to me — at Oxford? That if I were a lady, you would make me your wife. I am not a lady, Sir George."

"I did not say that," Sir George answered quickly.

"No! What then?"

"You know very well," he retorted with malice.

All of her cheek and neck that he could see turned scarlet. "Well, at any rate," she said, "let us be sure now that you are talking not to Clarissa but to Pamela?"

"I am talking to neither," he answered manfully. And he stood erect, his hat in his hand; they were almost of a height. "I am talking to the most beautiful woman in the world," he said, "whom I also believe to be the most virtuous — and whom I hope to make my wife. Shall it be so, Julia?"

She was trembling excessively; she used her fan that he might not see how her hand shook. "I — I will tell you tomorrow," she murmured breathlessly. "At Manton Corner."

"Now! Now!" he said.

But she cried "No, tomorrow," and fled from him into the house, deaf, as she passed through the hall, to the clatter of dishes and the cries of the waiters and the rattle of orders; for she had the singing of larks in her ears, and her heart rose on the throb of the song, rose until she felt that she must either cry or die — of very happiness.

Chapter XVI

THE BLACK FAN

I believe that Sir George, riding soberly to Estcombe in the morning, was not guiltless of looking back in spirit. Probably there are few men who, when the binding word has been said and the final step taken, do not feel a revulsion of mind, and for a moment question the wisdom of their choice. A more beautiful wife he could not wish; she was fair of face and faultless in shape, as beautiful as a Churchill or a Gunning. And in all honesty, and in spite of the undoubted advances she had made to him, he believed her to be good and virtuous. But her birth, her quality, or rather her lack of quality, her connections, these were things to cry him pause, to bid him reflect; until the thought — mean and unworthy, but not unnatural — that he was ruined, and what did it matter whom he wedded? came to him, and he touched his horse with the spur and cantered on by upland, down and clump, by Avebury, and Yatesbury, and Compton Bassett, until he came to his home.

Returning in the afternoon, sad at starting, but less sad with every added mile that separated him from the house to which he had bidden farewell in his heart — and which, much as he prized it now, he had not visited twice a year while it was his — it was another matter. He thought little of the future; of the past not at all. The present was sufficient for him. In an hour, in half an hour, in ten minutes, he would see her, would hold her hands in his, would hear her say that she loved him, would look unreproved into the depths of her proud eyes, would see them sink before his. Not a regret now for White's! Or the gaming table! Or Mrs. Cornelys' and Betty's! Gone the *blasé* insouciance of St. James's. The whole man was set on his mistress. Ruined, he had naught but her to look forward to, and he hungered for her. He cantered through Avebury, six miles short of Marlborough, and saw not one house.

Through West Kennet, where his shadow went long and thin before him; through Fyfield, where he well-nigh ran into a post-chaise, which seemed to be in as great a hurry to go west as he was to go east; under the Devil's Den, and by Clatford cross-lanes, nor drew rein until — as the sun sank finally behind him, leaving the downs cold and grey — he came in sight of Manton Corner.

Then, that no look of shy happiness, no downward quiver of the maiden eyelids might be lost — for the morsel, now it was within his grasp, was one to linger over and dwell on — Sir George, his own eyes shining with eagerness, walked his horse forward, his gaze greedily seeking the flutter of her kerchief or the welcome of her hand. Would she be at the meeting of the roads — shrinking aside behind the bend, her eyes laughing to greet him? No, he saw as he drew nearer that she was not there. Then he knew where she would be; she would be waiting for him on the foot-bridge in the lane, fifty yards from the high-road, yet within sight of it. She would have her lover come so far — to win her. The subtlety was like her, and pleased him.

But she was not there, nor was she to be seen elsewhere in the lane; for this descended a gentle slope until it plunged, still under his eyes, among the thatched roofs and quaint cottages of the village, whence the smoke of the evening meal rose blue among the trees. Soane's eyes returned to the main road; he expected to hear her laugh, and see her emerge at his elbow. But the length of the highway lay empty before, and empty behind; and all was silent. He began to look blank. A solitary house, which had been an inn, but was now unoccupied, stood in the angle formed by Manton Lane and the road; he scrutinized it. The big doors leading to the stable-yard were ajar; but he looked in and she was not there, though he noted that horses had stood there lately. For the rest, the house was closed and shuttered, as he had seen it that morning, and every day for days past.

Was it possible that she had changed her mind? That she had played or was playing him false? His heart said no. Nevertheless he felt a chill and a degree of disillusion as he rode down the lane to the foot-bridge; and over it, and on as far as the first house of the village. Still he saw nothing of her; and he turned. Riding back his search was rewarded with a discovery. Beside the ditch, at the corner where the road and lane met, and lying in such a position that it was not visible from the highway, but only from the lower ground of the lane, lay a plain black fan.

Sir George sprang down, picked it up, and saw that it was Julia's; and still possessed by the idea that she was playing him a trick he kissed it, and looked sharply round, hoping to detect her laughing face. Without result; then at last he began to feel misgiving. The road under the downs was growing dim and shadowy; the ten minutes he had lingered had stolen away the warmth and color of the day. The camps and tree-clumps stood black on the hills, the blacker for the creeping mist that stole beside the river where he stood. In another ten minutes night would fall in the valley. Sir George, his heart sinking under those vague and apparently foolish alarms which are among the penalties of affection, mounted his horse, stood in his stirrups, and called her name — "Julia! Julia!" — not loudly, but so that if she were within fifty yards of him she must hear.

He listened. His ear caught a confused Babel of voices in the direction of Marlborough; but only the empty house, echoing "Julia!" answered him. Not that he waited long for an answer; something in the dreary aspect of the evening struck cold to his heart, and touching his horse with the spur, he dashed off at a hand-gallop. Meeting the Bristol night-wagon beyond the bend of the road he was by it in a second. Nevertheless, the bells ringing at the horses' necks, the cracking whips, the tilt lurching white through the dusk somewhat reassured him. Reducing his pace, and a little ashamed of his fears, he entered the inn grounds by the stable entrance, threw his reins to a man — who seemed to have something to say, but did not say it — and walked off to the porch. He had been a fool to entertain such fears; in a minute he would see Julia.

Even as he thought these thoughts, he might have seen — had he looked that way — half a dozen men on foot and horseback, bustling out with lanterns through the great gates. Their voices reached him mellowed by distance; but immersed in thinking where he should find Julia, and what he should say to her, he crossed the roadway without heeding a commotion which in such a place was not unusual. On the contrary, the long lighted front of the house, the hum of life that rose from it, the sharp voices of a knot of men who stood a little on one side, arguing eagerly and all at once, went far to dissipate such of his fears as the pace of his horse had left. Beyond doubt Julia, finding herself in solitude, had grown alarmed and had returned, fancying him late; perhaps pouting because he had not forestalled the time!

But the moment he passed through the doorway his ear caught that buzz of excited voices, raised in all parts and in every key, that betokens disaster. And with a sudden chill at his heart, as of a cold hand gripping it, he stood, and looked down the hall. It was well perhaps that he had that moment of preparation, those few seconds in which to steady himself, before the full sense of what had happened struck him.

The lighted hall was thronged and in an uproar. A busy place, of much coming and going it ever was. Now the floor was crowded in every part with two or three score persons, all speaking, gesticulating, advising at once. Here a dozen men were proving something; there another group were controverting it; while twice as many listened, wide-eyed and open-mouthed, or in their turn dashed into the Babel. That something very serious had happened Sir George could not doubt. Once he caught the name of Lord Chatham, and the statement that he was worse, and he fancied that that was it. But the next moment the speaker added loudly, "Oh, he cannot be told! He is not to be told! The doctor has gone to him! I tell you, he is worse today!" And this, giving the lie to that idea, revived his fears. His eyes passing quickly over the crowd, looked everywhere for Julia; he found her nowhere. He touched the nearest man on the arm, and asked him what had happened.

The person he addressed was about to reply when an agitated figure, wig awry, cravat loosened, eyes staring, forced itself through the crowd, and, flinging itself on Sir George, clutched him by the open breast of his green riding-coat. It was Mr. Fishwick, but Mr. Fishwick transfigured by a great fright, his face grey, his cheeks trembling. For a moment such was his excitement he could not speak. Then "Where is she?" he stuttered, almost shaking Sir George on his feet. "What have you done with her, you — you villain?" Soane, with misgivings gnawing at his heart, was in no patient mood. In a blaze of passion he flung the attorney from him. "You madman!" he said; "what idiocy is this?"

Mr. Fishwick fell heavily against a stout gentleman in splashed boots and an old-fashioned Ramillies, who fortunately for the attorney, blocked the way to the wall. Even so the shock was no light one. But, breathless and giddy as he was the lawyer returned instantly to the charge. "I denounce you!" he cried furiously. "I denounce this man! You, and you," he continued, appealing with frantic gestures to those next him, "mark what I say! She is the claimant to his estates — estates he holds on sufferance! Tomorrow justice would have been done, and tonight he has kidnapped her. All he has is hers, I tell you, and he has kidnapped her. I denounce him! I —"

"What Bedlam stuff is this?" Sir George cried hoarsely; and he looked round the ring of curious starers, the sweat standing on his brow. Every eye in the hall was upon him, and there was a great silence; for the accusation to which the lawyer gave tongue had been buzzed and bruited since the first cry of alarm roused the house. "What stuff is this?" he repeated, his head giddy with the sense of that which Mr. Fishwick had said. "Who — who is it has been kidnapped? Speak! D——n you! Will no one speak?"

"Your cousin," the lawyer answered. "Your cousin, who claims —"

"Softly, man — softly," said the landlord, coming forward and laying his hand on the lawyer's shoulder. "And we shall the sooner know what to do. Briefly, Sir George," he continued, "the young lady who has been in your company the last day or two was seized and carried off in a post-chaise half an hour ago, as I am told — maybe a little more — from Manton Corner. For the rest, which this gentleman says, about who she is and her claim — which it does not seem to me can be true and your honor not know it — it is news to me. But, as I understand it, Sir George, he alleges that the young lady who has disappeared lays claim to your honor's estates at Estcombe."

"At Estcombe?"

"Yes, sir."

Sir George did not reply, but stood staring at the man, his mind divided between two thoughts. The first that this was the solution of the many things that had puzzled him in Julia; at once the explanation of her sudden amiability, her newborn forwardness, the mysterious fortune into which she had come, and of her education and her strange past. She was his cousin, the unknown claimant! She was his cousin, and —

He awoke with a start, dragged away by the second thought — hard following on the first. "From Manton Corner?" he cried, his voice keen, his eye terrible. "Who saw it?"

"One of the servants," the landlord answered, "who had gone to the top of the Mound to clean the mirrors in the summer-house. Here, you," he continued, beckoning to a man who limped forward reluctantly from one of the side passages in which he had been standing, "show yourself, and tell this gentleman the story you told me."

"If it please your honor," the fellow whimpered, "it was no fault of mine. I ran down to give the alarm as soon as I saw what was doing — they were forcing her into the carriage then — but I was in such a hurry I fell and rolled to the bottom of the Mound, and was that dazed and shaken it was five minutes before I could find anyone."

"How many were there?" Sir George asked. There was an ugly light in his eyes and his cheeks burned. But he spoke with calmness.

"Two I saw, and there may have been more. The chaise had been waiting in the yard of the empty house at the corner, the old Nag's Head. I saw it come out. That was the first thing I did see. And then the lady."

"Did she seem to be unwilling?" the man in the Ramillies asked. "Did she scream?"

"Aye, she screamed right enough," the fellow answered lumpishly. "I heard her, though the noise came faintlike. It is a good distance, your honor'll mind, and some would not have seen what I saw."

"And she struggled?"

"Aye, sir, she did. They were having a business with her when I left, I can tell you."

The picture was too much for Sir George. Gripping the landlord's shoulder so fiercely that Smith winced and cried out, "And you have heard this man," he said, "and you chatter here? Fools! This is no matter for words, but for horses and pistols! Get me a horse and pistols — and tell my servant. Are you so many dolls? D——n you, sir" — this to Mr. Fishwick — "stand out of my way!"

Chapter XVII

MR. FISHWICK, THE ARBITER

M<small>R.</small> Fishwick, who had stepped forward with a vague notion of detaining him, fell back. Sir George's stern aspect, which bore witness to the passions that raged in a heart at that moment cruelly divided, did not encourage interference; and though one or two muttered, no one moved. There is little doubt that he would have passed out without delay, mounted, and gone in pursuit — with what result in the direction of altering the issue, it is impossible to state — if an obstacle had not been cast in his way by an unexpected hand.

In every crowd, the old proverb has it, there are a knave and a fool. Between Sir George bursting with passion, and the door by which he had entered and to which he turned, stood Lady Dunborough. Her ladyship had been one of the first to hear the news and to take the alarm; it is safe to say, also, that for obvious reasons — and setting aside the lawyer and Sir George — she was of all present the person most powerfully affected by the news of the outrage. But she had succeeded in concealing alike her fears and her interest; she had exclaimed with others — neither more nor less; and had hinted, in common with three-fourths of the ladies present, that the minx's cries were forced, and her *bonne fortune* sufficiently to her mind. In a word she had comported herself so fitly that if there was one person in the hall whose opinion was likely to carry weight, as being coolly and impartially formed, it was her ladyship.

When she stepped forward therefore, and threw herself between Sir George and the door — still more when, with an intrepid gesture, she cried "Stay, sir; we have not done with you yet," there was a sensation. As the crowd pressed up to see and hear what passed, her accusing finger pointed steadily to Sir George's breast. "What is that you have there?" she continued. "That which peeps from your breast pocket, sir?"

Sir George, who, furious as he was, could go no farther without coming in contact with her ladyship, smothered an oath. "Madam," he said, "let me pass."

"Not until you explain how you came by that fan," she answered sturdily; and held her ground.

"Fan?" he cried savagely. "What fan?"

Unfortunately the passions that had swept through his mind during the last few minutes, the discovery he had made, and the flood of pity that would let him think of nothing but the girl — the girl carried away screaming and helpless, a prey to he knew not whom — left in his mind scant room for trifles. He had clean forgotten the fan. But the crowd gave him no credit for this; and some murmured, and some exchanged glances, when he asked "What fan?" Still more when my lady rejoined, "The fan in your breast," and drew it out and all saw it, was there a plain and general feeling against him.

Unheeding, he stared at the fan with grief-stricken eyes. "I picked it up in the road," he muttered, as much to himself as to them.

"It is hers?"

"Yes," he said, holding it reverently. "She must have dropped it — in the struggle!" And then "My God!" he continued fiercely, the sight of the fan bringing the truth more vividly before him, "Let me pass! Or I shall be doing someone a mischief! Madam, let me pass, I say!"

His tone was such that an ordinary woman must have given way to him; but the viscountess had her reasons for being staunch. "No," she said stoutly, "not until these gentlemen have heard more. You have her fan, which she took out an hour ago. She went to meet you — that we know from this person" — she indicated Mr. Fishwick; "and to meet you at your request. The time, at sunset, the place, the corner of Manton Lane. And what is the upshot? At that corner, at sunset, persons and a carriage were waiting to carry her off. Who besides you knew that she would be there?" Lady Dunborough continued, driving home the point with her finger. "Who besides you knew the time? And that being so, as soon as they are safely away with her, you walk in here with an innocent face and her fan in your pocket, and know naught about it! For shame! for shame! Sir George! You will have us think we see the Cock Lane Ghost next. For my part," her ladyship continued ironically, "I would as soon believe in the rabbit-woman."

"Let me pass, madam," Sir George cried between his teeth. "If you were not a woman —"

"You would do something dreadful," Lady Dunborough answered mockingly. "Nevertheless, I shall be much mistaken, sir, if some of these gentlemen have not a word to say in the matter."

Her ladyship's glance fell, as she spoke, on the stout red-faced gentle-man in the splashed boots and Ramillies, who had asked two questions of the servant; and who, to judge by the attention with which he followed my lady's words, was not proof against the charm which invests a viscountess. If she looked at him with intention, she reckoned well; for, as neatly as if the matter had been concerted between them, he stepped forward and took up the ball.

"Sir George," he said, puffing out his cheeks, "her ladyship is quite right. I — I am sorry to interfere, but you know me, and what my position is on the Rota. And I do not think I can stand by any longer — which might be *adaerere culpae*. This is a serious case, and I doubt I shall not be justified in allowing you to depart without some more definite explanation. Abduction, you know, is not bailable. You are a Justice yourself, Sir George, and must know that. If this person therefore — who I understand is an attorney — desires to lay a sworn information, I must take it."

"In heaven's name, sir," Soane cried desperately, "take it! Take what you please, but let me take the road."

"Ah, but that is what I doubt, sir, I cannot do," the Justice answered. "Mark you, there is motive, Sir George, and *praesentia in loco*," he continued, swelling with his own learning. "And you have a *partem delicti* on you. And, moreover, abduction is a special kind of case, seeing that if the *participes criminis* are free the *femme sole*, sometimes called the *femina capta*, is in greater danger. In fact, it is a continuing crime. An informa-tion being sworn therefore —"

"It has not been sworn yet!" Sir George retorted fiercely. "And I warn you that anyone who lays a hand on me shall rue it. God, man!" he continued, horror in his voice, "cannot you understand that while you prate here they are carrying her off, and that time is everything?"

"Some persons have gone in pursuit," the landlord answered with intent to soothe.

"Just so; some persons have gone in pursuit," the Justice echoed with dull satisfaction. "And you, if you went, could do no more than they can do. Besides, Sir George, the law must be obeyed. The sole point is" — he turned to Mr. Fishwick, who through all had stood by, his face distorted by grief and perplexity — "do you wish, sir, to swear the information?"

Mrs. Masterson had fainted at the first alarm and been carried to her room. Apart from her, it is probable that only Sir George and Mr. Fishwick really entered into the horror of the girl's position, realized the possible value of minutes, or felt genuine and poignant grief at what had occurred. On the decision of one of these two the freedom of the other now depended, and the conclusion seemed foregone. Ten minutes earlier Mr. Fishwick, carried away by the first sight of Sir George, and by the rage of an honest man who saw a helpless woman ruined, had been violent enough; Soane's possession of the fan — not then known to him — was calculated to corroborate his suspicions. The Justice in appealing to him felt sure of support; and was much astonished when Mr. Fishwick, in place of assenting, passed his hand across his brow, and stared at the speaker as if he had suddenly lost the power of speech.

In truth, the lawyer, harried by the expectant gaze of the room, and the Justice's impatience, was divided between a natural generosity, which was one of his oddities, and a suspicion born of his profession. He liked Sir George; his smaller manhood went out in admiration to the other's splendid personality. On the other hand, he had viewed Soane's approaches to his client with misgiving. He had scented a trap here and a bait there, and a dozen times, while dwelling on Dr. Addington's postponements and delays, he had accused the two of collusion and of some deep-laid chicanery. Between these feelings he had now to decide, and to decide in such a tumult of anxiety and dismay as almost deprived him of the power to think.

On the one hand, the evidence and inferences against Sir George pressed him strongly. On the other, he had seen enough of the futile haste of the ostlers and stable-helps, who had gone in pursuit, to hope little from them; while from Sir George, were he honest, everything was to be expected. In his final decision we may believe what he said afterwards, that he was determined by neither of these considerations, but by his old dislike of Lady Dunborough! For after a long silence, during which he seemed to be a dozen times on the point of speaking and as often disappointed his audience, he announced his determination in that sense. "No, sir; I — I will not!" he stammered, "or rather I will not — on a condition."

"Condition!" the Justice growled, in disgust.

"Yes," the lawyer answered staunchly; "that Sir George, if he be going in pursuit of them, permit me to go with him. I — I can ride, or at least

I can sit on a horse," Mr. Fishwick continued bravely; "and I am ready to go."

"Oh, la!" said Lady Dunborough, spitting on the floor — for there were ladies who did such things in those days — "I think they are all in it together. And the fair cousin too! Cousin be hanged!" she added with a shrill ill-natured laugh; "I have heard that before."

But Sir George took no notice of her words. "Come, if you choose," he cried, addressing the lawyer. "But I do not wait for you. And now, madam, if your interference is at an end —"

"And what if it is not?" she cried, insolently grimacing in his face. She had gained half an hour, and it might save her son. To persist farther might betray him, yet she was loath to give way. "What if it is not?" she repeated.

"I go out by the other door," Sir George answered promptly, and, suiting the action to the word, he turned on his heel, strode through the crowd, which subserviently made way for him, and in a twinkling he had passed through the garden door, with Mr. Fishwick, hat in hand, hurrying at his heels.

The moment they were gone, the Babel, suppressed while the altercation lasted, rose again, loud as before. It is not every day that the busiest inn or the most experienced traveler has to do with an elopement, to say nothing of an abduction. While a large section of the ladies, seated together in a corner, tee-hee'd and tossed their heads, sneered at Miss and her screams, and warranted she knew all about it, and had her jacket and night-rail in her pocket, another party laid all to Sir George, swore by the viscountess, and quoted the masked uncle who made away with his nephew to get his estate. One or two indeed — and, if the chronicler is to be candid, one or two only, out of as many scores — proved that they possessed both imagination and charity. These sat apart, scared and affrighted by their thoughts; or stared with set eyes and flushed faces on the picture they would fain have avoided. But they were young and had seen little of the world.

On their part the men talked fast and loud, at one time laughed, and at another dropped a curse — their form of pity; quoted the route and the inns, and weighed the chances of Devizes or Bath, Bristol or Salisbury; vaguely suggested highwaymen, an old lover, Mrs. Cornelys' ballet; and finally trooped out to stand in the road and listen, question the passers-by, and hear what the parish constable had to say of it. All except one very old man, who kept his seat and from time to time muttered, "Lord, what a shape she had! What a shape she had!" until he dissolved in maudlin tears.

Meanwhile a woman lay upstairs, tossing in passionate grief and tended by servants; who, more pitiful than their mistresses, stole to her to comfort her. And three men rode steadily along the western road.

Chapter XVIII

THE PURSUIT

*T*he attorney was brave with a coward's great bravery; he was afraid, but he went on. As he climbed into his saddle in the stable-yard, the muttering ostlers standing round, and the yellow-flaring light of the lanterns stretching fingers into the darkness, he could have wept for himself. Beyond the gates and the immediate bustle of the yard lay night, the road, and dimly-guessed violences; the meeting of man with man, the rush to grips under some dark wood, or where the moonlight fell cold on the heath. The prospect terrified; at the mere thought the lawyer dropped the reins and nervously gathered them. And he had another fear, and one more immediate. He was no horseman, and he trembled lest Sir George, the moment the gates were passed, should go off in a reckless gallop. Already he felt his horse heave and sidle under him, in a fashion that brought his heart into his mouth; and he was ready to cry for quarter. But the absurdity of the request where time was every-thing, the journey black earnest, and its issue life and death, struck him, and heroically he closed his mouth. Yet, at the remembrance that these things were, he fell into a fresh panic.

However, for a time there was to be no galloping. Sir George when all were up took a lantern from the nearest man, and bidding one of the others run at his stirrup, led the way into the road, where he fell into a sharp trot, his servant and Mr. Fishwick following. The attorney bumped in his saddle, but kept his stirrups and gradually found his hands and eyesight. The trot brought them to Manton Corner and the empty house; where Sir George pulled up and dismounted. Giving his reins to the stable boy, he thrust open the doors of the yard and entered, holding up his lantern, his spurs clinking on the stones and his skirts swaying.

"But she — they cannot be here?" the lawyer ejaculated, his teeth chattering.

Sir George, busy stooping and peering about the yard, which was grass-grown and surrounded by walls, made no answer; and the other two, as well as Mr. Fishwick, wondered what he would be at. But in a moment they knew. He stooped and took up a small object, smelt it, and held it out to them. "What is that?" he asked curtly.

The stable-man who was holding his horse stared at it. "Negro-head, your honor," he said. "It is sailors' tobacco."

"Who uses it about here?"

"Nobody to my knowing."

"They are from Bristol, then," Soane answered. And then "Make way!" he continued, addressing the other two who blocked the gateway; and springing into his saddle he pressed his horse between them, his stirrups dangling. He turned sharp to the left, and leaving the stable-man to stare after them, the lantern swaying in his hand, he led the way westward at the same steady trot.

The chase had begun. More than that, Mr. Fishwick was beginning to feel the excitement of it; the ring of the horses' shoes on the hard road, the rush of the night air past his ears exhilarated him. He began to feel confidence in his leader, and confidence breeds courage. Bristol? Then Bristol let it be. And then on top of this, his spirits being more composed, came a rush of rage and indignation at thought of the girl. The lawyer clutched his whip, and, reckless of consequences, dug his heels into his horse, and for the moment, in the heat of his wrath, longed to be up with the villains, to strike a blow at them. If his courage lasted, Mr. Fishwick might show them a man yet — when the time came!

Trot-trot, trot-trot through the darkness under the stars, the trees black masses that shot up beside the road and vanished as soon as seen, the downs grey misty outlines that continually fenced them in and went with them; and always in the van Sir George, a grim silent shape with face set immovably forward. They worked up Fyfield hill, and thence, looking back, bade farewell to the faint light that hung above Marlborough. Dropping into the bottom they cluntered over the wooden bridge and by Overton steeple — a dim outline on the left — and cantering up Avebury hill eased their horses through Little Kennet. Gathering speed again they swept through Beckhampton village, where the Bath road falls off to the left, and breasting the high downs towards Yatesbury, they trotted on to Cheril.

Here on the hills the sky hung low overhead, and the wind sweeping chill and drear across the upland was full of a melancholy soughing.

The world, it seemed to one of them, was uncreate, gone, and non-existent; only this remained — the shadowy downs stretching on every side to infinity, and three shadowy riders plodding across them; all shadowy, all unreal until a bellwether got up under the horses' heads, and with a confused rush and scurry of feet a hundred Southdowns scampered into the grey unknown.

Mr. Fishwick found it terrible, rugged, wild, a night foray. His heart began to sink again. He was sore too, sweating, and fit to drop from his saddle with the unwonted exertion.

And what of Sir George, hurled suddenly out of his age and world — the age *des philosophes,* and the smooth world of White's and Lord March — into this quagmire of feeling, this night of struggle upon the Wiltshire downs? A few hours earlier he had ridden the same road, and the prize he now stood in danger of losing had seemed — God forgive him! — of doubtful value. Now, as he thought of her, his heart melted in a fire of love and pity: of love that conjured up a thousand pictures of her eyes, her lips, her smile, her shape — all presently dashed by night and reality; of pity that swelled his breast to bursting, set his eyes burning and his brain throbbing — a pity near akin to rage.

Even so, he would not allow himself to dwell on the worst. He had formed his opinion of the abduction; if it proved correct he believed that he should be in time to save her from that. But from the misery of suspense, of fear, of humiliation, from the touch of rough hands and the shame of coarse eyes, from these things — and alone they kindled his blood into flame — he was powerless to save her!

Lady Dunborough could no longer have accused him of airs and graces. Breeding, habit, the custom of the gaming-table, the pride of caste availed to mask his passions under a veil of reserve, but were powerless to quell them. What was more remarkable, so set was he on the one object of recovering his mistress and putting an end to the state of terror in which he pictured her — ignorant what her fate would be, and dreading the worst — he gave hardly a thought to the astounding discovery which the lawyer had made to him. He asked him no questions, turned to him for no explanations. Those might come later; for the moment he thought not of his cousin, but of his mistress. The smiles that had brightened the dull passages of the inn, the figure that had glorified the quiet streets, the eyes that had now invited and now repelled him, these were become so many sharp thorns in his heart, so many goads urging him onward.

It was nine when they saw the lights of Calne below them, and trotting and stumbling down the hill, clattered eagerly into the town. A moment's delay in front of the inn, where their questions speedily gathered a crowd, and they had news of the chaise: it had passed through the town two hours before without changing horses. The canvas blinds were down or there were shutters; which, the ostler who gave them the information, could not say. But the fact that the carriage was closed had struck him, and together with the omission to take fresh horses, had awakened his suspicions.

By the time this was told a dozen were round them, listening open-mouthed; and cheered by the lights and company Mr. Fishwick grew brave again. But Sir George allowed no respite: in five minutes they were clear of the houses and riding hard for Chippenham, the next stage on the Bristol road; Sir George's horse cantering free, the lawyer's groaning as it bumped across Studley bridge and its rider caught the pale gleam of the water below. On through the village they swept, past Brumhill Lane-end, thence over the crest where the road branches south to Devizes, and down the last slope. The moon rose as they passed the fourth milestone out of Calne; another five minutes and they drew up, the horses panting and hanging their heads, in the main street of Chippenham.

A coach — one of the night coaches out of Bristol — was standing before the inn, the horses smoking, the lamps flaring cheerfully, a crowd round it; the driver had just unbuckled his reins and flung them either way. Sir George pushed his horse up to the splinter-bar and hailed him, asking whether he had met a closed chaise and four traveling Bristol way at speed.

"A closed chaise and four?" the man answered, looking down at the party; and then recognizing Sir George, "I beg your honor's pardon," he said. "Here, Jeremy," to the guard — while the stable-man and helpers paused to listen or stared at the heaving flanks of the riders' horses — "did we meet a closed chaise and four tonight?"

"We met a chaise and four at Cold Aston," the guard answered, ruminating. "But 'twas Squire Norris's of Sheldon, and there was no one but the Squire in it. And a chaise and four at Marshfield, but that was a burying party from Batheaston, going home very merry. No other, closed or open, that I can mind, sir, this side of Dungeon Cross, and that is but two miles out of Bristol."

"They are an hour and a half in front of us!" Sir George cried eagerly. "Will a guinea improve your memory?"

"Aye, sir, but 'twon't make it," the coachman answered, grinning. "Jeremy is right. I mind no others. What will your honor want with them?"

"They have carried off a young lady!" Mr. Fishwick cried shrilly. "Sir George's kinswoman!"

"To be sure?" ejaculated the driver, amid a murmur of astonishment; and the crowd which had grown since their arrival pressed nearer to listen. "Where from, sir, if I may make so bold?"

"From the Castle at Marlborough."

"Dear me, dear me, there is audaciousness, if you like! And you ha' followed them so far, sir?"

Sir George nodded and turned to the crowd. "A guinea for news!" he cried. "Who saw them go through Chippenham!"

He had not long to wait for the answer. "They never went through Chipnam!" a thick voice hiccoughed from the rear of the press.

"They came this way out of Calne," Sir George retorted, singling the speaker out, and signing to the people to make way that he might get at him.

"Aye, but they never — came to Chipnam," the fellow answered, leering at him with drunken wisdom. "D'you see that, master?"

"Which way, then?" Soane cried impatiently. "Which way did they go?"

But the man only lurched a step nearer. "That's telling!" he said with a beery smile. "You want to be — as wise as I be!"

Jeremy, the guard, seized him by the collar and shook him. "You drunken fool!" he said. "D'ye know that this is Sir George Soane of Estcombe? Answer him, you swine, or you'll be in the cage in a one, two!"

"You let me be," the man whined, straggling to release himself. "It's no business of yours. Let me be, master!"

Sir George raised his whip in his wrath, but lowered it again with a groan. "Can no one make him speak?" he said, looking round. The man was staggering and lurching in the guard's grasp.

"His wife, but she is to Marshfield, nursing her sister," answered one. "But give him his guinea, Sir George. 'Twill save time maybe."

Soane flung it to him. "There!" he said. "Now speak!"

"That'sh better," the man muttered. "That's talking! Now I'll tell you. You go back to Devizes Corner — corner of the road to De-vizes — you understand? There was a car — car — carriage there without lights an hour back. It was waiting under the hedge. I saw it, and I — I know what's what!"

Sir George flung a guinea to the guard, and wheeled his horse about. In the act of turning his eye fell on the lawyer's steed, which, chosen for sobriety rather than staying powers, was on the point of foundering. "Get another," he cried, "and follow!"

Mr. Fishwick uttered a wail of despair. To be left to follow — to follow alone, in the dark, through unknown roads, with scarce a clue and on a strange horse — the prospect might have appalled a hardier soul. He was saved from it by Sir George's servant, a stolid silent man, who might be warranted to ride twenty miles without speaking. "Here, take mine, sir," he said. "I must stop to get a lantern; we shall need one now. Do you go with his honor."

Mr. Fishwick slid down and was hoisted into the other's saddle. By the time this was done Sir George was almost lost in the gloom eat the farther end of the street. But anything rather than be left behind. The lawyer laid on his whip in a way that would have astonished him a few hours before, and overtook his leader as he emerged from the town. They rode without speaking until they had retraced their steps to the foot of the hill, and could discern a little higher on the ascent the turn for Devizes.

It is possible that Sir George hoped to find the chaise still lurking in the shelter of the hedge; for as he rode up to the corner he drew a pistol from his holster, and took his horse by the head. If so, he was disappointed. The moon had risen high and its cold light disclosed the whole width of the roadway, leaving no place in which even a dog could lie hidden. Nor as far as the eye could travel along the pale strip of road that ran southward was any movement or sign of life.

Sir George dropped from his saddle, and stooping, sought for proof of the toper's story. He had no difficulty in finding it. There were the deep narrow ruts which the wheels of a chaise, long stationary, had made in the turf at the side of the road; and south of them was a plat of poached ground where the horses had stood and shifted their feet uneasily. He walked forward, and by the moonlight traced the dusty indents of the wheels until they exchanged the sward for the hard road. There they were lost in other tracks, but the inference was plain. The chaise had gone south to Devizes.

For the first time Sir George felt the full horror of uncertainty. He climbed into his saddle and sat looking across the waste with eyes of misery, asking himself whither and for what? Whither had they taken her, and why? The Bristol road once left, his theory was at fault; he had no clue, and felt, where time was life and more than life, the slough of horrible conjecture rise to his very lips.

Only one thing, one certain thing remained — the road; the pale ribbon running southward under the stars. He must cling to that. The chaise had gone that way, and though the double might be no more than a trick to throw pursuers off the trail, though the first dark lane, the first roadside tavern, the first farmhouse among the woods might have swallowed the unhappy girl and the wretches who held her in their power, what other clue had he? What other chance but to track the chaise that way, though every check, every minute of uncertainty, of thought, of hesitation — and a hundred such there must be in a tithe of the miles — racked him with fears and dreadful surmises?

There was no other. The wind sweeping across the hill on the western extremity of which he stood, looking over the lower ground about the Avon, brought the distant howl of a dog to his ears, and chilled his blood heated with riding. An owl beating the coverts for mice sailed overhead; a hare rustled through the fence. The stars above were awake; in the intense silence of the upland he could almost hear the great spheres throb as they swept through space! But the human world slept, and while it slept what work of darkness might not be doing? That scream, shrill and ear-piercing, that suddenly rent the night — thank God, it was only a rabbit's death-cry, but it left the sweat on his brow! After that he could, he would, wait for nothing and no man. Lantern or no lantern, he must be moving. He raised his whip, then let it fall again as his ear caught far away the first faint hoof-beats of a horse traveling the road at headlong speed.

The sound was very distant at first, but it grew rapidly, and presently filled the night. It came from the direction of Chippenham. Mr. Fishwick, who had not dared to interrupt his companion's calculations, heard the sound with relief; and looking for the first gleam of the lantern, wondered how the servant, riding at that pace, kept it alight, and whether the man had news that he galloped so furiously. But Sir George sat arrested in his saddle, listening, listening intently; until the rider was within a hundred yards or less. Then, as his ear told him that the horse was slackening, he seized Mr. Fishwick's rein, and backing their horses nearer the hedge, once more drew a pistol from his holster.

The startled lawyer discerned what he did, looked in his face, and saw that his eyes were glittering with excitement. But having no ear for hoof-beats Mr. Fishwick did not understand what was afoot, until the rider appeared at the road-end, and coming plump upon them, drew rein.

Then Sir George's voice rang out, stern and ominous. "Good evening, Mr. Dunborough," he said, and raised his hat. "Well met! We are traveling the same road, and, if you please, will do the rest of our journey together."

Chapter XIX

AN UNWILLING ALLY

*U*nder the smoothness of Sir George's words, under the subtle mockery of his manner, throbbed a volcano of passion and vengeance. But this was for the lawyer only, even as he alone saw the moonlight gleam faintly on the pistol barrel that lurked behind his companion's thigh. For Mr. Dunborough, it would be hard to imagine a man more completely taken by surprise. He swore one great oath, for he saw, at least, that the meeting boded him 110 good; then he sat motionless in his saddle, his left hand on the pommel, his right held stiffly by his side. The moon, which of the two hung a little at Sir George's back, shone only on the lower part of Dunborough's face, and by leaving his eyes in the shadow of his hat, gave the others to conjecture what he would do next. It is probable that Sir George, whose hand and pistol were ready, was indifferent; perhaps would have hailed with satisfaction an excuse for vengeance. But Mr. Fishwick, the pacific witness of this strange meeting, awaited the issue with staring eyes, his heart in his mouth; and was mightily relieved when the silence, which the heavy breathing of Mr. Dunborough's horse did but intensify, was broken on the last comer's side, by nothing worse than a constrained laugh.

"Travel together?" he said, with an awkward assumption of jauntiness, "that depends on the road we are going."

"Oh, we are going the same road," Sir George answered, in the mocking tone he had used before.

"You are very clever," Mr. Dunborough retorted, striving to hide his uneasiness; "but if you know that, sir, you have the advantage of me."

"I have," said Sir George, and laughed rudely.

Dunborough stared, finding in the other's manner fresh cause for misgiving. At last, "As you please," he said contemptuously. "I am for Calne. The road is public. You may travel by it."

"We are not going to Calne," said Sir George.

Mr. Dunborough swore. "You are d——d impertinent!" he said,

reining back his horse, "and may go to the devil your own way. For me, I am going to Calne."

"No," said Sir George, "you are not going to Calne. She has not gone Calne way."

Mr. Dunborough drew in his breath quickly. Hitherto he had been uncertain what the other knew, and how far the meeting was accidental; now, forgetful what his words implied and anxious only to say something that might cover his embarrassment, "Oh," he said, "you are — you are in search of her?"

"Yes," said Sir George mockingly. "We are in search of her. And we want to know where she is."

"Where she is?"

"Yes, where she is. That is it; where she is. You were to meet her here, you know. You are late and she has gone. But you will know whither."

Mr. Dunborough stared; then in a tempest of wrath and chagrin, "D——n you!" he cried furiously. "As you know so much, you can find out the rest!"

"I could," said Sir George slowly. "But I prefer that you should help me. And you will."

"Will what?"

"Will help me, sir," Sir George answered quickly, "to find the lady we are seeking."

"I'll be hanged if I will," Dunborough cried, raging and furious.

"You'll be hanged if you won't," Sir George said in a changed tone; and he laughed contemptuously. "Hanged by the neck until you are dead, Mr. Dunborough — if money can bring it about. You fool," he continued, with a sudden flash of the ferocity that had from the first underlain his sarcasm, "we have got enough from your own lips to hang you, and if more be wanted, your people will peach on you. You have put your neck into the halter, and there is only one way, if one, in which you can take it out. Think, man; think before you speak again," he continued savagely, "for my patience is nearly at an end, and I would sooner see you hang than not. And look you, leave your reins alone, for if you try to turn, by G——d, I'll shoot you like the dog you are!"

Whether he thought the advice good or bad, Mr. Dunborough took it; and there was a long silence. In the distance the hoof-beats of the servant's horse, approaching from the direction of Chippenham, broke the stillness of the moonlit country; but round the three men who sat motionless in their saddles, glaring at one another and awaiting the word for action, was a kind of barrier, a breathlessness born of expectation. At length Dunborough spoke.

"What do you want?" he said in a low tone, his voice confessing his defeat. "If she is not here, I do not know where she is."

"That is for you," Sir George answered with a grim coolness that astonished Mr. Fishwick. "It is not I who will hang if aught happen to her."

Again there was silence. Then in a voice choked with rage Mr. Dunborough cried, "But if I do not know?"

"The worse for you," said Sir George. He was sorely tempted to put the muzzle of a pistol to the other's head and risk all. But he fancied that he knew his man, and that in this way only could he be effectually cowed; and he restrained himself.

"She should be here — that is all I know. She should have been here," Mr. Dunborough continued sulkily, "at eight."

"Why here?"

"The fools would not take her through Chippenham without me. Now you know."

"It is ten, now."

"Well, curse you," the younger man answered, flaring up again, "could I help it if my horse fell? Do you think I should be sitting here to be rough-ridden by you if it were not for this?" He raised his right arm, or rather his shoulder, with a stiff movement; they saw that the arm was bound to his side. "But for that she would be in Bristol by now," he continued disdainfully, "and you might whistle for her. But, Lord, here is a pother about a college-wench!"

"College-wench, sir?" the lawyer cried scarcely controlling his indignation. "She is Sir George Soane's cousin. I'd have you know that!"

"And my promised wife," Sir George said, with grim-ness.

Dunborough cried out in his astonishment. "It is a lie!" he said.

"As you please," Sir George answered.

At that, a chill such as he had never known gripped Mr. Dunborough's heart. He had thought himself in an unpleasant fix before; and that to escape scot free he must eat humble pie with a bad grace. But on this a secret terror, such as sometimes takes possession of a bold man who finds himself helpless and in peril seized on him. Given arms and the chance to use them, he would have led the forlornest of hopes, charged a battery, or fired a magazine. But the species of danger in which he now found himself — with a gallows and a silk rope in prospect, his fate to be determined by the very scoundrels he had hired — shook even his obstinacy. He looked about him; Sir George's servant had come up and was waiting a little apart.

Mr. Dunborough found his lips dry, his throat husky. "What do you want?" he muttered, his voice changed. "I have told you all I know. Likely enough they have taken her back to get themselves out of the scrape."

"They have not," said the lawyer. "We have come that way, and must have met them."

"They may be in Chippenham?"

"They are not. We have inquired."

"Then they must have taken this road. Curse you, don't you see that I cannot get out of my saddle to look?" he continued ferociously.

"They have gone this way. Have you any devil's shop — any house of call down the road?" Sir George asked, signing to the servant to draw nearer.

"Not I."

"Then we must track them. If they dared not face Chippenham, they will not venture through Devizes. It is possible that they are making for Bristol by cross-roads. There is a bridge over the Avon near Laycock Abbey, somewhere on our right, and a road that way through Pewsey Forest."

"That will be it," cried Mr. Dunborough, slapping his thigh. "That is their game, depend upon it."

Sir George did not answer him, but nodded to the servant. "Go on with the light," he said. "Try every turning for wheels, but lose no time. This gentleman will accompany us, but I will wait on him."

The man obeyed quickly, the lawyer going with him. The other two brought up the rear, and in that order they started, riding in silence. For a mile or more the servant held the road at a steady trot; then signing to those behind him to halt, he pulled up at the mouth of a by-road leading westwards from the highway. He moved the light once or twice across the ground, and cried that the wheels had gone that way; then got briskly to his saddle and swung along the lane at a trot, the others following in single file, Sir George last.

So far they had maintained a fair pace. But the party had not proceeded a quarter of a mile along the lane before the trot became a walk. Clouds had come over the face of the moon; the night had grown dark. The riders were no longer on the open downs, but in a narrow by-road, running across wastes and through thick coppices, the ground sloping sharply to the Avon. In one place the track was so closely shadowed by trees as to be as dark as a pit. In another it ran, unfenced, across a heath studded with water-pools, whence the startled moor-fowl squattered up unseen. Everywhere they stumbled: once a horse fell. Over such ground, founderous and scored knee-deep with ruts, it was plain that no wheeled carriage could move at speed; and the pursuers had this to cheer them. But the darkness of the night, the dreary glimpses of wood and water, which met the eye when the moon for a moment emerged, the solitude of this forest tract, the muffled tread of the horses' feet, the very moaning of the wind among the trees, suggested ideas and misgivings which Sir George strove in vain to suppress. Why had the scoundrels gone this way? Were they really bound for Bristol? Or for some den of villainy, some thieves' house in the old forest?

At times these fears stung him out of all patience, and he cried to the man with the light to go faster, faster! Again, the whole seemed unreal, and the shadowy woods and gleaming water-pools, the stumbling horses, the fear, the danger, grew to be the creatures of a disordered fancy. It was an immense joy to him when, at the end of an hour, the lawyer cried, "The road! the road!" and one by one the riders emerged with grunts of relief on a sound causeway. To make sure that the pursued had nowhere evaded them, the tracks of the chaise-wheels were sought and found, and forward the four went again. Presently they plunged through a brook, and this passed, were on Laycock bridge before they knew it, and across the Avon, and mounting the slope on the other side by Laycock Abbey.

There were houses abutting on the road here, black overhanging masses against a grey sky, and the riders looked, wavered, and drew rein. Before any spoke, however, an unseen shutter creaked open, and a voice from the darkness cried, "Hallo!"

Sir George found speech to answer. "Yes," he said, "what is it?" The lawyer was out of breath, and clinging to the mane in sheer weariness.

"Be you after a chaise driving to the devil?"

"Yes, yes," Sir George answered eagerly. "Has it passed, my man?"

"Aye, sure, Corsham way, for Bath most like, I knew 'twould be followed. Is't a murder, gentlemen?"

"Yes," Sir George cried hurriedly, "and worse! How far ahead are they?"

"About half an hour, no more, and whipping and spurring as if the old one was after them. My old woman's sick, and the apothecary from —"

"Is it straight on?"

"Aye, to be sure, straight on — and the apothecary from Corsham, as I was saying, he said, said he, as soon as he saw her —"

But his listeners were away again; the old man's words were lost in the scramble and clatter of the horses' shoes as they sprang forward. In a moment the stillness and the dark shapes of the houses were exchanged for the open country, the rush of wind in the riders' faces, and the pounding of hoofs on the hard road. For a brief while the sky cleared and the moon shone out, and they rode as easily as in the day. At the pace at which they were moving Sir George calculated that they must come up with the fugitives in an hour or less; but the reckoning was no sooner made than the horses, jaded by the heavy ground through which they had struggled, began to flag and droop their heads; the pace grew less and less; and though Sir George whipped and spurred, Corsham Corner was reached, and Pickwick Village on the Bath road, and still they saw no chaise ahead.

It was past midnight, and it seemed to some that they had been riding an eternity; yet even these roused at sight of the great western highway. The night coaches had long gone eastwards, and the road, so busy by day, stretched before them dim, shadowy, and empty, as solitary in the darkness as the remotest lane. But the knowledge that Bath lay at the end of it – and no more than nine miles away – and that there they could procure aid, fresh horses and willing helpers, put new life even into the most weary. Even Mr. Fishwick, now groaning with fatigue and now crying "Oh dear! oh dear!" as he bumped, in a way that at another time must have drawn laughter from a stone, took heart of grace; while Sir George settled down to a dogged jog that had something ferocious in its determination. If he could not trot, he would amble; if he could not amble, he would walk; if his horse could not walk, he would go on his feet. He still kept eye and ear bent forward, but in effect he had given up hope of overtaking the quarry before it reached Bath; and he was taken by surprise when the servant, who rode first and had eased his horse to a walk at the foot of Haslebury Hill, drew rein and cried to the others to listen.

For a moment the heavy breathing of the four horses covered all other sounds. Then in the darkness and the distance, on the summit of the rise before them, a wheel creaked as it grated over a stone. A few seconds and the sound was repeated; then all was silent. The chaise had passed over the crest and was descending the other side.

Oblivious of everything except that Julia was within his reach, forgetful even of Dunborough by whose side he had ridden all night – in silence but with many a look askance – Sir George drove his horse forward, scrambled and trotted desperately up the hill, and, gaining the summit a score of yards in front of his companions, crossed the brow and drew rein to listen. He had not been mistaken. He could hear the wheels creaking, and the wheelers stumbling and slipping in the darkness below him; and with a cry he launched his horse down the descent.

Whether the people with the chaise heard the cry or not, they appeared to take the alarm at that moment. He heard a whip crack, the carriage bound forward, the horses break into a reckless canter. But if they recked little he recked less; already he was plunging down the hill after them, his beast almost pitching on its head with every stride. The huntsman knows, however, that many stumbles go to a fall. The bottom was gained in safety by both, and across the flat they went, the chaise bounding and rattling behind the scared horses. Now Sir George had a glimpse of the black mass through the gloom, now it seemed to be gaining on him, now it was gone, and now again he drew up to it and the dim outline bulked bigger and plainer, and bigger and plainer, until he was close upon it, and the cracking whips and the shouts of the postboys rose above the din of hoofs and wheels. The carriage was swaying perilously, but Sir George saw that the ground was rising, and that up the hill he must win; and, taking his horse by the head, he lifted it on by sheer strength until his stirrup was abreast of the hind wheels. A moment, and he made out the bobbing figure of the leading postboy, and, drawing his pistol, cried to him to stop.

The answer was a blinding flash of light and a shot. Sir George's horse swerved to the right, and plunging headlong into the ditch, flung its rider six paces over its head.

The servant and Mr. Dunborough were no more than forty yards behind him when he fell; in five seconds the man had sprung from his saddle, let his horse go, and was at his master's side. There were trees there, and the darkness in the shadow, where Sir George lay across the roots of one of them, was intense. The man could not see his face, nor how he lay, nor if he was injured; and calling and getting no answer, he took fright and cried to Mr. Dunborough to get help.

But Mr. Dunborough had ridden straight on without pausing or drawing rein, and the man, finding himself deserted, wrung his hands in terror. He had only Mr. Fishwick to look to for help, and he was some way behind. Trembling, the servant knelt and groped for his master's face; to his joy, before he had found it, Sir George gasped, moved, and sat up; and, muttering an incoherent word or two, in a minute had recovered himself sufficiently to rise with help. He had fallen clear of the horse on the edge of the ditch, and the shock had taken his breath; otherwise he was rather shaken than hurt.

As soon as his wits and wind came back to him, "Why — why have you not followed?" he gasped.

"'Twill be all right, sir. All right, sir," the servant answered, thinking only of him.

"But after them, man, after them. Where is Fishwick?"

"Coming, sir, he is coming," the man answered, to soothe him; and remained where he was. Sir George was so shaken that he could not yet stand alone, and the servant did not know what to think. "Are you sure you are not hurt, sir?" he continued anxiously.

"No, no! And Mr. Dunborough? Is he behind?"

"He rode on after them, sir."

"Rode on after them?"

"Yes, sir, he did not stop."

"He has gone on — after them?" Sir George cried.

"But —" and with that it flashed on him, and on the servant, and on Mr. Fishwick, who had just jogged up and dismounted, what had happened. The carriage and Julia — Julia still in the hands of her captors — were gone. And with them was gone Mr. Dunborough! Gone far out of hearing; for as the three stood together in the blackness of the trees, unable to see one another's faces, the night was silent round them. The rattle of wheels, the hoof-beats of horses had died away in the distance.

Chapter XX

THE EMPTY POST-CHAISE

*I*t was one of those positions which try a man to the uttermost; and it was to Sir George's credit that, duped and defeated, astonishingly tricked in the moment of success, and physically shaken by his fall, he neither broke into execrations nor shod unmanly tears. He groaned, it is true, and his arm pressed more heavily on the servant's shoulder, as he listened and listened in vain for sign or so and of the runaways. But he still commanded himself, and in face of how great a misfortune! A more futile, a more wretched end to an expedition it was impossible to conceive. The villains had out-paced, out-fought, and out-maneuvered him; and even now were rolling merrily on to Bath, while he, who a few minutes before had held the game in his hands, lay belated here without horses and without hope, in a wretched plight, his every moment embittered by the thought of his mistress's fate.

In such crises — to give the devil his due — the lessons of the gaming-table, dearly bought as they are, stand a man in stead. Sir George's fancy pictured Julia a prisoner, trembling and disheveled, perhaps gagged and bound by the coarse hands of the brutes who had her in their power; and the picture was one to drive a helpless man mad. Had he dwelt on it long and done nothing it must have crazed him. But in his life he had lost and won great sums at a coup, and learned to do the one and the other with the same smile — it was the point of pride, the form of his time and class. While Mr. Fishwick, therefore, wrung his hands and lamented, and the servant swore, Sir George's heart bled indeed, but it was silently and inwardly; and meanwhile he thought, calculated the odds, and the distance to Bath and the distance to Bristol, noted the time; and finally, and with sudden energy, called on the men to be moving. "We must get to Bath," he said. "We will be upsides with the villains yet. But we must get to Bath. What horses have we?"

Mr. Fishwick, who up to this point had played his part like a man, wailed that his horse was dead lame and could not stir a step. The lawyer was sore, stiff, and beyond belief weary; and this last mishap, this terrible buffet from the hand of Fortune, left him cowed and spiritless.

"Horses or no horses, we must get to Bath," Sir George answered feverishly.

On this the servant made an attempt to drag Sir George's mount from the ditch, but the poor beast would not budge, and in the darkness it was impossible to discover whether it was wounded or not. Mr. Fishwick's was dead lame; the man's had wandered away. It proved that there was nothing for it but to walk. Dejectedly, the three took the road and trudged wearily through the darkness. They would reach Bathford village, the man believed, in a mile and a half.

That settled, not a word was said, for who could give any comfort? Now and then, as they plodded up the hill beyond Kingsdown, the servant uttered a low curse and Sir George groaned, while Mr. Fishwick sighed in sheer exhaustion. It was a strange and dreary position for men whose ordinary lives ran through the lighted places of the world. The wind swept sadly over the dark fields. The mud clung to the squelching, dragging boots; now Mr. Fishwick was within an ace of the ditch on one side, now on the other, and now he brought up heavily against one of his companions. At length the servant gave him an arm, and thus linked together they reached the crest of the hill, and after taking a moment to breathe, began the descent.

They were within two or three hundred paces of Bathford and the bridge over the Avon when the servant cried out that someone was awake in the village, for he saw a light. A little nearer and all saw the light, which grew larger as they approached but was sometimes obscured. Finally, when they were within a hundred yards of it, they discovered that it proceeded not from a window but from a lantern set down in the village street, and surrounded by five or six persons whose movements to and fro caused the temporary eclipses they noticed. What the men were doing was not at once clear; but in the background rose the dark mass of a post-chaise, and seeing that — and one other thing — Sir George uttered a low exclamation and felt for his hilt.

The other thing was Mr. Dunborough, who, seated at his ease on the step of the post-chaise, appeared to be telling a story, while he nursed his injured arm. His audience, who seemed to have been lately roused from their beds — for they were half-dressed — were so deeply engrossed in what he was narrating that the approach of our party was unnoticed; and Sir George was in the middle of the circle, his hand on the speaker's shoulder, and his point at his breast, before a man could move in his defense.

"You villain!" Soane cried, all the misery, all the labor, all the fears of the night turning his blood to fire, "you shall pay me now! Let a man stir, and I will spit you like the dog you are! Where is she? Where is she? For, by Heaven, if you do not give her up, I will kill you with my own hand!"

Mr. Dunborough, his eyes on the other's face, laughed.

That laugh startled Sir George more than the fiercest movement, the wildest oath. His point wavered and dropped. "My God!" he cried, staring at Dunborough. "What is it? What do you mean?"

"That is better," Mr. Dunborough said, nodding complacently but not moving a finger. "Keep to that and we shall deal."

"What is it, man? What does it mean?" Sir George repeated. He was all of a tremble and could scarcely stand.

"Better and better," said Mr. Dunborough, nodding his approval. "Keep to that, and your mouth shut, and you shall know all that I know. It is precious little at best. I spurred and they spurred, I spurred and they spurred — there you have it. When I got up and shouted to them to stop, I suppose they took me for you and thought I should stick to them and take them in Bath. So they put on the pace a bit, and drew ahead as they came to the houses here, and then began to pull in, recognizing me as I thought. But when I came up, fit and ready to curse their heads off for giving me so much trouble, the fools had cut the leaders' traces and were off with them, and left me the old rattle-trap there."

Sir George's face lightened; he took two steps forward and laid his hand on the chaise door.

"Just so," said Mr. Dunborough nodding coolly. "That was my idea. I did the same. But, Lord, what their game is I don't know! It was empty."

"Empty!" Sir George cried.

"As empty as it is now," Mr. Dunborough answered, shrugging his shoulders. "As empty as a bad nut! If you are not satisfied, look for yourself," he continued, rising that Sir George might come at the door.

Soane with a sharp movement plucked the door of the chaise open, and called hoarsely for a light. A big dingy man in a wrap-rascal coat, which left his brawny neck exposed and betrayed that under the coat he wore only his shirt, held up a lantern. Its light was scarcely needed. Sir George's hand, not less than, his eyes, told him that the carriage, a big roomy post-chaise, well-cushioned and padded, was empty.

Aghast and incredulous, Soane turned on Mr. Dunborough. "You know better," he said furiously. "She was here, and you sent her on with them!"

Mr. Dunborough pointed to the man in the wrap-rascal. "That man was up as soon as I was," he said. "Ask him if you don't believe me. He opened the chaise door."

Sir George turned to the man, who, removing the shining leather cap that marked him for a smith, slowly scratched his head. The other men pressed up behind him to hear, the group growing larger every moment as one and another, awakened by the light and hubbub, came out of his house and joined it. Even women were beginning to appear on the outskirts of the crowd, their heads muffled in hoods and mobs.

"The carriage was empty, sure enough, your honor," the smith said; "there is no manner of doubt about that. I heard the wheels coming, and looked out and saw it stop and the men go off. There was no woman with them."

"How many were they?" Soane asked sharply. The man seemed honest.

"Well, there were two went off with the horses," the smith answered, "and two again slipped off on foot by the lane 'tween the houses there. I saw no more, your honor, and there were no more."

"Are you sure," Sir George asked eagerly, "that no one of the four was a woman?"

The smith grinned. "How am I to know?" he answered with a chuckle. "That's none of my business. All I can say is, they were all dressed man fashion. And they all went willing, for they went one by one, as you may say."

"Two on foot?"

"By the lane there. I never said no otherwise. Seemingly they were the two on the carriage."

"And you saw no lady?" Sir George persisted, still incredulous.

"There was no lady," the man answered simply. "I came out, and the gentleman there was swearing and trying the door. I forced it with my chisel, and you may see the mark on the break of the lock now."

"Then we have been tricked," Sir George cried furiously. "We have followed the wrong carriage."

"Not you, sir," the smith answered. 'Twas fitted up for the job, or I should not have had to force the door. If 'twere not got ready for a job of this kind, why a half-inch shutter inside the canvas blinds, and the bolt outside, "swell as a lock? Mark that door! D'you ever see the like of that on an honest carriage? Why, 'tis naught but a prison!"

He held up the light inside the carriage, and Sir George, the crowd pressing forward to look over his shoulder, saw that it was as the man said. Sir George saw something more — and pounced on it greedily. At the foot of the doorway, between the floor of the carriage and the straw mat that covered it, the corner of a black silk kerchief showed. How it came to be in that position, whether it had been kicked thither by accident or thrust under the mat on purpose, it was impossible to say. But there it was, and as Sir George held it up to the lantern — jealously interposing himself between it and the curious eyes of the crowd — he felt something hard inside the folds and saw that the corners were knotted. He uttered an exclamation.

"More room, good people, more room!" he cried.

"Your honor ha' got something?" said the smith; and then to the crowd, "Here, you — keep back, will you?" he continued, "and give the gentleman room to breathe. Or will you ha' the constable fetched?"

"I be here!" cried a weakly voice from the skirts of the crowd.

"Aye, so be Easter," the smith retorted gruffly, as a puny atomy of a man with a stick and lantern was pushed with difficulty to the front. "But so being you are here, supposing you put Joe Hincks a foot or two back, and let the gentleman have elbow-room."

There was a laugh at this, for Joe Hincks was a giant a little taller than the smith. None the less, the hint had the desired effect. The crowd fell back a little. Meanwhile, Sir George, the general attention diverted from him, had untied the knot. When the smith turned to him again, it was to find him staring with a blank face at a plain black snuff-box, which was all he had found in the kerchief.

"Sakes!" cried the smith, "whose is that?"

"I don't know," Sir George answered grimly, and shot a glance of suspicion at Mr. Dunborough, who was leaning against the fore-wheel.

But that gentleman shrugged his shoulders. "You need not look at me," he said. "It is not my box; I have mine here."

"Whose is it?"

Mr. Dunborough raised his eyebrows and did not answer.

"Do you know?" Sir George persisted fiercely.

"No, I don't. I know no more about it than you do."

"Maybe the lady took snuff?" the smith said cautiously.

Many ladies did, but not this one; and Sir George sniffed his contempt. He turned the box over and over in his hand. It was a plain, black box, of smooth enamel, about two inches long.

"I believe I have seen one like it," said Mr. Dunborough, yawning. "But I'm hanged if I can tell where."

"Has your honor looked inside?" the smith asked. "Maybe there is a note in it."

Sir George cut him short with an exclamation, and held the box up to the light. "There is something scratched on it," he said.

There was. When he held the box close to the lantern, words rudely scratched on the enamel, as if with the point of a pin, became visible; visible, but not immediately legible, so scratchy were the letters and imperfectly formed the strokes. It was not until the fourth or fifth time of reading that Sir George made out the following scrawl:

"Take to Fishwick, Castle, Marlboro. Help!

"JULIA."

Sir George swore. The box, with its pitiful, scarce articulate cry, brought the girl's helpless position, her distress, her terror, more clearly to his mind than all that had gone before. Nor to his mind only, but to his heart; he scarcely asked himself why the appeal was made to another, or whence came this box — which was plainly a man's, and still had snuff in it — or even whither she had been so completely spirited away that there remained of her no more than this, and the black kerchief, and about the carriage a fragrance of her — perceptible only by a lover's senses. A whirl of pity and rage — pity for her, rage against her captors — swept such questions from his mind. He was shaken by gusty impulses, now to strike Mr. Dunborough across his smirking face, now to give some frenzied order, now to do some foolish act that must expose him to disgrace. He had much ado not to break into hysterical weeping, or into a torrent of frantic oaths. The exertions of the night, following on a day spent in the saddle, the tortures of fear and suspense, this last disappointment, the shock of his fall — had all told on him; and it was well that at this crisis Mr. Fishwick was at his elbow.

For the lawyer saw his face and read it aright, and interposing suggested an adjournment to the inn; adding that while they talked the matter over and refreshed themselves, a messenger could go to Bath and bring back new horses; in that way they might still be in Bristol by eight in the morning.

"Bristol!" Sir George muttered, passing his hand across his brow.

"Bristol! But — she is not with them. We don't know where she is."

Mr. Fishwick was himself sick with fatigue, but he knew what to do and did it. He passed his arm through Sir George's, and signed to the smith to lead the way to the inn. The man did so, the crowd made way for them, Mr. Dunborough and the servant followed; in less than a minute the three gentlemen stood together in the sanded tap-room at the tavern. The landlord hurried in and hung a lamp on a hook in the whitewashed wall; its glare fell strongly on their features, and for the first time that night showed the three to one another.

Even in that poor place, the light had seldom fallen on persons in a more pitiable plight. Of the three, Sir George alone stood erect, his glittering eyes and twitching nostrils belying the deadly pallor of his face. He was splashed with mud from head to foot, his coat was plastered where he had fallen, his cravat was torn and open at the throat. He still held his naked sword in his hand; apparently he had forgotten that he held it. Mr. Dunborough was in scarce better condition. White and shaken, his hand bound to his side, he had dropped at once into a chair, and sat, his free hand plunged into his breeches pocket, his head sunk on his breast. Mr. Fishwick, a pale image of himself, his knees trembling with exhaustion, leaned against the wall. The adventures of the night had let none of the travelers escape.

The landlord and his wife could be heard in the kitchen drawing ale and clattering plates, while the voices of the constable and his gossips, drawling their wonder and surmises, filled the passage. Sir George was the first to speak.

"Bristol!" he said dully. "Why Bristol?"

"Because the villains who have escaped us here," the lawyer answered, "we shall find there. And they will know what has become of her."

"But shall we find them?"

"Mr. Dunborough will find them."

"Ha!" said Sir George, with a somber glance. "So he will."

Mr. Dunborough spoke with sudden fury. "I wish to Heaven," he said, "that I had never heard the girl's name. How do I know where she is!"

"You will have to know," Sir George muttered between his teeth.

"Fine talk!" Mr. Dunborough retorted, with a faint attempt at a sneer, "when you know as well as I do that I have no more idea where the girl is or what has become of her than that snuff-box. And d——n me!" he continued sharply, his eyes on the box, which Sir George still held in his hand, "whose is the snuff-box, and how did she get it? That is what I want to know? And why did she leave it in the carriage? If we had found it dropped in the road now, and that kerchief round it, I could understand that! But in the carriage. Pho! I believe I am not the only one in this!"

Chapter XXI

IN THE CARRIAGE

*T*he man whose work had taken him that evening to the summit of the Druid's Mound, and whose tale roused the Castle Inn ten minutes later, had seen aright. But he had not seen all. Had he waited another minute, he would have marked a fresh actor appear at Manton Corner, would have witnessed the *dénouement* of the scene, and had that to tell when he descended, which must have allayed in a degree, not only the general alarm, but Sir George's private apprehensions.

It is when the mind is braced to meet a known emergency that it falls the easiest prey to the unexpected. Julia was no coward. But as she loitered along the lane beyond Préshute churchyard in the gentle hour before sunset, her whole being was set on the coming of the lover for whom she waited. As she thought over the avowal she would make to him, and conned the words she would speak to him, the girl's cheeks, though she believed herself alone, burned with happy blushes; her breath came more quickly, her body swayed involuntarily in the direction whence he, who had chosen and honored her, would come! The soft glow which overspread the heights, as the sun went down and left the vale to peace and rest, was not more real or more pure than the happiness that thrilled her. Her heart overflowed in a tender ecstasy, as she thanked God, and her lover. In the peace that lay around her, she who had flouted Sir George, not once or twice, who had mocked and tormented him, in fancy kissed his feet.

In such a mood as this she had neither eyes nor ears for aught but the coming of her lover. When she reached the corner, jealous that none but he should see the happy shining of her eyes — nor he until he stood beside her — she turned to walk back; in a luxury of anticipation. Her lot was wonderful to her. She sang in her heart that she was blessed among women.

And then, without the least warning, the grating of a stone even, or the sound of a footstep, a violent grip encircled her waist from behind; something thick, rough, suffocating, fell on her head and eyes, enveloped and blinded her. The shock of the surprise was so great that for a moment breath and even the instinct of resistance failed her; and she had been forced several steps, in what direction she had no idea, before sense and horror awoke together, and wresting herself, by the supreme effort of an active girl, from the grasp that confined her, she freed her mouth sufficiently to scream.

Twice and shrilly; then, before she could entirely rid her head of the folds that blinded her, a remorseless grip closed on her neck, and another round her waist; and choking and terrified, vainly struggling and fighting, she felt herself pushed along. Coarse voices, imprecating vengeance on her if she screamed, again, sounded in her ears: and then for a moment her course was stayed. She fancied that she heard a shout, the rush and scramble of feet in the road, new curses and imprecations. The grasp on her waist relaxed, and seizing her opportunity she strove with the strength of despair to wrest herself from the hands that still held the covering over her head. Instead, she felt herself lifted up, something struck her sharply on the knee; the next moment she fell violently and all huddled up on — it might have been the ground, for all she knew; it really was the seat of a carriage.

The shock was no slight one, but she struggled to her feet, and heard, as she tore the covering from her head, a report as of a pistol shot. The next moment she lost her footing, and fell back. She alighted on the place from which she had raised herself, and was not hurt. But the jolt, which had jerked her from her feet, and the subsequent motion, disclosed the truth. Before she had entirely released her head from the folds of the cloak, she knew that she was in a carriage, whirled along behind swift horses; and that the peril was real, and not of the moment, momentary!

This was horror enough. But it was not all. One wild look round, and her eyes began to penetrate the gloom of the closely shut carriage — and she shrank into her corner. She checked the rising sob that preluded a storm of rage and tears, stayed the frenzied impulse to shriek, to beat on the doors, to do anything that might scare the villains; she sat frozen, staring, motionless. For on the seat beside her, almost touching her, was a man.

In the dim light it was not easy to make out more than his figure.

He sat huddled up in his corner, his wig awry, one hand to his face; gazing at her, she fancied, between his fingers, enjoying the play of her rage, her agitation, her disorder. He did not move or speak when she discovered him, but in the circumstances that he was a man was enough. The violence with which she had been treated, the audacity of such an outrage in daylight and on the highway, the closed and darkened carriage, the speed at which they traveled, all were grounds for alarm as serious as a woman could feel; and Julia, though she was a brave woman, felt a sudden horror come over her. None the less was her mind made up; if the man moved nearer to her, if he stretched out so much as his hand towards her, she would tear his face with her fingers. She sat with them on her lap and felt them as steel to do her bidding.

The carriage rumbled on, and still he did not move. From her corner she watched him, her eyes glittering with excitement, her breath coming quick and short. Would he never move? In truth not three minutes had elapsed since she discovered him beside her; but it seemed to her that she had sat there an age watching him; aye, three ages. The light was dim and untrustworthy, stealing in through a crack here and a crevice there. The carriage swayed and shook with the speed at which it traveled. More than once she thought that the man's hand, which rested on the seat beside him, a fat white hand, hateful, dubious, was moving, moving slowly and stealthily along the cushion towards her; and she waited shuddering, a scream on her lips. The same terror which, a while before, had frozen the cry in her throat, now tried her in another way. She longed to speak, to shriek, to stand up, to break in one way or any way the hideous silence, the spell that bound her. Every moment the strain on her nerves grew tenser, the fear lest she should swoon, more immediate, more appalling; and still the man sat in his corner, motionless, peeping at her through his fingers, leering and biding his time.

It was horrible, and it seemed endless. If she had had a weapon it would have been better. But she had only her bare hands and her despair; and she might swoon. At last the carriage swerved sharply to one side, and jolted over a stone; and the man lurched nearer to her, and — and moaned!

Julia drew a deep breath and leaned forward, scarcely able to believe her ears. But the man moaned again; and then, as if the shaking had roused him from a state of stupor, sat up slowly in his corner; she saw, peering more closely at him, that he had been strangely huddled before. At last he lowered his hand from his face and disclosed his features. It was — her astonishment was immense — it was Mr. Thomasson!

In her surprise Julia uttered a cry. The tutor opened his eyes and looked languidly at her; muttered something incoherent about his head, and shut his eyes again, letting his chin fall on his breast.

But the girl was in a mood only one degree removed from frenzy. She leaned forward and shook his arm. "Mr. Thomasson!" she cried. "Mr. Thomasson!"

Apparently the name and the touch were more effectual. He opened his eyes and sat up with a start of recognition, feigned or real. On his temple just under the edge of his wig, which was awry, was a slight cut. He felt it gingerly with his fingers, glanced at them, and finding them stained with blood, shuddered. "I am afraid — I am hurt," he muttered.

His languor and her excitement went ill together. She doubted he was pretending, and had a hundred ill-defined, half-formed suspicions of him. Was it possible that he — he had dared to contrive this? Or was he employed by others — by another? "Who hurt you?" she cried sharply. At least she was not afraid of him.

He pointed in the direction of the horses. "They did," he said stupidly. "I saw it from the lane and ran to help you. The man I seized struck me — here. Then, I suppose they feared I should raise the country on them. And they forced me in — I don't well remember how."

"And that is all you know?" she cried imperiously.

His look convinced her. "Then help me now!" she replied, rising impetuously to her feet, and steadying herself by setting one hand against the back of the carriage. "Shout! Scream! Threaten them! Don't you see that every yard we are carried puts us farther in their power? Shout! — do you hear?"

"They will murder us!" he protested faintly. His cheeks were pale; his face wore a scared look, and he trembled visibly.

"Let them!" she answered passionately, beating on the nearest door. "Better that than be in their hands. Help! Help! Help here!"

Her shrieks rose above the rumble of the wheels and the steady trampling of the horses; she added to the noise by kicking and beating on the door with the fury of a mad woman. Mr. Thomasson had had enough of violence for that day; and shrank from anything that might bring on him the fresh wrath of his captors. But a moment's reflection showed him that if he allowed himself to be carried on he would, sooner or later, find himself face to face with Mr. Dunborough; and, in any case, that it was now his interest to stand by his companion; and presently he too fell to shouting and drumming on the panels. There was a quaver, indeed, in his "Help! Help!" that a little betrayed the man; but in the determined clamor which she raised and continued to maintain, it passed well enough.

"If we meet anyone — they must hear us!" she gasped, presently, pausing a moment to take breath. "Which way are we going?"

"Towards Calne, I think," he answered, continuing to drum on the door in the intervals of speech. "In the street we must be heard."

"Help! Help!" she screamed, still more recklessly. She was growing hoarse, and the prospect terrified her. "Do you hear? Stop, villains! Help! Help! Help!"

"Murder!" Mr. Thomasson shouted, seconding her with voice and fist. "Murder! Murder!"

But in the last word, despite his valiant determination to throw in his lot with her, was a sudden, most audible, quaver. The carriage was beginning to draw up; and that which he had imperiously demanded a moment before, he now as urgently dreaded. Not so Julia; her natural courage had returned, and the moment the vehicle came to a standstill and the door was opened, she flung herself towards it. The next instant she was pushed forcibly back by the muzzle of a huge horse-pistol which a man outside clapped to her breast; while the glare of the bull's-eye lantern which he thrust in her face blinded her.

The man uttered the most horrid imprecations. "You noisy slut," he growled, shoving his face, hideous in its crape mask, into the coach, and speaking in a voice husky with liquor, "will you stop your whining? Or must I blow you to pieces with my Toby? For you, you white-livered sneak," he continued, addressing the tutor, "give me anymore of your piping and I'll cut out your tongue! Who is hurting you, I'd like to know! As for you, my fine lady, have a care of your skin, for if I pull you out into the road it will be the worse for you! D'ye hear me?" he continued, with a volley of savage oaths. "A little more of your music, and I'll have you out and strip the clothes off your back! You don't hang me for nothing. D——n you, we are three miles from anywhere, and I have a mind to gag you, whether or no! And I will too, if you so much as open your squeaker again!"

"Let me go," she cried faintly. "Let me go."

"Oh, you will be let go fast enough — the other side of the water," he answered, with a villainous laugh. "I'm bail to that. In the meantime keep a still tongue, or it will be the worse for you! Once out of Bristol, and you may pipe as you like!"

The girl fell back in her corner with a low wail of despair. The man seeing the effect he had wrought, laughed his triumph, and in sheer brutality passed his light once or twice across her face. Then he closed the door with a crash and mounted; the carriage bounded forward again, and in a trice was traveling onward as rapidly as before.

Night had set in, and darkness, a darkness that could almost be felt, reigned in the interior of the chaise. Neither of the travelers could now see the other, though they sat within arm's length. The tutor, as soon as they were well started, and his nerves, shaken by the man's threats, permitted him to think of anything save his own safety, began to wonder that his companion, who had been so forward before, did not now speak; to look for her to speak, and to find the darkness and this silence, which left him to feed on his fears, strangely uncomfortable. He could almost believe that she was no longer there. At length, unable to bear it longer, he spoke.

"I suppose you know," he said — he was growing vexed with the girl who had brought him into this peril — "who is at the bottom of this?"

She did not answer, or rather she answered only by a sudden burst of weeping; not the light, facile weeping of a woman crossed or over-fretted, or frightened; but the convulsive heart-rending sobbing of utter grief and abandonment.

The tutor heard, and was at first astonished, then alarmed. "My dear, good girl, don't cry like that," he said awkwardly. "Don't! I — I don't understand it. You — you frighten me. You — you really should not. I only asked you if you knew whose work this was."

"I know! I know only too well!" she cried passionately. "God help me! God help all women!"

Mr. Thomasson wondered whether she referred to the future and her own fate. In that case, her complete surrender to despair seemed strange, seemed even inexplicable, in one who a few minutes before had shown a spirit above a woman's. Or did she know something that he did not know? Something that caused this sudden collapse. The thought increased his uneasiness; the coward dreads everything, and his nerves were shaken. "Pish! pish!" he said pettishly. "You should not give way like that! You should not, you must not give way!"

"And why not?" she cried, arresting her sobs. There was a ring of expectation in her voice, a hoping against hope. He fancied that she had lowered her hands and was peering at him.

"Because we — we may yet contrive something" he answered lamely. "We — we may be rescued. Indeed — I am sure we shall be rescued," he continued, fighting his fears as well as hers.

"And what if we are?" she cried with a passion that took him aback. "What if we are? What better am I if we are rescued? Oh, I would have done anything for him! I would have died for him!" she continued wildly. "And he has done this for me. I would have given him all, all freely, for no return if he would have it so; and this is his requital! This is the way he has gone to get it. Oh, vile! vile!"

Mr. Thomasson started. Metaphorically, he was no longer in the dark. She fancied that Sir George, Sir George whom she loved, was the contriver of this villainy. She thought that Sir George — Sir George, her cousin — was the abductor; that she was being carried off, not for her own sake, but as an obstacle to be removed from his path. The conception took the tutor's breath away; he was even staggered for the moment, it agreed as well with one part of the facts. And when an instant later his own certain information came to his aid and showed him its unreality, and he would have blurted out the truth — he hesitated. The words were on the tip of his tongue, the sentence was arranged, but he hesitated.

Why? Simply because he was Mr. Thomasson, and it was not in his nature to do the thing that lay before him until he had considered whether it might not profit him to do something else. In this case the bare statement that Mr. Dunborough, and not Sir George, was the author of the outrage, would go for little with her. If he proceeded to his reasons he might convince her; but he would also fix himself with a fore-knowledge of the danger — a fore-knowledge which he had not imparted to her, and which must sensibly detract from the merit of the service he had already and undoubtedly performed.

This was a risk; and there was a farther consideration. Why give Mr. Dunborough new ground for complaint by discovering him? True, at Bristol she would learn the truth. But if she did not reach Bristol? If they were overtaken midway? In that case the tutor saw possibilities, if he kept his mouth shut — possibilities of profit at Mr. Dunborough's hands.

In intervals between fits of alarm — when the carriage seemed to be about to halt — he turned these things over. He could hear the girl weeping in her corner, quietly, but in a heart-broken manner; and continually, while he thought and she wept, and an impenetrable curtain of darkness hid the one from the other, the chaise held on its course up-hill and down-hill, now bumping and rattling behind flying horses, and now rumbling and straining up Yatesbury Downs.

At last he broke the silence. "What makes you think," he said, "that it is Sir George has done this?"

She did not answer or stop weeping for a while. Then, "He was to meet me at sunset, at the Corner," she said. "Who else knew that I should be there? Tell me that."

"But if he is at the bottom of this, where is he?" he hazarded. "If he would play the villain with you —"

"He would play the thief," she cried passionately, "as he has played the hypocrite. Oh, it is vile! vile!"

"But — I don't understand," Mr. Thomasson stammered; he was willing to hear all he could.

"His fortune, his lands, all he has in the world are mine!" she cried.

"Mine! And he goes this way to recover them! But I could forgive him that, ah, I could forgive him that, but I cannot forgive him —"

"What?" he said.

"His love!" she cried fiercely. "That I will never forgive him! Never!"

He knew that she spoke, as she had wept, more freely for the darkness. He fancied that she was writhing on her seat, that she was tearing her handkerchief with her hands. "But — it may not be he," he said after a silence broken only by the rumble of wheels and the steady trampling of the horses.

"It is!" she cried. "It is!"

"It may not —"

"I say it is!" she repeated in a kind of fury of rage, shame, and impatience. "Do you think that I who loved him, I whom he fooled to the top of my pride, judge him too harshly? I tell you if an angel from heaven had witnessed against him I would have laughed the tale to scorn. But I have seen — I have seen with my own eyes. The man who came to the door and threatened us had lost a joint of the forefinger. Yesterday I saw that man with *him*; I saw the hand that held the pistol today give *him* a note yesterday. I saw *him* read the note, and I saw him point me out to the man who bore it — that he might know today whom he was to seize! Oh shame! Shame on him!" And she burst into fresh weeping.

At that moment the chaise, which had been proceeding for some time at a more sober pace, swerved sharply to one side; it appeared to sweep round a corner, jolted over a rough patch of ground, and came to a stand.

Chapter XXII

FACILIS DESCENSUS

Let not those who would judge her harshly forget that Julia, to an impulsive and passionate nature, added a special and notable disadvantage. She had been educated in a sphere alien from that in which she now moved. A girl, brought up as Sir George's cousin and among her equals, would have known him to be incapable of treachery as black as this. Such a girl, certified of his love, not only by his words and looks but by her own self-respect and pride, would have shut her eyes to the most pregnant facts and the most cogent inferences; and scorned all her senses, one by one, rather than believe him guilty. She would have felt, rightly or wrongly, that the thing was impossible; and would have believed everything in the world, yes, everything, possible or impossible — yet never that he had lied when he told her that he loved her.

But Julia had been bred in a lower condition, not far removed from that of the Pamela to whose good fortune she had humbly likened her own; among people who regarded a Macaroni or a man of fashion as a wolf ever seeking to devour. To distrust a gentleman and repel his advances had been one of the first lessons instilled into her opening mind; nor had she more than emerged from childhood before she knew that a laced coat forewent destruction, and held the wearer of it a cozener, who in ninety-nine cases out of a hundred kept no faith with a woman beneath him, but lived only to break hearts and bring grey hairs to the grave.

Out of this fixed belief she had been jolted by the upheaval that placed her on a level with Sir George. Persuaded that the convention no longer applied to herself, she had given the rein to her fancy and her girlish romance, no less than to her generosity; she had indulged in delicious visions, and seen them grow real; nor probably in all St. James's was there a happier woman than Julia when she found herself possessed of this lover of the prohibited class; who to the charms and attractions, the nice-ness and refinement, which she had been bred to consider beyond her reach, added a devotion, the more delightful — since he believed her to be only what she seemed — as it lay in her power to reward it amply. Some women would have swooned with joy over such a conquest effected in such circumstances. What wonder that Julia was deaf to the warnings and surmises of Mr. Fishwick, whom delay and the magnitude of the stakes rendered suspicious, as well as to the misgivings of old Mrs. Masterson, slow to grasp a new order of things? It would have been strange had she listened to either, when youth, and wealth, and love all beckoned one way.

But now, now in the horror and darkness of the post-chaise, the lawyer's warnings and the old woman's misgivings returned on her with crushing weight; and more and heavier than these, her old belief in the heartlessness, the perfidy of the man of rank. At the statement that a man of the class with whom she had commonly mixed could so smile,

while he played the villain, as to deceive not only her eyes but her heart
— she would have laughed. But on the mind that lay behind the smooth
and elegant mask of a *gentleman's* face she had no lights; or only the old
lights which showed it desperately wicked. Applying these to the circumstances, what a lurid glare they shed on his behavior! How quickly,
how suspiciously quickly, had he succumbed to her charms! How
abruptly had his insouciance changed to devotion, his impertinence to
respect! How obtuse, how strangely dull had he been in the matter of
her claims and her identity! Finally, with what a smiling visage had he
lured her to her doom, showed her to his tools, settled to a nicety the
least detail of the crime!

More weighty than any one fact, the thing he had said to her on the
staircase at Oxford came back to her mind. "If you were a lady," he had
lisped in smiling insolence, "I would kiss you and make you my wife."
In face of those words, she had been rash enough to think that she could
bend him, ignorant that she was more than she seemed, to her purpose.
She had quoted those very words to him when she had had it in her
mind to surrender — the sweetest surrender in the world. And all the
time he had been fooling her to the top of her bent. All the time he
had known who she was and been plotting against her devilishly —
appointing hour and place and — and it was all over.

It was all over. The sunny visions of love and joy were done! It was
all over. When the sharp, fierce pain of the knife had done its worst,
the consciousness of that remained a dead weight on her brain. When
the paroxysm of weeping had worn itself out, yet brought no relief to
her passionate nature, a kind of apathy succeeded. She cared nothing
where she was or what became of her; the worst had happened, the worst
been suffered. To be betrayed, cruelly, heartlessly, without scruple or care
by those we love — is there a sharper pain than this? She had suffered
that, she was suffering it still. What did the rest matter?

Mr. Thomasson might have undeceived her, but the sudden stoppage
of the chaise had left no place in the tutor's mind for aught but terror.
At any moment, now the chaise was at a stand, the door might open
and he be hauled out to meet the fury of his pupil's eye, and feel the
smart of his brutal whip. It needed no more to sharpen Mr. Thomasson's
long ears — his eyes were useless; but for a time crouching in his corner
and scarce daring to breathe, he heard only the confused muttering of
several men talking at a distance. Presently the speakers came nearer, he
caught the click of flint on steel, and a bright gleam of light entered the
chaise through a crack in one of the shutters. The men had lighted a
lamp.

It was only a slender shaft that entered, but it fell athwart the girl's face and showed him her closed eyes. She lay back in her corner, her cheeks colorless, an expression of dull, hopeless suffering stamped on her features. She did not move or open her eyes, and the tutor dared not speak lest his words should be heard outside. But he looked, having nothing to check him, and looked; and in spite of his fears and his preoccupation, the longer he looked the deeper was the impression which her beauty made on his senses.

He could hear no more of the men's talk than muttered grumblings plentifully bestrewn with curses; and wonder what was forward and why they remained inactive grew more and more upon him. At length he rose and applied his eyes to the crack that admitted the light; but he could distinguish nothing outside, the lamp, which was close to the window, blinding him. At times he caught the clink of a bottle, and fancied that the men were supping; but he knew nothing for certain, and by-and-by the light was put out. A brief — and agonizing — period of silence followed, during which he thought that he caught the distant tramp of horses; but he had heard the same sound before, it might be the beating of his heart, and before he could decide, oaths and exclamations broke the silence, and there was a sudden bustle. In less than a minute the chaise lurched forward, a whip cracked, and they took the road again.

The tutor breathed more freely, and, rid of the fear of being overheard, regained a little of his unctuousness. "My dear good lady," he said, moving a trifle nearer to Julia, and even making a timid plunge for her hand, "you must not give way. I protest you must not give way. Depend on me! Depend on me, and all will be well. I — oh dear, what a bump! I" — this as he retreated precipitately to his corner — "I fear we are stopping!"

They were, but only for an instant, that the lamps might be lighted. Then the chaise rolled on again, but from the way in which it jolted and bounded, shaking its passengers this way and that, it was evident that it no longer kept the main road. The moment this became clear to Mr. Thomasson his courage vanished as suddenly as it had appeared.

"Where are they taking us?" he cried, rising and sitting down again; and peering first this way and then the other. "My G——d, we are undone! We shall be murdered — I know we shall! Oh dear! what a jolt! They are taking us to some cutthroat place! There again! Didn't you feel it? Don't you understand, woman? Oh, Lord," he continued, piteously wringing his hands, "why did I mix myself up with this trouble?"

She did not answer, and enraged by her silence and insensibility, the cowardly tutor could have found it in his heart to strike her. Fortunately the ray of light which now penetrated the carriage suggested an idea which he hastened to carry out. He had no paper, and, given paper, he had no ink; but falling back on what he had, he lugged out his snuff-box and pen-knife, and holding the box in the ray of light, and himself as still as the road permitted, he set to work, laboriously and with set teeth, to scrawl on the bottom of the box the message of which we know. To address it to Mr. Fishwick and sign it Julia were natural precautions, since he knew that the girl, and not he, would be the object of pursuit. When he had finished his task, which was no light one — the road growing worse and the carriage shaking more and more — he went to thrust the box under the door, which fitted ill at the bottom. But stooping to remove the straw, he reflected that probably the road they were in was a country lane, where the box would be difficult to find; and in a voice trembling with fear and impatience, he called to the girl to give him her black kerchief.

She did not ask him why or for what, but complied without opening her eyes. No words could have described her state more eloquently.

He wrapped the thing loosely in the kerchief — which he calculated would catch the passing eye more easily than the box — and knotted the ends together. But when he went to push the package under the door, it proved too bulky; and, with an exclamation of rage, he untied it, and made it up anew and more tightly. At last he thought that he had got it right, and he stooped to feel for the crack; but the carriage, which had been traveling more and more heavily and slowly, came to a sudden standstill, and in a panic he sat up, dropping the box and thrusting the straw over it with his foot.

He had scarcely done this when the door was opened, and the masked man, who had threatened them before, thrust in his head. "Come out!" he said curtly, addressing the tutor, who was the nearer. "And be sharp about it!"

But Mr. Thomasson's eyes, peering through the doorway, sought in vain the least sign of house or village. Beyond the yellow glare cast by the lamp on the wet road, he saw nothing but darkness, night, and the gloomy shapes of trees; and he hung back. "No," he said, his voice quavering with fear. "I — my good man, if you will promise —"

The man swore a frightful oath. "None of your tongue!" he cried, "but out with you unless you want your throat cut. You cursed, whining, psalm-singing sniveler, you don't know when you are well off! Out with you!"

Mr. Thomasson waited for no more, but stumbled out, shaking with fright.

"And you!" the ruffian continued, addressing the girl, "unless you want to be thrown out the same way you were thrown in! The sooner I see your back, my sulky Madam, the better I shall be pleased. No more meddling with petticoats for me! This comes of working with fine gentlemen, say I!"

Julia was but half roused. "Am. I — to get out?" she said dully.

"Aye you are! By G——d, you are a cool one!" the man continued, watching her in a kind of admiration, as she rose and stepped by him like one in a dream. "And a pretty one for all your temper! The master is not here, but the man is; and if —"

"Stow it, you fool!" cried a voice from the darkness, "and get aboard!"

"Who said anything else?" the ruffian retorted, but with a look that, had Julia been more sensible of it, must have chilled her blood. "Who said anything else? So there you are, both of you, and none the worse, I'll take my davy! Lash away, Tim! Make the beggars fly!"

As he uttered the last words he sprang on the wheel, and before the tutor could believe his good fortune, or feel assured that there was not some cruel deceit playing on him, the carriage splashed up the mud, and rattled away. In a trice the lights grew small and were gone, and the two were left standing side by side in the darkness. On one hand a mass of trees rose high above them, blotting out the grey sky; on the other the faint outline of a low wall appeared to divide the lane in which they stood — the mud rising rapidly about their shoes — from a flat aguish expanse over which the night hung low.

It was a strange position, but neither of the two felt this to the fall; Mr. Thomasson in his thankfulness that at any cost he had eluded Mr. Dunborough's vengeance, Julia because at the moment she cared not what became of her. Naturally, however, Mr. Thomasson, whose satisfaction knew no drawback save that of their present condition, and who had to congratulate himself on a risk safely run, and a good friend gained, was the first to speak.

"My dear young lady," he said, in an insinuating tone very different from that in which he had called for her kerchief, "I vow I am more thankful than I can say, that I was able to come to your assistance! I shudder to think what those ruffians might not have done had you been alone, and — and unprotected! Now I trust all danger is over. We have only to find a house in which we can pass the night, and tomorrow we may laugh at our troubles!"

She turned her head towards him, "Laugh?" she said, and a sob took her in the throat.

He felt himself set back; then remembered the delusion under which she lay, and went to dispel it — pompously. But his evil angel was at his shoulder; again at the last moment he hesitated. Something in the despondency of the girl's figure, in the hopelessness of her tone, in the intensity of the grief that choked her utterance, wrought with the remembrance of her beauty and her disorder in the coach, to set his crafty mind working in a new direction. He saw that she was for the time utterly hopeless; utterly heedless what became of herself. That would not last; but his cunning told him that with returning sensibility would come pique, resentment, the desire to be avenged. In such a case one man was sometimes as good as another. It was impossible to say what she might not do or be induced to do, if full advantage were taken of a moment so exceptional. Fifty thousand pounds! And her fresh young beauty! What an opening it was! The way lay far from clear, the means were to find; but faint heart never won fair lady, and Mr. Thomasson had known strange things come to pass.

He was quick to choose his part. "Come, child," he said, assuming a kind of paternal authority. "At least we must find a roof. We cannot spend the night here."

"No," she said dully, "I suppose not."

"So — shall we go this way?"

"As you please," she answered.

They started, but had not moved far along the miry road before she spoke again. "Do you know," she asked drearily, "why they set us down?"

He was puzzled himself as to that, but, "They may have thought that the pursuit was gaining on them," he answered, "and become alarmed." Which was in part the truth; though Mr. Dunborough's failure to appear at the rendezvous had been the main factor in determining the men.

"Pursuit?" she said. "Who would pursue us?"

"Mr. Fishwick," he suggested.

"Ah!" she answered bitterly; "he might. If I had listened to him! If I had — but it is over now."

"I wish we could see a light," Mr. Thomasson said, anxiously looking into the darkness, "or a house of any kind. I wonder where we are." She did not speak.

"I do not know — even what time it is," he continued pettishly; and he shivered. "Take care!" She had stumbled and nearly fallen. "Will you be pleased to take my arm, and we shall be able to proceed more quickly. I am afraid that your feet are wet."

Absorbed in her thoughts she did not answer.

"However the ground is rising," he said. "By-and-by it will be drier under foot."

They were an odd couple to be trudging a strange road, in an unknown country, at the dark hour of the night. The stars must have twinkled to see them. Mr. Thomasson began to own the influence of solitude, and longed to pat the hand she had passed through his arm —

it was the sort of caress that came natural to him; but for the time discretion withheld him. He had another temptation: to refer to the past, to the old past at the College, to the part he had taken at the inn, to make some sort of apology; but again discretion intervened, and he went on in silence.

As he had said, the ground was rising; but the outlook was cheerless enough, until the moon on a sudden emerged from a bank of cloud and disclosed the landscape. Mr. Thomasson uttered a cry of relief. Fifty paces before them the low wall on the right of the lane was broken by a pillared gateway, whence the dark thread of an avenue trending across the moonlit flat seemed to point the way to a house.

The tutor pushed the gate open. "Diana favors you, child," he said, with a smirk which was lost on Julia. "It was well she emerged when she did, for now in a few minutes we shall be safe under a roof. 'Tis a gentleman's house too, unless I mistake."

A more timid or a more suspicious woman might have refused to leave the road, or to tempt the chances of the dark avenue, in his company. But Julia, whose thoughts were bitterly employed, complied without thought or hesitation, perhaps unconsciously. The gate swung to behind them, and they plodded a hundred yards between the trees arm in arm; then one and then a second light twinkled out in front. These as they approached were found to proceed from two windows in the ground floor of a large house. The travelers had not advanced many paces towards them before the peaks of three gables rose above them, vandyking the sky and docking the last sparse branches of the elms.

Mr. Thomasson's exclamation of relief, as he surveyed the building, was cut short by the harsh rattle of a chain, followed by the roar of a watchdog, as it bounded from the kennel; in a second a horrid raving and baying, as of a score of hounds, awoke the night. The startled tutor came near to dropping his companion's hand, but fortunately the threshold, dimly pillared and doubtfully Palladian, was near, and resisting the impulse to put himself back to back with the girl — for the protection of his calves rather than her skirts — the reverend gentleman hurried to occupy it. Once in that coign of refuge, he hammered on the door with the energy of a frightened man.

When his anxiety permitted him to pause, a voice made itself heard within, cursing the dogs and roaring for Jarvey. A line of a hunting song, bawled at the top of a musical voice and ending in a shrill "View Halloa!" followed; then "To them, beauties; to them!" and the crash of an overturned chair. Again the house echoed with "Jarvey, Jarvey!" on top of which the door opened and an elderly man-servant, with his wig set on askew, his waistcoat unbuttoned, and his mouth twisted into a tipsy smile, confronted the wanderers.

Chapter XXIII

BULLY POMEROY

*T*he man held a candle in a hand that wavered and strewed tallow broadcast; the light from this for a moment dazzled the visitors. Then the draft of air extinguished it, and looking over the servant's shoulder — he was short and squat — Mr. Thomasson's anxious eyes had a glimpse of a spacious old-fashioned hall, paneled and furnished in oak, with here a blazon, and there antlers or a stuffed head. At the farther end of the hall a wide easy staircase rose, to branch at the first landing into two flights, that returning formed a gallery round the apartment. Between the door and the foot of the staircase, in the warm glow of an unseen fire, stood a small heavily-carved oak table, with Jacobean legs, like stuffed trunk-hose. This was strewn with cards, liquors, glasses, and a china punch-bowl; but especially with cards, which lay everywhere, not only on the table, but in heaps and batches beneath and around it, where the careless hands of the players had flung them.

Yet, for all these cards, the players were only two. One, a man something under forty, in a peach coat and black satin breeches, sat on the edge of the table, his eyes on the door and his chair lying at his feet. It was his voice that had shouted for Jarvey and that now saluted the arrivals with a boisterous "Two to one in guineas, it's a catchpoll! D'ye take me, my lord?" — the while he drummed merrily with his heels on a leg of the table. His companion, an exhausted young man, thin and pale, remained in his chair, which he had tilted on its hinder feet; and contented himself with staring at the doorway.

The latter was our old friend, Lord Almeric Doyley; but neither he nor Mr. Thomasson knew one another, until the tutor had advanced some paces into the room. Then, as the gentleman in the peach coat cried, "Curse me, if it isn't a parson! The bet's off! Off!" Lord Almeric dropped his hand of cards on the table, and opening his mouth gasped in a paroxysm of dismay.

"Oh, Lord," he exclaimed, at last. "Hold me, someone! If it isn't Tommy! Oh, I say," he continued, rising and speaking in a tone of querulous remonstrance, "you have not come to tell me the old man's gone! And I'd pitted him against Bedford to live to — to — but it's like him! It is like him, and monstrous unfeeling. I vow and protest it is! Eh! oh, it is not that! Hal — loa!"

He paused there, his astonishment greater even than that which he had felt on recognizing the tutor. His eye had lighted on Julia, whose figure was now visible on the threshold.

His companion did not notice this. He was busy identifying the tutor. "Gad! it is old Thomasson!" he cried, for he too had been at Pembroke. "*And* a petticoat! *And* a petticoat!" he repeated. "Well, I am spun!"

The tutor raised his hands in astonishment. "Lord!" he said, with a fair show of enthusiasm, "do I really see my old friend and pupil, Mr. Pomeroy of Bastwick?"

"Who put the cat in your valise? When you got to London — kittens? You do, Tommy."

"I thought so!" Mr. Thomasson answered effusively. "I was sure of it! I never forget a face when my — my heart has once gone out to it! And you, my dear, my very dear Lord Almeric, there is no danger I shall ever —"

"But, crib me, Tommy," Lord Almeric shrieked, cutting him short without ceremony, so great was his astonishment, "it's the Little Masterson!"

"You old fox!" Mr. Pomeroy chimed in, shaking his finger at the tutor with leering solemnity; he, belonging to an older generation at the College, did not know her. Then, "The Little Masterson, is it?" he continued, advancing to the girl, and saluting her with mock ceremony. "Among friends, I suppose? Well, my dear, for the future be pleased to count me among them. Welcome to my poor house! And here's to bettering your taste — for, fie, my love, old men are naughty. Have naught to do with them!" And he laughed wickedly. He was a tall, heavy man, with a hard, bullying, sneering face; a Dunborough grown older.

"Hush! my good sir. Hush!" Mr. Thomasson cried anxiously, after making more than one futile effort to stop him. Between his respect for his companion, and the deference in which he held a lord, the tutor was in agony. "My good sir, my dear Lord Almeric, you are in error," he continued strenuously. "You mistake, I assure you, you mistake —"

"Do we, by Gad!" Mr. Pomeroy cried, winking at Julia. "Well, you and I, my dear, don't, do we? We understand one another very well."

The girl only answered by a fierce look of contempt. But Mr. Thomasson was in despair. "You do not, indeed!" he cried, almost wringing his hands. "This lady has lately come into a — a fortune, and tonight was carried off by some villains from the Castle Inn at Marlborough in a — in a post-chaise. I was fortunately on the spot to give her such protection as I could, but the villains overpowered me, and to prevent my giving the alarm, as I take it, bundled me into the chaise with her."

"Oh, come," said Mr. Pomeroy, grinning. "You don't expect us to swallow that?"

"It is true, as I live," the tutor protested. "Every word of it."

"Then how come you here?"

"Not far from your gate, for no reason that I can understand, they turned us out, and made off."

"Honest Abraham?" Lord Almeric asked; he had listened open-mouthed.

"Every word of it," the tutor answered.

"Then, my dear, if you have a fortune, sit down," cried Mr. Pomeroy; and seizing a chair he handed it with exaggerated gallantry to Julia, who still remained near the door, frowning darkly at the trio; neither ashamed nor abashed, but proudly and coldly contemptuous. "Make yourself at home, my pretty," he continued familiarly, "for if you have a fortune it is the only one in this house, and a monstrous uncommon thing. Is it not, my lord?"

"Lord! I vow it is!" the other drawled; and then, taking advantage of the moment when Julia's attention was engaged elsewhere — she dumbly refused to sit, "Where is Dunborough?" my lord muttered.

"Heaven knows," Mr. Thomasson whispered, with a wink that postponed inquiry. "What is more to the purpose," he continued aloud, "if I may venture to make the suggestion to your lordship and Mr. Pomeroy, Miss Masterson has been much distressed and fatigued this evening. If there is a respectable elderly woman in the house, therefore, to whose care you could entrust her for the night, it were well."

"There is old Mother Olney," Mr. Pomeroy answered, assenting with a readier grace than the tutor expected, "who locked herself up an hour ago for fear of us young bloods. She should be old and ugly enough! Here you, Jarvey, go and kick in her outworks, and bid her come down."

"Better still, if I may suggest it," said the tutor, who was above all things anxious to be rid of the girl before too much was said — "Might not your servant take Miss above stairs to this good woman — who will doubtless see to her comfort? Miss Masterson has gone through some surprising adventures this evening, and I think it were better if you allowed her to withdraw at once, Mr. Pomeroy."

"Jarvey, take the lady," Mr. Pomeroy cried. "A sweet pretty toad she is. Here's to your eyes and fortune, child!" he continued with an impudent grin; and filling his glass he pledged her as she passed.

After that he stood watching while Mr. Thomasson opened the door and bowed her out; and this done and the door closed after her, "Lord, what ceremony!" he said, with an ugly sneer. "Is't real, man, or are you bubbling her? And what is this Cock-lane story of a chaise and the rest? Out with it, unless you want to be tossed in a blanket."

"True, upon my honor!" Mr. Thomasson asseverated.

"Oh, but Tommy, the fortune?" Lord Almeric protested seriously. "I vow you are sharping us."

"True too, my lord, as I hope to be saved!"

"True? Oh, but it is too monstrous absurd," my lord wailed. "The Little Masterson? As pretty a little tit as was to be found in all Oxford. The Little Masterson a fortune?"

"She has eyes and a shape," Mr. Pomeroy admitted generously. "For the rest, what is the figure, Mr. Thomasson?" he continued. "There are fortunes and fortunes."

Mr. Thomasson looked at the gallery above, and thence, and slyly, to his companions and back again to the gallery; and swallowed something that rose in his throat. At length he seemed to make up his mind to speak the truth, though when he did so it was in a voice little above a whisper. "Fifty thousand," he said, and looked guiltily round him.

Lord Almeric rose from his chair as if on springs. "Oh, I protest!" he said. "You are roasting us. Fifty thousand! It's a bite?"

But Mr. Thomasson nodded. "Fifty thousand," he repeated softly. "Fifty thousand."

"Pounds?" gasped my lord. "The Little Masterson?"

The tutor nodded again; and without asking leave, with a dogged air unlike his ordinary bearing when he was in the company of those above him, he drew a decanter towards him, and filling a glass with a shaking hand raised it to his lips and emptied it. The three were on their feet round the table, on which several candles, luridly lighting up their faces, still burned; while others had flickered down, and smoked in the guttering sockets, among the empty bottles and the litter of cards. In one corner of the table the lees of wine had run upon the oak, and dripped to the floor, and formed a pool, in which a broken glass lay in fragments beside the overturned chair. An observant eye might have found on the panels below the gallery the vacant nails and dusty lines whence Lelys and Knellers, Cuyps and Hondekoeters had looked down on two generations of Pomeroys. But in the main the disorder of the scene centered in the small table and the three men standing round it;

a lighted group, islanded in the shadows of the hall.

Mr. Pomeroy waited with impatience until Mr. Thomasson lowered his glass. Then, "Let us have the story," he said. "A guinea to a China orange the fool is tricking us."

The tutor shook his head, and turned to Lord Almeric. "You know Sir George Soane," he said. "Well, my lord, she is his cousin."

"Oh, tally, tally!" my lord cried. "You — you are romancing, Tommy!"

"And under the will of Sir George's grandfather she takes fifty thousand pounds, if she make good her claim within a certain time from today."

"Oh, I say, you are romancing!" my lord repeated, more feebly. "You know, you really should not! It is too uncommon absurd, Tommy."

"It's true!" said Mr. Thomasson.

"What? That this porter's wench at Pembroke has fifty thousand pounds?" cried Mr. Pomeroy. "She is the porter's wench, isn't she?" he continued. Something had sobered him. His eyes shone, and the veins stood out on his forehead. But his manner was concise and harsh, and to the point.

Mr. Thomasson. glanced at him stealthily, as one gamester scrutinizes another over the cards. "She is Masterson, the porter's, foster-child," he said.

"But is it certain that she has the money?" the other cried rudely. "Is it true, man? How do you know? Is it public property?"

"No," Mr. Thomasson answered, "it is not public property. But it is certain and it is true!" Then, after a moment's hesitation, "I saw some papers — by accident," he said, his eyes on the gallery.

"Oh, d——n your accident!" Mr. Pomeroy cried brutally. "You are very fine tonight. You were not used to be a Methodist! Hang it, man, we know you," he continued violently, "and this is not all! This does not bring you and the girl tramping the country, knocking at doors at midnight with Cock-lane stories of chaises and abductions. Come to it, man, or —"

"Oh, I say," Lord Almeric protested weakly. "Tommy is an honest man in his way, and you are too stiff with him."

"D——n him! my lord; let him come to the point then," Mr. Pomeroy retorted savagely. "Is she in the way to get the money?"

"She is," said the tutor sullenly.

"Then what brings her here — with you, of all people?"

"I will tell you if you will give me time, Mr. Pomeroy," the tutor said plaintively. And he proceeded to describe in some detail all that had happened, from the *fons et origo mali* — Mr. Dunborough's passion for the girl — to the stay at the Castle Inn, the abduction at Manton Corner, the strange night journey in the chaise, and the stranger release.

When he had done, "Sir George was the girl's fancy-man, then?" Pomeroy said, in the harsh overbearing tone he had suddenly adopted.

The tutor nodded.

"And she thinks he has tricked her?"

"But for that and the humor she is in," Mr. Thomasson answered, with a subtle glance at the other's face, "you and I might talk here till Doomsday, and be none the better, Mr. Pomeroy."

His frankness provoked Mr. Pomeroy to greater frankness. "Consume your impertinence!" he cried. "Speak for yourself."

"She is not that kind of woman," said Mr. Thomasson firmly.

"Kind of woman?" cried Mr. Pomeroy furiously. "I am this kind of man. Oh, d——n you! If you want plain speaking you shall have it! She has fifty thousand, and she is in my house; well, I am this kind of man! I'll not let that money go out of the house without having a fling at it! It is the devil's luck has sent her here, and it will be my folly will send her away — if she goes. Which she does not if I am the kind of man I think I am. So there for you! There's plain speaking."

"You don't know her," Mr. Thomasson answered doggedly. "Mr. Dunborough is a gentleman of mettle, and he could not bend her."

"She was not in his house!" the other retorted, with a grim laugh. Then, in a lower, if not more amicable tone, "Look here, man," he continued, "d'ye mean to say that you had not something of this kind in your mind when you knocked at this door?"

"I!" Mr. Thomasson cried, virtuously indignant.

"Aye, you! Do you mean to say you did not see that here was a chance in a hundred? In a thousand? Aye, in a million? Fifty thousand pounds is not found in the road any day?"

Mr. Thomasson grinned in a sickly fashion. "I know that," he said.

"Well, what is your idea? What do you want?"

The tutor did not answer on the instant, but after stealing one or two furtive glances at Lord Almeric, looked down at the table, a nervous smile distorting his mouth. At length, "I want — her," he said; and passed his tongue furtively over his lips.

"The girl?"

"Yes."

"Oh Lord!" said Mr. Pomeroy, in a voice of disgust.

But the ice broken, Mr. Thomasson had more to say. "Why not?" he said plaintively. "I brought her here — with all submission. I know her, and — and am a friend of hers. If she is fair game for anyone, she is fair game for me. I have run a risk for her," he continued pathetically, and touched his brow, where the slight cut he had received in the struggle with Dunborough's men showed below the border of his wig, "and — and for that matter, Mr. Pomeroy is not the only man who has bailiffs to avoid."

"Stuff me, Tommy, if I am not of your opinion!" cried Lord Almeric. And he struck the table with unusual energy.

Pomeroy turned on him in surprise as great as his disgust. "What?" he cried. "You would give the girl and her money — fifty thousand — to this old hunks!"

"I? Not I! I would have her myself!" his lordship answered stoutly. "Come, Pomeroy, you have won three hundred of me, and if I am not to take a hand at this, I shall think it low! Monstrous low I shall think it!" he repeated in the tone of an injured person. "You know. Pom, I want money as well as another — want it devilish bad —"

"You have not been a Sabbatarian, as I was for two months last year," Mr. Pomeroy retorted, somewhat cooled by this wholesale rising among his allies, "and walked out Sundays only for fear of the catchpolls."

"No, but —"

"But I am not now, either. Is that it? Why, d'ye think, because I pouched six hundred of Flitney's, and three of yours, and set the mare going again, it will last forever?"

"No, but fair's fair, and if I am not in this, it is low. It is low, Pom," Lord Almeric continued, sticking to his point with abnormal spirit. "And here is Tommy will tell you the same. You have had three hundred of me —"

"At cards, dear lad; at cards," Mr. Pomeroy answered easily. "But this is not cards. Besides," he continued, shrugging his shoulders and pouncing on the argument, "we cannot all marry the girl!"

"I don't know," my lord answered, passing his fingers tenderly through his wig. "I — I don't commit myself to that."

"Well, at any rate, we cannot all have the money!" Pomeroy replied, with sufficient impatience.

"But we can all try! Can't we, Tommy?"

Mr. Thomasson's face, when the question was put to him in that form, was a curious study. Mr. Pomeroy had spoken aright when he called it a chance in a hundred, in a thousand, in a million. It was a chance, at any rate, that was not likely to come in Mr. Thomasson's way again. True, he appreciated more correctly than the others the obstacles in the way of success — the girl's strong will and wayward temper; but he knew also the humor which had now taken hold of her, and how likely it was that it might lead her to strange lengths if the right man spoke at the right moment.

The very fact that Mr. Pomeroy had seen the chance and gauged the possibilities, gave them a more solid aspect and a greater reality in the tutor's mind. Each moment that passed left him less willing to resign pretensions which were no longer the shadowy creatures of the brain, but had acquired the aspect of solid claims — claims made his by skill and exertion.

But if he defied Mr. Pomeroy, how would he stand? The girl's position in this solitary house, apart from her friends, was half the battle; in a sneaking way, though he shrank from facing the fact, he knew that she was at their mercy; as much at their mercy as if they had planned the abduction from the first. Without Mr. Pomeroy, therefore, the master of the house and the strongest spirit of the three —

He got no farther, for at this point Lord Almeric repeated his question; and the tutor, meeting Pomeroy's bullying eye, found it necessary to say something. "Certainly," he stammered at a venture, "we can all try, my lord. Why not?"

"Aye, why not?" said Lord Almeric. "Why not try?"

"Try? But how are you going to try?" Mr. Pomeroy responded with a jeering laugh. "I tell you, we cannot all marry the girl."

Lord Almeric burst in a sudden fit of chuckling. "I vow and protest I have it!" he cried. "We'll play for her! Don't you see, Pom? We'll cut for her! Ha! Ha! That is surprising clever of me; don't you think? We'll play for her!"

Chapter XXIV

CUTTING FOR THE QUEEN

*I*t was a suggestion so purely in the spirit of a day when men betted on every contingency, public or private, decorous or the reverse, from the fecundity of a sister to the longevity of a sire, that it sounded less indecent in the cars of Lord Almeric's companions than it does in ours. Mr. Thomasson indeed, who was only so far a gamester as every man who had pretensions to be a gentleman was one at that time, and who had seldom, since the days of Lady Harrington's faro bank, staked more than he could afford, hesitated and looked dubious. But Mr. Pomeroy, a reckless and hardened gambler, gave a boisterous assent, and in the face of that the tutor's objections went for nothing. In a trice, all the cards and half the glasses were swept pell-mell to the floor, a new pack was torn open, the candles were snuffed, and Mr. Pomeroy, smacking him on the back, was bidding him draw up.

"Sit down, man! Sit down!" cried that gentleman, who had regained his jovial humor as quickly as he had lost it, and whom the prospect of the stake appeared to intoxicate. "May I burn if I ever played for a girl before! Hang it! man, look cheerful, We'll toast her first — and a daintier bit never swam in a bowl — and play for her afterwards! Come, no heel-taps, my lord. Drink her! Drink her! Here's to the Mistress of Bastwick!"

"Lady Almeric Doyley!" my lord cried, rising, and bowing with his hand to his heart, while he ogled the door through which she had disappeared. "I drink you! Here's to your pretty face, my dear!"

"Mrs. Thomasson!" cried the tutor, "I drink to you. But —"

"But what shall it be, you mean?" Pomeroy cried briskly. "Loo, Quinze, Faro, Lansquenet? Or cribbage, all-fours, put, Mr. Parson, if you like! It's all one to me. Name your game and I am your man!"

"Then let us shuffle and cut, and the highest takes," said the tutor.

"Sho! man, where is the sport in that?" Pomeroy cried, receiving the suggestion with disgust.

"It is what Lord Almeric proposed," Mr. Thomasson answered. The two glasses of wine he had taken had given him courage. "I am no player, and at games of skill I am no match for you."

A shadow crossed Mr. Pomeroy's face; but he recovered himself immediately. "As you please," he said, shrugging his shoulders with a show of carelessness. "I'll match any man at anything. Let's to it!"

But the tutor kept his hands on the cards, which lay in a heap face downwards on the table. "There is a thing to be settled," he said, hesitating somewhat, "before we draw. If she will not take the winner — what then?"

"What then?"

"Yes, what then?"

Mr. Pomeroy grinned. "Why, then number two will try his luck with her, and if he fail, number three! There, my bully boy, that is settled. It seems simple enough, don't it?"

"But how long is each to have?" the tutor asked in a low voice. The three were bending over the cards, their faces near one another. Lord

Almeric's eyes turned from one to the other of the speakers.

"How long?" Mr. Pomeroy answered, raising his eyebrows. "Ah. Well, let's say — what do you think? Two days?"

"And if the first fail, two days for the second?"

"There will be no second if I am first," Pomeroy answered grimly.

"But otherwise," the tutor persisted; "two days for the second?"

Bully Pomeroy nodded.

"But then, the question is, can we keep her here?"

"Four days?"

"Yes."

Mr. Pomeroy laughed harshly. "Aye," he said, "or six if needs be and I lose. You may leave that to me. We'll shift her to the nursery tomorrow."

"The nursery?" my lord said, and stared.

"The windows are barred. Now do you understand?"

The tutor turned a shade paler, and his eyes sank slyly to the table. "There'll — there'll be no violence, of course," he said, his voice a trifle unsteady.

"Violence? Oh, no, there will be no violence," Mr. Pomeroy answered with an unpleasant sneer. And they all laughed; Mr. Thomasson tremulously, Lord Almeric as if he scarcely entered into the other's meaning and laughed that he might not seem outside it. Then, "There is another thing that must not be," Pomeroy continued, tapping softly on the table with his forefinger, as much to command attention as to emphasize his words, "and that is peaching! Peaching! We'll have no Jeremy Twitcher here, if you please."

"No, no!" Mr. Thomasson stammered. "Of course not."

"No, damme!" said my lord grandly. "No peaching!"

"No," Mr. Pomeroy said, glancing keenly from one to the other, "and by token I have a thought that will cure it. D'ye see here, my lord! What do you say to the losers taking five thousand each out of Madam's money? That should bind all together if anything will — though I say it that will have to pay it," he continued boastfully.

My lord was full of admiration. "Uncommon handsome!" he said. "Pom, that does you credit. You have a head! I always said you had a head!"

"You are agreeable to that, my lord?"

"Burn me, if I am not."

"Then shake hands upon it. And what say you, Parson?"

Mr. Thomasson proffered an assent fully as enthusiastic as Lord Almeric's, but for a different reason. The tutor's nerves, never strong, were none the better for the rough treatment he had undergone, his long drive, and his longer fast. He had taken enough wine to obscure remoter terrors, but not the image of Mr. Dunborough — *impiger, iracundus, inexorabilis, acer* — Dunborough doubly and trebly offended! That image recurred when the glass was not at his lips; and behind it, sometimes the angry specter of Sir George, sometimes the face of the girl, blazing with rage, slaying him with the lightning of her contempt.

He thought that it would not suit him ill, therefore, though it was a sacrifice, if Mr. Pomeroy took the fortune, the wife, and the risk — and five thousand only fell to him. True, the risk, apart from that of Mr. Dunborough's vengeance, might be small; no one of the three had had act or part in the abduction of the girl. True, too, in the atmosphere of this unfamiliar house — into which he had been transported as suddenly as Bedreddin Hassan to the palace in the fairy tale — with the fumes of wine and the glamour of beauty in his head, he was in a mood to minimize even that risk. But under the jovial good-fellowship which Mr. Pomeroy affected, and strove to instill into the party, he discerned at odd moments a something sinister that turned his craven heart to water and loosened the joints of his knees.

The lights and cards and jests, the toasts and laughter were a mask that sometimes slipped and let him see the death's head that grinned behind it. They were three men, alone with the girl in a country house, of which the reputation, Mr. Thomasson had a shrewd idea, was no better than its master's. No one outside knew that she was there; as far as her friends were concerned, she had vanished from the earth. She was a woman, and she was in their power. What was to prevent them bending her to their purpose?

It is probable that had she been of their rank from the beginning, bred and trained, as well as born, a Soane, it would not have occurred even to a broken and desperate man to frame so audacious a plan. But scruples grew weak, and virtue — the virtue of Vauxhall and the masquerades — languished where it was a question of a woman who a month before had been fair game for undergraduate gallantry, and who now carried fifty thousand pounds in her hand.

Mr. Pomeroy's next words showed that this aspect of the case was in his mind. "Damme, she ought to be glad to marry anyone of us!" he said, as he packed the cards and handed them to the others that each might shuffle them. "If she is not, the worse for her! We'll put her on bread and water until she sees reason!"

"D'you think Dunborough knew, Tommy?" said Lord Almeric, grinning at the thought of his friend's disappointment. "That she had the money?"

Dunborough's name turned the tutor grave. He shook his head.

"He'll be monstrous mad! Monstrous!" Lord Almeric said with a chuckle; the wine he had drunk was beginning to affect him. "He has paid the postboys and we ride. Well, are you ready? Ready all? Hallo! Who is to draw first?"

"Let's draw for first," said Mr. Pomeroy. "All together!"

"All together!"

"For it's hey, derry down, and it's over the lea.
And it's out with the fox in the dawning!"

sang my lord in an uncertain voice. And then, "Lord! I've a d——d deuce! Tommy has it! Tommy's Pam has it! No, by Gad! Pomeroy, you have won it! Your Queen takes!"

"And I shall take the Queen!" quoth Mr. Pomeroy. Then ceremoniously, "My first draw, I think?"

"Yes," said Mr. Thomasson nervously.

"Yes," said Lord Almeric, gloating with flushed face on the blind backs of the cards as they lay in a long row before him. "Draw away!"

"Then here's for a wife and five thousand a year!" cried Pomeroy. "One, two, three — oh, hang and sink the cards!" he continued with a violent execration, as he flung down the card he had drawn. "Seven's the main! I have no luck! Now, Mr. Parson, get on! Can you do better?"

Mr. Thomasson, a damp flush on his brow, chose his card gingerly, and turned it with trembling fingers. Mr. Pomeroy greeted it with a savage oath, Lord Almeric with a yell of tipsy laughter. It was an eight.

"It is bad to be crabbed, but to be crabbed by a smug like you!" Mr. Pomeroy cried churlishly. Then, "Go on, man!" he said to his lordship. "Don't keep us all night."

Lord Almeric, thus adjured, turned a card with a flourish. It was a King!

"Fal-lal-lal, lal-lal-la!" he sang, rising with a sweep of the arm that brought down two candlesticks. Then, seizing a glass and filling it from the punch-bowl, "Here's your health once more, my lady. And drink her, you envious beggars! Drink her! You shall throw the stocking for us. Lord, we'll have a right royal wedding! And then —"

"Don't you forget the five thousand," said Pomeroy sulkily. He kept his seat, his hands thrust deep into his breeches pockets; he looked the picture of disappointment.

"Not I, dear lad! Not I! Lord, it is as safe as if your banker had it. Just as safe!"

"Umph! She has not taken you yet!" Pomeroy muttered, watching him; and his face relaxed. "No, hang me! she has not!" he continued in a tone but half audible. "And it is even betting she will not. She might take you drunk, but d——n me if she will take you sober!" And, cheered by the reflection, he pulled the bowl to him, and, filling a glass, "Here's to her, my lord," he said, raising it to his lips. "But remember you have only two days."

"Two days!" my lord cried, reeling slightly; the last glass had been too much for him. "We'll be married in two days. See if we are not."

"The Act notwithstanding?" Mr. Pomeroy said, with a sneer.

"Oh, sink the Act!" his lordship retorted. "But where's — where's the door? I shall go," he continued, gazing vacantly about him, "go to her at once, and tell her — tell her I shall marry her! You — you fellows are hiding the door! You are — you are all jealous! Oh, yes! Such a shape and such eyes! You are jealous, hang you!"

Mr. Pomeroy leaned forward and leered at the tutor. "Shall we let him go?" he whispered. "It will mend somebody's chance. What say you, Parson? You stand next. Make it six thousand instead of five, and I'll see to it."

"Let me go to her!" my lord hiccoughed. He was standing, holding by the back of a chair. "I tell you — I — where is she? You are jealous! That's what you are! Jealous! She is fond of me — pretty charmer — and I shall go to her!"

But Mr. Thomasson shook his head; not so much because he shrank from the outrage which the other contemplated with a grin, as because he now wished Lord Almeric to succeed. He thought it possible and even likely that the girl, dazzled by his title, would be willing to take the young sprig of nobility. And the influence of the Doyley family was great.

He shook his head therefore, and Mr. Pomeroy rebuffed, solaced himself with a couple of glasses of punch. After that, Mr. Thomasson pleaded fatigue as his reason for declining to take a hand at any game whatever, and my lord continuing to maunder and flourish and stagger, the host reluctantly suggested bed; and going to the door bawled for Jarvey and his lordship's man. They came, but were found to be incapable of standing when apart. The tutor and Mr. Pomeroy, therefore, took my lord by the arms and partly shoved and partly supported him to his room.

There was a second bed in the chamber. "You had better tumble in there, Parson," said Mr. Pomeroy. "What say you? Will't do?"

"Finely," Tommy answered. "I am obliged to you." And when they had jointly loosened his lordship's cravat, and removed his wig and set the cool jug of small beer within his reach, Mr. Pomeroy bade the other a curt good-night, and took himself off.

Mr. Thomasson waited until his footsteps ceased to echo in the gallery, and then, he scarcely knew why, he furtively opened the door and peeped out. All was dark; and save for the regular tick of the pendulum on the stairs, the house was still. Mr. Thomasson, wondering which way Julia's room lay, stood listening until a stair creaked; and then, retiring precipitately, locked his door. Lord Almeric, in the gloom of the green moreen curtains that draped his huge four-poster, had fallen into a drunken slumber. The shadow of his wig, which Pomeroy had clapped on the wig-stand by the bed, nodded on the wall, as the draft moved the tails. Mr. Thomasson shivered, and, removing the candle — as was his prudent habit of nights — to the hearth, muttered that a goose was walking over his grave, undressed quickly, and jumped into bed.

Chapter XXV

LORD ALMERIC'S SUIT

*W*hen Julia awoke in the morning, without start or shock, to the dreary consciousness of all she had lost, she was still under the influence of the despair which had settled on her spirits overnight, and had run like a dark stain through her troubled dreams. Fatigue of body and lassitude of mind, the natural consequences of the passion and excitement of her adventure, combined to deaden her faculties. She rose aching in all her limbs — yet most at heart — and wearily dressed herself; but neither saw nor heeded the objects round her. The room to which poor puzzled Mrs. Olney had hastily consigned her looked over a sunny stretch of park, sprinkled with gnarled thorn trees that poorly filled the places of the oaks and chestnuts which the gaming-table had consumed. Still, the outlook pleased the eye, nor was the chamber itself lacking in liveliness. The panels on the walls, wherein needlework cockatoos and flamingoes, wrought under Queen Anne, strutted in the care of needlework black-boys, were faded and dull; but the pleasant white dimity with which the bed was hung relieved and lightened them.

To Julia it was all one. Wrapped in bitter thoughts and reminiscences, her bosom heaving from time to time with ill-restrained grief, she gave no thought to such things, or even to her position, until Mrs. Olney appeared and informed her that breakfast awaited her in another room.

Then, "Can I not take it here?" she asked, shrinking painfully from the prospect of meeting anyone.

"Here?" Mrs. Olney repeated. The housekeeper never closed her mouth, except when she spoke; for which reason, perhaps, her face faithfully mirrored the weakness of her mind.

"Yes," said Julia. "Can I not take it here, if you please? I suppose — we shall have to start by-and-by?" she added, shivering.

"By-and-by, ma'am?" Mrs. Olney answered. "Oh, yes."

"Then I can have it here."

"Oh, yes, if you please to follow me, ma'am." And she held the door open.

Julia shrugged her shoulders, and, contesting the matter no further, followed the good woman along a corridor and through a door which shut off a second and shorter passage. From this three doors opened, apparently into as many apartments. Mrs. Olney threw one wide and ushered her into a room damp-smelling, and hung with drab, but of good size and otherwise comfortable. The windows looked over a neglected Dutch garden, which was so rankly overgrown that the box hedges scarce rose above the wilderness of parterres. Beyond this, and divided from it by a deep-sunk fence, a pool fringed with sedges and marsh-weeds carried the eye to an alder thicket that closed the prospect.

Julia, in her relief on finding that the table was laid for one only, paid no heed to the outlook or to the bars that crossed the windows, but sank into a chair and mechanically ate and drank. Apprised after a while that Mrs. Olney had returned and was watching her with fatuous good nature, she asked her if she knew at what hour she was to leave.

"To leave?" said the housekeeper, whose almost invariable custom it was to repeat the last words addressed to her. "Oh, yes, to leave. Of course."

"But at what time?" Julia asked, wondering whether the woman was as dull as she seemed.

"Yes, at what time?" Then after a pause and with a phenomenal effort, "I will go and see — if you please."

She returned presently. "There are no horses," she said. "When they are ready the gentleman will let you know."

"They have sent for some?"

"Sent for some," repeated Mrs. Olney, and nodded, but whether in assent or imbecility it was hard to say.

After that Julia troubled her no more, but rising from her meal had recourse to the window and her own thoughts. These were in unison with the neglected garden and the sullen pool, which even the sunshine failed to enliven. Her heart was torn between the sense of Sir George's treachery — which now benumbed her brain and now awoke it to a fury of resentment — and fond memories of words and looks and gestures, that shook her very frame and left her sick — love-sick and trembling. She did not look forward or form plans; nor, in the dull lethargy in which she was for the most part sunk, was she aware of the passage of time until Mrs. Olney came in with mouth and eyes a little wider than usual, and announced that the gentleman was coming up.

Julia supposed that the woman referred to Mr. Thomasson; and, recalled to the necessity of returning to Marlborough, she gave a reluctant permission. Great was her astonishment when, a moment later, not the tutor, but Lord Almeric, fanning himself with a laced handkerchief and carrying his little French hat under his arm, appeared on the threshold, and entered simpering and bowing. He was extravagantly dressed in a mixed silk coat, pink satin waistcoat, and a mushroom stock, with breeches of silver net and white silk stockings; and had a large pearl pin thrust through his wig. Unhappily, his splendor, designed to captivate the porter's daughter, only served to exhibit more plainly the nerveless hand and sickly cheeks which he owed to last night's debauch.

Apparently he was aware of this, for his first words were, "Oh, Lord! What a twitter I am in! I vow and protest, ma'am, I don't know where you get your roses of a morning. But I wish you would give me the secret."

"Sir!" she said, interrupting him, surprise in her face. "Or" — with a momentary flush of confusion — "I should say, my lord, surely there must be some mistake here."

"None, I dare swear," Lord Almeric answered, bowing gallantly. "But I am in such a twitter" — he dropped his hat and picked it up again — "I hardly know what I am saying. To be sure, I was devilish cut last night! I hope nothing was said to — to — oh, Lord! I mean I hope you were not much incommoded by the night air, ma'am."

"The night air has not hurt me, I thank you," said Julia, who did not take the trouble to hide her impatience.

However, my lord, nothing daunted, expressed himself monstrously glad to hear it; monstrously glad. And after looking about him and humming and hawing, "Won't you sit?" he said, with a killing glance.

"I am leaving immediately," Julia answered, and declined with coldness the chair which he pushed forward. At another time his foppish dress might have moved her to smiles, or his feebleness and vapid oaths

to pity. This morning she needed her pity for herself, and was in no
smiling mood. Her world had crashed around her; she would sit and
weep among the ruins, and this butterfly insect flitted between. After a
moment, as he did not speak, "I will not detain your lordship," she
continued, curtseying frigidly.

"Cruel beauty!" my lord answered, dropping his hat and clasping his
hands in an attitude. And then, to her astonishment, "Look, ma'am,"
he cried with animation, "look, I beseech you, on the least worthy of
your admirers and deign to listen to him. Listen to him while — and
don't, oh, I say, don't stare at me like that," he continued hurriedly,
plaintiveness suddenly taking the place of grandiloquence. "I vow and
protest I am in earnest."

"Then you must be mad!" Julia cried in great wrath. "You can have
no other excuse, sir, for talking to me like that!"

"Excuse!" he cried rapturously. "Your eyes are my excuse, your lips,
your shape! Whom would they not madden, ma'am? Whom would they
not charm — insanitate — intoxicate? What man of sensibility, seeing
them at an immeasurable distance, would not hasten to lay his homage
at the feet of so divine, so perfect a creature, whom even to see is to taste
of bliss! Deign, madam, to — Oh, I say, you don't mean to say you are
really of — offended?" Lord Almeric stuttered in amazement, again
falling lamentably from the standard of address which he had conned
while his man was shaving him. "You — you — look here —"

"You must be mad!" Julia cried, her eyes flashing lightning on the
unhappy beau. "If you do not leave me, I will call for someone to put
you out! How dare you insult me? If there were a bell I could reach —"

Lord Almeric stared in the utmost perplexity; and fallen from his
high horse, alighted on a kind of dignity. "Madam," he said with a little
bow and a strut, "'tis the first time an offer of marriage from one of my
family has been called an insult! And I don't understand it. Hang me!
If we have married fools, we have married high!"

It was Julia's turn to be overwhelmed with confusion. Having nothing
less in her mind than marriage, and least of all an offer of marriage
from such a person, she had set down all he had said to impudence and
her unguarded situation. Apprised of his meaning, she experienced a
degree of shame, and muttered that she had not understood; she craved
his pardon.

"Beauty asks and beauty has!" Lord Almeric answered, bowing and
kissing the tips of his fingers, his self-esteem perfectly restored.

Julia frowned. "You cannot be in earnest," she said.

"Never more in earnest in my life!" he replied. "Say the word — say
you'll have me," he continued, pressing his little hat to his breast and

gazing over it with melting looks, "most adorable of your sex, and I'll call up Pomeroy, I'll call up Tommy, the old woman, too, if you choose, and tell 'em, tell 'em all."

"I must be dreaming," Julia murmured, gazing at him in a kind of fascination.

"Then if to dream is to assent, dream on, fair love!" his lordship spouted with a grand air. And then, "Hang it! that's — that's rather clever of me," he continued. "And I mean it too! Oh, depend upon it, there's nothing that a man won't think of when he's in love! And I am fallen confoundedly in love with — with you, ma'am."

"But very suddenly," Julia replied. She was beginning to recover from her amazement.

"You don't think that I am sincere?" he protested plaintively. "You doubt me! Then —"he advanced a pace towards her with hat and arms extended, "let the eloquence of a — a feeling heart plead for me; a heart, too — yes, too sensible of your charms, and — and your many merits, ma'am! Yes, most adorable of your sex. But there," he added, breaking off abruptly, "I said that before, didn't I? Yes. Lord! what a memory I have got! I am all of a twitter. I was so cut last night, I don't know what I am saying."

"That I believe," Julia said with chilling severity.

"Eh, but — but you do believe I am in earnest?" he cried anxiously. "Shall I kneel to you? Shall I call up the servants and tell them? Shall I swear that I mean honorably? Lord! I am no Mr. Thornhill! I'll make it as public as you like," he continued eagerly. "I'll send for a bishop —"

"Spare me the bishop," Julia rejoined with a faint smile, "and any farther appeals. They come, I am convinced, my lord, rather from your head than your heart."

"Oh, Lord, no!" he cried.

"Oh, Lord, yes," she answered with a spice of her old archness. "I may have a tolerable opinion of my own attractions — women commonly have, it is said. But I am not so foolish, my lord, as to suppose that on the three or four occasions on which I have seen you I can have gained your heart. To what I am to attribute your sudden — shall I call it whim or fancy —" Julia continued with a faint blush, "I do not know. I am willing to suppose that you do not mean to insult me."

Lord Almeric denied it with a woeful face.

"Or to deceive me. I am willing to suppose," she repeated, stopping him by a gesture as he tried to speak, "that you are in earnest for the time, my lord, in desiring to make me your wife, strange and sudden as the desire appears. It is a great honor, but it is one which I must as earnestly and positively decline."

"Why?" he cried, gaping, and then, "O 'swounds, ma'am, you don't mean it?" he continued piteously. "Not have me? Not have me? And why?"

"Because," she said modestly, "I do not love you, my lord."

"Oh, but — but when we are married," he answered eagerly, rallying his scattered forces, "when we are one, sweet maid —"

"That time will never come," she replied cruelly. And then gloom overspreading her face, "I shall never marry, my lord. If it be any consolation to you, no one shall be preferred to you."

"Oh, but, damme, the desert air and all that!" Lord Almeric cried, fanning himself violently with his hat. "I — oh, you mustn't talk like that, you know. Lord! you might be some queer old put of a dowager!" And then, with a burst of sincere feeling, for his little heart was inflamed by her beauty, and his manhood — or such of it as had survived the lessons of Vauxhall, and Mr. Thomasson — rose in arms at sight of her trouble, "See here, child," he said in his natural voice, "say yes, and I'll swear I'll be kind to you! Sink me if I am not! And, mind you, you'll be my lady. You'll to Ranelagh and the masquerades with the best. You shall have your box at the opera and the King's House; you shall have your frolic in the pit when you please, and your own money for loo and brag, and keep your own woman and have her as ugly as the bearded lady, for what I care — I want nobody's lips but yours, sweet, if you'll be kind. And, so help me, I'll stop at one bottle, my lady, and play as small as a Churchwarden's club! And, Lord, I don't see why we should not be as happy together as James and Betty!"

She shook her head; but kindly, with tears in her eyes and a trembling lip. She was thinking of another who might have given her all this, or as much as was to her taste; one with whom she had looked to be as happy as any James and Betty. "It is impossible, my lord," she said.

"Honest Abraham?" he cried, very downcast.

"Oh, yes, yes!"

"S'help me, you are melting!"

"No, no!" she cried, "it is not — it is not that! It is impossible, I tell you. You don't know what you ask," she continued, struggling with the emotion that almost mastered her.

"But, curse me, I know what I want!" he answered gloomily. "You may go farther and fare worse! Lord, I swear you may. I'd be kind to you, and it is not everybody would be that!"

She had turned from him that he might not see her face, and she did not answer. He waited a moment, twiddling his hat; his face was overcast, his mood hung between spite and pity. At last, "Well, 'tisn't my fault," he said; and then relenting again, "But there, I know what women are

— vapors one day, kissing the next. I'll try again, my lady. I am not proud."

She flung him a gesture that meant assent, dissent, dismissal, as he pleased to interpret it. He took it to mean the first, and muttering, "Well, well, have it your own way. I'll go for this time. But hang all prudes, say I," he withdrew reluctantly, and slowly closed the door on her.

As soon as he was gone the tempest, which Julia's pride had enabled her to stern for a time, broke forth in a passion of tears and sobs, and, throwing herself on the shabby window-seat, she gave free vent to her grief. The happy future which the little bean had dangled before her eyes, absurdly as he had fashioned and bedecked it, reminded her all too sharply of that which she had promised herself with one, in whose affections she had fancied herself secure, despite the attacks of the prettiest Abigail in the world. How fondly had her fancy depicted life with him! With what happy blushes, what joyful tremors! And now? What wonder that at the thought a fresh burst of grief convulsed her frame, or that she presently passed from the extremity of grief to the extremity of rage, and, realizing anew Sir George's heartless desertion and more cruel perfidy, rubbed her tear-stained face in the dusty chintz of the window-seat — that had known so many childish sorrows — and there choked the fierce, hysterical words that rose to her lips?

Or what wonder that her next thought was revenge? She sat up, with her back to the window and the unkempt garden, whence the light stole through the disordered masses of her hair; her face to the empty room. Revenge? Yes, she could punish him; she could take this money from him, she could pursue him with a woman's unrelenting spite, she could hound him from the country, she could have all but his life. But none of these things would restore her maiden pride; would remove from her the stain of his false love, or rebut the insolent taunt of the eyes to which she had bowed herself captive. If she could so beat him with his own weapons that he should doubt his conquest, doubt her love; if she could effect that, there was no method she would not adopt, no way she would not take.

Pique in a woman's mind, even in the mind of the best, finds a rival the tool readiest to hand. A wave of crimson swept across Julia's pale face, and she stood up on her feet. Lady Almeric! Lady Almeric Doyley! Here was a revenge, the fittest of revenges, ready to her hand, if she could bring herself to take it. What if, in the same hour in which he heard that his plan had gone amiss, he heard that she was to marry another? and such another that marry almost whom he might she would take precedence of his wife. That last was a small thought, a petty thought, worthy of a smaller mind than Julia's; but she was a woman, and passionate, and the charms of such a revenge in the general, came home to her. It would show him that others valued what he had cast away; it would convince him — she hoped, him I yet, alas! she doubted — that she had taken his suit as lightly as he had meant it. It would give her a home, a place, a settled position in the world.

She followed it no farther; perhaps because she would act on impulse rather than on reason, blindly rather than on foresight. In haste, with trembling fingers, she set a chair below the broken, frayed end of a bell-rope that hung on the wall. Reaching it, as if she feared her resolution might fail before the event, she pulled and pulled frantically, until hurrying footsteps came along the passage, and Mrs. Olney with a foolish face of alarm entered the room.

"Fetch — tell the gentleman to come back," Julia cried, breathing quickly.

"To come back?"

"Yes! The gentleman who was here now."

"Oh, yes, the gentleman," Mrs. Olney murmured. "Your ladyship wishes him?"

Julia's very brow turned crimson; but her resolution held. "Yes, I wish to see him," she said imperiously. "Tell him to come to me!"

She stood erect, panting and defiant, her eyes on the door while the woman went to do her bidding — waited erect, refusing to think, her face set hard, until far down the outer passage — Mrs. Olney had left the door open — the sound of shuffling feet and a shrill prattle of words heralded Lord Almeric's return. Presently he came tripping in with a smirk and a bow, the inevitable little hat under his arm. Before he had recovered the breath the ascent of the stairs had cost him, he was in an attitude that made the best of his white silk stockings.

"See at your feet the most obedient of your slaves, ma'am!" he cried. "To hear was to obey, to obey was to fly! If it's Pitt's diamond you need, or Lady Mary's soap-box, or a new conundrum, or — hang it all! I cannot think of anything else, but command me! I'll forth and get it, stap me if I won't!"

"My lord, it is nothing of that kind," Julia answered, her voice steady, though her cheeks burned.

"Eh? what? It's not!" he babbled. "Then what is it? Command me, whatever it is."

"I believe, my lord," she said, smiling faintly, "that a woman is always privileged to change her mind — once."

My lord stared. Then, gathering her meaning as much from her heightened color as from her words, "What!" he screamed. "Eh? O Lord! Do you mean that you will have me? Eh? Have you sent for me for that?

Do you really mean that?" And he fumbled for his spy-glass that he might see her face more clearly.

"I mean," Julia began; and then, more firmly, "Yes, I do mean that," she said, "if you are of the same mind, my lord, as you were half an hour ago."

"Crikey, but I am!" Lord Almeric cried, fairly skipping in his joy. "By jingo! I am! Here's to you, my lady! Here's to you, ducky! Oh, Lord! but I was fit to kill myself five minutes ago, and those fellows would have done naught but roast me. And now I am in the seventh heaven. Ho! ho!" he continued, with a comical pirouette of triumph, "he laughs best who laughs last. But there, you are not afraid of me, pretty? You'll let me buss you?"

But Julia, with a face grown suddenly white, shrank back and held out her hand.

"Sakes! but to seal the bargain, child," he remonstrated, trying to get near her.

She forced a faint smile, and, still retreating, gave him her hand to kiss. "Seal it on that," she said graciously. Then, "Your lordship will pardon me, I am sure. I am not very well, and — and yesterday has shaken me. Will you be so good as to leave me now, until tomorrow?"

"Tomorrow!" he cried. "Tomorrow! Why, it is an age! An eternity!"

But she was determined to have until tomorrow — God knows why. And, with a little firmness, she persuaded him, and he went.

Chapter XXVI

BOON COMPANIONS

Lord Almeric flew down the stairs on the wings of triumph, rehearsing at each corner the words in which he would announce his conquest. He found his host and the tutor sitting together in the parlor, in the middle of a game of shilling hazard; which they were playing, the former with as much enjoyment and the latter with as much good-humor as consisted with the fact that Mr. Pomeroy was losing, and Mr. Thomasson played against his will. The weather had changed for the worse since morning. The sky was leaden, the trees were dripping, the rain hung in rows of drops along the rails that flanked the avenue. Mr. Pomeroy cursed the damp hole he owned and sighed for town and the Cocoa Tree. The tutor wished he were quit of the company — and his debts. And both were so far from suspecting what had happened upstairs, though the tutor had his hopes, that Mr. Pomeroy was offering three to one against his friend, when Lord Almeric danced in upon them.

"Give me joy!" he cried breathless. "D'you hear, Pom? She'll take me, and I have bussed her! March could not have done it quicker! She's mine, and the pool! She is mine! Give me joy!"

Mr. Thomasson lost not a minute in rising and shaking him by the hand. "My dear lord," he said, in a voice rendered unusually rich and mellow by the prospect of five thousand pounds, "you make me infinitely happy. You do indeed! I give your lordship joy! I assure you that it will ever be a matter of the deepest satisfaction to me that I was the cause under Providence of her presence here! A fine woman, my lord, and a — a commensurate fortune!"

"A fine woman? Gad! you'd say so if you had held her in your arms!" cried my lord, strutting and lying.

"I am sure," Mr. Thomasson hastened to say, "your lordship is every way to be congratulated."

"Gad! you'd say so, Tommy!" the other repeated with a wink. He was in the seventh heaven of delight.

So far all went swimmingly, neither of them remarking that Mr. Pomeroy kept silence. But at this point the tutor, whose temper it was to be uneasy unless all were on his side, happened to turn, saw that he kept his seat, and was struck with the blackness of his look. Anxious to smooth over any unpleasantness, and to recall him to the requirements of the occasion, "Come, Mr. Pomeroy," he cried jestingly, "shall we drink her ladyship, or is it too early in the day?"

Bully Pomeroy thrust his hands deep into his breeches pockets and did not budge. "'Twill be time to drink her when the ring is on!" he said, with an ugly sneer.

"Oh, I vow and protest that's ungenteel," my lord complained. "I vow and protest it is!" he repeated querulously. "See here, Pom, if you had won her I'd not treat you like this!"

"Your lordship has not won her yet," was the churlish answer.

"But she has said it, I tell you. She said she'd have me."

"She won't be the first woman has altered her mind, nor the last,"

Mr. Pomeroy retorted with an oath. "You may be amazing sure of that, my lord." And muttering something about a woman and a fool being near akin, he spurned a dog out of his way, overset a chair, and strode cursing from the room.

Lord Almeric stared after him, his face a queer mixture of vanity and dismay. At last, "Strikes me, Tommy, he's uncommon hard hit," he said, with a simper. "He must have made surprising sure of her. Ah!" he continued with a chuckle, as he passed his hand delicately over his well-curled wig, and glanced at a narrow black-framed mirror that stood between the windows. "He is a bit too old for the women, is Pom. They run to something lighter in hand. Besides, there's a — a way with the pretty creatures, if you take me, and Pom has not got it. Now I flatter myself I have, Tommy, and Julia — it is a sweet name, Julia, don't you think? — Julia is of that way of thinking. Lord! I know women," his lordship continued, beaming the happier the longer he talked. "It is not what a man has, or what he has done, or even his taste in a coat or a wig — though, mind you, a French friseur does a deal to help men to *bonnes fortunes* — but it is a sort of a way one has. The silly creatures cannot stand against it."

Mr. Thomasson hastened to agree, and to vouch her future ladyship's flame in proof of my lord's prowess. But the tutor was a timid man; and the more perfect the contentment with which he viewed the turn things had taken, and the more nearly within his grasp seemed his five thousand, the graver was the misgiving with which he regarded Mr. Pomeroy's attitude. He had no notion what shape that gentleman's hostility might take, nor how far his truculence might aspire. But he guessed that Lord Almeric's victory had convinced the elder man that his task would have been easy had the cards favored him; and when a little later in the day he saw Pomeroy walking in the park in the drenching rain, his hands thrust deep into the pockets of his wrap-rascal and his chin bent on his breast, he trembled. He knew that when men of Mr. Pomeroy's class take to thinking, someone is likely to lose.

At dinner the tutor's fears were temporarily lulled. Mr. Pomeroy put in a sulky appearance, but his gloom, it was presently manifest, was due to the burden of an apology; which, being lamely offered and readily accepted, he relapsed into his ordinary brusque and reckless mood, swearing that they would have the lady down and drink her, or if that were not pleasing, "Damme, we'll drink her any way!" he continued. "I was a toad this morning. No offence meant, my lord. Lover's license, you know. You can afford to be generous, having won the pool."

"And the maid," my lord said with a simper. "Burn me! you are a good fellow, Pom. Give me your hand. You shall see her after dinner.

She said tomorrow; but, hang me! I'll to her this evening."

Mr. Pomeroy expressed himself properly gratified, adding demurely that he would play no tricks.

"No, hang me! no tricks!" my lord cried somewhat alarmed. "Not that —"

"Not that I am likely to displace your lordship, her affections once gained," said Mr. Pomeroy.

He lowered his face to hide a smile of bitter derision, but he might have spared his pains; for Lord Almeric, never very wise, was blinded by vanity. "No, I should think not," he said, with a conceit which came near to deserving the other's contempt. "I should think not, Tommy. Give me twenty minutes of a start, as Jack Wilkes says, and you may follow as you please. I rather fancy I brought down the bird at the first shot?"

"Certainly, my lord."

"I did, didn't I?"

"Most certainly, your lordship did," repeated the obsequious tutor; who, basking in the smiles of his host's good-humor, began to think that things would run smoothly after all. So the lady was toasted, and toasted again. Nay, so great was Mr. Pomeroy's complaisance and so easy his mood, he must needs have up three or four bottles of Brooks and Hellier that had lain in the cellar half a century — the last of a batch — and give her a third time in bumpers and no heel-taps.

But that opened Mr. Thomasson's eyes. He saw that Pomeroy had reverted to his idea of the night before, and was bent on making the young fop drunk, and exposing him in that state to his mistress; perhaps had the notion of pushing him on some rudeness that, unless she proved very compliant indeed, must ruin him forever with her. Three was their dinner hour; it was not yet four, yet already the young lord was flushed and a little flustered, talked fast, swore at Jarvey, and bragged of the girl lightly and without reserve. By six o'clock, if something were not done, he would be unmanageable.

The tutor stood in no little awe of his host. He had tremors down his back when he thought of his violence; nor was this dogged persistence in a design, as cruel as it was cunning, calculated to lessen the feeling. But he had five thousand pounds at stake, a fortune on which he had been pluming himself since noon; it was no time for hesitation. They were dining in the hall at the table at which they had played cards the night before, Jarvey and Lord Almeric's servant attending them. Between the table and the staircase was a screen. The next time Lord Almeric's glass was filled, the tutor, in reaching something, upset the glass and its contents over his own breeches, and amid the laughter of the other two retired behind the screen to be wiped. There he slipped a crown into the servant's hand, and whispered him to keep his master sober and he should have another.

Mr. Pomeroy saw nothing and heard nothing, and for a time suspected nothing. The servant was a crafty fellow, a London rascal, deft at whipping away full bottles. He was an age finding a clean glass, and slow in drawing the next cork. He filled the host's bumper, and Mr. Thomasson's, and had but half a glass for his master. The next bottle he impudently pronounced corked, and when Pomeroy cursed him for a liar, brought him some in an unwashed glass that had been used for Bordeaux. The wine was condemned, and went out; and though Pomeroy, with unflagging spirits, roared to Jarvey to open the other bottles, the butler had got the office, and was slow to bring them. The cheese came and went, and left Lord Almeric cooler than it found him. The tutor was overjoyed at the success of his tactics.

But when the board was cleared, and the bottles were set on, and the men withdrawn, Bully Pomeroy began to push what remained of the Brooks and Hellier after a fashion that boded an early defeat to the tutor's precautions. It was in vain Thomasson clung to the bottle and sometimes returned it Hertfordshire fashion. The only result was that Mr. Pomeroy smelt a rat, gave Lord Almeric a back-hander, and sent the bottle on again, with a grin that told the tutor he was understood.

After that Mr. Thomasson had the choice between sitting still and taking his own part. It was neck or nothing. Lord Almeric was already hiccoughing and would soon be talking thickly. The next time the bottle came round, the tutor retained it, and when Lord Almeric reached, for it, "No, my lord," he said, laughing; "Venus first and Bacchus afterwards. Your lordship has to wait on the lady. When you come down, with Mr. Pomeroy's leave, we'll crack another bottle."

My lord withdrew his hand more readily than the other had hoped. "Right, Tommy," he said. "I'll wait till I come down. What's that song, 'Rich the treasure, sweet the pleasure, sweet is pleasure after pain?' Oh, no, damme! I don't mean that," he continued. "No. How does it go?"

Mr. Pomeroy thrust the bottle into his hands, looking daggers the while at the tutor. "Take another glass," he cried boisterously. "'Swounds, the girl will like you the better for it."

"D'ye think so, Pom? Honest?"

"Sure of it. 'Twill give you spirit, my lord."

"So it will."

"At her and kiss her! Are you going to be governed all your life by that whey-faced old Methodist? Or be your own man? Tell me that."

"My lord, there's fifty thousand pounds upon it," Thomasson said, his face red. And he pushed back the bottle. The setting sun, peeping a moment through the rain clouds and the low-browed lattice windows, flung an angry yellow light on the board and the three flushed faces round it. "Fifty thousand pounds," repeated Mr. Thomasson firmly.

"Damme! so there is!" my lord answered, settling his chin in his cravat and dusting the crumbs from his breeches. "I'll take no more. So there!"

"I thought your lordship was a good-humored man and no flincher," Mr. Pomeroy retorted with a sneer.

"Oh, I vow and protest — if you put it that way," the weakling answered, once more extending his hand, the fingers of which closed lovingly round the bottle, "I cannot refuse. Positively I cannot."

"Fifty thousand pounds!" the tutor said, shrugging his shoulders.

Lord Almeric drew back his hand.

"Why, she'll like you the better!" Pomeroy cried fiercely, as he thrust the bottle to him again. "D'you think a woman doesn't love an easy husband? And wouldn't rather have a good fellow than a thread-paper?"

"Mr. Pomeroy! Mr. Pomeroy!" the tutor said. Such words used of a lord shocked him.

"A milksop! A thing of curds and whey!"

"After marriage, yes," the tutor muttered, pitching his voice cleverly in Lord Almeric's ear, and winking as he leant towards him. "But your lordship has a great stake in't; and to abstain one night — why, sure, my lord, it's a small thing to do for a fine woman and a fortune."

"Hang me! so it is!" Lord Almeric answered. "You are a good friend to me, Tommy." And he flung his glass crashing into the fireplace. "No, Pom; you'd bubble me. You want the pretty charmer yourself. But I'll be hanged if you shall have her. I'll walk, my boy, I'll walk, and at six I'll go to her, and take you too. And mind you, no tricks, Pom. Lord! I know women as well as I know my own head in the glass. You don't bite me."

Pomeroy, with a face like thunder, did not answer; and Lord Almeric, walking a little unsteadily, went to the door, and a moment later became visible through one of the windows. He stood awhile, his back towards them, now sniffing the evening air, and now, with due regard to his mixed silk coat, taking a pinch of snuff.

Mr. Thomasson, his heart beating, wished he had had the courage to go with him. But this would have been to break with his host beyond mending; and it was now too late. He was still seeking a propitiatory phrase with which to break the oppressive silence, when Pomeroy anticipated him.

"You think yourself vastly clever, Mr. Tutor," he growled, his voice hoarse with anger. "You think a bird in the hand is worth two in the bush, I see."

"Ten in the bush," Mr. Thomasson answered, affecting an easiness he did not feel. "Ten fives are fifty."

"Two in the bush I said, and two in the bush I mean," the other retorted, his voice still low. "Take it or leave it," he continued, with a muttered oath and a swift side glance at the windows, through which Lord Almeric was still visible, walking slowly to and fro, and often standing. "If you want it firm, I'll put it in black and white. Ten thousand, or security, the day after we come from church."

The tutor was silent a moment. Then, "It is too far in the bush," he answered in a low voice. "I am willing enough to serve you, Mr. Pomeroy. I assure you, my dear sir, I desire nothing better. But if — if his lordship were dismissed, you'd be as far off as ever. And I should lose my bird in hand."

"She took him. Why should she not take me?"

"He has — no offence — a title, Mr. Pomeroy."

"And is a fool."

Mr. Thomasson raised his hands in deprecation. Such a saying, spoken of a lord, really offended him. But his words went to another point. "Besides, it's a marriage-brocage contract, and void," he muttered. "Void in law."

"You don't trust me?"

"'Twould be of no use, Mr. Pomeroy," the tutor answered, gently shaking his head, and avoiding the issue presented to him. "You could not persuade her. She was in such a humor today, my lord had special advantages. Break it off between them, and she'll come to herself. And she is willful — Lord! you don't know her! Petruchio could not tame her."

"I know nothing about Petruchio," Mr. Pomeroy answered grimly. "Nor who the gentleman was. But I've ways of my own. You can leave that to me."

But Mr. Thomasson, who had only parleyed out of compliance, took fright at that, and rose from the table, shaking his head.

"You won't do it?" Mr. Pomeroy said.

The tutor shook his head again, with a sickly smile. "'Tis too far in the bush," he said.

"Ten thousand," Mr. Pomeroy persisted, his eyes on the other's face. "Man," he continued forcibly, "Do you think you will ever have such a chance again? Ten thousand! Why, 'tis eight hundred a year. 'Tis a gentleman's fortune."

For a moment Mr. Thomasson did waver. Then he put the temptation from him, and shook his head. "You must pardon me, Mr. Pomeroy," he said. "I cannot do it."

"Will not!" Pomeroy cried harshly. "Will not!" And would have said more, but at that moment Jarvey entered behind him.

"Please, your honor," the man said, "the lady would see my lord."

"Oh!" Pomeroy answered coarsely, "she is impatient, is she? Devil take her for me! And him too!" And he sat sulkily in his place.

But the interruption suited Mr. Thomasson perfectly. He went to the outer door, and, opening it, called Lord Almeric, who, hearing what was afoot, hurried in.

"Sent for me!" he cried, pressing his hat to his breast. "Dear creature!" and he kissed his fingers to the gallery. "Positively she is the daintiest, sweetest morsel ever wore a petticoat! I vow and protest I am in love with her! It were brutal not to be, and she so fond! I'll to her at once! Tell her I fly! I stay for a dash of bergamot, and I am with her!"

"I thought that you were going to take us with you," said Mr. Pomeroy, watching him sourly.

"I will! 'Pon honor, I will!" replied the delighted beau. "But she will soon find a way to dismiss you, the cunning baggage! and then, 'Sweet is pleasure after pain.' Ha! Ha! I have it aright this time. Sweet is Plea — oh! the doting rascal! But let us to her! I vow, if she is not civil to you, I'll — I'll be cold to her!"

Chapter XXVII

MR. FISHWICK'S DISCOVERY

We left Sir George Soane and his companions stranded in the little alehouse at Bathford, waiting through the small hours of the night for a conveyance to carry them forward to Bristol. Soap and water, a good meal, and a brief dog's sleep, in which Soane had no share — he spent the night walking up and down — and from which Mr. Fishwick was continually starting with cries and moanings, did something to put them in better plight, if in no better temper. When the dawn came, and with it the chaise-and-four for which they had sent to Bath, they issued forth haggard and unshaven, but resolute; and long before the shops in Bristol had begun to look for custom, the three, with Sir George's servant, descended before the old Bush Inn, near the Docks.

The attorney held strongly the opinion that they should not waste a second before seeking the persons whom Mr. Dunborough had employed; the least delay, he urged, and the men might be gone into hiding. But on this a wrangle took place, in the empty street before the half-roused inn; with a milk-girl and a couple of drunken sailors for witnesses. Mr. Dunborough, who was of the party will-he, nill-he, and asked nothing better than to take out in churlishness the pressure put upon him, stood firmly to it, he would take no more than one person to the men. He would take Sir George, if he pleased, but he would take no one else.

"I'll have no lawyer to make evidence!" he cried boastfully. "And I'll take no one but on terms. I'll have no Jemmy Twitcher with me. That's flat."

Mr. Fishwick in a great rage was for insisting; but Sir George stopped him. "On what terms?" he asked the other.

"If the girl be unharmed, we go unharmed. One and all!" Mr. Dunborough answered. "Damme!" he continued with a great show of bravado, "do you think I am going to peach on 'em? Not I. There's the offer, take it or leave it."

Sir George might have broken down his opposition by the same arguments addressed to his safety which had brought him so far. But time was everything, and Soane was on fire to know the best or worst. "Agreed!" he cried. "Lead the way, sir! And do you, Mr. Fishwick, await me here."

"We must have time," Mr. Dunborough grumbled, hesitating, and looking askance at the attorney — he hated him. "I can't answer for an hour or two. I know a place, and I know another place, and there is another place. And they may be at one or another, or the other. D'you see?"

"I see that it is your business," Sir George answered with a glance, before which the other's eyes fell. "Wait until noon, Mr. Fishwick. If we have not returned at that hour, be good enough to swear an information against this gentleman, and set the constables to work."

Mr. Dunborough muttered that it lay on Sir George's head if ill came of it; but that said, swung sulkily on his heel. Mr. Fishwick, when the two were some way down the street, ran after Soane, and asked in a whisper if his pistols were primed; when he returned satisfied on that point, the servant, whom he had left at the door of the inn, had vanished. The lawyer made a shrewd guess that he would have an eye to his master's safety, and retired into the house with less misgiving.

He got his breakfast early, and afterwards dozed awhile, resting his aching bones in a corner of the coffee-room. It was nine and after, and the tide of life was roaring through the channels of the city when he roused himself, and to divert his suspense and fend off his growing stiffness went out to look about him. All was new to him, but he soon wearied of the main streets, where huge drays laden with puncheons of rum and bales of tobacco threatened to crush him, and tarry seamen, their whiskers hanging in ringlets, jostled him at every crossing. Turning aside into a quiet court he stood to stare at a humble wedding which was leaving a church. He watched the party out of sight, and then, the church-door standing open, he took the fancy to stroll into the building. He looked about him at the maze of dusty green-cushioned pews with little alleys winding hither and thither among them; at the great three-decker with its huge sounding-board; at the royal escutcheon, and the faded tables of the law, and was about to leave as aimlessly as he had entered, when he espied the open vestry door. Popping in his head, his eye fell on a folio bound in sheepskin, that lay open on a chest, a pen and ink beside it.

The attorney was in that state of fatigue of body and languor of mind in which the least trifle amuses. He tiptoed in, his hat in his hand, and licking his lips as he thought of the law-cases that lay enshrined between those covers, he perused a couple of entries with a kind of professional enthusiasm. He was beginning a third, which, being by a different hand, was a little hard to decipher, when a black gown that hung on a hook over against him swung noiselessly outward from the wall, and a little old man emerged from the doorway which it masked.

The lawyer, who was stooping over the register, raised himself guiltily. "Hallo!" he said, to cover his confusion.

"Hallo!" the old man answered with a wintry smile. "A shilling, if you please." And he held out his hand.

"Oh!" said Mr. Fishwick, much chap-fallen, "I was only just — looking out of curiosity."

"It is a shilling to look," the newcomer retorted with a chuckle. "Only one year, I think? Just so, anno domini seventeen hundred and sixty-seven. A shilling, if you please."

Mr. Fishwick hesitated, but in the end professional pride swayed him, he drew out the coin, and grudgingly handed it over. "Well," he said, "it is a shilling for nothing. But, I suppose, as you have caught me, I must pay."

"I've caught a many that way," the old fellow answered as he pouched the shilling. "But there, I do a lot of work upon them. There is not a better register kept anywhere than that, nor a parish clerk that knows more about his register than I do, though I say it that should not. It is clear and clean from old Henry Eighth, with never a break except at the time of the siege, and, by the way, there is an entry about that that you could see for another shilling. No? Well, if you would like to see a year for nothing — No? Now, I know a lad, an attorney's clerk here, name of Chatterton, would give his ears for the offer. Perhaps your name is Smith?" the old fellow continued, looking curiously at Mr. Fishwick. "If it is, you may like to know that the name of Smith is in the register of burials just three hundred-and eighty-three times — was last Friday! Oh, it is not Smith? Well, if it is Brown, it is there two hundred and seventy times — and one over!"

"That is an odd thought of yours," said the lawyer, staring at the conceit.

"So many have said," the old man chuckled. "But it is not Brown? Jones, perhaps? That comes two hundred and — Oh, it is not Jones?"

"It is a name you won't be likely to have once, let alone four hundred times!" the lawyer answered, with a little pride — heaven knows why.

"What may it be, then?" the clerk asked, fairly put on his mettle. And he drew out a pair of glasses, and settling them on his forehead looked fixedly at his companion.

"Fishwick."

"Fishwick! Fishwick? Well, it is not a common name, and I cannot speak to it at this moment. But if it is here, I'll wager I'll find it for you. D'you see, I have them here in alphabet order," he continued, bustling with an important air to a cupboard in the wall, whence he produced a thick folio bound in roughened calf. "Aye, here's Fishwick, in the burial book, do you see, volume two, page seventeen, anno domini 1750, seventeen years gone, that is. Will you see it? 'Twill be only a shilling. There's many pays out of curiosity to see their names."

Mr. Fishwick shook his head.

"Dods! man, you shall!" the old clerk cried generously; and turned the pages. "You shall see it for what you have paid. Here you are. *'Fourteenth of September, William Fishwick, aged eighty-one, barber, West Quay, died the eleventh of the month.'* No, man, you are looking too low. Higher on the page! Here 'tis, do you see? Eh — what is it? What's the matter with you?"

"Nothing," Mr. Fishwick muttered. But he continued to stare at the page with a face struck suddenly sallow, while the hand that rested on the corner of the book shook as with the ague.

"Nothing?" the old man said, staring suspiciously at him. "I do believe it is something. I do believe it is money. Well, it is five shillings to extract. So there!"

That seemed to change Mr. Fishwick's view. "It might be money," he confessed, still speaking thickly, and as if his tongue were too large for his mouth. "It might be," he repeated. "But — I am not very well this morning. Do you think you could get me a glass of water?"

"None of that!" the old man retorted sharply, with a sudden look of alarm. "I would not leave you alone with that book at this moment for all the shillings I have taken! So if you want water you've got to get it."

"I am better now," Mr. Fishwick answered. But the sweat that stood on his brow went far to belie his words. "I — yes, I think I'll take an extract. Sixty-one, was he?"

"Eighty-one, eighty-one, it says. There's pen and ink, but you'll please to give me five shillings before you write. Thank you kindly. Lord save us, but that is not the one. You're taking out the one above it."

"I'll have 'em all — for identification," Mr. Fishwick replied, wiping his forehead nervously.

"Sho! You have no need."

"I think I will."

"What, all?"

"Well, the one before and the one after."

"Dods! man, but that will be fifteen shillings!" the clerk cried, aghast at such extravagance.

"You'll only charge for the entry I want?" the lawyer said with an effort.

"Well — we'll say five shillings for the other two."

Mr. Fishwick closed with the offer, and with a hand which was still unsteady paid the money and extracted the entries. Then he took his hat, and hurriedly, his eyes averted, turned to go.

"If it's money," the old clerk said, staring at him as if he could never satisfy his inquisitiveness, "you'll not forget me?"

"If it's money," Mr. Fishwick said with a ghastly smile, "it shall be some in your pocket."

"Thank you kindly. Thank you kindly, sir! Now who would ha' thought when you stepped in here you were stepping into fortune, so to speak?"

"Just so," Mr. Fishwick answered, a spasm distorting his face. "Who'd have thought it? Good morning!"

"And good-luck!" the clerk bawled after him. "Good-luck!"

Mr. Fishwick fluttered a hand backward, but made no answer. His first object was to escape from the court; this done, he plunged through a stream of traffic, and having covered his trail, went on rapidly, seeking a quiet corner. He found one in a square among some warehouses, and standing, pulled out the copy he had made from the register. It was neither on the first nor the second entry, however, that his eyes dwelled, while the hand that held the paper shook as with the ague. It was the third fascinated him: —

"*September 19th,*" it ran, "*at the Bee in Steep Street, Julia, daughter of Anthony and Julia Soane of Estcombe, aged three, and buried the 21st of the month.*"

Mr. Fishwick read it thrice, his lips quivering; then he slowly drew from a separate pocket a little sheaf of papers, frayed at the corners, and soiled with much and loving handling. He selected from these a slip; it was one of those which Mr. Thomasson had surprised on the table in the room at the Castle Inn. It was a copy of the attestation of birth "of Julia, daughter of Anthony Soane, of Estcombe, England, and Julie his wife"; the date, August, 1747; the place, Dunquerque.

The Attorney drew a long quivering breath, and put the papers up again, the packet in the place from which he had taken it, the extract from the Bristol register in another pocket. Then, after drawing one or two more sighs as if his heart were going out of him, he looked dismally upwards as in protest against heaven. At length he turned and went back to the thoroughfare, and there, with a strangely humble air, asked a passer-by the nearest way to Steep Street.

The man directed him; the place was near at hand. In two minutes Mr. Fishwick found himself at the door of a small but decent grocer's shop, over the portal of which a gilded bee seemed to prognosticate more business than the fact performed. An elderly woman, stout and comfortable-looking, was behind the counter. Eyeing the attorney as he came forward, she asked him what she could do for him, and before he could answer reached for the snuff canister.

He took the hint, requested an ounce of the best Scotch and Havannah mixed, and while she weighed it, asked her how long she had lived there.

"Twenty-six years, sir," she answered heartily, "Old Style. For the New, I don't hold with it nor them that meddle with things above them. I am sure it brought me no profit," she continued, rubbing her nose. "I have buried a good husband and two children since they gave it us!"

"Still, I suppose people died Old Style?" the lawyer ventured.

"Well, well, may be."

"There was a death in this house seventeen years gone this September," he said, "if I remember rightly."

The woman pushed away the snuff and stared at him. "Two, for the matter of that," she said sharply. "But should I remember you?"

"No."

"Then, if I may make so bold, what is't to you?" she retorted. "Do you come from Jim Masterson?"

"He is dead," Mr. Fishwick answered.

She threw up her hands. "Lord! And he a young man, so to speak! Poor Jim! Poor Jim! It is ten years and more — aye, more — since I heard from him. And the child? Is that dead too?"

"No, the child is alive," the lawyer answered, speaking at a venture, "I am here on her behalf, to make some inquiries about her kinsfolk."

The woman's honest red face softened and grew motherly. "You may inquire," she said, "you'll learn no more than I can tell you. There is no one left that's kin to her. The father was a poor Frenchman, a monsieur that taught the quality about here; the mother was one of his people — she came from Canterbury, where I am told there are French and to spare. But according to her account she had no kin left. He died the year after the child was born, and she came to lodge with me, and lived by teaching, as he had; but 'twas a poor livelihood, you may say, and when she sickened, she died — just as a candle goes out."

"When?" Mr. Fishwick asked, his eyes glued to the woman's face.

"The week Jim Masterson came to see us bringing the child from foreign parts — that was buried with her. 'Twas said his child took the fever from her and got its death that way. But I don't know. I don't know. It is true they had not brought in the New Style then; but —"

"You knew him before? Masterson, I mean?"

"Why, he had courted me!" was the good-tempered answer. "You don't know much if you don't know that. Then my good man came along and I liked him better, and Jim went into service and married Oxford-shire way. But when he came to Bristol after his journey in foreign parts, 'twas natural he should come to see me; and my husband, who was always easy, would keep him a day or two — more's the pity, for in twenty-four hours the child he had with him began to sicken, and died. And never was man in such a taking, though he swore the child was not his, but one he had adopted to serve a gentleman in trouble; and because his wife had none. Any way, it was buried along with my lodger, and nothing would serve but he must adopt the child she had left. It seemed ordainedlike, they being of an age, and all. And I had two children to care for, and was looking for another that never came; and the mother had left no more than buried her with a little help. So he took it with him, and we heard from him once or twice, how it fared, and that his wife took to it, and the like; and then — well, writing's a burden. But," with renewed interest, "she's a well-grown girl by now, I guess?"

"Yes," the attorney answered absently, "she — she's a well-grown girl."

"And is poor Jim's wife alive?"

"Yes."

"Ah," the good woman answered, looking thoughtfully into the street. "If she were not — I'd think about taking to the girl myself. It's lonely at times without chick or child. And there's the shop to tend. She could help with that."

The attorney winced. He was looking ill; wretchedly ill. But he had his back to the light, and she remarked nothing save that he seemed to be a somber sort of body and poor company. "What was the Frenchman's name?" he asked after a pause.

"Parry," said she. And then, sharply, "Don't they call her by it?"

"It has an English sound," he said doubtfully, evading her question.

"That is the way he called it. But it was spelled Pare, just Pare."

"Ah," said Mr. Fishwick. "That explains it." He wondered miserably why he had asked what did not in the least matter; since, if she were not a Soane, it mattered not who she was. After an interval he recovered himself with a sigh. "Well, thank you," he continued, "I am much obliged to you. And now — for the moment — good-morning, ma'am. I must wish you good-morning," he repeated, hurriedly; and took up his snuff.

"But that is not all?" the good woman exclaimed in astonishment. "At any rate you'll leave your name?"

Mr. Fishwick pursed up his lips and stared at her gloomily. "Name?" he said at last. "Yes, ma'am, certainly. Brown. Mr. Peter Brown, the — the Poultry —"

"The Poultry!" she cried, gaping at him helplessly.

"Yes, the Poultry, London. Mr. Peter Brown, the Poultry, London. And now I have other business and shall — shall return another day. I must wish you good-morning, ma'am, Good-morning." And thrusting his face into his hat, Mr. Fishwick bundled precipitately into the street, and with singular recklessness made haste to plunge into the thickest of the traffic, leaving the good woman in a state of amazement.

Nevertheless, he reached the inn safely. When Mr. Dunborough returned from a futile search, his failure in which condemned him to another twenty-four hours in that company, the first thing he saw was the attorney's gloomy face awaiting them in a dark corner of the coffee-room. The sight reproached him subtly, he knew not why; he was in the worst of tempers, and, for want of a better outlet, he vented his spleen on the lawyer's head.

"D——n you!" he cried, brutally. "Your hangdog phiz is enough to spoil any sport! Hang me if I believe that there is such another mumping, whining, whimpering sneak in the 'varsal world! D'you think anyone will have luck with your tallow face within a mile of him?" Then longing, but not daring, to turn his wrath on Sir George, "What do you bring him for?" he cried.

"For my convenience," Sir George retorted, with a look of contempt that for the time silenced the other. And that said, Soane proceeded to explain to Mr. Fishwick, who had answered not a word, that the rogues had got into hiding; but that by means of persons known to Mr. Dunborough it was hoped that they would be heard from that evening or the next. Then, struck by the attorney's sickly face, "I am afraid you are not well, Mr. Fishwick," Sir George continued, more kindly. "The night has been too much for you. I would advise you to lie down for a few hours and take some rest. If anything is heard I will send word to you."

Mr. Fishwick thanked him, without meeting his eyes; and after a minute or two retired. Sir George looked after him, and pondered a little on the change in his manner. Through the stress of the night Mr. Fishwick had shown himself alert and eager, ready and not lacking in spirit; now he had depression written large on his face, and walked and bore himself like a man sinking under a load of despondency.

All that day the messenger from the slums was expected but did not come; and between the two men who sat downstairs, strange relations prevailed. Sir George did not venture to let the other out of his sight; yet there were times when they came to the verge of blows, and nothing but the knowledge of Sir George's swordsmanship kept Mr. Dunborough's temper within bounds. At dinner, at which Sir George insisted that the attorney should sit down with them, Dunborough drank his two bottles of wine, and in his cups fell into a strain peculiarly provoking.

"Lord! you make me sick," he said. "All this pother about a girl that a month ago your high mightiness would not have looked at in the street. You are vastly virtuous now, and sneer at me; but, damme! which of us loves the girl best? Take away her money, and will you marry her? I'd 'a done it, without a rag to her back. But take away her money, and will you do the same, Mr. Virtuous?"

Sir George listening darkly, and putting a great restraint on himself, did not answer. Mr. Fishwick waited a moment, then got up suddenly, and hurried from the room — with a movement so abrupt that he left his wine-glass in fragments on the floor.

Chapter XXVIII

A ROUGH AWAKENING

Lord Almeric continued to vapor and romance as he mounted the stairs. Mr. Pomeroy attended, sneering, at his heels. The tutor followed, and longed to separate them. He had his fears for the one and of the other, and was relieved when his lordship at the last moment hung back, and with a foolish chuckle proposed a plan that did more honor to his vanity than his taste.

"Hist!" he whispered. "Do you two stop outside a minute, and you'll hear how kind she'll be to me! I'll leave the door ajar, and then in a minute do you come in and roast her! Lord, 'twill be as good as a play!"

Mr. Pomeroy shrugged his shoulders. "As you please," he growled. "But I have known a man go to shear and be shorn!"

Lord Almeric smiled loftily, and waiting for no more, winked to them, turned the handle of the door, and simpered in.

Had Mr. Thomasson entered with him, the tutor would have seen at a glance that he had wasted his fears; and that whatever trouble threatened brooded in a different quarter. The girl, her face a blaze of excitement and shame and eagerness, stood in the recess of the farther window seat, as far from the door as she could go; her attitude the attitude of one driven into a corner. And from that alone her lover should have taken warning. But Lord Almeric saw nothing, feared nothing. Crying "Most lovely Julia!" he tripped forward to embrace her, and, the wine emboldening him, was about to clasp her in his arms, when she checked him by a gesture unmistakable even by a man in his flustered state.

"My lord," she said hurriedly, yet in a tone of pleading — and her head hung a little, and her cheeks began to flame. "I ask your forgiveness for having sent for you. Alas, I have also to ask your forgiveness for a more serious fault. One — one which you may find it less easy to pardon," she added, her courage failing.

"Try me!" the little beau answered with ardor; and he struck an attitude. "What would I not forgive to the loveliest of her sex?" And under cover of his words he made a second attempt to come within reach of her.

She waved him back. "No!" she said. "You do not understand me."

"Understand?" he cried effusively. "I understand enough to — but why, my Chloe, these alarms, this bashfulness? Sure," he spouted,

"How can I see you, and not love,
    While you as Opening East are fair?
While cold as Northern Blasts you prove,
    How can I love and not despair?"

And then, in wonder at his own readiness, "S'help me! that's uncommon clever of me," he said. "But when a man is in love with the most beautiful of her sex —"

"My lord!" she cried, stamping the floor in her impatience. "I have something serious to say to you. Must I ask you to return to me at another time? Or will you be good enough to listen to me now?"

"Sho, if you wish it, child," he said lightly, taking out his snuff-box. "And to be sure there is time enough. But between us two, sweet —"

"There is nothing between us!" she cried, impetuously snatching at the word. "That is what I wanted to tell you. I made a mistake when I said that there should be. I was mad; I was wicked, if you like. Do you hear me, my lord?" she continued passionately. "It was a mistake. I did not know what I was doing. And, now I do understand, I take it back."

Lord Almeric gasped. He heard the words, but the meaning seemed incredible, inconceivable; the misfortune, if he heard aright, was too terrible; the humiliation too overwhelming! He had brought listeners — and for this! "Understand?" he cried, looking at her in a confused, chap-fallen way. "Hang me if I do understand! You don't mean to say — Oh, it is impossible, stuff me! it is. You don't mean that — that you'll not have me? After all that has come and gone, ma'am?"

She shook her head; pitying him, blaming herself, for the plight in which she had placed him. "I sent for you, my lord," she said humbly, "that I might tell you at once. I could not rest until I had told you. I did what I could. And, believe me, I am very, very sorry."

"But do you mean — that you — you jilt me?" he cried, still fighting off the dreadful truth.

"Not jilt!" she said, shivering.

"That you won't have me?"

She nodded.

"After — after saying you would?" he wailed.

"I cannot," she answered. Then, "Cannot you understand?" she cried, her face scarlet. "I did not know until — until you went to kiss me."

"But — oh, I say — but you love me?" he protested.

"No, my lord," she said firmly. "No. And there, you must do me the justice to acknowledge that I never said I did."

He dashed his hat on the floor: he was almost weeping. "Oh, damme!" he cried, "a woman should not — should not treat a man like this. It's low. It's cruel! It's —"

A knock on the door stopped him. Recollection of the listeners, whom he had momentarily forgotten, revived, and overwhelmed him. With an oath he sprang to shut the door, but before he could intervene Mr. Pomeroy appeared smiling on the threshold; and behind him the reluctant tutor.

Lord Almeric swore, and Julia, affronted by the presence of strangers at such a time, drew back, frowning. But Bully Pomeroy would see nothing. "A thousand pardons if I intrude," he said, bowing this way and that, that he might hide a lurking grin. "But his lordship was good enough to say a while ago, that he would present us to the lady who had consented to make him happy. We little thought last night, ma'am, that so much beauty and so much goodness were reserved for one of us."

Lord Almeric looked ready to cry. Julia, darkly red, was certain that they had overheard; she stood glaring at the intruders, her foot tapping the floor. No one answered, and Mr. Pomeroy, after looking from one to the other in assumed surprise, pretended to hit on the reason. "Oh, I see; I spoil sport!" he cried with coarse joviality. "Curse me if I meant to! I fear we have come *mal à propos,* my lord, and the sooner we are gone the better.

"And though she found his usage rough,
  Yet in a man 'twas well enough!"

he hummed, with his head on one side and an impudent leer. "We are interrupting the turtledoves, Mr. Thomasson, and had better be gone."

"Curse you! Why did you ever come?" my lord cried furiously. "But she won't have me. So there! Now you know."

Mr. Pomeroy struck an attitude of astonishment.

"Won't have you?" he cried, "Oh, stap me! you are biting us."

"I'm not! And you know it!" the poor little blood answered, tears of vexation in his eyes. "You know it, and you are roasting me!"

"Know it?" Mr. Pomeroy answered in tones of righteous indignation.

"I know it? So far from knowing it, my dear lord, I cannot believe it! I understood that the lady had given you her word."

"So she did."

"Then I cannot believe that a lady would anywhere, much less under my roof, take it back. Madam, there must be some mistake here," Mr. Pomeroy continued warmly. "It is intolerable that a man of his lordship's rank should be so treated. I'm forsworn if he has not mistaken you."

"He does not mistake me now," she answered, trembling and blushing painfully. "What error there was I have explained to him."

"But, damme —"

"Sir!" she said with awakening spirit, her eyes sparkling. "What has happened is between his lordship and myself. Interference on the part of anyone else is an intrusion, and I shall treat it as such. His lordship understood —"

"Curse me! He does not look as if he understood," Mr. Pomeroy cried, allowing his native coarseness to peep through. "Sink me, ma'am, there is a limit to prudishness. Fine words butter no parsnips. You plighted your troth to my guest, and I'll not see him thrown over i' this fashion. These airs and graces are out of place. I suppose a man has some rights under his own roof, and when his guest is jilted before his eyes" — here Mr. Pomeroy frowned like Jove — "it is well you should know, ma'am, that a woman no more than a man can play fast and loose at pleasure."

She looked at him with disdain. "Then the sooner I leave your roof the better, sir," she said.

"Not so fast there, either," he answered with an unpleasant smile. "You came to it when you chose, and you will leave it when we choose; and that is flat, my girl. This morning, when my lord did you the honor to ask you, you gave him your word. Perhaps tomorrow morning you'll be of the same mind again. Any way, you will wait until tomorrow and see."

"I shall not wait on your pleasure," she cried, stung to rage.

"You will wait on it, ma'am! Or 'twill be the worse for you."

Burning with indignation she turned to the other two, her breath coming quick. But Mr. Thomasson gazed gloomily at the floor, and would not meet her eyes; and Lord Almeric, who had thrown himself into a chair, was glowering sulkily at his shoes. "Do you mean," she cried, "that you will dare to detain me, sir?"

"If you put it so," Pomeroy answered, grinning, "I think I dare take it on myself."

His voice full of mockery, his insolent eyes, stung her to the quick.

"I will see if that be so," she cried, fearlessly advancing on him. "Lay a finger on me if you dare! I am going out. Make way, sir."

"You are not going out!" he cried between his teeth. And held his ground in front of her.

She advanced until she was within touch of him, then her courage failed her; they stood a second or two gazing at one another, the girl with heaving breast and cheeks burning with indignation, the man with cynical watchfulness. Suddenly, shrinking from actual contact with him, she sprang aside, and was at the door before he could intercept her. But with a rapid movement he turned on his heel, seized her round the waist before she could open the door, dragged her shrieking from it, and with an oath — and not without an effort — flung her panting and breathless into the window-seat. "There!" he cried ferociously, his blood fired by the struggle; "lie there! And behave yourself, my lady, or I'll find means to quiet you. For you," he continued, turning fiercely on the tutor, whose face the sudden scuffle and the girl's screams had blanched to the hue of paper, "did you never hear a woman squeak before? And you, my lord? Are you so dainty? But, to be sure, 'tis your lordship's mistress," he continued ironically. "Your pardon. I forgot that. I should not have handled her so roughly. However, she is none the worse, and 'twill bring her to reason."

But the struggle and the girl's cries had shaken my lord's nerves. "D——n you!" he cried hysterically, and with a stamp of the foot, "you should not have done that."

"Pooh, pooh," Mr. Pomeroy answered lightly. "Do you leave it to me, my lord. She does not know her own mind. 'Twill help her to find it. And now, if you'll take my advice, you'll leave her to a night's reflection."

But Lord Almeric only repeated, "You should not have done that."

Mr. Pomeroy's face showed his scorn for the man whom a cry or two and a struggling woman had frightened. Yet he affected to see art in it. "I understand. And it is the right line to take," he said; and he laughed unpleasantly. "No doubt it will be put to your lordship's credit. But now, my lord," he continued, "let us go. You will see she will have come to her senses by tomorrow."

The girl had remained passive since her defeat. But at this she rose from the window-seat where she had crouched, slaying them with furious glances. "My lord," she cried passionately, "if you are a man, if you are a gentleman — you'll not suffer this."

But Lord Almeric, who had recovered from his temporary panic, and was as angry with her as with Pomeroy, shrugged his shoulders. "Oh, I don't know," he said resentfully. "It has naught to do with me, ma'am.

I don't want you kept, but you have behaved uncommon low to me; uncommon low. And 'twill do you good to think on it. Stap me, it will!"

And he turned on his heel and sneaked out.

Mr. Pomeroy laughed insolently. "There is still Tommy," he said. "Try him. See what he'll say to you. It amuses me to hear you plead, my dear; you put so much spirit into it. As my lord said, before we came in, 'tis as good as a play."

She flung him a look of scorn, but did not answer. For Mr. Thomasson, he shuffled his feet uncomfortably. "There are no horses," he faltered, cursing his indiscreet companion. "Mr. Pomeroy means well, I know. And as there are no horses, even if nothing prevented you, you could not go tonight, you see."

Mr. Pomeroy burst into a shout of laughter and clapped the stammering tutor (fallen miserably between two stools) on the back. "There's a champion for you!" he cried. "Beauty in distress! Lord! how it fires his blood and turns his look to flame! What! going, Tommy?" he continued, as Mr. Thomasson, unable to bear his raillery or the girl's fiery scorn, turned and fled ignobly. "Well, my pretty dear, I see we are to be left alone. And, damme! quite right too, for we are the only man and the only woman of the party, and should come to an understanding."

Julia looked at him with shuddering abhorrence. They were alone; the sound of the tutor's retreating footsteps was growing faint. She pointed to the door. "If you do not go," she cried, her voice shaking with rage, "I will rouse the house! I will call your people! Do you hear me? I will so cry to your servants that you shall not for shame dare to keep me! I will break this window and cry for help?"

"And what do you think I should be doing meanwhile?" he retorted with an ugly leer. "I thought I had shown you that two could play at that game. But there, child, I like your spirit! I love you for it! You are a girl after my own heart, and, damme! we'll live to laugh at those two old women yet!"

She shrank farther from him with an expression of loathing. He saw the look, and scowled, but for the moment he kept his temper. "Fie! the Little Masterson playing the grand lady!" he said. "But there, you are too handsome to be crossed, my dear. You shall have your own way tonight, and I'll come and talk to you tomorrow, when your head is cooler and those two fools are out of the way. And if we quarrel then, my beauty, we can but kiss and make it up. Look on me as your friend," he added, with a leer from which she shrank, "and I vow you'll not repent it."

She did not answer, she only pointed to the door, and finding that he could draw nothing from her, he went at last. On the threshold he turned, met her eyes with a grin of meaning, and took the key from the inside of the lock. She heard him insert it on the outside, and turn it, and had to grip one hand with the other to stay the scream that arose in her throat. She was brave beyond most women; but the ease with which he had mastered her, the humiliation of contact with him, the conviction of her helplessness in his grasp lay on her still. They filled her with fear; which grew more definite as the light, already low in the corners of the room, began to fail, and the shadows thickened about the dingy furniture, and she crouched alone against the barred window, listening for the first tread of a coming foot — and dreading the night.

Chapter XXIX

MR. POMEROY'S PLAN

M<small>r.</small> Pomeroy chuckled as he went down the stairs. Things had gone so well for him, he owed it to himself to see that they went better, he had mounted with a firm determination to effect a breach even if it cost him my lord's enmity. He descended, the breach made, the prize open to competition, and my lord obliged by friendly offices and unselfish service.

Mr. Pomeroy smiled. "She is a saucy baggage," he muttered, "but I've tamed worse. 'Tis the first step is hard, and I have taken that. Now to deal with Mother Olney. If she were not such a fool, or if I could be rid of her and Jarvey, and put in the Tamplins, all's done. But she'd talk! The kitchen wench need know nothing; for visitors, there are none in this damp old hole. Win over Mother Olney and the Parson — and I don't see where I can fail. The wench is here, safe and tight, and bread and water, damp and loneliness will do a great deal. She don't deserve better treatment, hang her impudence!"

But when he appeared in the hall an hour later, his gloomy face told a different story. "Where's Doyley?" he growled; and stumbled over a dog, kicked it howling into a corner. "Has he gone to bed?"

The tutor, brooding sulkily over his wine, looked up. "Yes," he said, as rudely as he dared — he was sick with disappointment. "He is going in the morning."

"And a good riddance!" Pomeroy cried with an oath. "He's off it, is he? He gives up?"

The tutor nodded gloomily. "His lordship is not the man," he said, with an attempt at his former manner, "to — to —"

"To win the odd trick unless he holds six trumps," Mr. Pomeroy cried. "No, by God! he is not. You are right, Parson. But so much the better for you and me!"

Mr. Thomasson sniffed. "I don't follow you," he said stiffly.

"Don't you? You weren't so dull years ago," Mr. Pomeroy answered, filling a glass as he stood. He held it in his hand and looked over it at the other, who, ill at ease, fidgeted in his chair, "You could put two and two together then, Parson, and you can put five and five together now. They make ten — thousand."

"I don't follow you," the tutor repeated, steadfastly looking away from him.

"Why? Nothing is changed since we talked — except that he is out of it! And that that is done for me for nothing, which I offered you five thousand to do. But I am generous, Tommy. I am generous."

"The next chance is mine," Mr. Thomasson cried, with a glance of spite.

Mr. Pomeroy, looking down at him, laughed — a galling laugh. "Lord! Tommy, that was a hundred years ago," he said contemptuously.

"You said nothing was changed!"

"Nothing is changed in my case," Mr. Pomeroy answered confidently, "except for the better. In your case everything is changed — for the worse. Did you take her part upstairs? Are your hands clean now? Does she see through you or does she not? Or, put it in another way, my friend. It is your turn; what are you going to do?"

"Go," the tutor answered viciously. "And glad to be quit."

Mr. Pomeroy sat down opposite him. "No, you'll not go," he said in a low voice; and drinking off half his wine, set down the glass and regarded the other over it. "Five and five are ten, Tommy. You are no fool, and I am no fool."

"I am not such a fool as to put my neck in a noose," the tutor retorted. "And there is no other way of coming at what you want, Mr. Pomeroy."

"There are twenty," Pomeroy returned coolly. "And, mark you, if I fail, you are spun, whether you help rue or no. You are blown on, or I can blow on you! You'll get nothing for your cut on the head."

"And what shall I get if I stay?"

"I have told you."

"The gallows."

"No, Tommy. Eight hundred a year."

Mr. Thomasson sneered incredulously, and having made it plain that he refused to think — thought! He had risked so much in this enterprise, gone through so much; and to lose it all! He cursed the girl's fickleness, her coyness, her obstinacy! He hated her. And do what he might for her now, he doubted if he could cozen her or get much from her. Yet in that lay his only chance, apart from Mr. Pomeroy. His eye was cunning and his tone sly when he spoke.

"You forget one thing," he said. "I have only to open my lips after I leave."

"And I am nicked?" Mr. Pomeroy answered. "True. And you will get a hundred guineas, and have a worse than Dunborough at your heels."

The tutor wiped his brow. "What do you want?" he whispered.

"That old hag of a housekeeper has turned rusty," Pomeroy answered. "She has got it into her head something is going to be done to the girl. I sounded her and I cannot trust her. I could send her packing, but Jarvey is not much better, and talks when he is drunk. The girl must be got from here."

Mr. Thomasson raised his eyebrows scornfully.

"You need not sneer, you fool!" Pomeroy cried with a little spirt of rage. "'Tis no harder than to get her here."

"Where will you take her?"

"To Tamplin's farm by the river. There, you are no wiser, but you may trust me. I can hang the man, and the woman is no better. They have done this sort of thing before. Once get her there, and, sink me! she'll be glad to see the parson!"

The tutor shuddered. The water was growing very deep. "I'll have no part in it!" he said hoarsely. "No part in it, so help me God!"

"There's no part for you!" Mr. Pomeroy answered with grim patience. "Your part is to thwart me."

Mr. Thomasson, half risen from his chair, sat down again. "What do you mean?" he muttered.

"You are her friend. Your part is to help her to escape. You're to sneak to her room tomorrow, and tell her that you'll steal the key when I'm drunk after dinner. You'll bid her be ready at eleven, and you'll let her out, and have a chaise waiting at the end of the avenue. The chaise will be there, you'll put her in, you'll go back to the house. I suppose you see it now?"

The tutor stared in wonder. "She'll get away," he said.

"Half a mile," Mr. Pomeroy answered dryly, as he filled his glass. "Then I shall stop the chaise — with a pistol if you like, jump in — a merry surprise for the nymph; and before twelve we shall be at Tamplin's. And you'll be free of it."

Mr. Thomasson pondered, his face flushed, his eyes moist. "I think you are the devil!" he said at last.

"Is it a bargain? And see here. His lordship has gone silly on the girl. You can tell him before he leaves what you are going to do. He'll leave easy, and you'll have an evidence — of your good intentions!" Mr. Pomeroy added with a chuckle. "Is it a bargain?"

"I'll not do it!" Mr. Thomasson cried faintly. "I'll not do it!"

But he sat down again, their heads came together across the table; they talked long in low voices. Presently Mr. Pomeroy fetched pen and paper from a table in one of the windows; where they lay along with one or two odd volumes of Crebillon, a tattered Hoyle on whist, and Foote's jest book. A note was written and handed over, and the two rose.

Mr. Thomasson would have liked to say a word before they parted as to no violence being contemplated or used; something smug and fair-seeming that would go to show that his right hand did not understand what his left was doing. But even his impudence was unequal to the task, and with a shamefaced good-night he secured the memorandum in his pocketbook and sneaked up to bed.

He had every opportunity of carrying out Pomeroy's suggestion to make Lord Almeric his confidant. For when he entered the chamber which they shared, he found his lordship awake, tossing and turning in the shade of the green moreen curtains; in a pitiable state between chagrin and rage. But the tutor's nerve failed him. He had few scruples — it was not that; but he was weary and sick at heart, and for that night he felt that he had done enough. So to all my lord's inquiries he answered as sleepily as consisted with respect, until the effect which he did not wish to produce was produced. The young roué's suspicions were aroused, and on a sudden he sat up in bed, his nightcap quivering on his head.

"Tommy!" he cried feverishly. "What is afoot downstairs? Now, do you tell me the truth."

"Nothing," Mr. Thomasson answered soothingly.

"Because — well, she's played it uncommon low on me, uncommon low she's played it," my lord complained pathetically; "but fair is fair, and willing's willing! And I'll not see her hurt. Pom's none too nice, I know, but he's got to understand that. I'm none of your Methodists, Tommy, as you are aware, no one more so! But, s'help me! no one shall lay a hand on her against her will!"

"My dear lord, no one is going to!" the tutor answered, quaking in his bed.

"That is understood, is it? Because it had better be!" the little lord continued with unusual vigor. "I vow I have no cause to stand up for her. She's a d——d saucy baggage, and has treated me with — with d——d disrespect. But, oh Lord! Tommy, I'd have been a good husband to her. I would indeed. And been kind to her. And now — she's made a fool of me! She's made a fool of me!"

And my lord took off his nightcap, and wiped his eyes with it.

Chapter XXX

A GREEK GIFT

*J*ulia, left alone, and locked in the room, passed such a night as a girl instructed in the world's ways might have been expected to pass in her position, and after the rough treatment of the afternoon. The room grew dark, the dismal garden and weedy pool that closed the prospect faded from sight; and still as she crouched by the barred window, or listened breathless at the door, all that part of the house lay silent. Not a sound of life came to the ear.

By turns she resented and welcomed this. At one time, pacing the floor in a fit of rage and indignation, she was ready to dash herself against the door, or scream and scream and scream until someone came to her. At another the recollection of Pomeroy's sneering smile, of his insolent grasp, revived to chill and terrify her; and she hid in the darkest corner, hugged the solitude, and, scarcely daring to breathe, prayed that the silence might endure forever.

But the hours in the dark room were long and cold; and at times the fever of rage and fear left her in the chill. Of this came another phase through which she passed, as the night wore on and nothing happened.

Her thoughts reverted to him who should have been her protector, but had become her betrayer — and by his treachery had plunged her into this misery; and on a sudden a doubt of his guilt flashed into her mind and blinded her by its brilliance. Had she done him an injustice? Had the abduction been, after all, concerted not by him but by Mr. Thomasson and his confederates? The setting down near Pomeroy's gate, the reception at his house, the rough, hasty suit paid to her — were these all parts of a drama cunningly arranged to mystify her? And was he innocent? Was *he* still her lover, true, faithful, almost her husband?

If she could think so! She rose, and softly walked the floor in the darkness, tears raining down her face. Oh, if she could be sure of it! At the thought, the thought only, she glowed from head to foot with happy shame. And fear? If this were so, if his love were still hers, and hers the only fault — of doubting him, she feared nothing! Nothing! She felt her way to a tray in the corner where her last meal remained untasted, and ate and drank humbly, and for him. She might need her strength.

She had finished, and was groping her return to the window-seat, when a faint rustle as of someone moving on the other side of the door caught her ear. She had fancied herself brave enough an instant before, but in the darkness a great horror of fear came on her. She stood rooted to the spot; and heard the noise again. It was followed by the sound of a hand passed stealthily over the panels; a hand seeking, as she thought, for the key; and she could have shrieked in her helplessness. But while she stood, her face turned to stone, came instant relief, A voice, subdued in fear, whispered, "Hist, ma'am, hist! Are you asleep?"

She could have fallen on her knees in her thankfulness. "No! no!" she cried eagerly. "Who is it?"

"It is me — Olney!" was the answer. "Keep a heart, ma'am! They are gone to bed. You are quite safe."

"Can you let me out?" Julia cried. "Oh, let me out!"

"Let you out?"

"Yes, yes! Let me out? Please let me out."

"God forbid, ma'am!" was the horrified answer. "He'd kill me. And he has the key. But —"

"Yes? yes?"

"Keep your heart up, ma'am, for Jarvey'll not see you hurt; nor will I. You may sleep easy. And good-night!"

She stole away before Julia could answer; but she left comfort. In a glow of thankfulness the girl pushed a chair against the door, and, wrapping herself for warmth in the folds of the shabby curtains, lay down on the window seat. She was willing to sleep now, but the agitation of her thoughts, the whirl of fear and hope that prevailed in them, as she went again and again over the old ground, kept her long awake. The moon had risen and run its course, decking the old garden with a solemn beauty as of death, and was beginning to retreat before the dawn, when Julia slept at last.

When she awoke it was broad daylight. A moment she gazed upwards, wondering where she was; the next a harsh grating sound, and the echo of a mocking laugh brought her to her feet in a panic of remembrance.

The key was still turning in the lock — she saw it move, saw it withdrawn; but the room was empty. And while she stood staring and listening heavy footsteps retired along the passage. The chair which she had set against the door had been pushed back, and milk and bread stood on the floor beside it.

She drew a deep breath; he had been there. But her worst terrors had passed with the night. The sun was shining, filling her with scorn of her jailer. She panted to be face to face with him, that she might cover him with ridicule, overwhelm him with the shafts of her woman's wit, and show him how little she feared and how greatly she despised him.

But he did not appear; the hours passed slowly, and with the afternoon came a clouded sky, and weariness and reaction of spirits; fatigue of body, and something like illness; and on that a great terror. If they drugged her in her food? The thought was like a knife in the girl's heart, and while she still writhed on it, her ear caught the creak of a board in the passage, and a furtive tread that came, and softly went again, and once more returned. She stood, her heart beating; and fancied she heard the sound of breathing on the other side of the door. Then her eye alighted on a something white at the foot of the door, that had not been there a minute earlier. It was a tiny note. While she gazed at it the footsteps stole away again.

She pounced on the note and opened it, thinking it might be from Mrs. Olney. But the opening lines smacked of other modes of speech than hers; and though Julia had no experience of Mr. Thomasson's epistolary style, she felt no surprise when she found the initials F.T. appended to the message.

"Madam," it ran. "You are in danger here, and I in no less of being held to account for acts which my heart abhors. Openly to oppose myself to Mr. P. — the course my soul dictates — were dangerous for us both, and another must be found. If he drink deep tonight, I will, heaven assisting, purloin the key, and release you at ten, or as soon after as may be. Jarvey, who is honest, and fears the turn things are taking, will have a carriage waiting in the road. Be ready, hide this, and when you are free, though I seek no return for services attended by much risk, yet if you desire to find one, an easy way may appear of requiting,

"Madam, your devoted, obedient servant, F.T."

Julia's face glowed. "He cannot do even a kind act as it should be done," she thought. "But once away it will be easy to reward him. At worst he shall tell me how I came to be set down here."

She spent the rest of the day divided between anxiety on that point — for Mr. Thomasson's intervention went some way to weaken the theory she had built up with so much joy — and impatience for night to come and put an end to her suspense. She was now as much concerned to escape the ordeal of Mr. Pomeroy's visit as she had been earlier in the day to see him. And she had her wish. He did not come; she fancied he might be willing to let the dullness and loneliness, the monotony and silence of her prison, work their effect on her mind.

Night, as welcome today as it had been yesterday unwelcome, fell at last, and hid the dingy familiar room, the worn furniture, the dusky outlook. She counted the minutes, and before it was nine by the clock was the prey of impatience, thinking the time past and gone and the tutor a poor deceiver. Ten was midnight to her; she hoped against hope, walking her narrow bounds in the darkness. Eleven found her lying on her face on the floor, heaving dry sobs of despair, her hair disheveled. And then, on a sudden she sprang up; the key was grating in the lock! While she stared, half demented, scarcely believing her happiness, Mr. Thomasson appeared on the threshold, his head — he wore no wig — muffled in a woman's shawl, a shaded lantern in his hand.

"Come!" he said. "There is not a moment to be lost."

"Oh!" she cried hysterically, yet kept her shaking voice low; "I thought you were not coming. I thought it was all over."

"I am late," he answered nervously; his face was pale, his shifty eyes avoided hers. "It is eleven o'clock, but I could not get the key before. Follow me closely and silently, child; and in a few minutes you will be safe."

"Heaven bless you!" she cried, weeping. And would have taken his hand.

But at that he turned from her so abruptly that she marveled, for she had not judged him a man averse from thanks. But setting his manner down to the danger and the need of haste, she took the hint and controlling her feelings, prepared to follow him in silence. Holding the lantern so that its light fell on the floor he listened an instant, then led the way on tiptoe down the dim corridor. The house was hushed round them; if a board creaked under their feet, it seemed to her scared ears a pistol shot. At the entrance to the gallery which was partly illumined by lights still burning in the hall below, the tutor paused anew an instant to listen, then turned quickly from it, and by a narrow passage on the right gained a back staircase. Descending the steep stairs he guided her by devious turnings through dingy offices and servants' quarters until they stood in safety before an outer door. To withdraw the bar that secured it, while she held the lantern, was for the tutor the work of an instant. They passed through, and he closed the door softly behind them.

After the confinement of her prison, the night air that blew on her temples was rapture to Julia; for it breathed of freedom. She turned her face up to the dark boughs that met and interlaced above her head, and whispered her thankfulness. Then, obedient to Mr. Thomasson's impatient gesture, she hastened to follow him along a dank narrow path that skirted the wall of the house for a few yards, then turned off among the trees.

They had left the wall no more than a dozen paces behind them, when Mr. Thomasson paused, as in doubt, and raised his light. They were in a little beech-coppice that grew close up to the walls of the servants' offices. The light showed the dark shining trunks, running in solemn rows this way and that; and more than one path trodden smooth across the roots. The lantern disclosed no more, but apparently this was enough for Mr. Thomasson. He pursued the path he had chosen, and less than a minute's walking brought them to the avenue.

Julia drew a breath of relief and looked behind and before. "Where is the carriage?" she whispered, shivering with excitement.

The tutor before he answered raised his lantern thrice to the level of his head, as if to make sure of his position. Then, "In the road," he answered. "And the sooner you are in it the better, child, for I must return and replace the key before he sobers. Or 'twill, be worse for me," he added snappishly, "than for you."

"You are not coming with me?" she exclaimed in surprise.

"No, I — I can't quarrel with him," he answered hurriedly. "I — I am under obligations to him. And once in the carriage you'll be safe."

"Then please to tell me this," Julia rejoined, her breath a little short. "Mr. Thomasson, did you know anything of my being carried off before it took place?"

"I?" he cried effusively. "Did I know?"

"I mean — were you employed — to bring me to Mr. Pomeroy's?"

"I employed? To bring you to Mr. Pomeroy's? Good heavens! ma'am, what do you take me for?" the tutor cried in righteous indignation. "No, ma'am, certainly not! I am not that kind of man!" And then blurting out the truth in his surprise, "Why, 'twas Mr. Dunborough!" he said. "And like him too! Heaven keep us from him!"

"Mr. Dunborough?" she exclaimed.

"Yes, yes."

"Oh," she said, in a helpless, foolish kind of way. "It was Mr. Dunborough, was it?" And she begged his pardon. And did it too so humbly, in a voice so broken by feeling and gratitude, that, bad man as he was, his soul revolted from the work he was upon; and for an instant, he stood still, the lantern swinging in his hand.

She misinterpreted the movement. "Are we right?" she said, anxiously. "You don't think that we are out of the road?" Though the night was dark, and it was difficult to discern, anything beyond the circle of light thrown by the lantern, it struck her that the avenue they were traversing was not the one by which she had approached the house two nights before. The trees seemed to stand farther from one another and to be smaller. Or was it her fancy?

But it was not that had moved him to stand; for in a moment, with a curious sound between a groan and a curse he led the way on, without answering her. Fifty paces brought them to the gate and the road. Thomasson held up his lantern and looked over the gate.

"Where is the carriage?" she whispered, startled by the darkness and silence.

"It should be here," he answered, his voice betraying his perplexity. "It should be here at this gate. But I — I don't see it."

"Would it have lights?" she asked anxiously. He had opened the gate by this time, and as she spoke they passed through, and stood together looking up and down the road. The moon was obscured, and the lantern's rays were of little use to find a carriage which was not there.

"It should be here, and it should have lights," he said in evident dismay. "I don't know what to think of it. I — ha! What is that? It is coming, I think. Yes, I hear it. The coachman must have drawn off a little for some reason, and now he has seen the lantern."

He had only the sound of wheels to go upon, but he proved to be right; she uttered a sigh of relief as the twin lights of a carriage apparently approaching round a bend of the road broke upon them. The lights drew near and nearer, and the tutor waved his lamp. For a second the driver appeared to be going to pass them; then, as Mr. Thomasson again waved his lantern and shouted, he drew up.

"Halloa!" he said.

Mr. Thomasson did not answer, but with a trembling hand opened the door and thrust the girl in. "God bless you!" she murmured; "and —"
He slammed the door, cutting short the sentence.

"Well?" the driver said, looking down at him, his face in shadow; "I am —"

"Go on!" Mr. Thomasson cried peremptorily, and waving his lantern again, startled the horses; which plunged away wildly, the man tugging vainly at the reins. The tutor fancied that, as it started, he caught a faint scream from the inside of the chaise, but he set it down to fright caused by the sudden jerk; and, after he had stood long enough to assure himself that the carriage was keeping the road, he turned to retrace his steps to the house.

He was feeling for the latch of the gate — his thoughts no pleasant ones, for the devil pays scant measure — when his ear was surprised by a new sound of wheels approaching from the direction whence the chaise had come. He stood to listen, thinking he heard an echo; but in a second or two he saw lights approaching through the night precisely as the other lights had approached. Once seen they came on swiftly, and he was still standing gaping in wonder when a carriage and pair, a postboy riding and a servant sitting outside, swept by, dazzling him a moment; the next it was gone, whirled away into the darkness.

Chapter XXXI

THE INN AT CHIPPENHAM

*T*he road which passed before the gates at Bastwick was not a highway, and Mr. Thomasson stood a full minute, staring after the carriage, and wondering what chance brought a traveler that way at that hour. Presently it occurred to him that one of Mr. Pomeroy's neighbors might have dined abroad, have sat late over the wine, and be now returning; and that so the incident might admit of the most innocent explanation. Yet it left him uneasy. Until the last hum of wheels died in the distance he stood listening and thinking. Then he turned from the gate, and with a shiver betook himself towards the house. He had done his part.

Or had he? The road was not ten paces behind him, when a cry rent the darkness, and he paused to listen. He caught the sound of hasty footsteps crossing the open ground on his right, and apparently approaching; and he raised his lantern in alarm. The next moment a dark form vaulted the railings that fenced the avenue on that side, sprang on the affrighted tutor, and, seizing him violently by the collar, shook him to and fro as a terrier shakes a rat.

It was Mr. Pomeroy, beside himself with rage. "What have you done with her?" he cried. "You treacherous hound! Answer, or by heaven I shall choke you!"

"Done – done with whom?" the tutor gasped, striving to free himself. "Mr. Pomeroy, I am not – what does this – mean?"

"With her? With the girl?"

"She is – I have put her in the carriage! I swear I have! Oh!" he shrieked, as Mr. Pomeroy, in a fresh access of passion, gripped his throat and squeezed it. "I have put her in the carriage, I tell you! I have done everything you told me!"

"In the carriage? What carriage? In what carriage?"

"The one that was there."

"At the gate?"

"Yes, yes."

"You fool! You imbecile!" Mr. Pomeroy roared, as he shook him with all his strength. "The carriage is at the other gate."

Mr. Thomasson gasped, partly with surprise, partly under the influence of Pomeroy's violence. "At the other gate?" he faltered. "But – there was a carriage here. I saw it. I put her in it. Not a minute ago!"

"Then, by heaven, it was your carriage, and you have betrayed me," Pomeroy retorted; and shook his trembling victim until his teeth chattered and his eyes protruded. "I thought I heard wheels and I came to see. If you don't tell me the truth this instant," he continued furiously, "I'll have the life out of you."

"It is the truth," Mr. Thomasson stammered, blubbering with fright. "It was a carriage that came up – and stopped. I thought it was yours, and I put her in. And it went on."

"A lie, man – a lie!"

"I swear it is true! I swear it is! If it were not should I be going back to the house? Should I be going to face you?" Mr. Thomasson protested.

The argument impressed Pomeroy; his grasp relaxed. "The devil is in it, then!" he muttered. "For no one else could have set a carriage at that gate at that minute! Anyway, I'll know. Come on!" he continued recklessly snatching up the lantern, which had fallen on its side and was not extinguished. "We'll after her! By the Lord, we'll after her. They don't trick me so easily!"

The tutor ventured a terrified remonstrance, but Mr. Pomeroy, deaf to his entreaties and arguments, bundled him over the fence, and, gripping his arm, hurried him as fast as his feet would carry him across the sward to the other gate. A carriage, its lamps burning brightly, stood in the road. Mr. Pomeroy exchanged a few curt words with the driver, thrust in the tutor, and followed himself. On the instant the vehicle dashed away, the coachman cracking his whip and shouting oaths at his horses.

The hedges flew by, pale glimmering walls in the lamplight; the mud flew up and splashed Mr. Pomeroy's face; still he hung out of the window, his hand on the fastening of the door, and a brace of pistols on the ledge before him; while the tutor, shuddering at these preparations, hoping against hope that they would overtake no one, cowered in the farther corner. With every turn of the road or swerve of the horses Pomeroy expected to see the fugitives' lights. Unaware or oblivious that the carriage he was pursuing had the start of him by so much that at top speed he could scarcely look to overtake it under the hour, his rage increased with every disappointment. Although the pace at which they traveled over a rough road was such as to fill the tutor with instant terror and urgent thoughts of death — although first one lamp was extinguished and then another, and the carriage swung so violently as from moment to moment to threaten an overturn, Mr. Pomeroy never ceased to hang out of the window, to yell at the horses and upbraid the driver.

And with all, the labor seemed to be wasted. With wrath and a volley of curses he saw the lights of Chippenham appear in front, and still no sign of the pursued. Five minutes later the carriage awoke the echoes in the main street of the sleeping town, and Mr. Thomasson drew a deep breath of relief as it came to a stand.

Not so Mr. Pomeroy. He dashed the door open and sprang out, prepared to overwhelm the driver with reproaches. The man anticipated him. "They are here," he said with a sulky gesture.

"Here? Where?"

A man in a watchman's coat, and carrying a staff and lantern — of whom the driver had already asked a question — came heavily round, from the off-side of the carriage. "There is a chaise and pair just come in from the Melksham Road," he said, "and gone to the Angel, if that is what you want, your honor."

"A lady with them?"

"I saw none, but there might be."

"How long ago?"

"Ten minutes."

"We're right!" Mr. Pomeroy cried with a jubilant oath, and turning back to the door of the carriage, slipped the pistols into his skirt pockets. "Come," he said to Thomasson. "And do you," he continued, addressing his driver, who was no other than the respectable Tamplin, "follow at a walking pace. Have they ordered on?" he asked, slipping a crown into the night-watchman's hand.

"I think not, your honor," the man answered. "I believe they are staying."

With a word of satisfaction Mr. Pomeroy hurried his unwilling companion towards the inn. The streets were dark; only an oil lamp or two burned at distant points. But the darkness of the town was noon-day light in comparison of the gloom which reigned in Mr. Thomasson's mind. In the grasp of this headstrong man, whose temper rendered him blind to obstacles and heedless of danger, the tutor felt himself swept along, as incapable of resistance as the leaf that is borne upon the stream. It was not until they turned into the open space before the Angel, and perceived a light in the doorway of the inn that despair gave him courage to remonstrate.

Then the risk and folly of the course they were pursuing struck him so forcibly that he grew frantic. He clutched Mr. Pomeroy's sleeve, and dragging him aside out of earshot of Tamplin, who was following them, "This is madness!" he urged vehemently. "Sheer madness! Have you considered, Mr. Pomeroy? If she is here, what claim have we to interfere with her? What authority over her? What title to force her away? If we had overtaken her on the road, in the country, it might have been one thing. But here —"

"Here?" Mr. Pomeroy retorted, his face dark, his under-jaw thrust out hard as a rock. "And why not here?"

"Because — why, because she will appeal to the people."

"What people?"

"The people who have brought her hither."

"And what is their right to her?" Mr. Pomeroy retorted, with a brutal oath.

"The people at the inn, then."

"Well, and what is their right? But — I see your point, parson! Damme, you are a cunning one. I had not thought of that. She'll appeal to them, will she? Then she shall be my sister, run off from her home! Ha! Ha! Or no, my lad," he continued, chuckling savagely, and slapping the tutor on the back; "they know me here, and that I have no sister. She shall be your daughter!" And while Mr. Thomasson stared aghast, Pomeroy laughed recklessly. "She shall be your daughter, man! My guest, and run off with an Irish ensign! Oh, by Gad, we'll nick her! Come on!"

Mr. Thomasson shuddered. It seemed to him the wildest scheme — a folly beyond speech. Resisting the hand with which Pomeroy would have impelled him towards the lighted doorway, "I will have nothing to do with it!" he cried, with all the firmness he could muster. "Nothing! Nothing!"

"A minute ago you might have gone to the devil!" Mr. Pomeroy answered grimly, "and welcome! Now, I want you. And, by heaven, if you don't stand by me I'll break your back! Who is there here who is likely to know you? Or what have you to fear?"

"She'll expose us!" Mr. Thomasson whimpered. "She'll tell them!"

"Who'll believe her?" the other answered with supreme contempt. "Which is the more credible story — hers about a lost heir, or ours? Come on, I say!"

Mr. Thomasson had been far from anticipating a risk of this kind when he entered on his career of scheming. But he stood in mortal terror of his companion, whose reckless passions were fully aroused; and after a brief resistance he succumbed. Still protesting, he allowed himself to be urged past the open doors of the inn-yard — in the black depths of which the gleam of a lantern, and the form of a man moving to and fro, indicated that the strangers' horses were not yet bedded — and up the hospitable steps of the Angel Inn.

A solitary candle burning in a room on the right of the hall, guided their feet that way. Its light disclosed a red-curtained snuggery, well furnished with kegs and jolly-bodied jars, and rows of bottles; and in the middle of this cheerful profusion the landlord himself, stooping over a bottle of port, which he was lovingly decanting. His array, a horseman's coat worn over night-gear, with bare feet thrust into slippers, proved him newly risen from bed; but the hum of voices and clatter of plates which came from the neighboring kitchen were signs that, late as it was, the good inn was not caught napping.

The host heard their steps behind him, but crying "Coming, gentlemen, coming!" finished his task before he turned. Then "Lord save us!" he ejaculated, staring at them — the empty bottle in one hand, the decanter in the other. "Why, the road's alive tonight! I beg your honor's pardon, I am sure, and yours, sir! I thought 'twas one of the gentlemen that arrived, awhile ago — come down to see why supper lagged. Squire Pomeroy, to be sure! What can I do for you, gentlemen? The fire is scarce out in the Hertford, and shall be rekindled at once?"

Mr. Pomeroy silenced him by a gesture. "No," he said; "we are not staying. But you have some guests here, who arrived half an hour ago?"

"To be sure, your honor. The same I was naming." "Is there a young lady with them?"

The landlord looked hard at him. "A young lady?" he said.

"Yes! Are you deaf, man?" Pomeroy retorted wrathfully, his impatience getting the better of him. "Is there a young lady with them? That is what I asked."

But the landlord still stared; and it was only after an appreciable interval that he answered cautiously: "Well, to be sure, I am not — I am not certain. I saw none, sir. But I only saw the gentlemen when they had gone upstairs. William admitted them, and rang up the stables. A young lady?" he continued, rubbing his head as if the question perplexed him. "May I ask, is't someone your honor is seeking?"

"Damme, man, should I ask if it weren't?" Mr. Pomeroy retorted angrily. "If you must know, it is this gentleman's daughter, who has run away from her friends."

"Dear, dear!"

"And taken up with a beggarly Irishman!"

The landlord stared from one to the other in great perplexity. "Dear me!" he said. "That is sad! The gentleman's daughter!" And he looked at Mr. Thomasson, whose fat sallow face was sullenness itself. Then, remembering his manners, "Well, to be sure, I'll go and learn," he continued briskly. "Charles!" to a half-dressed waiter, who at that moment appeared at the foot of the stairs, "set lights in the Yarmouth and draw these gentlemen what they require. I'll not be many minutes, Mr. Pomeroy."

He hurried up the narrow staircase, and an instant later appeared on the threshold of a room in which sat two gentlemen, facing one another in silence before a hastily-kindled fire. They had traveled together from Bristol, cheek by jowl in a post-chaise, exchanging scarce as many words as they had traversed miles. But patience, whether it be of the sullen or the dignified cast, has its limits; and these two, their tempers exasperated by a chilly journey taken fasting, had come very near to the end of sufferance. Fortunately, at the moment Mr. Dunborough — for he was the one — made the discovery that he could not endure Sir George's impassive face for so much as the hundredth part of another minute — and in consequence was having recourse to his invention for the most brutal remark with which to provoke him — the port and the landlord arrived together; and William, who had carried up the cold beef and stewed kidneys by another staircase, was heard on the landing. The host helped to place the dishes on the table. Then he shut out his assistant.

"By your leave, Sir George," he said diffidently. "But the young lady you were inquiring for? Might I ask — ?"

He paused as if he feared to give offence. Sir George laid down his knife and fork and looked at him. Mr. Dunborough did the same. "Yes, yes, man," Soane said. "Have you heard anything? Out with it!"

"Well, sir, it is only — I was going to ask if her father lived in these parts."

"Her father?"

"Yes, sir."

Mr. Dunborough burst into rude laughter. "Oh, Lord!" he said. "Are we grown so proper of a sudden? Her father, damme!"

Sir George shot a glance of disdain at him. Then, "My good fellow," he said to the host, "her father has been dead these fifteen years."

The landlord reddened, annoyed by the way Mr. Dunborough had taken him. "The gentleman mistakes me, Sir George," he said stiffly. "I did not ask out of curiosity, as you, who know me, can guess; but to be plain, your honor, there are two gentlemen below stairs, just come in; and what beats me, though I did not tell them so, they are also in search of a young lady."

"Indeed?" Sir George answered, looking gravely at him. "Probably they are from the Castle Inn at Marlborough, and are inquiring for the lady we are seeking."

"So I should have thought," the landlord answered, nodding sagely; "but one of the gentlemen says he is her father, and the other —"

Sir George stared. "Yes?" he said, "What of the other?"

"Is Mr. Pomeroy of Bastwick," the host replied, lowering his voice. "Doubtless your honor knows him?"

"By name."

"He has naught to do with the young lady?"

"Nothing in the world."

"I ask because — well, I don't like to speak ill of the quality, or of those by whom one lives, Sir George; but he has not got the best name in the county; and there have been wild doings at Bastwick of late, and writs and bailiffs and worse. So I did not up and tell him all I knew."

On a sudden Dunborough spoke. "He was at College, at Pembroke," he said. "Doyley knows him. He'd know Tommy too; and we know Tommy is with the girl, and that they were both dropped Laycock way. Hang me, if I don't think there is something in this!" he continued, thrusting his feet into slippers: his boots were drying on the hearth. "Thomasson is rogue enough for anything! See here, man," he went on, rising and flinging down his napkin; "do you go down and draw them into the hall, so that I can hear their voices. And I will come to the head of the stairs. Where is Bastwick?"

"Between here and Melksham, but a bit off the road, sir."

"It would not be far from Laycock?"

"No, your honor; I should think it would be within two or three miles of it. They are both on the flat the other side of the river."

"Go down! go down!" Mr. Dunborough answered. "And pump him, man! Set him talking. I believe we have run the old fox to earth. It will be our fault if we don't find the vixen!"

Chapter XXXII

CHANCE MEDLEY

*B*y this time the arrival of a second pair of travelers hard on the heels of the first had roused the inn to full activity. Half-dressed servants flitted this way and that through the narrow passages, setting nightcaps in the chambers, or bringing up clean snuffers and snuff trays. One was away to the buttery, to draw ale for the driver, another to the kitchen with William's orders to the cook. Lights began to shine in the hall and behind the diamond panes of the low-browed windows; a pleasant hum, a subdued bustle, filled the hospitable house.

On entering the Yarmouth, however, the landlord was surprised to find only the clergyman awaiting him. Mr. Pomeroy, irritated by his long absence, had gone to the stables to learn what he could from the postboy. The landlord was nearer indeed than he knew to finding no one; for when he entered, Mr. Thomasson, unable to suppress his fears, was on his feet; another ten seconds, and the tutor would have fled panic-stricken from the house.

The host did not suspect this, but Mr. Thomasson thought he did; and the thought added to his confusion. "I — I was coming to ask what had happened to you," he stammered. "You will understand, I am very anxious to get news."

"To be sure, sir," the landlord answered comfortably. "Will you step this way, and I think we shall be able to ascertain something for certain?"

But the tutor did not like his tone; moreover, he felt safer in the room than in the public hall. He shrank back. "I — I think I will wait here until Mr. Pomeroy returns," he said.

The landlord raised his eyebrows. "I thought you were anxious, sir," he retorted, "to get news?"

"So I am, very anxious!" Mr. Thomasson replied, with a touch of the stiffness that marked his manner to those below him. "Still, I think I had better wait here. Or, no, no!" he cried, afraid to stand out, "I will come with you. But, you see, if she is not here, I am anxious to go in search of her as quickly as possible, where — wherever she is."

"To be sure, that is natural," the landlord answered, holding the door open that the clergyman might pass out, "seeing that you are her father, sir. I think you said you were her father?" he continued, as Mr. Thomasson, with a scared look round the hall, emerged from the room.

"Ye — yes," the tutor faltered; and wished himself in the street. "At least — I am her step-father."

"Oh, her step-father!"

"Yes," Mr. Thomasson answered, faintly. How he cursed the folly that had put him in this false position! How much more strongly he would have cursed it, had he known what it was cast that dark shadow, as of a lurking man, on the upper part of the stairs!

"Just so," the landlord answered, as he paused at the foot of the staircase. "And, if you please — what might your name be, sir?"

A cold sweat rose on the tutor's brow; he looked helplessly towards the door. If he gave his name and the matter were followed up, he would be traced, and it was impossible to say what might not come of it. At last, "Mr. Thomas," he said, with a sneaking guilty look.

"Mr. Thomas, your reverence?"

"Yes."

"And the young lady's name would be Thomas, then?"

"N-no," Mr. Thomasson faltered. "No. Her name — you see," he continued, with a sickly smile, "she is my step-daughter."

"To be sure, your reverence. So I understood. And her name?"

The tutor glowered at his persecutor. "I protest, you are monstrous inquisitive," he said, with a sudden sorry air of offence. "But, if you must know, her name is Masterson; and she has left her friends to join — to join a — an Irish adventurer."

It was unfortunately said; the more as the tutor in order to keep his eye on the door, by which he expected Mr. Pomeroy to reenter, had turned his back on the staircase. The lie was scarcely off his lips when a heavy hand fell on his shoulder, and, twisting him round with a jerk, brought him face to face with an old friend. The tutor's eyes met those of Mr. Dunborough, he uttered one low shriek, and turned as white as paper. He knew that Nemesis had overtaken him.

But not how heavy a Nemesis! For he could not know that the landlord of the Angel owned a restive colt, and no farther back than the last fair had bought a new whip; nor that that very whip lay at this moment where the landlord had dropped it, on a chest so near to Mr. Dunborough's hand that the tutor never knew how he became possessed of it. Only he saw it imminent, and would have fallen in sheer terror, his coward's knees giving way under him, if Mr. Dunborough had not driven him back against the wall with a violence that jarred the teeth in his head.

"You liar!" the infuriated listener cried; "you lying toad!" and shook him afresh with each sentence. "She has run away from her friends, has she? With an Irish adventurer, eh? And you are her father? And your name is Thomas? Thomas, eh! Well, if you do not this instant tell me where she is, I'll Thomas you! Now, come! One! Two! Three!"

In the last words seemed a faint promise of mercy; alas! it was fallacious. Mr. Thomasson, the lash impending over him, had time to utter one cry; no more. Then the landlord's supple cutting-whip, wielded by a vigorous hand, wound round the tenderest part of his legs — for at the critical instant Mr. Dunborough dragged him from the wall — and with a gasping shriek of pain, pain such as he had not felt since boyhood, Mr. Thomasson leapt into the air. As soon as his breath returned, he strove frantically to throw himself down; but struggle as he might, pour forth screams, prayers, execrations, as he might, all was vain. The hour of requital had come. The cruel lash fell again and again, raising great wheals on his pampered body: now he clutched Mr. Dunborough's arm only to be shaken off; now he groveled on the floor; now he was plucked up again, now an ill-directed cut marked his cheek. Twice the landlord, in pity and fear for the man's life, tried to catch Mr. Dunborough's arm and stay the punishment; once William did the same — for ten seconds of this had filled the hall with staring servants. But Mr. Dunborough's arm and the whirling whip kept all at a distance; nor was it until a tender-hearted housemaid ran in at risk of her beauty, and clutched his wrist and hung on it, that he tossed the whip away, and allowed Mr. Thomasson to drop, a limp moaning rag on the floor.

"For shame!" the girl cried hysterically. "You blackguard! You cruel blackguard!"

"'Tis he's the blackguard, my dear!" the honorable Mr. Dunborough answered, panting, but in the best of tempers. "Bring me a tankard of something; and put that rubbish outside, landlord. He has got no more than he deserved, my dear."

Mr. Thomasson uttered a moan, and one of the waiters stooping over him asked him if he could stand. He answered only by a faint groan, and the man raising his eyebrows, looked gravely at the landlord; who, recovered from the astonishment into which the fury and suddenness of the assault had thrown him, turned his indignation on Mr. Dunborough.

"I am surprised at you, sir," he cried, rubbing his hands with vexation. "I did not think a gentleman in Sir George's company would act like this! And in a respectable house! For shame, sir! For shame! Do, some of you," he continued to the servants, "take this gentleman to his room and put him to bed. And softly with him, do you hear?"

"I think he has swooned," the man answered, who had stooped over him.

The landlord wrung his hands. "Fie, sir — for shame!" he said. "Stay, Charles; I'll fetch some brandy."

He bustled away to do so, and to acquaint Sir George; who through all, and though from his open door he had gathered what was happening, had resolutely held aloof. The landlord, as he went out, unconsciously evaded Mr. Pomeroy who entered at the same moment from the street. Ignorant of what was forward — for his companion's cries had not reached the stables — Pomeroy advanced at his ease and was surprised to find the hall, which he had left empty, occupied by a chattering crowd of half-dressed servants; some bending over the prostrate man with lights, some muttering their pity or suggesting remedies; while others again glanced askance at the victor, who, out of bravado rather than for any better reason, maintained his place at the foot of the stairs, and now and then called to them "to rub him — they would not rub that off!"

Mr. Pomeroy did not at first see the fallen man, so thick was the press round him. Then someone moved, and he did; and the thing that had happened bursting on him, his face, gloomy before, grew black as a thundercloud. He flung the nearest to either side, that he might see the better; and, as they recoiled, "Who has done this?" he cried in a voice low but harsh with rage. "Whose work is this?" And standing over the tutor he turned himself, looking from one to another.

But the servants knew his reputation, and shrank panic-stricken from his eye; and for a moment no one answered. Then Mr. Dunborough, who, whatever his faults, was not a coward, took the word. "Whose work is it?" he answered with assumed carelessness. "It is my work. Have you any fault to find with it?"

"Twenty, puppy!" the elder man retorted, foaming with rage. And then, "Have I said enough, or do you want me to say more?" he cried.

"Quite enough," Mr. Dunborough answered calmly. He had wreaked the worst of his rage on the unlucky tutor. "When you are sober I'll talk to you."

Mr. Pomeroy with a frightful oath cursed his impudence. "I believe I have to pay you for more than this!" he panted. "Is it you who decoyed a girl from my house tonight?"

Mr. Dunborough laughed aloud. "No, but it was I sent her there," he said. He had the advantage of knowledge. "And if I had brought her away again, it would have been nothing to you."

The answer staggered Bully Pomeroy in the midst of his rage.

"Who are you?" he cried.

"Ask your friend there!" Dunborough retorted with disdain. "I've written my name on him! It should be pretty plain to read"; and he turned on his heel to go upstairs.

Pomeroy took two steps forward, laid his hand on the other's shoulder, and, big man as he was, turned him round. "Will you give me satisfaction?" he cried.

Dunborough's eyes met his. "So that is your tone, is it?" he said slowly; and he reached for the tankard of ale that had been brought to him, and that now stood on a chest at the foot of the stairs.

But Mr. Pomeroy's hand was on the pot first; in a second its contents were in Dunborough's face and dripping from his cravat. "Now will you fight?" Bully Pomeroy cried; and as if he knew his man, and that he had done enough, he turned his back on the stairs and strode first into the Yarmouth.

Two or three women screamed as they saw the liquor thrown, and a waiter ran for the landlord. A second drawer, more courageous, cried, "Gentlemen, gentlemen — for God's sake, gentlemen!" and threw himself between the younger man and the door of the room. But Dunborough, his face flushed with anger, took him by the shoulder, and sent him spinning; then with an oath he followed the other into the Yarmouth, and slammed the door in the faces of the crowd. They heard the key turned.

"My God!" the waiter who had interfered cried, his face white, "there will be murder done!" And he sped away for the kitchen poker that he might break in the door. He had known such a case before. Another ran to seek the gentleman upstairs. The others drew round the door and stooped to listen; a moment, and the sound they feared reached their ears — the grinding of steel, the trampling of leaping feet, now a yell and now a taunting laugh. The sounds were too much for one of the men who heard them: he beat on the door with his fists. "Gentlemen!" he cried, his voice quavering, "for the Lord's sake don't, gentlemen! Don't!" On which one of the women who had shrieked fell on the floor in wild hysterics.

That brought to a pitch the horror without the room, where lights shone on frightened faces and huddled forms. In the height of it the landlord and Sir George appeared. The woman's screams were so violent that it was rather from the attitude of the group about the door than from anything they could hear that the two took in the position. The instant they did so Sir George signed to the servants to stand aside, and drew back to hurl himself against the door. A cry that the poker was come, and that with this they could burst the lock with ease, stayed him just in time — and fortunately; for as they went to adjust the point of the tool between the lock and the jamb the nearest man cried "Hush!" and raised his hand, the door creaked, and in a moment opened inwards. On the threshold, supporting himself by the door, stood Mr. Dunborough, his face damp and pale, his eyes furtive and full of a strange horror. He looked at Sir George.

"He's got it!" he muttered in a hoarse whisper. "You had better — get a surgeon. You'll bear me out," he continued, looking round eagerly, "he began it. He flung it in my face. By God — it may go near to hanging me!"

Sir George and the landlord pushed by him and went in. The room was lighted by one candle, burning smokily on the high mantelshelf; the other lay overturned and extinguished in the folds of a tablecloth which had been dragged to the floor. On a wooden chair beside the bare table sat Mr. Pomeroy, huddled chin to breast, his left hand pressed to his side, his right still resting on the hilt of his small-sword. His face was the color of chalk, and a little froth stood on his lips; but his eyes, turned slightly upwards, still followed his rival with a grim fixed stare. Sir George marked the crimson stain on his lips, and raising his hand for silence — for the servants were beginning to crowd in with exclamations of horror — knelt down beside the chair, ready to support him in case of need. "They are fetching a surgeon," he said. "He will be here in a minute."

Mr. Pomeroy's eyes left the door, through which Dunborough had disappeared, and for a few seconds they dwelt unwinking on Sir George: but for a while he said nothing. At length, "Too late," he whispered. "It was my boots — I slipped, or I'd have gone through him. I'm done. Pay Tamplin — five pounds I owe him."

Soane saw that it was only a matter of minutes, and he signed to the landlord, who was beginning to lament, to be silent.

"If you can tell me where the girl is — in two words," he said gently, "will you try to do so?"

The dying man's eyes roved over the ring of faces. "I don't know," he whispered, so faintly that Soane had to bring his ear very near his lips. "The parson — was to have got her to Tamplin's — for me. He put her in the wrong carriage. He's paid. And — I'm paid."

With the last word the small-sword fell clinking to the floor. The

dying man drew himself up, and seemed to press his hand more and
more tightly to his side. For a brief second a look of horror — as if the
consciousness of his position dawned on his brain — awoke in his eyes.
Then he beat it down. "Tamplin's staunch," he muttered. "I must stand
by Tamplin. I owe — pay him five pounds for —"

A gush of blood stopped his utterance. He gasped and with a groan
but no articulate word fell forward in Soane's arms. Bully Pomeroy had
lost his last stake!

Not this time the spare thousands the old squire, good saving man,
had left on bond and mortgage; not this time the copious thousands
he had raised himself for spendthrift uses: nor the old oaks his great-
grand-sire had planted to celebrate His Majesty's glorious Restoration:
nor the Lelys and Knellers that great-grand-sire's son, shrewd old connoisseur, commissioned: not this time the few hundreds hardly squeezed
of late from charge and jointure, or wrung from the unwilling hands of
friends — but life; life, and who shall say what besides life!

Chapter XXXIII

IN THE CARRIAGE

M r. Thomasson was mistaken in supposing that it was the jerk,
caused by the horses' start, which drew from Julia the scream he heard
as the carriage bounded forward and whirled into the night. The girl,
indeed, was in no mood to be lightly scared; she had gone through too
much. But as, believing herself alone, she sank back on the seat — at the
moment that the horses plunged forward — her hand, extended to save
herself, touched another hand: and the sudden contact in the dark,
conveying to her the certainty that she had a companion, with all the
possibilities the fact conjured up, more than excused an involuntary
cry.

The answer, as she recoiled, expecting the worst, was a sound between
a sigh and a grunt; followed by silence. The coachman had got the horses

in hand again, and was driving slowly; perhaps he expected to be stopped. She sat as far into her corner as she could, listening and staring, enraged rather than frightened. The lamps shed no light into the interior of the carriage, she had to trust entirely to her ears; and, gradually, while she sat shuddering, awaiting she knew not what, there stole on her senses, mingling with the roll of the wheels, a sound the least expected in the world — a snore!

Irritated, puzzled, she stretched out a hand and touched a sleeve, a man's sleeve; and at that, remembering how she had sat and wasted fears on Mr. Thomasson before she knew who he was, she gave herself entirely to anger. "Who is it?" she cried sharply. "What are you doing here?"

The snoring ceased, the man turned himself in his corner. "Are we there?" he murmured drowsily; and, before she could answer, was asleep again.

The absurdity of the position pricked her. Was she always to be traveling in dark carriages beside men who mocked her? In her impatience she shook the man violently. "Who are you? What are you doing here?" she cried again.

The unseen roused himself. "Eh?" he exclaimed. "Who — who spoke? I — oh, dear, dear, I must have been dreaming. I thought I heard —"

"Mr. Fishwick!" she cried; her voice breaking between tears and laughter. "Mr. Fishwick!" And she stretched out her hands, and found his, and shook and held them in her joy.

The lawyer heard and felt; but, newly roused from sleep, unable to see her, unable to understand how she came to be by his side in the post-chaise, he shrank from her. He was dumbfounded. His mind ran on ghosts and voices; and he was not to be satisfied until he had stopped the carriage, and with trembling fingers brought a lamp, that he might see her with his eyes. That done, the little attorney fairly wept for joy.

"That I should be the one to find you!" he cried. "That I should be the one to bring you back! Even now I can hardly believe that you are here! Where have you been, child? Lord bless us, we have seen strange things!"

"It was Mr. Dunborough!" she cried with indignation.

"I know, I know," he said. "He is behind with Sir George Soane. Sir George and I followed you. We met him, and Sir George compelled him to accompany us."

"Compelled him?" she said.

"Aye, with a pistol to his head," the lawyer answered; and chuckled and leapt in his seat — for he had reentered the carriage — at the remembrance. "Oh, Lord, I declare I have lived a year in the last two days. And to think that I should be the one to bring you back!" he repeated. "To bring you back! But there, what happened to you? I know that they set you down in the road. We learned that at Bristol this afternoon from the villains who carried you off."

She told him how they had found. Mr. Pomeroy's house, and taken shelter there, and —

"You have been there until now?" he said in amazement. "At a gentleman's house? But did you not think, child, that we should be anxious? Were there no horses? No servants? Didn't you think of sending word to Marlborough?"

"He was a villain," she answered, shuddering. Brave as she was, Mr. Pomeroy had succeeded in frightening her. "He would not let me go. And if Mr. Thomasson had not stolen the key of the room and released me, and brought me to the gate tonight, and put me in with you —"

"But how did he know that I was passing?" Mr. Fishwick cried, thrusting back his wig and rubbing his head in perplexity. He could not yet believe that it was chance and only chance had brought them together.

And she was equally ignorant. "I don't know," she said. "He only told me — that he would have a carriage waiting at the gate."

"And why did he not come with you?"

"He said — I think he said he was under obligations to Mr. Pomeroy."

"Pomeroy? Pomeroy?" the lawyer repeated slowly. "But sure, my dear, if he was a villain, still, having the clergyman with you you should have been safe. This Mr. Pomeroy was not in the same case as Mr. Dunborough. He could not have been deep in love after knowing you a dozen hours."

"I think," she said, but mechanically, as if her mind ran on something else, "that he knew who I was, and wished to make me marry him."

"Who you were!" Mr. Fishwick repeated; and — and he groaned.

The sudden check was strange, and Julia should have remarked it. But she did not; and after a short silence, "How could he know?" Mr. Fishwick asked faintly.

"I don't know," she answered, in the same absent manner. Then with an effort which was apparent in her tone, "Lord Almeric Doyley was there," she said. "He was there too."

"Ah!" the lawyer replied, accepting the fact with remarkable apathy. Perhaps his thoughts also were far away. "He was there, was he?"

"Yes," she said. "He was there, and he —" then, in a changed tone, "Did you say that Sir George was behind us?"

"He should be," he answered; and, occupied as she was with her own trouble, she was struck with the gloom of the attorney's tone. "We settled," he continued, "as soon as we learned where the men had left you, that I should start for Calne and make inquiries there, and they should start an hour later for Chippenham and do the same there. Which reminds me that we should be nearing Calne. You would like to rest there?"

"I would rather go forward to Marlborough," she answered feverishly, "if you could send to Chippenham to tell them I am safe? I would rather go back at once, and quietly."

"To be sure," he said, patting her hand. "To be sure, to be sure," he repeated, his voice shaking as if he wrestled with some emotion. "You'll he glad to be with — with your mother."

Julia wondered a little at his tone, but in the main he had described her feelings. She had gone through so many things that, courageous as she was, she longed for rest and a little time to think. She assented in silence therefore, and, wonderful to relate, he fell silent too, and remained so until they reached Calne. There the inn was roused; a messenger was dispatched to Chippenham; and while a relay of horses was prepared he made her enter the house and eat and drink. Had he stayed at that, and preserved when he reentered the carriage the discreet silence he had maintained before, it is probable that she would have fallen asleep in sheer weariness, and deferred to the calmer hours of the morning the problem that occupied her. But as they settled themselves in their corners, and the carriage rolled out of the town, the attorney muttered that he did not doubt Sir George would be at Marlborough to breakfast. This set the girl's mind running. She moved restlessly, and presently, "When did you hear what had happened to me?" she asked.

"A few minutes after you were carried off," he answered; "but until Sir George appeared, a quarter of an hour later, nothing was done."

"And he started in pursuit?" To hear it gave her a delicious thrill between pain and pleasure.

"Well, at first, to confess the truth," Mr. Fishwick answered humbly, "I thought it was his doing, and —"

"You did?" she cried in surprise.

"Yes, I did; even I did. And until we met Mr. Dunborough, and Sir George got the truth from him — I had no certainty. More shame to me!"

She bit her lips to keep back the confession that rose to them, and for a little while was silent. Then, to his astonishment, "Will he ever forgive me?" she cried, her voice tremulous. "How shall I tell him? I was mad — I must have been mad."

"My dear child," the attorney answered in alarm, "compose yourself. What is it? What is the matter?"

"I, too thought it was he! I, even I. I thought that he wanted to rid himself of me," she cried, pouring forth her confession in shame and abasement. "There! I can hardly bear to tell you in the dark, and how shall I tell him in the light?"

"Tut-tut!" Mr. Fishwick answered. "What need to tell anyone? Thoughts are free."

"Oh, but" — she laughed hysterically — "I was not free, and I — what do you think I did?" She was growing more and more excited.

"Tut-tut!" the lawyer said. "What matter?"

"I promised — to marry someone else."

"Good Lord!" he said. The words were forced from him.

"Someone else!" she repeated. "I was asked to be my lady, and it tempted me! Think! It tempted me," she continued with a second laugh, bitterly contemptuous. "Oh, what a worm — what a thing I am! It tempted me. To be my lady, and to have my jewels, and to go to Ranelagh and the masquerades! To have my box at the King's House and my frolic in the pit! And my woman as ugly as I liked — if he might have my lips! Think of it, think of it! That anyone should be so low! Or no, no, no!" she cried in a different tone. "Don't believe me! I am not that! I am not so vile! But I thought he had tricked me, I thought he had cheated me, I thought that this was his work, and I was mad! I think I was mad!"

"Dear, dear," Mr. Fishwick said rubbing his head. His tone was sympathetic; yet, strange to relate, there was no real smack of sorrow in it. Nay, an acute ear might have caught a note of relief, of hope, almost of eagerness. "Dear, dear, to be sure!" he continued; "I suppose — it was Lord Almeric Doyley, the nobleman I saw at Oxford?"

"Yes!"

"And you don't know what to do, child?"

"To do?" she exclaimed.

"Which — I mean which you shall accept. Really," Mr. Fishwick continued, his brain succumbing to a kind of vertigo as he caught himself balancing the pretensions of Sir George and Lord Almeric, "it is a very remarkable position for any young lady to enjoy, however born. Such a choice —"

"Choice!" she cried fiercely, out of the darkness. "There is no choice. Don't you understand? I told him No, no, no, a thousand times No!"

Mr. Fishwick sighed. "But I understood you to say," he answered meekly, "that you did not know what to do."

"How to tell Sir George! How to tell him."

Mr. Fishwick was silent a moment. Then he said earnestly, "I would not tell him. Take my advice, child. No harm has been done. You said No to the other."

"I said Yes," she retorted.

"But I thought —"

"And then I said No," she cried, between tears and foolish laughter. "Cannot you understand?"

Mr. Fishwick could not; but, "Anyway, do not tell him," he said. "There is no need, and before marriage men think much of that at which they laugh afterwards."

"And much of a woman of whom they think nothing afterwards," she answered.

"Yet do not tell him," he pleaded. From the sound of his voice she knew that he was leaning forward. "Or at least wait. Take the advice of one older than you, who knows the world, and wait."

"And talk to him, listen to him, smile on his suit with a lie in my heart? Never?" she cried. Then with a new strange pride, a faint touch of stateliness in her tone, "You forget who I am, Mr. Fishwick," she said. "I am as much a Soane as he is, and it becomes me to — to remember that. Believe me, I would far rather resign all hope of entering his house, though I love him, than enter it with a secret in my heart."

Mr. Fishwick groaned. He told himself that this would be the last straw. This would give Sir George the handle he needed. She would never enter that house.

"I have not been true to him," she said. "But I will be true now."

"The truth is — is very costly," Mr. Fishwick murmured almost under his breath. "I don't know that poor people can always afford it, child."

"For shame!" she cried hotly. "For shame! But there," she continued, "I know you do not mean it. I know that what you bid me do you would not do yourself. Would you have sold my cause, would you have hidden the truth for thousands? If Sir George had come to you to bribe you, would you have taken anything? Any sum, however large? I know you would not. My life on it, you would not. You are an honest man," she cried warmly.

The honest man was silent awhile. Presently he looked out of the carriage. The moon had risen over Savernake; by its light he saw that they were passing Manton village. In the vale on the right the tower of Preshute Church, lifting its head from a dark bower of trees, spoke a solemn language, seconding hers. "God bless you!" he said in a low voice. "God bless you."

A minute later the horses swerved to the right, and half a dozen lights keeping vigil in the Castle Inn gleamed out along the dark front. The post-chaise rolled across the open, and drew up before the door. Julia's strange journey was over. Its stages, somber in the retrospect, rose before her as she stepped from the carriage: yet, had she known all, the memories at which she shuddered would have worn a darker hue. But it was not until a late hour of the following morning that even the lawyer heard what had happened at Chippenham.

Chapter XXXIV

BAD NEWS

*T*he attorney entered the Mastersons' room a little before eleven next morning; Julia was there, and Mrs. Masterson. The latter on seeing him held up her hands in dismay. "Lord's wakes, Mr. Fishwick!" the good woman cried, "why, you are the ghost of yourself! Adventuring does not suit you, that's certain. But I don't wonder. I am sure I have not slept a wink these three nights that I have not dreamt of Bessy Canning and that horrid old Squires; which, she did it without a doubt. Don't go to say you've bad news this morning."

Certain it was that Mr. Fishwick looked woefully depressed. The night's sleep, which had restored the roses to Julia's cheeks and the light to her eyes, had done nothing for him; or perhaps he had not slept. His eyes avoided the girl's look of inquiry. "I've no news this morning," he said awkwardly. "And yet I have news."

"Bad?" the girl said, nodding her comprehension; and her color slowly faded.

"Bad," he said gravely, looking down at the table.

Julia took her fostermother's hand in hers, and patted it; they were sitting side by side. The elder woman, whose face was still furrowed by the tears she had shed in her bereavement, began to tremble. "Tell us," the girl said bravely. "What is it?"

"God help me," Mr. Fishwick answered, his face quivering. "I don't know how I shall tell you. I don't indeed. But I must." Then, in a voice harsh with pain, "Child, I have made a mistake," he cried. "I am wrong, I was wrong, I have been wrong from the beginning. God help me! And God help us all!"

The elder woman broke into frightened weeping. The younger grew pale and paler: grew presently white to the lips. Still her eyes met his, and did not flinch. "Is it — about our case?" she whispered.

"Yes! Oh, my dear, will you ever forgive me?"

"About my birth?"

He nodded.

"I am not Julia Soane? Is that it?"

He nodded again.

"Not a Soane — at all?"

"No; God forgive me, no!"

She continued to hold the weeping woman's hand in hers, and to look at him; but for a long minute she seemed not even to breathe. Then in a voice that, notwithstanding the effort she made, sounded harsh in his ears, "Tell me all," she muttered. "I suppose — you have found something!"

"I have," he said. He looked old, and worn, and shabby; and was at once the surest and the saddest corroboration of his own tidings. "Two days ago I found, by accident, in a church at Bristol, the death certificate of the — of the child."

"Julia Soane?"

"Yes."

"But then — who am I?" she asked, her eyes growing wild: the world was turning, turning with her.

"Her husband," he answered, nodding towards Mrs. Masterson, "adopted a child in place of the dead one, and said nothing. Whether he intended to pass it off for the child entrusted to him, I don't know. He never made any attempt to do so. Perhaps," the lawyer continued drearily, "he had it in his mind, and when the time came his heart failed him."

"And I am that child?"

Mr. Fishwick looked away guiltily, passing his tongue over his lips. He was the picture of shame and remorse.

"Yes," he said. "Your father and mother were French. He was a teacher of French at Bristol, his wife French from Canterbury. No relations are known."

"My name?" she asked, smiling piteously.

"Paré," he said, spelling it. And he added, "They call it Parry."

She looked round the room in a kind of terror, not unmixed with wonder. To that room they had retired to review their plans on their first arrival at the Castle Inn — when all smiled on them. Thither they had fled for refuge after the brush with Lady Dunborough and the rencontre with Sir George. To that room she had betaken herself in the first flush and triumph of Sir George's suit; and there, surrounded by the same objects on which she now gazed, she had sat, rapt in rosy visions, through the livelong day preceding her abduction. Then she had been a gentlewoman, an heiress, the bride in prospect of a gallant gentleman. Now?

What wonder that, as she looked round in dumb misery, recognizing these things, her eyes grew wild again; or that the shrinking lawyer expected an outburst. It came, but from another quarter. The old woman rose and trembling pointed a palsied finger at him. "Yo' eat your words!" she said. "Yo' eat your words and seem to like them. But didn't yo' tell me no farther back than this day five weeks that the law was clear? Didn't yo' tell me it was certain? Yo' tell me that!"

"I did! God forgive me," Mr. Fishwick murmured from the depths of his abasement.

"Didn't yo' tell me fifty times, and fifty times to that, that the case was clear?" the old woman continued relentlessly. "That there were thousands and thousands to be had for the asking? And her right besides, that no one could cheat her of, no more than me of the things my man left me?"

"I did, God forgive me!" the lawyer said.

"But yo' did cheat me!" she continued with quavering insistence, her withered face faintly pink. "Where is the home yo' ha' broken up? Where are the things my man left me? Where's the bit that should ha' kept me from the parish? Where's the fifty-two pounds yo' sold all for and ha' spent on us, living where's no place for us, at our betters' table? Yo' ha' broken my heart! Yo' ha' laid up sorrow and suffering for the girl that is dearer to me than my heart. Yo' ha' done all that, and yo' can come to me smoothly, and tell me yo' ha' made a mistake. Yo' are a rogue, and, what maybe is worse, I mistrust me yo' are a fool!"

"Mother! mother!" the girl cried.

"He is a fool!" the old woman repeated, eyeing him with a dreadful sternness. "Or he would ha' kept his mistake to himself. Who knows of it? Or why should he be telling them? 'Tis for them to find out, not for him! Yo' call yourself a lawyer? Yo' are a fool!" And she sat down in a palsy of senile passion. "Yo' are a fool! And yo' ha' ruined us!"

Mr. Fishwick groaned, but made no reply. He had not the spirit to defend himself. But Julia, as if all through which she had gone since the day of her reputed father's death had led her to this point, only that she might show the stuff of which she was wrought, rose to the emergency.

"Mother," she said firmly, her hand resting on the older woman's shoulder, "you are wrong — you are quite wrong. He would have ruined

us indeed, he would have ruined us hopelessly and forever, if he had
kept silence! He has never been so good a friend to us as he has shown
himself today, and I thank him for his courage. And I honor him!" She
held out her hand to Mr. Fishwick, who having pressed it, his face
working ominously, retired to the window.

"But, my deary, what will yo' do?" Mrs. Masterson cried peevishly.
"He ha' ruined us!"

"What I should have done if we had never made this mistake," Julia
answered bravely; though her lips trembled and her face was white, and
in her heart she knew that hers was but a mockery of courage, that must
fail her the moment she was alone. "We are but fifty pounds worse than
we were."

"Fifty pounds!" the old woman cried aghast. "Yo' talk easily of fifty
pounds. And, Lord knows, it is soon spent here. But where will yo' get
another?"

"Well, well," the girl answered patiently, "that is true. Yet we must
make the best of it. Let us make the best of it," she continued, appealing
to them bravely, yet with tears in her voice. "We are all losers together.
Let us bear it together. I have lost most," she continued, her voice
trembling. Fifty pounds? Oh, God! what was fifty pounds to what she
had lost. "But perhaps I deserve it. I was too ready to leave you, mother.
I was too ready to — to take up with new things and — and richer things,
and forget those who had been kin to me and kind to me all my life.
Perhaps this is my punishment. You have lost your all, but that we will
get again. And our friend here — he, too, has lost."

Mr. Fishwick, standing, dogged and downcast, by the window, did
not say what he had lost, but his thoughts went to his old mother at
Wallingford and the empty stocking, and the weekly letters he had sent
her for a month past, letters full of his golden prospects, and the great
case of Soane *v.* Soane, and the grand things that were to come of it.
What a home-coming was now in store for him, his last guinea spent,
his hopes wrecked, and Wallingford to be faced!

There was a brief silence. Mrs. Masterson sobbed querulously, or now
and again uttered a wailing complaint: the other two stood sank in bitter
retrospect. Presently, "What must we do?" Julia asked in a faint voice.
"I mean, what step must we take? Will you let them know?"

"I will see them," Mr. Fishwick answered, wincing at the note of pain
in her voice. "I — I was sent for this morning, for twelve o'clock. It is a
quarter to eleven now."

She looked at him, startled, a spot of red in each cheek. "We must go
away," she said hurriedly, "while we have money. Can we do better than
return to Oxford?"

The attorney felt sure that at the worst Sir George would do something for her: that Mrs. Masterson need not lament for her fifty pounds. But he had the delicacy to ignore this. "I don't know," he said mournfully. "I dare not advise. You'd be sorry, Miss Julia — anyone would be sorry who knew what I have gone through. I've suffered — I can't tell you what I have suffered — the last twenty-four hours! I shall never have any opinion of myself again. Never!"

Julia sighed. "We must cut a month out of our lives," she murmured. But it was something else she meant — a month out of her heart!

Chapter XXXV

DORMITAT HOMERUS

*I*f Julia's return in the middle of the night balked the curiosity of some who would fain have had her set down at the door that they might enjoy her confusion as she passed through the portico, it had the advantage, appreciated by others, of leaving room for conjecture. Before breakfast her return was known from, one end of the Castle Inn to the other; within half an hour a score had private information. Sir George had brought her back, after marrying her at Salisbury. The attorney had brought her back, and both were in custody, charged with stealing Sir George's title-deeds. Mr. Thomasson had brought her back; he had wedded her at Calne, the reverend gentleman himself performing the ceremony with a curtain-ring at a quarter before midnight, in the presence of two chambermaids, in a room hung with drab moreen. Sir George's servant had brought her back; he was the rogue in the play; it was Lady Harriet Wentworth and footman Sturgeon over again. She had come back in a Flemish hat and a white cloth Joseph with black facings; she had come back in her night-rail; she had come back in a tabby gauze, with a lace head and lappets. Nor were there wanting other rumors, of an after-dinner Wilkes-and-Lord-Sandwich flavor, which we refrain from detailing; but which the Castle Inn, after the mode of the eighteenth century, discussed with freedom in a mixed company.

Of all these reports and the excitement which they created in an assemblage weary of waiting on the great man's recovery and in straits for entertainment, the attorney knew nothing until he set forth to keep the appointment in Lord Chatham's apartments; which, long the object of desire, now set his teeth on edge. Nor need he have learned much of them then; for he had only to cross the lobby of the east wing, and was in view of the hall barely three seconds. But, unluckily, Lady Dunborough, cackling shrewishly with a kindred dowager, caught sight of him as he passed; and in a trice her old limbs bore her in pursuit. Mr. Fishwick heard his name called, had the weakness to turn, and too late found that he had fallen into the clutches of his ancient enemy.

The absence of her son's name from the current rumors had relieved the Viscountess of her worst fears, and left her free to enjoy herself. Seeing his dismay, "La, man! I am not going to eat you!" she cried; for the lawyer, nervous and profoundly dispirited, really shrank before her. "So you have brought back your fine madam, I hear? And made an honest woman of her!"

Mr. Fishwick glared at her, but did not answer.

"I knew what would come of pushing out of your place, my lad!" she continued, nodding complacently. "It wasn't likely she'd behave herself. When the master is away the man will play, and the maid too. I mind me perfectly of the groom. A saucy fellow and a match for her; 'tis to be hoped he'll beat some sense into her. Was she tied up at Calne?"

"No!" Mr. Fishwick blurted, wincing under her words; which hurt him a hundred times more sharply than if the girl had been what he had thought her. Then he might have laughed at the sneer and the spite that dictated it. Now — something like this all the world would say.

The Viscountess eyed him cunningly, her head on one side. "Was it at Salisbury, then?" she cried. "Wherever 'twas. I hear she had need of haste. Or was it at Bristol? D'you hear me speak to you, man?" she continued impatiently. "Out with it."

"At neither," he cried.

My lady's eyes sparkled with rage. "Hoity-toity!" she answered. "D'you say No to me in that fashion? I'll thank you to mend your manners, Fishwick, and remember to whom you are speaking. Hark ye, sirrah, is she Sir George's cousin or is she not?"

"She is not, my lady," the attorney muttered miserably.

"But she is married?"

"No," he said; and with that, unable to bear more, he turned to fly.

She caught him by the sleeve. "Not married?" she cried, grinning with ill-natured glee. "Not married? And been of three days with a man! Lord, 'tis a story as bald as Granby! She ought to be whipped, the hussy! Do you hear? She ought to the Roundhouse, and you with her, sirrah, for passing her of on us!"

But that was more than the attorney, his awe of the peerage notwithstanding, could put up with. "God forgive you!" he cried. "God forgive you, ma'am, your hard heart!"

She was astonished. "You impudent fellow!" she exclaimed. "What do you know of God? And how dare you name Him in the same breath with me? D'you think He'd have people of quality be Methodists and live as the like of you? God, indeed! Hang your impudence! I say, she should to the Roundhouse — and you, too, for a vagabond! And so you shall!"

The lawyer shook with rage. "The less your ladyship talks of the Roundhouse," he answered, his voice trembling, "the better! There's one is in it now who may go farther and fare worse — to your sorrow, my lady!"

"You rogue!" she cried. "Do you threaten me?"

"I threaten no one," he answered. "But your son, Mr. Dunborough, killed a man last night, and lies in custody at Chippenham at this very time! I say no more, my lady!"

He had said enough. My lady glared; then began to shake in her turn. Yet her spirit was not easily quelled; "You lie!" she cried shrilly, the stick, with which she vainly strove to steady herself, rattling on the floor. "Who dares to say that my son has killed a man?"

"It is known," the attorney answered.

"Who — who is it?"

"Mr. Pomeroy of Bastwick, a gentleman living near Calne."

"In a duel! 'Twas in a duel, you lying fool!" she retorted hoarsely. "You are trying to scare me! Say 'twas in a duel and I — I'll forgive you."

"They shut themselves up in a room, and there were no seconds," the lawyer answered, beginning to pity her. "I believe that Mr. Pomeroy gave the provocation, and that may bring your ladyship's son off. But, on the other hand —"

"On the other hand, what? What?" she muttered.

"Mr. Dunborough had horsewhipped a man that was in the other's company."

"A man?"

"It was Mr. Thomasson."

Her ladyship's hands went up. Perhaps she remembered that but for her the tutor would not have been there. Then "Sink you! I wish he had flogged you all!" she shrieked, and, turning stiffly, she went mumbling and cursing down the stairs, the lace lappets of her head trembling, and her gold-headed cane now thumping the floor, now waving uncertainly in the air.

A quarter of an hour earlier, in the apartments for which Mr. Fishwick was bound when her ladyship intercepted him, two men stood talking at a window. The room was the best in the Castle Inn — a lofty paneled chamber with a southern aspect looking upon the smooth sward and sweet-briar hedges of Lady Hertford's terrace, and commanding beyond these a distant view of the wooded slopes of Savernake. The men spoke in subdued tones, and more than once looked towards the door of an adjacent room, as if they feared to disturb someone.

"My dear Sir George," the elder said, after he had listened patiently to a lengthy relation, in the course of which he took snuff a dozen times, "your mind is quite made up, I suppose?"

"Absolutely."

"Well, it is a remarkable series of events; a — most remarkable series," Dr. Addington answered with professional gravity. "And certainly, if the lady is all you paint her — and she seems to set you young bloods on fire — no ending could well be more satisfactory. With the addition of a comfortable place in the Stamps or the Pipe Office, if we can take his lordship the right way — it should do. It should do handsomely. But," with a keen glance at his companion, "even without that — you know that he is still far from well?"

"I know that all the world is of one of two opinions," Sir George answered, smiling. "The first, that his lordship ails nothing save politically; the other, that he is at death's door and will not have it known."

The physician shrugged his shoulders contemptuously. "Neither is true," he said. "The simple fact is, he has the gout; and the gout is an odd thing, Sir George, as you'll know one of these days," with another sharp glance at his companion. "It flies here and there, and everywhere."

"And where is it now?" Soane asked innocently.

"It has gone to his head," Addington answered, in a tone so studiously jejune that Sir George glanced at him. The doctor, however, appeared unaware of the look, and merely continued: "So, if he does not take things quite as you wish, Sir George, you'll — but here his lordship comes!"

The doctor thought that he had sufficiently prepared Soane for a change in his patron's appearance. Nevertheless, the younger man was greatly shocked when through the door, obsequiously opened — and held open while a man might count fifty, so that eye and mind grew expectant — the great statesman, the People's Minister at length appeared. For the stooping figure that moved to a chair only by virtue of a servant's arm, and seemed the taller for its feebleness, for dragging legs and shrunken, frame and features sharpened by illness and darkened by the great peruke it was the Earl's fashion to wear, he was in a degree prepared. But for the languid expression of the face that had been so eloquent, for the lackluster eyes and the dullness of mind that noticed little and heeded less, he was not prepared; and these were so marked and so unlike the great minister —

"A daring pilot in extremity
Pleased with the danger when the waves went high"

— so unlike the man whose eagle gaze had fluttered Courts and imposed the law on Senates, that it was only the presence of Lady Chatham, who followed her lord, a book and cushion in her hands, that repressed the exclamation which rose to Sir George's lips. So complete was the change indeed that, as far as the Earl was concerned, he might have uttered it! His lordship, led to the head of the table, sank without a word into the chair placed for him, and propping his elbow on the table and his head on his hand, groaned aloud.

Lady Chatham compressed her lips with evident annoyance as she took her stand behind her husband's chair; it was plain from the glance she cast at Soane that she resented the presence of a witness. Even Dr. Addington, with his professional *sang-froid* and his knowledge of the invalid's actual state, was put out of countenance for a moment. Then he signed to Sir George to be silent, and to the servant to withdraw.

At last Lord Chatham spoke. "This business?" he said in a hollow voice and without uncovering his eyes, "is it to be settled now?"

"If your lordship pleases," the doctor answered in a subdued tone.

"Sir George Soane is there?"

"Yes."

"Sir George," the Earl said with an evident effort, "I am sorry I cannot receive you better."

"My lord, as it is I am deeply indebted to your kindness."

"Dagge finds no flaw in their case," Lord Chatham continued apathetically. "Her ladyship has read his report to me. If Sir George likes to contest the claim, it is his right."

"I do not propose to do so."

Sir George had not this time subdued his voice to the doctor's pitch; and the Earl, whose nerves seemed alive to the slightest sound, winced visibly. "That is your affair," he answered querulously. "At any rate the trustees do not propose to do so."

Sir George, speaking with more caution, replied that he acquiesced; and then for a few seconds there was silence in the room, his lordship continuing to sit in the same attitude of profound melancholy, and the others to look at him with compassion, which they vainly strove to dissemble. At last, in a voice little above a whisper, the Earl asked if the man was there.

"He waits your lordship's pleasure," Dr. Addington answered. "But before he is admitted," the physician continued diffidently and with a manifest effort, "may I say a word, my lord, as to the position in which this places Sir George Soane?"

"I was told this morning," Lord Chatham answered, in the same muffled tone, "that a match had been arranged between the parties, and that things would remain as they were. It seemed to me, sir, a prudent arrangement."

Sir George was about to answer, but Dr. Addington made a sign to him to be silent. "That is so," the physician replied smoothly. "But your lordship is versed in Sir George Soane's affairs, and knows that he must now go to his wife almost empty-handed. In these circumstances it has occurred rather to his friends than to himself, and indeed I speak against his will and by sufferance only, that — that, in a word, my lord —"

Lord Chatham lowered his hand as Dr. Addington paused. A faint flush darkened his lean aquiline features, set a moment before in the mold of hopeless depression. "What?" he said. And he raised himself sharply in his chair. "What has occurred to his friends?"

"That some provision might be made for him, my lord."

"From the public purse?" the Earl cried in a startling tone. "Is that your meaning, sir?" And, with the look in his eyes which had been more dreaded by the Rigbys and Dodingtons of his party than the most scathing rebuke from the lips of another, he fixed the unlucky doctor where he stood. "Is that your proposal, sir?" he repeated.

The physician saw too late that he had ventured farther than his interest would support him; and he quailed. On the other hand, it is possible he had been neither so confident before, nor was so entirely crushed now, as appeared. "Well, my lord, it did occur to me," he stammered, "as not inconsistent with the public welfare."

"The public welfare!" the minister cried in biting accents. "The public plunder, sir, you mean! It were not inconsistent with that to quarter on the nation as many ruined gentlemen as you please! But you mistake if you bring the business to me to do — you mistake. I have dispersed thirteen millions of His Majesty's money in a year, and would have spent as much again and as much to that, had the affairs of this nation required it; but the gentleman is wrong if he thinks it has gone to my friends. My hands are clean," his lordship continued with an expressive gesture. "I have said, in another place, none of it sticks to them. *Virtute me involvo!*" And then, in a lower tone, but still with a note of austerity in his voice, "I rejoice to think," he continued, "that the gentleman was not himself the author of this application. I rejoice to think that it did not come from him. These things have been done freely; it concerns me not to deny it; but since I had to do with His Majesty's exchequer, less freely. And that only concerns me!"

Sir George Soane bit his lip. He felt keenly the humiliation of his position. But it was so evident that the Earl was not himself — so evident that the tirade to which he had just listened was one of those outbursts, noble in sentiment, but verging on the impracticable and the ostentatious, in which Lord Chatham was prone to indulge in his weaker moments, that he felt little inclination to resent it. Yet to let it pass unnoticed was impossible.

"My lord," he said firmly, but with respect, "it is permitted to all to make an application which the custom of the time has sanctioned. That is the extent of my action — at the highest. The propriety of granting such requests is another matter and rests with your lordship. I have nothing to do with that."

The Earl appeared to be as easily disarmed as he had been lightly aroused. "Good lad! good lad!" he muttered. "Addington is a fool!" Then drowsily, as his head sunk on his hand again, "The man may enter. I will tell him!"

Chapter XXXVI

THE ATTORNEY SPEAKS

It was into an atmosphere highly charged, therefore, in which the lightning had scarcely ceased to play, and might at any moment dart its fires anew, that Mr. Fishwick was introduced. The lawyer did not know this; yet it was to be expected that without that knowledge he would bear himself but ill in the company in which he now found himself. But the task which he had come to perform raised him above himself; moreover, there is a point of depression at which timidity ceases, and he had reached this point. Admitted by Dr. Addington, he looked round, bowed stiffly to the physician, and lowly and with humility to Lord Chatham and her ladyship; then, taking his stand at the foot of the table, he produced his papers with an air of modest self-possession.

Lord Chatham did not look up, but he saw what was passing. "We have no need of documents," he said in the frigid tone which marked his dealings with all save a very few. "Your client's suit is allowed, sir, so far as the trustees are concerned. That is all it boots me to say."

"I humbly thank your lordship," the attorney answered, speaking with an air of propriety which surprised Sir George. "Yet I have with due submission to crave your lordship's leave to say somewhat."

"There is no need," the Earl answered, "the claim being allowed, sir."

"It is on that point, my lord."

The Earl, his eyes smoldering, looked his displeasure, but controlled himself. "What is it?" he said irritably.

"Some days ago, I made a singular discovery, my lord," the attorney answered sorrowfully. "I felt it necessary to communicate it to my client, and I am directed by her to convey it to your lordship and to all others concerned." And the lawyer bowed slightly to Sir George Soane.

Lord Chatham raised his head, and for the first time since the attorney's entrance looked at him with a peevish attention. "If we are to go into this, Dagge should be here," he said impatiently. "Or your lawyer, Sir George." with a look as fretful in that direction. "Well, man, what is it?"

"My lord," Mr. Fishwick answered, "I desire first to impress upon your lordship and Sir George Soane that this claim was set on foot in good faith on the part of my client, and on my part; and, as far as I was concerned, with no desire to promote useless litigation. That was the position up to Tuesday last, the day on which the lady was forcibly carried off. I repeat, my lord, that on that day I had no more doubt of the justice of our claim than I have today that the sky is above us. But on Wednesday I happened in a strange way — at Bristol, my lord, whither but for that abduction I might never have gone in my life — on a discovery, which by my client's direction I am here to communicate."

"Do you mean, sir," the Earl said with sudden acumen, a note of keen surprise in his voice, "that you are here — to abandon your claim?"

"My client's claim," the attorney answered with a sorrowful look.

"Yes, my lord, I am."

For an instant there was profound silence in the room; the astonishment was as deep as it was general. At last, "are the papers which were submitted to Mr. Dagge — are they forgeries then?" the Earl asked.

"No, my lord; the papers are genuine," the attorney answered. "But my client, although the identification seemed to be complete, is not the person indicated in them." And succinctly, but with sufficient clearness, the attorney narrated his chance visit to the church, the discovery of the entry in the register, and the story told by the good woman at the "Golden Bee." "Your lordship will perceive," he concluded, "that, apart from the exchange of the children, the claim was good. The identification of the infant whom the porter presented to his wife with the child handed to him by his late master three weeks earlier seemed to be placed beyond doubt by every argument from probability. But the child was not the child," he added with a sigh. And, forgetting for the moment the presence in which he stood, Mr. Fishwick allowed the despondency he felt to appear in his face and figure.

There was a prolonged silence. "Sir!" Lord Chatham said at last — Sir George Soane, with his eyes on the floor and a deep flush on his face, seemed to be thunderstruck by this sudden change of front — "it appears to me that you are a very honest man! Yet let me ask you. Did it never occur to you to conceal the fact?"

"Frankly, my lord, it did," the attorney answered gloomily, "for a day. Then I remembered a thing my father used to say to us, 'Don't put molasses in the punch!' And I was afraid."

"Don't put molasses in the punch!" his lordship ejaculated, with a lively expression of astonishment. "Are you mad, sir?"

"No, my lord and gentlemen," Mr. Fishwick answered hurriedly. "But it means — don't help Providence, which can very well help itself. The thing was too big for me, my lord, and my client too honest. I thought, if it came out afterwards, the last state might be worse than the first. And — I could not see my way to keep it from her; and that is the truth," he added candidly.

The statesman nodded. Then,

> "Dissimulare etiam sperasti, perfide tantum
> Posse nefas, tacitusque meam subducere terram?"

he muttered in low yet sonorous tones.

Mr. Fishwick stared. "I beg your lordship's pardon," he said. "I do not quite understand."

"There is no need. And that is the whole truth, sir, is it?"

"Yes, my lord, it is."

"Very good. Very good," Lord Chatham replied, pushing away the papers which the attorney in the heat of his argument had thrust before him. "Then there is an end of the matter as far as the trustees are concerned. Sir George, you have nothing to say, I take it?"

"No, I thank you, my lord — nothing here," Soane answered vaguely. His face continued to wear the dark flush which had overspread it a few minutes before. "This, I need not say, is an absolute surprise to me," he added.

"Just so. It is an extraordinary story. Well, good-morning, sir," his lordship continued, addressing the attorney. "I believe you have done your duty. I believe you have behaved very honestly. You will hear from me."

Mr. Fishwick knew that he was dismissed, but after a glance aside, which showed him Sir George standing in a brown study, he lingered. "If your lordship," he said desperately, "could see your way to do anything — for my client?"

"For your client? Why?" the Earl cried, with a sudden return of his gouty peevishness. "Why, sir — why?"

"She has been drawn," the lawyer muttered "out of the position in which she lived, by an error, not her own, my lord."

"Yours!"

"Yes, my lord."

"And why drawn?" the Earl continued regarding him severely. "I will tell you, sir. Because you were not content to await the result of investigation, but must needs thrust yourself in the public eye! You must needs assume a position before it was granted! No, sir, I allow you honest; I allow you to be well-meaning; but your conduct has been indiscreet, and your client must pay for it. Moreover, I am in the position of a trustee, and can do nothing. You may go, sir."

After that Mr. Fishwick had no choice but to withdraw. He did so; and a moment later Sir George, after paying his respects, followed him. Dr. Addington was clear-sighted enough to fear that his friend had gone after the lawyer, and, as soon as he decently could, he went himself in pursuit. He was relieved to find Sir George alone, pacing the floor of the room they shared.

The physician took care to hide his real motive and his distrust of Soane's discretion under a show of heartiness. "My dear Sir George, I congratulate you!" he cried, shaking the other effusively by the hand. "Believe me, 'tis by far the completest way out of the difficulty; and though I am sorry for the — for the young lady, who seems to have behaved very honestly — well, time brings its repentances as well as its revenges. It is possible the match would have done tolerably well, assuming you to be equal in birth and fortune. But even then 'twas a risk; 'twas a risk, my dear sir! And now —"

"It is not to be thought of, I suppose?" Sir George said; and he looked at the other interrogatively.

"Good Lord, no!" the physician answered. "No, no, no!" he added weightily.

Sir George nodded, and, turning, looked thoughtfully through the window. His face still wore a flush. "Yet something must be done for her," he said in a low voice. "I can't let her here, read that."

Dr. Addington took the open letter the other handed to him, and, eyeing it with a frown while he fixed his glasses, afterwards proceeded to peruse it.

"Sir," it ran — it was pitifully short — "when I sought you I deemed myself other than I am. Were I to seek you now I should be other than I deem myself. We met abruptly, and can part after the same fashion. This from one who claims to be no more than your well-wisher. — JULIA."

The doctor laid it down and took a pinch of snuff. "Good girl!" he muttered. "Good girl. That — that confirms me. You must do something for her, Sir George. Has she — how did you get that, by the way?"

"I found it on the table. I made inquiry, and heard that she left Marlboro' an hour gone."

"For?"

"I could not learn."

"Good girl! Good girl! Yes, certainly you must do something for her."

"You think so?" Sir George said, with a sudden queer look at the doctor, "Even you?"

"Even I! An allowance of — I was going to suggest fifty guineas a year," Dr. Addington continued impulsively. "Now, after reading that letter, I say a hundred. It is not too much, Sir George! 'Fore Gad, it is not too much. But —"

"But what?"

The physician paused to take an elaborate pinch of snuff. "You'll forgive me," he answered. "But before this about her birth came out, I fancied that you were doing, or going about to do the girl no good. Now, my dear Sir George, I am not strait-laced," the doctor continued, dusting the snuff from the lappets of his coat, "and I know very well what your friend, my Lord March, would do in the circumstances. And you have lived much, with him, and think yourself, I dare swear, no better. But you are, my dear sir — you are, though you may not know it. You are wondering what I am at? Inclined to take offence, eh? Well, she's a good girl, Sir George" — he tapped the letter, which lay on the table beside him — "too good for that! And you'll not lay it on your conscience, I hope."

"I will not," Sir George said quietly.

"Good lad!" Dr. Addington muttered, in the tone Lord Chatham had used; for it is hard to be much with the great without trying on their shoes. "Good lad! Good lad!"

Soane did not appear to notice the tone. "You think an allowance of a hundred guineas enough?" he said, and looked at the other.

"I think it very handsome," the doctor answered. "D——d handsome."

"Good!" Sir George rejoined. "Then she shall have that allowance;" and after staring awhile at the table he nodded assent to his thoughts and went out.

Chapter XXXVII

A HANDSOME ALLOWANCE

*T*he physician might not have deemed his friend so sensible — or so insensible — had he known that the young man proposed to make the offer of that allowance in person. Nor to Sir George Soane himself, when he alighted five days later before The George Inn at Wallingford, did the offer seem the light and easy thing,

"Of smiles and tears compact,"

it had appeared at Marlborough. He recalled old clashes of wit, and here and there a spark struck out between them, that, alighting on the flesh, had burned him. Meanwhile the arrival of so fine a gentleman, traveling in a post-chaise and four, drew a crowd about the inn. To give the idlers time to disperse, as well as to remove the stains of the road, he entered the house, and, having bespoken dinner and the best rooms, inquired the way to Mr. Fishwick the attorney's. By this time his servant had blabbed his name; and the story of the duel at Oxford being known, with some faint savor of his fashion, the landlord was his most obedient, and would fain have guided his honor to the place cap in hand.

Rid of him, and informed that the house he sought was neighbor on the farther side, of the Three Tuns, near the bridge, Sir George strolled down the long clean street that leads past Blackstone's Church, then in the building, to the river; Sinodun Hill and the Berkshire Downs, speaking evening peace, behind him. He paused before a dozen neat houses with brass knockers and painted shutters, and took each in turn for the lawyer's. But when he came to the real Mr. Fishwick's, and found it a mere cottage, white and decent, but no more than a cottage, he thought that he was mistaken. Then the name of "Mr. Peter Fishwick, Attorney-at-Law," not in the glory of brass, but painted in white letters on the green door, undeceived him; and, opening the wicket of the tiny garden, he knocked with the head of his cane on the door.

The appearance of a stately gentleman in a laced coat and a sword, waiting outside Fishwick's, opened half the doors in the street; but not that one at which Sir George stood. He had to knock again and again before he heard voices whispering inside. At last a step came tapping down the bricked passage, a bolt was withdrawn, and an old woman, in a coarse brown dress and a starched mob, looked out. She betrayed no surprise on seeing so grand a gentleman, but told his honor, before he could speak, that the lawyer was not at home.

"It is not Mr. Fishwick I want to see," Sir George answered civilly. Through the brick passage he had a glimpse, as through a funnel, of green leaves climbing on a tiny treillage, and of a broken urn on a scrap of sward. "You have a young lady staying here?" he continued.

The old woman's stiff grey eyebrows grew together. "No!" she said sharply. "Nothing of the kind!"

"A Miss Masterson."

"No" she snapped, her face more and more forbidding. "We have no Misses here, and no baggages for fine gentlemen! You have come to the wrong house!" And she tried to shut the door in his face.

He was puzzled and a little affronted; but he set his foot between the door and the post, and balked her. "One moment, my good woman," he said. "This is Mr. Fishwick's, is it not?"

"Aye, 'tis," she answered, breathing hard with indignation. "But if it is him your honor wants to see, you must come when he is at home. He is not at home today."

"I don't want to see him," Sir George said. "I want to speak to the young lady who is staying here."

"And I tell you that there is no young lady staying here!" she retorted wrathfully. "There is no soul in the house but me and my serving girl, and she's at the wash-tub. It is more like the Three Tuns you want! There's a flaunting gypsy-girl there if you like — but the less said about her the better."

Sir George stood and stared at the woman. At last, on a sudden suspicion, "Is your servant from Oxford?" he said.

She seemed to consider him before she answered. "Well, if she is?" she said grudgingly. "What then?"

"Is her name Masterson?"

Again she seemed to hesitate. At last, "May be and may be not!" she snapped, with a sniff of contempt.

He saw that it was, and for an instant the hesitation was on his side. Then, "Let me come in!" he said abruptly. "You are doing your son's client little good by this!" And when she had slowly and grudgingly made way for him to enter, and the door was shut behind him, "Where is she?" he asked almost savagely. "Take me to her!"

The old dame muttered something unintelligible. Then, "She's in the back part," she said, "but she'll not wish to see you. Don't blame me if she pins a clout to your skirts."

Yet she moved aside, and the way lay open — down the brick passage. It must be confessed that for an instant, just one instant, Sir George wavered, his face hot; for the third part of a second the dread of the ridiculous, the temptation to turn and go as he had come were on him. Nor need he, for this, forfeit our sympathies, or cease to be a hero. It was the age, be it remembered, of the artificial. Nature, swathed in perukes and ruffles, powder and patches, and stifled under a hundred studied airs and grimaces, had much ado to breathe. Yet it did breathe; and Sir George, after that brief hesitation, did go on. Three steps carried him down the passage. Another, and the broken urn and tiny treillage brought him up short, but on the greensward, in the sunlight, with the air of heaven fanning his brow. The garden was a very duodecimo; a single glance showed him its whole extent — and Julia.

She was not at the wash-tub, as the old lady had said; but on her knees, scouring a step that led to a side-door, her drugget gown pinned up about her. She raised her head as he appeared, and met his gaze defiantly, her face flushing red with shame or some kindred feeling. He was struck by a strange likeness between her hard look and the frown with which the old woman at the door had received him; and this, or something in the misfit of her gown, or the glimpse he had of a stocking grotesquely fine in comparison of the stuff from which it peeped — or perhaps the cleanliness of the step she was scouring, since he seemed to instant, just one instant, Sir George wavered, his face hot; for the third part of a second the dread of the ridiculous, the temptation to turn and go as he had come were on him. Nor need he, for this, forfeit our sympathies, or cease to be a hero. It was the age, be it remembered, of the artificial. Nature, swathed in perukes and ruffles, powder and patches, and stifled under a hundred studied airs and grimaces, had much ado to breathe. Yet it did breathe; and Sir George, after that brief hesitation, did go on. Three steps carried him down the passage. Another, and the broken urn and tiny treillage brought him up short, but on the greensward, in the sunlight, with the air of heaven fanning his brow. The garden was a very duodecimo; a single glance showed him its whole extent — and Julia.

She was not at the wash-tub, as the old lady had said; but on her knees, scouring a step that led to a side-door, her drugget gown pinned up about her. She raised her head as he appeared, and met his gaze defiantly, her face flushing red with shame or some kindred feeling. He was struck by a strange likeness between her hard look and the frown with which the old woman at the door had received him; and this, or something in the misfit of her gown, or the glimpse he had of a stocking grotesquely fine in comparison of the stuff from which it peeped — or perhaps the cleanliness of the step she was scouring, since he seemed to see everything without looking at it — put an idea into his head. He checked the exclamation that sprang to his lips; and as she rose to her feet he saluted her with an easy smile. "I have found you, child," he said. "Did you think you had hidden yourself?"

She met his gaze sullenly. "You have found me to no purpose," she said. Her tone matched her look.

The look and the words together awoke an odd pang in his heart. He had seen her arch, pitiful, wrathful, contemptuous, even kind; but never sullen. The new mood gave him the measure of her heart; but his tone lost nothing of its airiness. "I hope not," he said, "for we think you have behaved vastly well in the matter, child. Remarkably well! And that, let me tell you, is not only my own sentiment, but the opinion of my friends who perfectly approve of the arrangement I have come to propose. You may accept it, therefore, without the least scruple."

"Arrangement?" she muttered. Her cheeks, darkly red a moment before, began to fade.

"Yes," he said. "I hope you will think it not ungenerous. It will rid you of the need to do this — sort of thing, and put you — put you in a comfortable position. Of course, you know," he continued in a tone of patronage, under which her heart burned if her cheeks did not, "that a good deal of water has run under the bridge since we talked in the garden at Marlborough? That things are changed."

Her eyelids quivered under the cruel stroke. But her only answer was, "They are." Yet she wondered how and why; for if she had thought herself an heiress, he had not — then.

"You admit it, I am sure?" he persisted.

"Yes," she answered resolutely.

"And that to — to resume, in fact, the old terms would be — impossible,"

"Quite impossible." Her tone was as hard as his was easy.

"I thought so," Sir George continued complacently. "Still, I could not, of course, leave you here, child. As I have said, my friends think that something should be done for you; and I am only too happy to do it. I have consulted them, and we have talked the matter over. By the way," with a look round, "perhaps your mother should be here — Mrs. Masterson, I mean? Is she in the house?"

"No," she answered, her face flaming scarlet; for pride had conquered pain. She hated him. Oh, how she hated him and the hideous dress which in her foolish dream — when, hearing him at the door, she had looked for something very different — she had hurriedly put on; and the loose tangle of hair which she had dragged with trembling fingers from its club so that it now hung sluttishly over her ear. She longed, as she had never longed before, to confront him in all her beauty; to be able to say to him, "Choose where you will, can you buy form or face like this?" Instead she stood before him, prisoned in this shapeless dress, a slattern, a drab, a thing whereat to curl the lip.

"Well, I am sorry she is not here," he resumed. "It would have given a — a kind of legality to the offer," he continued with an easy laugh. "To tell you the truth, the amount was not fixed by me, but by my friend, Dr. Addington, who interested himself in your behalf. He thought that an allowance of a hundred guineas a year, child, properly secured, would place you in comfort, and — and obviate all this," with a negligent wave of the hand that took in the garden and the half-scoured stone, "at the same time," he added, "that it would not be unworthy of the donor." And he bowed, smiling.

"A hundred guineas?" she said slowly. "A year?"

"Yes."

"Properly secured?"

"To be sure, child."

"On your word?" with a sudden glance at him. "Of course, I could not ask better security! Surely, sir, there's but one thing to be said. 'Tis too generous, too handsome!"

"Tut-tut!" he answered, wondering at her way of taking it.

"Far too handsome — seeing that I have no claim on you, Sir George, and have only put you to great expense."

"Pooh! Pooh!"

"And — trouble. A vast deal of trouble," she repeated in an odd tone of raillery, while her eyes, grown hard and mocking, raked him mercilessly. "So much for so little! I could not — I could not accept it. A hundred guineas a year, Sir George, from one in your position to one in mine, would only lay me open to the tongue of slander. You had better say — fifty."

"Oh, no!"

"Or — thirty, I am sure thirty were ample! Say thirty guineas a year, dear sir; and leave me my character."

"Nonsense," he answered, a trifle discomfited. Strange, she was seizing her old position. The weapon he had wrought for her punishment was being turned against himself.

"Or, I don't know that thirty is not too much!" she continued, her eyes unnaturally bright, her voice keen as a razor. "'Twould have been enough if offered through your lawyers. But at your own mouth, Sir George, ten shillings a week should do, and handsomely! Which reminds me — it was a kind thought to come yourself to see me; I wonder why you did."

"Well," he said, "to be frank, it was Dr. Addington —"

"Oh, Dr. Addington — Dr. Addington suggested it! Because I fancied — it could not give you pleasure to see me like this?" she continued with a flashing eye, her passion for a brief moment breaking forth. "Or to go back a month or two and call me child? Or to speak to me as to your chambermaid? Or even to give me ten shillings a week?"

"No," he said gravely; "perhaps not, my dear."

She winced and her eyes flashed; but she controlled herself. "Still, I shall take your ten shillings a week," she said. "And — and is that all? Or is there anything else?"

"Only this," he said firmly. "You'll please to remember that the ten shillings a week is of your own choosing. You'll do me that justice at least. A hundred guineas a year was the allowance I proposed. And — I bet a guinea you ask for it, my dear, before the year is out!"

She was like a tigress outraged; she writhed under the insult. And yet, because to give vent to her rage were also to bare her heart to his eyes, she had to restrain herself, and endure even this with a scarlet cheek. She had thought to shame him by accepting the money he offered; by accepting it in the barest form. The shame was hers; it did not seem to touch him a whit. At last, "You are mistaken," she answered, in a voice she strove to render steady. "I shall not! And now, if there is nothing more, sir —"

"There is," he said. "Are you sufficiently punished?"

She looked at him wildly — suddenly, irresistibly compelled to do so by a new tone in his voice. "Punished!" she stammered, almost inaudibly. "For what?"

"Do you not know?"

"No," she muttered, her heart fluttering strangely.

"For this travesty," he answered; and coolly, as he stood before her, he twitched the sleeve of her shapeless gown, looking masterfully down at her the while, so that her eyes fell before his. "Did you think it kind to me or fair to me," he continued, almost sternly, "to make that difficult, Julia, which my honor required, and which you knew that my honor required? Which, if I had not come to do, you would have despised me in your heart, and presently with your lips? Did you think it fair to widen the distance between us by this — this piece of play-acting? Give me your hand."

She obeyed, trembling, tongue-tied. He held it an instant, looked at it, and dropped it almost contemptuously. "It has not cleaned that step before," he said. "Now put up your hair."

She did so with shaking fingers, her cheeks pale, tears oozing from under her lowered eyelashes. He devoured her with his gaze.

"Now go to your room," he said. "Take off that rag and come to me properly dressed."

"How?" she whispered.

"As my wife."

"It is impossible," she cried with a gesture of despair; "It is impossible."

"Is that the answer you would have given me at Manton Corner?"

"Oh no, no!" she cried. "But everything is changed."

"Nothing is changed."

"You said so," she retorted feverishly. "You said that it was changed!"

"And have you, too, told the whole truth?" he retorted. "Go, silly child! If you are determined to play Pamela to the end, at least you shall play it in other guise than this. 'Tis impossible to touch you! And yet, if you stand long and tempt me, I vow, sweet, I shall fall!"

To his astonishment she burst into hysterical laughter. "I thought men wooed — with promises!" she cried. "Why don't you tell me I shall have my jewels; and my box at the Opera and the King's House? And go to Vauxhall and the Masquerades? And have my frolic in the pit with the best? And keep my own woman as ugly as I please? He did; and I said Yes to him! Why don't you say the same?"

Sir George was prepared for almost anything, but not for that. His face grew dark. "He did? Who did?" he asked grimly, his eyes on her face.

"Lord Almeric! And I said Yes to him — for three hours."

"Lord Almeric?"

"Yes! For three hours," she answered with a laugh, half hysterical, half despairing. "If you must know, I thought you had carried me off to — to get rid of my claim — and me! I thought — I thought you had only been playing with me," she continued, involuntarily betraying by her tone how deep had been her misery. "I was only Pamela, and 'twas cheaper, I thought, to send me to the Plantations than to marry me."

"And Lord Almeric offered you marriage?"

"I might have been my lady," she cried in bitter abasement. "Yes."

"And you accepted him?"

"Yes! Yes, I accepted him."

"And then — 'Pon honor, ma'am, you are good at surprises. I fear I don't follow the course of events," Sir George said icily.

"Then I changed my mind — the same day," she replied. She was shaking on her feet with emotion; but in his jealousy he had no pity on her weakness. "You know, a woman may change her mind once, Sir George," she added with a feeble smile.

"I find that I don't know as much about women — as I thought I did," Sir George answered grimly. "You seem, ma'am, to be much sought after. One man can hardly hope to own you. Pray have you any other affairs to confess?"

"I have told you — all," she said.

His face dark, he hung a moment between love and anger; looking at her. Then, "Did he kiss you?" he said between his teeth. "No!" she cried fiercely.

"You swear it?"

She flashed a look at him.

But he had no mercy. "Why not?" he persisted, moving a step nearer her. "You were betrothed to him. You engaged yourself to him, ma'am. Why not?"

"Because — I did not love him," she answered so faintly he scarcely heard.

He drew a deep breath. "May I kiss you?" he said.

She looked long at him, her face quivering between tears and smiles, a great joy dawning in the depths of her eyes. "If my lord wills," she said at last, "when I have done his bidding and — and changed — and dressed as —"

But he did not wait.

Chapter XXXVIII

THE CLERK OF THE LEASES

*W*hen Sir George left the house, an hour later, it happened that the first person he met in the street was Mr. Fishwick. For a day or two after the conference at the Castle Inn the attorney had gone about, his ears on the stretch to catch the coming footstep. The air round him quivered with expectation. Something would happen. Sir George would do something. But with each day that passed eventless, the hope and expectation grew weaker; the care with which the attorney avoided his guest's eyes, more marked; until by noon of this day he had made up his mind that if Sir George came at all, it would be as the wolf and not as the sheep-dog. While Julia, proud and mute, was resolving that if her lover came she would save him from himself by showing him how far he had to stoop, the attorney in the sourness of defeat and a barren prospect — for he scarcely knew which way to turn for a guinea — was resolving that the ewe-lamb must be guarded and all precautions taken to that end.

When he saw the gentleman issue from his door therefore, still more when Sir George with a kindly smile held out his hand, a condescension which the attorney could not remember that he had ever extended to him before, Mr. Fishwick's prudence took fright. "Too much honored, Sir George," he said, bowing low. Then stiffly, and looking from his visitor to the house and back again, "But, pardon me, sir, if there is any matter of business, any offer to be made to my client, it were well, I think — if it were made through me."

"I thank you," Sir George answered. "I do not think that there is anything more to be done. I have made my offer."

"Oh!" the lawyer cried.

"And it has been accepted," Soane continued, smiling at his dismay. "I believe that you have been a good friend to your client, Mr. Fishwick. I shall be obliged if you will allow her to remain under your roof until tomorrow, when she has consented to honor me by becoming my wife."

"Your wife?" Mr. Fishwick ejaculated, his face a picture of surprise.

"Tomorrow?"

"I brought a license with me," Sir George answered. "I am now on my way to secure the services of a clergyman."

The tears stood in Mr. Fishwick's eyes, and his voice shook. "I felicitate you, sir," he said, taking off his hat. "God bless you, sir. Sir George, you are a very noble gentleman!" And then, remembering himself, he hastened to beg the gentleman's pardon for the liberty he had taken.

Sir George nodded kindly. "There is a letter for you in the house, Mr. Fishwick," he said, "which I was asked to convey to you. For the present, good-day."

Mr. Fishwick stood and watched him go with eyes wide with astonishment; nor was it until he had passed from sight that the lawyer turned and went into his house. On a bench in the passage he found a letter. It was formally directed after the fashion of those days "To Mr. Peter Fishwick, Attorney at Law, at Wallingford in Berkshire, by favor of Sir George Soane of Estcombe, Baronet."

"Lord save us, 'tis an honor," the attorney muttered. "What is it?" and with shaking hands he cut the thread that confined the packet. The letter, penned by Dr. Addington, was to this effect:

"SIR, —

"I am directed by the Right Honorable the Earl of Chatham, Lord Keeper of His Majesty's Privy Seal, to convey to you his lordship's approbation of the conduct displayed by you in a late transaction. His lordship, acknowledging no higher claim to employment than probity, nor anymore important duty in the disposition of patronage than the reward of integrity, desires me to intimate that the office of Clerk of the Leases in the Forest of Dean, which is vacant and has been placed at his command, is open for your acceptance. He is informed that the emoluments of the office arising from fees amount in good years to five hundred pounds, and in bad years seldom fall below four hundred.

"His lordship has made me the channel of this communication, that I may take the opportunity of expressing my regret that a misunderstanding at one time arose between us. Accept, sir, this friendly assurance of a change of sentiment, and allow me to

"Have the honor to be, sir,

"Your obedient servant,
"J. ADDINGTON"

"Clerk of the Leases — in the Forest of Dean — have been known in bad years — to fall to four hundred!" Mr. Fishwick ejaculated, his eyes like saucers. "Oh, Lord, I am dreaming! I must be dreaming! If I don't get my cravat untied, I shall have a lit! Four hundred in bad years! It's a — oh, it's incredible! They'll not believe it! I vow they'll not believe it!"

But when he turned to seek them, he saw that they had stolen a march on him, that they knew it already and believed it! Between him and the tiny plot of grass, the urn, and the espalier, which, still caught the last beams of the setting sun, he surprised two happy faces spying on his joy — the one beaming through a hundred puckers with a mother's tearful pride; the other, the most beautiful in the world, and now softened and elevated by every happy emotion.

*M*r. Dunborough stood his trial at the next Salisbury assizes, and, being acquitted of the murder of Mr. Pomeroy, was found guilty of manslaughter. He pleaded his clergy, went through the formality of being branded in the hand with a cold iron, and was discharged on payment of his fees. He lived to be the fifth Viscount Dunborough, a man neither much worse nor much better than his neighbors; and dying at a moderate age — in his bed, of gout in the stomach — escaped the misfortune which awaited some of his friends; who, living beyond the common span, found themselves shunned by a world which could find no worse to say of them than that they lived in their age as all men of fashion had lived in their youth.

Mr. Thomasson was less fortunate. Bully Pomeroy's dying words and the evidence of the man Tamplin were not enough to bring the crime home to him. But representations were made to his college, and steps were taken to compel him to resign his Fellowship. Before these came to an issue, he was arrested for debt, and thrown into the Fleet. There he lingered for a time, sinking into a lower and lower state of degradation, and making ever more and more piteous appeals to the noble pupils who owed so much of their knowledge of the world to his guidance. Beyond this point his career is not to be traced, but it is improbable that it was either creditable to him or edifying to his friends.

Today the old Bath road is silent, or echoes only the fierce note of the cyclist's bell. The coaches and curricles, wigs and hoops, bolstered saddles and carriers' wagons are gone with the beaux and fine ladies and gentlemen's gentlemen whose environment they were; and the Castle Inn is no longer an inn. Under the wide eaves that sheltered the love passages of Sir George and Julia, in the paneled halls that echoed the steps of Dutch William and Duke Chandos, through the noble rooms that a Seymour built that Seymours might be born and die under their frescoed ceilings, the voices of boys and tutors now sound. The boys are divided from the men of that day by four generations, the tutors from the man we have depicted, by a moral gulf infinitely greater. Yet is the change in a sense outward only; for where the heart of youth beats, there, and not behind fans or masks, the "Stand!" of the highwayman, or the "Charge!" of the hero, lurks the high romance.

Nor on the outside is all changed at the Castle Inn. Those who in this quiet lap of the Wiltshire Downs are busy molding the life of the future are reverent of the past. The old house stands stately, high-roofed, almost unaltered, its great pillared portico before it; hard by are the Druids' Mound, and Preshute Church in the lap of trees. Much water has run under the bridge that spans the Kennet since Sir George and Julia sat on the parapet and watched the Salisbury coach come in; the bridge that was of wood is of brick — but there it is, and the Kennet still flows under it, watering the lawns and flowering shrubs that Lady Hertford loved. Still can we trace in fancy the sweet-briar hedge and the border of pinks which she planted by the trim canal; and a bowshot from the great school can lose all knowledge of the present in the crowding memories which the Dueling Green and the Bowling Alley, trodden by the men and women of a past generation, awaken in the mind.

THE END